TARNISHED

THE ELDER TREE TRILOGY
BOOK ONE

ERICA ROSE EBERHART

Published in the United States by Creative James Media.

www.creativejamesmedia.com

978-1-956183-02-3 (trade paperback)

First U.S. Edition 2025

AUTHOR'S NOTE

Tarnished is a high fantasy. While it ends on a positive note, a lot occurs to reach that point and, like with much of life, getting to the end of a story is not always pleasant. This novel depicts fantasy violence (sword fights, arrow strikes, etc.); death of a parent and (the temporary death) of a child; discussion of fantasy genocide; talk of superior race and social persecution; body horror and transformation including descriptions of blood, burning of people, injuries and scars; implied sex; nightmares about traumatic events; complicated parent-child relationships; and themes of anxiety. If you are sensitive to any of these areas, please take care. Only you can best decide what you can handle.

For those who loved and wanted to be
both the princess and the knight.

PRONUNCIATION GUIDE

Many of the names of places and people are influenced from Gaelic, Scandinavian, German, and English pronunciations but some variances from those languages of our world may defer to the world of Visennore.

People

Ailith: *Ay-l-ith*
Caitriona: *Kah-tree-nah*
Greer: *Gh-rear*
Barden: *Bar-den*
Isla: *Eye-lah*
Kayl: *K-ale*
Cearny: *Kear-knee*
Róisín: *Ro-sheen*
Ceenear: *See-near*
Raum: *R-ah-mm*
Niveem: *Nive-ee-mm*

Places

Visennore: *V-iss-en-nor*
Wimleigh: *Whim-lee*
Braewick: *Brr-aye-wick*
Ulla Syrmin: *Ooo-la Sear-min*
Invarlwen: *In-varl-when*
Mazgate: *Mah-zz-gate*
Avorkaz: *Ah-vore-kah-zz*
Beaslig: *Bees-ll-ig*
Caermythlin: *Care-myth-lynn*
Umberfend: *Uhm-burr-fend*

Ailith MacCree

CHAPTER ONE

AILITH

The blood from the body on the cart smelled like crushed berries left in the summer sun for too long: sickeningly sweet while still bitter, and wrongly enticing. When the royal hunters approached the northern gate, the scent hung thick in the late summer air. Midnight blue blood spread over the haphazardly tossed white cloth that covered the decapitated form of a woman, gathering at the tips of the fabric and dripping off in a trail behind the cart. The cart rolled to a stop in front of Ailith MacCree who frowned at the corpse.

"She took three of our men. We'll come back for what remains of them later." The hunter walking beside the cart smiled at Ailith. The short sword hanging at his side still dripped blue blood. "But we got her anyway."

He patted the uncovered head placed proudly on top of the cart. A woman's head, by all appearance, until you noticed her pale skin had a slightly green hue, the ripple of gills just behind her ears, and rows of pointed teeth in her open mouth, all the tell-tale imagery of a caroling countess. A tickling of unease rose along Ailith's neck as she looked at the corpse. She shifted on her feet, attempting to appear unbothered. The guard didn't notice her discomfort, or perhaps he didn't care. "King Cearny will be glad; don't you agree?"

"Aye, leave her be," the driver of the cart chided. Another hunter, older than the one on foot, and more kind, offered Ailith a soft smile. "You're the same guard when we left yesterday afternoon. Haven't you finished your shift?"

Ailith pressed her lips together and shook her head. The scent of the countess' blood filled her nostrils and made her queasy. This was the closest she ever came to a countess, although she heard the creature's song for a fortnight and witnessed men leave through the northern gate never to return. Now she lay before Ailith on the cart, her eyes vacant and cloudy. One of her hands, so human-like besides her nails ending in clawed points, stretched forward as if begging Ailith for aid.

"I worked a double," she admitted, pulling her gaze from the creature to the driver. Beyond them, on the path toward the city, another guard appeared. Ailith nodded toward him, relief filling her. "And that is my replacement now."

"Hop on back, we'll give you a ride as far as the castle. You can sit with me," the hunter standing beside her said, grinning with stained teeth and hungry eyes. Ailith took a step back and felt her insides curl.

"Or you can ride up front with me," the driver offered, patting the seat. Ailith *was* tired and riding the cart would at least get her home sooner.

His was an offer that Ailith could stomach.

Castle walls loomed beside them before yips and cheers from royal guards sounded from above. Everyone was seemingly thrilled to see one more magical creature dead, understandable considering their existence was illegal. But the cheers left Ailith shrinking into her seat, brushing her loose brown hair from her face whilst willing the cart forward, unwilling to be perceived by anyone else.

"It's nasty business," said the driver, his voice softer, only for Ailith's ears. "She put up quite the fight and consumed two of our men. She broke the third in half and scattered him like grain tossed to chickens. But that's the expectation of our job. Same as you're expected to check the carts that pass through the northern gate. In the end—just keep this between you and me—she was only doing what she was born to do. Singing by that lake, killing anyone who came too close; I doubt she knew any other way; it was what she was meant for. We all do what we have to in order to get by."

Ailith smiled at that, glancing at the man as the cart turned toward the castle entrance. "Well, thank you for the ride. I'm sure King Cearny will be thrilled by your accomplishment."

"He always is," the man replied with a smile that didn't reach his eyes. Slowing the cart, Ailith climbed off and continued down the main thoroughfare towards home.

She worked doubles frequently, gathering as much coin as she could to help her household survive, but the exhaustion from constant work was poisoning her body, making her muscles ache and her joints stiff. She only wanted the comfort of her mattress in the little room she shared with her parents' caregiver, Gwen, until she had to rise for the next shift that night. Such desires seemed foolish, she realized, as her dilapidated home came into view and a figure waited outside. It could never be so simple as to go home and take a nap.

Pausing her step, Ailith sucked in a deep breath before propelling herself forward, turning her gaze down as she side-stepped the figure and pulled at the doorknob to her home.

"Excuse me, are you Ailith MacCree?" The figure moved forward, ignoring Ailith's unwelcoming posture. The door clung to the frame, sticking closed as the hinges succumbed to rust. Ailith cursed under her breath at the door not for the first time, nor likely the last until she had enough coin for supplies to fix it. She glanced at the figure who shifted closer and pulled back their hood, revealing a kind, round face surrounded by a graying mass of curls. Her brown eyes were large and tender, and she offered a tentative smile with the air of a woman who wiped away tears and healed scraped knees. "I apologize for bothering you. I know you've been working long shifts at the gate, but I must speak with you."

Ailith bristled and threw her shoulder into the door, finally pushing it open with an audible groan. The stranger's accent was of Braewick City locals, yet with a crispness often associated with the royal family. That, paired with the high quality of her clothes and alarming familiarity with Ailith's work schedule, seemed to confirm she was from the palace.

"I have no interest in working for the king," Ailith replied as she stepped into her home and pulled off her cloak to hang it on the peg by the door. Her fingers drifted over Gwen's cloak hanging next to it sporting moth-made holes, another expense that only soured Ailith's mood further. She turned back to the woman now in her doorway, finding her blinking with surprise. The woman hadn't expected Ailith to figure out her ties and she nearly smiled with self-satisfaction.

Nearly.

"You wouldn't be working for the king," she admitted, her voice soft but sincere. "In fact, it's better if he's never involved."

Ailith pressed her lips together, not moving her stance and narrowing her brown eyes, and the woman's shoulders dropped. She continued; her tone hesitant. "Allow me to start over: my name is Etta. I work for the royal family, but my loyalty isn't directly tied to the king. I've sworn not to go into too much detail, but I can offer you this: a hefty sum of gold as an advance payment, whether you accept the job or not. Enough that you and your parents won't have to worry about their well-being while you're away. More upon agreeing to the task and completion of it."

"While I'm away?" Ailith blurted and immediately snapped her mouth shut, not wanting to appear eager. Away from the northern gate, away from long shifts, away from the boring solitude of rummaging through carts of grain, potatoes, and carrots. But also away from her parents, away from ensuring they were fine, that they were safe, but the coin—

"You would be gone for a few weeks, at least," Etta continued, breaking through Ailith's thoughts.

Ailith stepped back, the door groaning against her hand as she continued to hold it open. Ailith's eyes traveled upward, avoiding Etta's gaze. The roof was leaking and rotting away. It wouldn't last another winter without collapsing. Already, it welcomed a chill on cold nights. But to repair the roof would leave them without enough coin for food. To eat left them without coin to repair the roof. With *this* coin, perhaps they could afford both.

"And this coin you're offering, it'll be enough to care for my parents through the rest of autumn? Will it be enough for winter?"

Etta glanced behind her and stepped closer to Ailith with pleading eyes. "Perhaps we should step inside before we continue this conversation?"

Ailith looked around the woman toward the busy street. Morning slipped precariously close to afternoon. The weather was pleasant with bright sunshine, and the city was alive with the movement of people. Ailith stepped back and held the door open for the woman to enter.

The MacCree household was simple and lacked any sense of personality. A place to sleep, eat, and hold items for jobs. The doorway opened to the living area with a table before dying embers of a fire, and bread rising in a bowl Gwen left behind when she took Ailith's parents to the market that morning. Ailith's mother, Cari, kept a basket of wool and tools for yarn making between two thinly cushioned chairs overlooking the street beyond the singular dusty window. In the back of the room was her parents' bedroom door and up crooked stairs was another to Ailith and Gwen's room.

Ailith glanced around the small room, briefly embarrassed by the lack of personality of the house, and motioned to the chairs by the window. "You can sit there if you'd like."

Etta nodded, dutifully taking a seat. She brushed at her skirts before placing her hands upon her lap. "You'll receive coin thereafter, should you not return. I've heard your parents are not well; this coin is enough to lend them medicinal aid from royal healers."

Ailith took the seat across from Etta and tried to make eye contact with Etta but found it immediately unnerving, so she let her gaze roam to the window, her hands, and Etta's as she organized her thoughts. This woman was serious and so was the job. She nervously bit the edge of her shirt sleeve. "Tell me more."

"Your task is to take something beyond Braewick Valley to the Endless Mountains. We're searching for a man, Kayl, who's believed to live somewhere within the mountain range. You must go to him and he'll decide what to do." Etta pressed her fingertips gently against her leg for each step. "There's no need to bring anything; we'll fully supply and arm you. It's best to travel on foot to the outpost on the edge of Umberfend Marsh. You can purchase a horse and continue from there. If you agree to take this task, arrive at the Elder Tree by first morning's light on the first day of autumn. Additional information will be provided then."

Ailith narrowed her eyes. From what she could read of Etta, the way she maintained eye contact, how she spoke earnestly and was devoid of any apparent discomfort, she was honest. But why would Etta approach her with this task? She kept to herself, never growing close to any of the other guards, and was careful not to draw attention. The vague description of the job offer made sense; being called upon by the royals was often surrounded by mystery because the royal family was nothing *but* mystery. Still ...

"How do I trust your word?" Ailith asked, dropping her hands to her lap. "I don't know you beyond this meeting. I don't know if you truly work for the royal family beyond your accent and the quality of your clothes. How do I trust you'll care for my parents?"

Etta reached into the folds of her skirts, pulling a leather bag free and tossing it for Ailith to catch. The heaviness and bulging sides made Ailith's eyebrows rise. "The advanced payment I mentioned. If you're at the Elder Tree, we'll immediately dispatch more coin to your home."

Ailith looked from Etta to the bag as she shifted it in her hands. Her fingers made quick work of the ties and tipped the pouch onto the table. Gold coins spilled out. Not even silver or bronze. *Gold*. Ailith withheld a smile—Etta surely *did* work for the royal family. They had no true understanding of how much it cost to exist in these lower ranks of the valley and there was enough gold coin to last the entirety of winter, not just half of it. If they got half as much from agreeing to the job, the roof could be fixed, the front door, too.

She kept her face blank and placed the coins into the bag. "I have to think this over."

"Wonderful." Etta grinned and got to her feet, moving to the door and opening it on her own. Ailith followed, stopping short when Etta turned and slipped her plump hand into hers and squeezed tightly. "Thank you."

She left, closing the door behind her, and Ailith stared at the wood grain. If she wasn't mistaken, the woman not only sounded relieved when she thanked her, but had tears in her eyes.

That evening, Ailith discussed the job with her parents who listened with quiet, sincere attention. They had gotten a ride home from the market mid-afternoon, leaving Gwen behind to search for deals on winter clothes and long-lasting vegetables.

"When you were born, you cried for months," Cari began after quiet contemplation, tapping her finger to her chin, her skin tanner than Ailith's and complementing her still-dark hair despite being sixty years of age. "I felt like we took you from some adventure and you were mourning your loss because you've always had your eyes to the horizon. Now it's time to see what's there."

Cari's hands grazed her daughter's cheek, and her brow furrowed as she studied Ailith's face. Cari's peripheral vision was the first to go years before and the rest of her sight was funneling down to a pinpoint.

"If we get the rest of the coin they're offering we can pay for the royal healers to make you glasses so you can see a little better."

"Oh, don't worry about me," Cari laughed, cupping Ailith's face with her hand. "We'll fix the house and make sure there's enough firewood for winter. Perhaps we can pay for a sign to hang out front promoting your father's expertise."

"A splendid idea," Taren joined in, squeezing Ailith's shoulder from his seat beside his daughter. He once was a stonemason for the king until the dragon attacked. When the warning bells came, he was required to report to the castle and help. But stones from an eastern wall collapsed and partially crushed him. Now he couldn't walk without pain and spent most of his time moving from chair to chair, only able to go out once a week to the market by riding on the back of the neighbor's cart. "See? We'll be fine. That additional coin will do us wonders and knowing you'll see more of Visennore will fill our hearts. Take the job, Ailith."

"The world is great and large; if only we could all be so lucky to see it," her mother added reassuringly.

Ailith's interest in seeing different landscapes and meeting different people was in her blood. When she was younger, her mother told stories of the people from her home in the Umberfend Marsh decades before she ever met Ailith's father. The people traveled on Gilway Road with pointed ears and magic at their disposal, some imposingly tall and others fascinatingly short. Her father had trained under a half-fae man, who taught him to listen to stones before breaking them so the break would be clean. Taren often recounted stories the man had told him of lands far and away, including the mysterious mist of the Endless Mountains.

Yet, while Ailith daydreamt of adventuring past the city walls, she was never away from her parents. Ailith spent nights in the city guard barracks during training and overnight shifts at the gate, but she remained within the city proper. Ailith found comfort knowing she could get to her parents should anything go wrong. Now, however, she faced weeks away from the two people who meant the most to her.

"I'm not sure what to do," Ailith admitted.

The front door burst forward; Gwen stumbled inside with a curse, wisps of her light brown hair falling into her face and her cheeks flushed. The girl looked defeated. "The prices at the markets have gone up again. Our market was more expensive than it was a week ago, so I tried the market on the western side of the city and their prices are double. I was only able to get half of what I went for."

Ailith's father leaned forward and pressed his hand against Ailith's.

"I think you know what needs to be done."

Days later, the morning dawned fresh with autumn's arrival. Perfect autumn days left everyone rushing to prepare for the oncoming winter, but there was also an undercurrent of discomfort for anyone old enough to remember the attack fifteen years prior. The white dragon attack occurred on the first day of autumn with similar weather, forever ruining the pleasantry of summer heat calming down and crisp mornings creeping in. It felt like a bad omen that left Ailith fidgeting with the dagger she kept strapped to her leg. Despite that she was only five when the attack happened, the terror of it still bled into her movements when she felt uneasy, even now at twenty-years-old.

"Papa," she murmured as she pulled herself away from looking out the window. It was still dark, but the faintest outline of dawn's light shone along the ridge of the eastern valley. Taren was pushing sixty-five; the accident aged him all the more. His wrinkles ran deep, his hair, once brown, now white, but he still had the familiar light in his eyes that sparked when Ailith entered a room. She knelt beside his chair and reached for his hand. "Papa, you need to keep hold of these coins. Give Gwen what she needs for errands and expect more today."

"I'll guard them with my life," Taren teased, reaching to brush stray hairs from Ailith's face. She leaned her cheek into his hand and closed her eyes. "My little dove, you've dreamt of seeing the world your entire life. Don't worry. It's time you *live*."

"I still worry," Ailith murmured with a frown.

"A child shouldn't worry about their parents. That's the parents' job," Cari said, moving from the bedroom with a cane to guide her. Ailith rushed to her side, taking her free arm and guiding her to the seat opposite Taren. Cari settled and reached for Ailith's hand, squeezing it tight.

A creak from the floorboards above announced Gwen's footfall as she emerged from their bedroom, now hers for the time being. She remained at the top of the steps, tightly wrapping an old shawl over her thin shoulders and bowed her head. Ailith nodded before turning back to her mother. Reaching forward, Ailith hugged her. Her mother's fingers, once callused and now smooth from lack of work, grazed over Ailith's cheeks one final time before Ailith reached for her father. He held her and Ailith buried her face into his shirt as she remembered her father's muscular arms, now slight, yet still capable of strong embraces.

Her parents stood in the doorway of their small home as she slipped into the gray hours of early dawn. She waved goodbye before stepping out of sight and felt such fullness in her chest she was sure it would burst.

Moving north through the city, past the ramparts of the castle on the familiar path she took to the northern gate, she hastily wiped at warm tears gathering in her eyes. Ailith's only company were the scurrying rats and homeless dogs, following her in hopes of finding scraps of food until they realized she had nothing. It was too late for drunks to be stumbling through the streets, too early for early morning cobblers. Per the instructions, she left with only the clothing on her back, although she couldn't go without having the assurance of the dagger on her thigh.

She arrived at the Elder Tree, pausing at the clearing near its base and finding the area quiet, empty. Nestling between the roots where she found safety during the dragon attack years before—a smaller nook now that she had grown—she leaned her head against the trunk to look into its broad branches. They were covered in strings and ribbons of different colors. Some had coins or small bells tied to the ends. All were wishes and desires of those who tied them to the ancient tree. If the wish was granted, the wish maker returned to remove their wish or risk it being lost.

As a child, Ailith loved lying beneath the branches and staring at the limbs while the sun filtered through, making the coins glitter and ribbons glow. Now the tree sighed; its leaves dark in the dying night but already beginning to sport golden veins. The branches stirred, seemingly to reach down and wipe the tears dotting Ailith's cheek, and tenderly hush her worries and sorrows. After a moment, Ailith pulled her dagger free and reached toward the edge of her cloak. Making quick work, she cut off the edge and got to her feet to snatch at a branch.

"Bring me home," she whispered as she tied the cut piece of fabric to the bough, "so that I may care for my parents. Let me accomplish this task. Let me be happy." She stepped back, letting the branch return to its lofty place above. The cut gray fabric of Ailith's cloak waved lazily at her from above then grew still.

The slight glow of impending dawn brought the edges of leaves and curves of the tree limbs to life. The crickets were silent, and a crow cawed in the distance. What if she wasn't cut out for this task and simply fell apart? What if she couldn't find her way home? Perhaps she could just return home now. Just forget it all and continue working at that wretched gate. Maybe this was the taste of freedom she needed, just the opportunity and open door.

Footfall pulled Ailith free from her thoughts. She peered around the Elder Tree's base, searching the brush.

"Hello?" a voice called hesitantly, as if searching for someone while fearing discovery. The sky above rapidly dashed towards sunrise, a palette of pinks and oranges burning the heavens, heralding a beautiful day. It cast the brush in a hushed, peachy glow, revealing the young man who stepped into the clearing. He was near Ailith's age, tall and thin with metal-rimmed glasses sliding down his nose as he awkwardly carried a bow and filled quiver. Another figure followed and Ailith recognized Etta moving with certainty while carrying a traveler's bag and cloak. They stopped in the clearing beneath the Elder Tree.

"Ailith MacCree?" he called. "If you're there, we've come to see you."

His shoulders were curved and his head bowed as he nervously glanced around the clearing. His clean, simple clothing, the expensive glasses he wore—something Ailith could perhaps afford after this job— and his accent that wasn't quite the commoner accent she grew up around gave away his status as an employee of the crown. Someone who didn't have to fight tooth and nail for the position, whatever it was, but was born into it. Ailith frowned and stepped around the tree.

"I'm here," Ailith replied, finding a spark of humor when the man jumped. He quickly recovered, pushing his glasses up and brushing through his shaggy brown hair as she approached.

"Ailith, I'm glad to see you." Etta stepped forward and touched Ailith's arm lightly.

"I'm Callan," the man said, offering his hand. "It's nice to meet you."

Ailith looked at his hand then back at him, her frown continued— an expression she wore more than she realized. Callan dropped his hand.

"We have your supplies. Bread, cheese, a waterskin, dried meats and fruits. I was told you're skilled with a bow, so there's one for you, plus arrows, flint and ..." He shifted to his waist and pulled free a short sword. "This is for you as well."

The blade was top quality, something the royal guard used but was rarely found amongst the city guard. They were never the ones to get the best quality weapons.

Etta gestured to the items. "That bag has your supplies, as well as a traveler's blanket and a pair of extra pants, a warm vest, and a tunic. I've also brought this cloak for you. We wouldn't want anyone to recognize your current cloak as you leave the city."

"And one from the royal house is better?" Ailith asked, going to the ties at her throat. The pair glanced at one another and Ailith sighed; she hadn't meant to be offensive, but sometimes her thoughts didn't stay within her brain and found their way out of her mouth. Changing tactics, she pulled her cloak free and held it to Etta. "When you bring the expected coin to my parents, can you please take this to them? Their caretaker is due for another cloak."

"Certainly," Etta replied, exchanging it with the new one made of a deep green fabric thick enough to keep away the early autumn chill. The royal guard had the same make of cloak, except theirs were adorned with the crest of the royal family. This cloak was less conspicuous, absent from any embroidery.

"And what am I taking out of the valley, exactly?" Ailith looked down at the bag of items as she looped the sword belt around her waist and placed the short sword into the scabbard. Etta's smile faded and Callan looked uncomfortable.

"Oh," he began, succumbing to the pressure of Ailith's stare. "I ... I don't have what you're taking ..."

"I do," a cool voice said from the shadows. The accent was clear, rigid ... a royal accent. A *true* royal, not just an employee within the castle. More interesting, the accent belonged to a royal Ailith recognized, the only one she had any interaction with. The figure stepped from the brush with her hood pulled up, another figure with a cloak similar to Ailith's and a traveler's pack followed close behind.

The figure stopped beside Callan and pulled down her hood, exposing thick, blonde hair in an elaborate braid. Ailith was immediately aware of her own brown braid that hung down her back, sloppy and unkempt. Princess Greer stood before her as she had a few years prior when Ailith was sworn into the guard. King Cearny and Princess Greer had stood at the helm of the room, beneath the open mouth of the white dragon's head that loomed above, sharing the same scowl. Ailith stared at Greer the entire time, the princess who would one day be queen, rather than allowing her eyes to be drawn upward to the terrifying, imposing face of the dragon that still gave her nightmares. Despite her best efforts, Ailith's anxiety grew in strength within her gut and clutched at her throat. At one point during the ceremony, Greer locked her caramel-brown eyes with Ailith, and she'd looked away then, her cheeks hot with embarrassment but her anxiety diminishing. Ailith doubted the princess remembered her, but now that Greer's attention was fully on her she wasn't so sure.

The city seemed satisfied that Princess Greer was heir to the throne. She was always proper and a prettier version of her father; good with a sword and willing to defend the kingdom. Many said she was serious, her strong jaw tight and her lips pitched down, and never seemed to joke. She displayed a confidence that all the guards aspired to despite the fact she wasn't yet thirty. Greer wore fitted pants, leather boots, a white tunic and black bodice edged in golden thread with the familiar Elder Tree crest embroidered on the breast. Ailith hated to find herself standing straighter, hands at her sides as she was trained; the proper stance in front of royalty until given the grace to relax.

Greer looked down her nose at Ailith—fitting, Ailith thought—and the items at their feet before turning her attention to Callan and Etta. "Do you have the coin for the MacCrees?"

"Yes, ma'am," Callan replied with a bow of his head. He reached to his waist and pulled free a coin purse similar to what Ailith received two days before.

"Good, I'll need you to deliver it to their home when we've finished here."

Callan bowed his head and Etta stepped back to stand beside the silent, cloaked individual who arrived with Greer. The heir to the throne turned her attention to Ailith and looked her over before continuing. "I know we've been vague about what we need from you and I'll explain but allow me to assure you that you are *not* doing this for the king, but for me."

Ailith blinked, not immediately comforted by this admission. The king was the cause of her family's struggles. Her father's dependable job was dashed when he was injured, and the king only provided a cart to bring his mangled body home. The memory left Ailith with rage she never felt toward anyone else. He was power hungry and focused on expanding his empire while his people struggled, and it was no wonder Ailith wasn't comfortable with the rest of the royal family. Even being a city guard, Ailith felt she had betrayed her morals by working for the king's army, but the coin to support her family won out against her unease.

The princess continued.

"I'm sure you're aware my father has made repeated attempts to overtake the Mazgate Dominion. Apart from the outlier islands of Visennore he's gained control of, he's begun speaking of expanding the empire overseas. Beyond that, he continues my grandfather's crusade to empty the world of magic.

"To be blunt, he has no idea how drawn out the royal guard is nor that the rest of the continent has rapidly growing resentment toward him. We're facing an uprising if he doesn't stop this, but he refuses to listen to reason. I'm hopeful we can find the guidance of an old friend, Kayl, and that he may come to our aid."

"Why don't you summon him to court?" Ailith asked, the question leaving her mouth before she thought twice. A spike of shame crawled up her spine and nestled around her throat as she saw Callan cringe and Greer's eyebrows rise.

"It's a bit more complicated than that," she admitted before beckoning the other cloaked figure forward. The figure pulled back her hood and Ailith's eyes grew wide.

While Greer became a public figure, her younger sister remained hidden away since the dragon attack and was a mystery to the commoners. There were always those who knew a palace worker and spouted what they claimed was true. Rumors spread. Some said the youngest princess was insane, others that she was gravely ill, and a few assumed something was off with her that could threaten the king's reputation, so it was best she was hidden away within the castle.

Ailith's only clear memory of Caitriona was from the king's last birthday celebration, the summer before the attack, then a toddler with hair a deeper shade of crimson than her mother's and a happy disposition. The woman who now stood beside Greer, with red hair in elaborate braids similar to her older sister's, was decidedly more reserved than the toddler Ailith remembered. While Caitriona was an adult now, she still had a youthful plumpness to her cheeks. In body, she was thinner than her sister, and sported a shy expression compared to Greer's seriousness. Her skin was paler, and her red eyebrows and eyelashes made her large sky-blue eyes bright.

"Ailith, this is my sister, Caitriona," Greer began, taking her sister's hand and leading her a step closer. Ailith glanced at Greer, surprised that the future queen's tone had suddenly grown softer; even her expression was gentler. "Your task is to take Caitriona out of the valley and locate Kayl. Bring her to him and do so safely."

CHAPTER TWO

AILITH

"Wait a minute." Ailith raised her hand and brushed her fingers along the edge of her hairline. She shook her head and felt her cheeks growing warm as she stepped back. Clenching her jaw, her rising nerves made her skin prickle with uncertainty. "You want me to take the *princess* out of the city, out of the *kingdom*, to a mountain range to convince *someone* ... to persuade the *king* to stop his wars? The king doesn't know about this. Does the queen?"

"Neither know," Greer rushed, her tone turning serious. She stepped closer, her voice lowering to a whisper. "You've surely heard talk about his ... mind."

Ailith had. The king changed after the white dragon attack, becoming a haunted man. His father, King Donal, outlawed magic years before, but Cearny became obsessed with removing it as well as all magic creatures from their world. Just a year prior, a fever swept through the city and death bringers—small black birds whose appearance foretold death—gathered en masse. The king set up nets to catch the birds then drowned them in oil upon the castle steps before an audience. He watched the nets plunge into the oil and laughed as the birds screamed and attempted to escape. Since then, the king was discussed in hushed tones because who was to question the king and his decisions? Who other than Greer, his own daughter and the next in line to the throne?

"He's created more enemies than he realizes and there's distrust amongst the guard. I worry if he doesn't change his ways, we'll all be destroyed. Not just the royal crown, but Braewick Valley and its citizens. There won't be a kingdom left and Caitriona ... she has a special tie to Kayl. He knows her."

"And a letter isn't enough?" Ailith asked, looking at Caitriona who lowered her gaze.

"He's a known recluse; he interacts with no one. It's essential she goes because she may be the only one he's willing to speak to."

"And what can he do about all this?" Ailith asked.

Greer frowned. "We're at the end of our rope. We need help and are running out of options. We have to try."

The creeping sense of apprehension touched Ailith, running its fingers along her arms and wrapping around her skull to bear down and stir up the sense of unease. It pressed down on her until she could no longer hold it in. The unease shivered up her spine and turned to words that spilled from her mouth. "But why *me*?"

"I may not be constantly present with the city guard, but I certainly review guard performances. You've always been an outstanding individual and shown great promise. Your strengths expand beyond your physical skills. I know how hard you work and how you provide for your parents. I know you stay to yourself, and you don't cause trouble or draw attention which are great attributes for this mission since we must be discreet.

"When we realized this venture was necessary, I looked to the city guard. Remembering your performance, I kept an eye on you from that point forward. But when I saw you returning home from one of your shifts, I knew you were the right choice."

Ailith licked her lips and studied Greer for a moment as discomfort spread in her stomach from the idea Greer had watched her and Ailith hadn't known. "What did you see?"

The corner of Greer's lip curved upward with the hint of a smile before she spoke again. "You were coming home mid-day, walking past the castle walls. I watched you from there. The roads were busy with carts coming and going, and a group of children were playing a game. Running, as they do, from one side of the road to the other as the carts passed, trying to make it to the other side before a horse spooked or they were crushed by wagon wheels. Foolish games, really."

Ailith's eyes slowly widened as the memory surfaced. It had been raining, leaving the roadway thick with mud. Ailith was half asleep, having worked since the evening before when it happened. She hadn't thought she'd make it in time, she was sure she would fail, but she had to try ...

"A child ran out ahead of you," Greer continued. "Slipped in the roadway and fell. The driver of the carriage didn't see the child and they were going too quickly to stop even if they had. You darted out though, ran forward and pulled the child out of harm's way."

"Anyone would have done that." Ailith shifted on her feet, the gaze of everyone bearing down on her.

Greer shook her head. "We live in a kingdom ruled by a king who makes sport of hunting and executing creatures on the steps of his castle. Where magic users and fae must remain secret. Not everyone would do that; we're surrounded by people too focused on their own survival and appeasing the king to worry about children playing a foolish, dangerous game.

"I feel you are the perfect person for this task. Quiet, unassuming, a rule follower with a good heart stationed at a gate not many people pass through; you're the perfect person to lead Caitriona out of the valley."

Ailith looked at the ground, and her cheeks grew hot under Greer's praise. She blinked and licked her lips. She always had kept her head down and worked hard, she was always driven toward caring for her family and never wanting to disrupt the forward movement she had. Despite that, all this time she was observed, studied, and judged. The fact Greer had such a positive opinion of her was a surprise because Ailith had never sought what others thought of her. A hand reached forward and touched Ailith's shoulder, squeezing it. She looked up and met Greer's eyes. The princess pulled back and gave her a reassuring look. Ailith rolled her shoulders, ridding herself of her temporary shyness and discomfort. "Alright." Ailith gave a small nod. "I'll get Caitriona to Kayl."

"I'm certain you will," Greer replied, the softness in her voice returning. She smiled and stepped back, pointing to the bag at Callan's feet. "Caitriona has her own supplies as well as maps and extra coin. Go to the Umberfend outpost where you can obtain horses. Send a message to Etta or Callan indicating your arrival. Be discreet in your messages, but please send them from any village or city where you're able.

"Cait," Greer turned to her sister, her tone filled with pain. Her lips pitched down, and Caitriona had tears welling in her eyes. Greer touched Caitriona's hair and caressed her cheek, the motion similar to how Ailith's parents interacted with her that morning. Maternal, protective, and not at all what Ailith would have expected. "Be safe and come home to me."

Ailith looked away from the sisters, the interaction too private to observe.

"Don't fret over me, Ree. I'll be home and all will be well in no time," Caitriona said, and the use of the nickname brought a tightness to Ailith's chest. Ailith's dislike of the king bubbled over into distrust of the royal family and all in such lofty positions of power. In many ways, her distance from them as she struggled to make ends meet made her paint them as people entirely separate from her. People who didn't have the same type of love or worries that she and fellow peasants shared. But hearing their nicknames brought forth a realization that perhaps they weren't as separate as she assumed.

"I'll see you soon, sister." Greer embraced Caitriona before they pulled Etta into the embrace as well. Callan picked up the travel bag for Ailith and offered to help it onto her back. She slipped the bag over her new cloak then secured the bow and quiver.

"We should head back," Greer announced, pulling away from Caitriona. Etta fussed over Caitriona's face for a moment, a motherly touch to wipe away tears and straighten her hair and cloak. Greer's cheeks were flushed and eyes slightly red, but she hadn't shed any tears. "I ensured the northern gate is guarded by one of my personal guards. He'll let you out of the city walls without issue. All your future shifts at the gate are covered. After working so much, it shouldn't be too noticeable that you've taken a break from shifts.

"Travel fast and quietly. Stay well." Greer gave Caitriona's hand a quick squeeze before she turned and disappeared into the brush toward the castle.

"Travel well," Callan said. Caitriona's cheeks turned red as she looked down.

"Don't finish that map of Agatiroth without me," Caitriona replied.

"Never." Callan grinned.

"Stay safe, my dear," Etta said softly, moving forward to embrace Caitriona. "I'll see you soon." She and Callan disappeared into the brush, following Greer's footsteps.

"I feel I should mention," Caitriona said as she turned to Ailith, "I'm not particularly skilled with a bow or blade, but I have a short sword."

"Splendid, because unskilled swordsmen are never a danger to themselves," Ailith murmured. Color immediately rose on Caitriona's cheek, and Ailith grimaced. "Sorry. It's been a long morning."

"It's fine." Caitriona reached into her cloak and withdrew a folded paper, handing it over. "I'm better at maps than battle. So hopefully I can help in other ways."

Ailith unfolded the paper and stared at a carefully drawn map showing the expanse of Visennore. "Oh, this *will* help." She studied the guard's maps the day prior, hoping to memorize their details, but wasn't able to obtain a copy herself.

A crow cawed loudly, startling the pair. It flapped its wings from an overhead branch then fixed its gaze on them. The sun had risen, its light coming over the eastern hills although it hadn't yet spilled its bright light into the valley.

The pair left the Elder Tree, the scrap of cloth Ailith hung overhead waved goodbye with the aid of the morning breeze. They approached the quiet northern gate and pulled their hoods up. Ailith recognized Barden, a tall legacy guard following in his father's footsteps. He was one of the best, with excellent weapon skills rumored to be better than Greer herself, which was likely why she named him her right-hand man.

As they stepped to the checkpoint, she drew her hood back enough for Barden to see her. He nodded to Ailith and bowed to Caitriona, stepping aside to let them pass through the gate without a word. The pair immediately turned off the road to the farmlands and into the woods. Both lost in thought, comfortable enough to scramble over boulders and begin their slow ascent to the valley ridge in silence. They planned to avoid main roads and climb the hills bordering Braewick Valley on game trails.

After a few hours, they paused to eat apples from their bags as they sat in silence. The further into the hills they climbed, they glimpsed more evidence that autumn arrived. Here, leaves occasionally dropped from the relatively still-green trees. Some rushed ahead with autumnal colors, eager to greet the first day of the season in their most festive attire before slipping to the ground in heavenly bliss. Squirrels rummaged, desperately searching for nuts and seeds. Had they been there for pleasantries, it would have had the makings of a perfect afternoon.

"It's so quiet here," Caitriona commented, her soft-spoken voice breaking the silence. "You know, I began working within the castle library this year. I love its silence. The rest of the castle has a constant hum of conversation."

Ailith didn't respond, finding it easier to ignore Caitriona's occasional commentary. She still nursed her initial discomfort of the royal family but had to move her feelings aside in order for this to be bearable. Ultimately, the princess's positive personality wasn't causing her dark mood. If Ailith was honest, she was nervous about the task before her. Taking an item out of Braewick was one thing; sneaking the king's youngest child beyond the gates was something entirely different and much more dangerous. With Ailith's unease, her mood soured.

"Callan is set to take over the library from his father when Greer becomes queen. He wants to expand it and make it public to the rest of the city, so long as Greer agrees," Caitriona continued, unwrapping a cloth that had a mix of late summer berries.

Ailith shifted on the boulder where she sat, swallowing the last bite of her apple. She considered what her mother would say, envisioning her brown eyes and soft smile. She could hear her mother's laugh curve over her words: *Princesses aren't the only ones on high horses. Make an attempt to befriend her, she's certainly trying* her *best.*

"That would be … nice," she admitted. "I always wanted to learn more about the world, and we don't have access to many books in the lower ward."

"Yes! It's such a large library and despite the many books within, it's empty and meaningless without people. What's the point of a book if there's no one to read it?" Caitriona popped a blackberry into her mouth and grinned.

A smile appeared on Ailith's face as well, curling slightly on one side, much more mischievous than Caitriona's openly honest grin. "And of course, there's *Callan*. How long have the two of you been together?"

Caitriona choked. Coughing, a hand going to her chest, she gasped, "No." Shaking her head, she swallowed. "We aren't together. Not at all."

Ailith raised her eyebrows with warm pleasure when the princess's cheeks grew red.

"We grew up together, that's all," Caitriona began, her cheeks deepening. "I mean … I've had the worst crush on him in recent years, if I'm honest."

"I could tell," Ailith replied, finding herself laughing when Caitriona's eyes grew all the wider. "Come on, love-sick princess, let's keep going."

As the pair traveled further up the valley side, the sun settled closer to the western horizon. Shadows stretched curious tendrils over the valley to cast cool fingers down the travelers' backs. Ailith paused on an outcrop of stone a few leagues from the top of the valley ridge and looked west. "We should stop soon, gather wood, and make a fire to keep the darkness at bay."

"Wouldn't a fire be noticeable here?" Caitriona asked as she came to stand beside Ailith, wrapping the edges of her cloak around her body as the temperature continued its decline. The valley was in shadow and flickers of light within Braewick City dotted the view. Down below, fires were lit, meals prepared, and families returned home. Homesickness welled up in Ailith's heart; her family's evening rituals were occurring without her. Her parents wouldn't ask about her day, and she couldn't tell them she was on this adventure with the princess. Ailith glanced at Caitriona, wondering what her evenings were like and if the king already realized his youngest daughter was missing. A shiver rushed up her spine.

"Have *you* ever noticed a fire on the hillside? You live high enough to have a clear view," Ailith asked, her tone blunter than intended. Caitriona frowned as she looked down upon the city with wisps of red hair drifting about her face in the cool breeze. Ailith had to admit that for a library mouse, Caitriona kept up with Ailith whilst they traveled and hardly complained. But, despite her happy demeanor, there seemed to be a shadow of sadness creeping closer to tug down the corners of the princess's lips. A shadow not created by Ailith's poor mood.

Caitriona didn't take Ailith's bitter bait and simply shook her head. "Not that I recall."

"There you have it," Ailith responded before turning and walking further into the trees bordering the outcrop of rocks. "Even if they did, it wouldn't be out of the norm. The hunting parties camp here. But I believe the tree cover is thick enough to not provide too much sight of a fire; we can camp here for the night."

Caitriona offered to build the fire while Ailith hunted a squirrel, but when Ailith returned there was only a tidy pile of sticks and no flame. Ailith sighed, dropping the dead squirrel and began to search for tinder. "You weren't taught how to light a fire?"

"We always have someone start fires for us," Caitriona said softly, her cheeks coloring with embarrassment. Ailith's lips went flat, her annoyance bubbling and overwhelming her expression. Caitriona's eyes turned away. "It looked easy to do. I'm sorry."

As the last of the sunlight slipped beyond the horizon, the fire blazed to life under Ailith's trained hand. When she skinned the squirrel, Ailith found herself biting her tongue as Caitriona began to gag over the sight of skin being tugged off the meat.

"I suppose you've never seen your cooks prep the meat you ate either?" Ailith asked as she pushed the squirrel's body onto a spit and settled it over the flames. This time, Caitriona didn't answer. Perhaps from embarrassment, but at least a little bit because she heaved into the bushes again.

Later, Ailith glanced at Caitriona who sat near the fire, silently watching the flames while hugging her legs to her chest and resting her chin on her knees. Evening settled and so had Ailith's irritation. Taking in a deep breath, Ailith asked the one question that was on her mind.

"Do you suspect your father sent a search party by now?"

Firelight reflected in Caitriona's eyes as she shook her head. "Not yet," she said before returning her chin to her knee. "I often go many days without seeing him. He rarely has time for us as a family, only for whatever services he needs."

She reached over her shoulder and pulled out her long braid, made messy from traveling underneath her cloak hood. She started to unbraid her hair. "I do my work in the library, then return to my quarters. Greer and Etta often have supper with me, perhaps my mother, but my father is constantly locked in the war room."

"What do you suppose will happen when he realizes you're gone?" Ailith asked. Caitriona's hand stilled in the tangles of her waist-length hair.

"Send a search party and message the guards at the towers along the border. He'll likely ask Greer to look for me; for what little he knows of me; he recognizes that she knows me best. But, if we're lucky, we'll get a few days of travel before he notices."

Other than days that kept Ailith from home due to a shift at the gate, she had every meal with her father. She couldn't fathom going days without her parents noticing she was missing. Caitriona's only company was Etta, Greer, and the library staff she worked with; perhaps riches didn't immediately indicate a fulfilling life. Loneliness could still be present.

Caitriona gave a lazy shrug of her shoulders. "Greer will try to keep him at bay. Sometimes when they meet, he asks for a report of how I'm doing—I suppose it saves time from actually seeing me."

Ailith frowned. "I'm sorry. That's ..." Ailith knew what she was about to say would toe the line into blasphemy but somehow she felt Caitriona wouldn't care. "... really awful behavior for a father."

The princess's eyebrows rose briefly, before rewarding Ailith with a genuine smile.

"Thank you, Ailith MacCree," she replied, her arms wrapping more tightly around her legs, her smile brighter than before.

Ailith shifted and chewed on the inside of her cheek for a moment before offering, "You can just call me Ailith."

"Alright. Thank you, Ailith. And you can call me Caitriona, if you'd like."

The pair shared bread and squirrel meat in quiet companionship. Once the sun fully sunk beyond the horizon and into the western sea, night let its hair down in a quiet hush of cool, frosty air. Ailith spent many nights at the gate through various forms of weather, making her less sensitive to the changing elements. On the ridge of the valley while the temperature dropped and the wind traveled up over the curves of the earth, Ailith found she didn't mind very much as her gaze was drawn upward. It was rare to see so many stars in the city.

It became rapidly clear that Caitriona had no experience with such nights. Caitriona settled as Ailith declared first watch. The princess wrapped herself in her traveling cloak and covered herself with the blanket from her pack. She slipped beautifully-made gray gloves over her hands and pulled the hood of her cloak over her head. All her movements were specific, tidy. She seemed unable to make herself comfortable on the hard ground or to pull her cloak any more tightly around her. Each time Ailith glanced at the princess's curled form she seemed to have curled up tighter until a slight quiver shook her body.

"Princess, are you cold?" Ailith asked, unable to speak Caitriona's name yet. It felt wrong, unprofessional, and they still knew little of each other. Ailith squatted beside the small fire and placed more sticks and branches onto it. It had been barely enough to cook the squirrel and didn't make much of a difference for warming a sleeping body on the cold earth.

"I'm fine," Caitriona murmured from beneath her heap of cloak and blanket. Ailith reached for her own pack, pulling from it the blanket Etta provided and unfurled it over the princess. Grabbing her bag, she positioned it against Caitriona's back to block some of the night air from blowing against her. Caitriona's shivering stopped, then a tentative, gloved hand reached out from the cloth and pulled it down to expose her face; nose pink, cheeks too, she looked over the small flames of the tiny fire. "Wake me halfway through the night and I'll keep watch."

"Sure thing."

"And Ailith?" Caitriona pushed herself up on her elbows, pulling the blankets down and looking serious. Ailith raised her brows. "Thank you for helping my sister and I, it means more than I can express."

The princess settled amongst her blankets, burrowing her face beneath her cloak, and Ailith let her head tilt back as she looked to the heavens, glad to not have to respond. She was exhausted, less so from the physical exertion of the day, but more from having to interact with another human, and she welcomed the quiet night.

Caitriona was a ball of light and observation. Neither woman had much experience beyond the city gates, but while Ailith made quiet observations of her surroundings, Caitriona shared her joy, eagerly pointing out the different beauties on their path. How the sunset looked from the hills, the peace of the streambed, a doe and her fawn.

Ailith had no intention of waking Caitriona halfway through the night. She was trained to stay awake for long hours while she suspected Caitriona wasn't. She would let the princess sleep until dawn and take this time to enjoy the silence of the woods.

Ailith's experience with the woods beyond the city gate was brief. At the city gate, despite being near the brush and wooded area surrounding the Elder Tree, the rumble of city life drowned out sounds of the forest.

Now sitting in the woods beside the runaway princess, Ailith was surprised by how loud the forest could be. Owls, foxes, a wolf somewhere far off in the hills—thankfully—and more insect noises than Ailith ever heard from the gate. For the first hour of her watch, Ailith was on edge, listening intently to every sound and wondering if monstrous creatures would draw near. They often remained out of the valley, seemingly understanding that Cearny's hunters would kill any discovered there, but that didn't stop them from appearing every now and again. The caroling countess that was killed that week, a cockatrice the summer before that peacefully pecked at the forest floor beyond the gate until the hunters arrived. Farmers occasionally reported spotting the hidden ones, childlike creatures that appeared lost in the woods and would devour any well-meaning helper. But as the night continued, she allowed herself to relax.

When dawn neared, birdsong replaced hooting owls and a chill hung heavy in the air. The earth, and their clothes, grew damp as dew ran its wet fingers along the ground. The dew would surely turn into etchings of heavy frost soon and Ailith hoped they found warmer outfits before that, mentally taking note to shop for thicker clothes once they reached one of the cities.

Ailith remained by the fire, closing her eyes briefly overnight and jolting awake only twice when her body began to slump. The sun had not yet crested the hillside and Braewick still lay in shadow, peaceful in darkness when Caitriona sat up, her red hair a mess surrounding her shoulders and falling down her back, and the crease of her glove indented her cheek.

"You should've woken me so I could have a shift," she stated, her voice soft. She pulled the gray gloves off her hands and reached to her hair to make a quick plait. "Good morning, though. Thank you for letting me sleep."

"You aren't one of those cheerful morning people, are you?"

Caitriona grinned and it was the only answer Ailith needed.

They gathered their supplies and ate the remaining fruit. They would make it over the ridge and begin the descent toward the Umberfend Marsh that day. The outpost was along Gilway Road, south of the Avorkaz battlefields. It was a risk to go to the outpost as Braewick guardsmen and cavalries often passed through, but it was the only post outside of the valley before the few days' travel to Stormhaven and where Greer instructed them to get horses.

They made good time, scrambling over the boulder-covered hillside crests before beginning their way down the other side. Springs leaked from rocks, trickling water downhill. One stone outcrop allowed the pair a clear view of the eastern expanse of land beyond Braewick Valley. The Endless Mountains were not yet visible on the horizon, but the Umberfend Marsh showed speckled flecks of skyward reflection with tall grasses, a scattering of dead trees, and hungry carrion birds in the distance. Gilway Road was clear—a stripe of sandy-colored earth that cut through the wetlands with spots of travelers scattered along its length. Tufts of smoke rose from the chimneys of a few homes, each one quite a distance from the other. But the light blue sky with a sprinkle of puffed clouds left Ailith realizing that she was but a speck, much like the rest of humanity, ultimately meaningless when paired with the expanse of the world.

"Are you alright?" Caitriona stood beside Ailith and reached toward her, as if to touch her shoulder. Ailith blinked and stepped away, ignoring the brief blush over Caitriona's face as her hand dropped.

"I'm fine," Ailith responded, quick and guarded, her own cheeks growing hot. She frowned. She *had* to be more open with Caitriona, not only for the longevity of their travel, but because Caitriona was nothing but an open book to her. Her mother would have scolded her if she was there. "I've just ... never seen the sky this *large* before."

"Nor have I, friend. How lucky are we to see the beauty of something new?"

They moved down the hillside, slipping between the watchtowers without notice. They made their way toward more even ground by the marsh as the sun began to dip behind the hillside and shadows grew, stretching further away from them and enveloping the ground to the east. Within the sight of Gilway Road toward Stormhaven and the outpost, a nervous energy grew in each of them until day truly escaped them and night drew close.

"We should stop," Caitriona suggested, tugging on her cloak and pulling it closed over her chest. "I don't believe we can make it to the outpost today. Greer said by horse we could make it there in a day along the road, but based on my maps, I don't think we'll make it for a few hours more."

Ailith paused and looked toward Gilway Road. They intentionally remained in the woods, sheltered by brush so as not to draw attention to themselves from the few travelers spotted on the road. "You're right. Best to find somewhere to rest."

They tucked themselves against a wide oak with a broad canopy where Ailith showed Caitriona how to stoke the fire with quiet patience before skinning another squirrel out of sight.

"It's like the Elder Tree," Caitriona offered, peering at the oak's leaves gently stirring from the rising heat of the fire. The women looked at one another and simultaneously shook their heads. Nothing could compare to the Elder Tree. Tales told before warm fires explained that from the Elder Tree's roots came the creatures of night, drowning dukes who devour passersby in the Umberfend Marsh, marrow maidens who feast on the men they tricked, fool makers who mirror anything they pleased, as well as dragons, wyverns, cockatrice, and smoke fiends. The tender fibers produced the desires of greed and destruction, ill will and poor luck. From the Elder Tree's fallen leaves, men, fae, phoenixes, and dryads were born amongst the light of creation, hope and joy. This oak could never compare.

They ate in silence, exhausted from the last two days, and, as Ailith settled against the tree, she attempted friendliness.

"Caitriona," she began, the princess's name feeling odd on her tongue. "Is this what you hoped for beyond the kingdom's borders? At least what you have already seen?"

Caitriona settled beside Ailith; their arms pressed together as they shared the base of the oak. "A little bit, yes, although I hoped to explore the world in different ways. Greer has plenty of opportunities to travel, and not all for the guard. I always assumed if I were to ever travel, it would be with a horse and frequent beds to sleep in ... and yet ... there's a certain quality of excitement to this, isn't there?"

"Wandering the woods, hoping we're following the map correctly, eating squirrel, and sleeping in the dirt?" Ailith asked with a smirk.

"Seeing the foliage begin to change," Caitriona laughed, picking up a stick and poking at the flames with it. "Spotting waterfalls I otherwise wouldn't have seen if I traveled by horse and carriage. Sleeping under the stars—something I *never* would've done if I traveled under the pretenses of the crown; they always make Greer take a tent. The stars are shy near the castle, don't you think? But out here, they're on full display."

Ailith studied the princess as she gazed at the tree above them. Something gently pressed into Ailith's mind since they left the Elder Tree, a shadow of a thought that grew until it became a fully formed thing. A form of curiosity and the craving for truth that took firm hold of Ailith until she was unable to think of little else: What caused Caitriona to be so hidden from the rest of the world?

Beyond her better judgment, Ailith fell asleep with her back pressed against the oak tree, head bowed and resting against Caitriona. She'd been watching the fire, their conversation quiet, when her eyes closed, and sleep pulled her down. She was trapped in its embrace, vaguely aware of her surroundings, but couldn't quite free herself from the exhaustion that kept her under. She felt the weight of Caitriona press against her and wondered if she had fallen asleep too, knowing that it was a bad idea.

It never takes long for darkness to gather itself to strike. It only took two days before the creatures Ailith was so worried about found them.

The initial rustling in the brush went unheard. The darkness and all it held eased in and caught the taste of the women in the night air, its salivating desire too much for the gathering creatures to remain silent. With drooling fangs and hanging tongues, clicking, clawed-nails scratched into the boulders along the earth as the shades lapped at the air and laughed over the luck of their discovery in finding such delicacies ripe for the taking.

No stories stated that shades were particularly smart. Perhaps because the smart ones were more discreet. They were hound-like creatures, lanky, the color of darkness, and covered in matted hair and rotting flesh. They weaved between noxious mist and solid mass, switching their forms with ease to travel through night. But when solid, they hunted. In their solid forms, they feasted on life, swallowing the emotions of the creatures they killed and humming from the heat of their prey's blood.

Their laughing growls were enough to snap Ailith out of the paralyzed shell she became in her sleep, shaking her from the hold it had on her body as she witnessed the creatures draw near. Cackling faces of the shades with their eyes glowing, teeth flashing, and lengthened forms bent toward her and Caitriona as wet snouts snuffled to taste the air the pair breathed. She gasped, one hand quickly grabbing her bow and the other reaching for Caitriona. The shades tittered, their teeth clattering together as they chuckled.

Caitriona, awake now, scrambled to her feet. She pulled out her short sword, but the shades already had enough time to study the women. They seemed to determine Ailith was sturdier, her brow wrinkled and lips in a frown even in sleep. She had the most weapons, and her fingers were calloused. She didn't shy away from work. She could fight. But Caitriona was a wisp, gentle and soft, sleeping beside Ailith with her rounded cheek pressed against Ailith's shoulder. They seemed to understand what Ailith already knew. Caitriona was weak, inexperienced, perfectly easy prey, so long as they separated the two.

A shade lunged, snatching at Caitriona's cloak with its teeth and sending her stumbling into Ailith as she tried to pull her cloak free. The short sword dropped from the princess's hand, but Ailith twisted, pulling the string of her bow and letting an arrow fly into the skull of the ghastly beast. The arrow caused it to stagger back and sink to the ground in a pile of putrid rotted hair and bones. Another shade jumped, biting at Ailith's sleeve, its teeth grazing her skin and saliva bitter with the fetid scent of decay. Her arm jolted from the attack and the arrow she pulled from her quiver dropped to her feet.

"Get behind me!" Ailith yelled as she retrieved another arrow. Caitriona pressed her back against the tree as Ailith sent an arrow into the side of one more shade. Another slipped along the edge of the fire, pausing to let out a short howl that rippled into the night air. A peppering of other haunting howls rose from the shadows around the campfire, their calls catching on the wind and moving through the trees.

The shades' eyes glinted in the dark, too far for mortal eyes to see their forms but close enough for the firelight to highlight their hungry gazes. They were surrounded. Caitriona screeched when a shade grabbed her cloak again. Ailith spun on her heel and shot a blind arrow beyond the oak tree. A sigh confirmed her success. Another shade rushed forward, its large paws striking her side, as jaws clamped down on her arm's leather bracer. The impact knocked her off her feet, her bow flying, and the air left her lungs as she hit the ground. Ailith gasped, trying to recall how to breathe as she stared at the leaves of the oak lit by firelight. The shade let go of her arm when she fell, but moved before her vision, fangs dripping as it placed a paw on Ailith's shoulder. Cold pressure seeped through her clothes into her skin like ice. Time slowed, each passing second unbearably long. Had the shade bit her? Had it pressed its fangs down into her skull to finally satisfy its hunger? Was this simply death? She could have done more, Ailith panicked in reflection. If she died, who would help Caitriona? Who would care for Ailith's parents? Her poor parents who were so happy to see her go and *live*?

Blindly, Ailith reached for the dagger on her leg, pulling it free with renewed focus and energy before plunging it into the creature's chest. The blade released a gag-inducing scent of decay and splattered the ground and Ailith's side with foul, black sludge as the shade howled in pain.

Without warning, the world flashed white overhead, a burning light consumed the beast as Ailith's face was shocked by heat. The radiance shifted and moved to the side, the heat going with it and leaving a startling coolness of the air. Ailith focused on the underside of the oak leaves high above once more. The passing white light was a sheet of flame that flew over her body and made her skin sun-hot. An inferno that sent the shades into screaming pain.

As rapidly as it appeared, the flames vanished and Ailith was left blinking. The sudden loss of light, even with the small campfire still sputtering, left her blind for a moment. The forest was silent.

"Caitriona?" Ailith croaked, still lying flat on her back.

"Are you alright?" Caitriona whispered. Ailith rolled onto her elbow and pushed herself upright. They were finally alone with Caitriona sitting on her knees a few feet away.

Ailith nodded as she mirrored Caitriona's position on the ground, her lips parted, her jaw dropped. Caitriona returned Ailith's gaze, her cheeks tear stained, and eyes no longer blue but a dull *gold* that glowed with an internal light.

The smell of blood, decay, burnt fur and flesh hung in the air. Ailith suspected the dead shades weren't far in the brush. Black smoke curled from what remained and small embers winked out one by one. Caitriona's glowing eyes continued to stare straight ahead. Cautiously, so as not to frighten her—but perhaps to also not frighten herself— Ailith crawled forward and took hold of Caitriona's hands. She steeled herself from the heat of Caitriona's palms that nearly burned her on contact and the shocking change of the princess's fingers. Her nails were longer, sharpened, but Ailith only afforded them a passing glance as she tried to remain calm.

"Caitriona?" Ailith whispered, but the princess continued to stare, her glowing eyes boring through Ailith. Ailith felt her heart racing in her chest, but she tried again, leaning closer and whispering the nickname she heard from Greer. "*Cait?*"

Caitriona blinked and the glow of her eyes lessened, her pupils became visible. Ailith tried to smile, something her father would do when Ailith was younger and frightened, but she was certain her smile looked more like a grimace. "Cait, what *was* that?"

Caitriona sucked in a breath and pulled her hands free from Ailith's grasp. Turning her gaze downward she stared at her palms. A sob caught in her throat before she said, "... *I don't know.*"

CHAPTER THREE

CAITRIONA

Fifteen Years Prior

The castle bustled. In fact, it always bustled, but today it was heightened. A visitor arrived, someone who Caitriona's mother knew before she was queen, and Caitriona was in her best dress with hair braided and looped around her head. She was told to be careful, not to get messy, but to busy herself in the nursery until Etta came to retrieve her.

Etta had not yet come and that was part of the problem. A small child has only so much patience and the princess's had run out. So, she found herself drawing figures in the soot of the fireplace, and discovered she could leave handprints across the floor if she put her hands into the soot itself—still warm from the fire that burned out earlier in the morning—and pressed hard against the wood planks. It was a fun game, entertaining, and better than listening to the droning voices of her parents and whatever court guest was there today. Even Greer sat patiently during such talks, back straight and hands folded in her lap.

She would bat Caitriona away when she tried to convince her elder sister to play. Overall, the time in her nursery was better than anything beyond.

Caitriona hummed to herself as she sat upon the ground, turning her attention to her skirts. They were green, perpetually, to set off the color of her hair—just like her mother's—but with soot she made swirls and lines. A beautiful design she was proud of although she suspected Etta would be less pleased. So entranced by decorating her dress, she did not at first hear the rhythmic hum of wind outside the windows of the nursery. She did not notice the bells begin to toll and when she did, it still made no difference. She knew of the warning tolls of the bells. Once upon a time, they frightened her, but Etta comforted Caitriona, reassuring her as she did, "they'll happen weekly, little one. You mustn't let them scare you, otherwise you'll have a lifetime of tears. They only are to be tested in case we ever need them. If we did, it would call all the men who work for the king to the castle to keep us all safe. But for now, ignore them."

She never heard them used for an actual warning. She never knew of a time when they were to be taken seriously.

Never is a very short span of time when you are not yet four.

Caitriona was too young to understand the change of tone in the city, too young to understand the normal hum of noise heightened to gasps and screams. When the white dragon flew to the city and let forth its first blast of flame, Caitriona was too young to know what to do when the room began to slowly fill with smoke.

It wouldn't have mattered either way. The white dragon circled the castle, likely seeing the glimmer of the white marble walls and clean stone, smelling the scent of meat cooked in its large kitchens. Its powerful tail thrashed down into the roof of the nursery, showering the tiny soot handprints with burning beams. The dragon's taloned fingers clawed at the building, not caring for the terror its presence brought.

Caitriona *was* old enough to know fear. She was old enough to hide. She crawled under the table where she ate her morning meals, covered her ears as the dragon howled in the sky above, and buried her face into her decorated skirts. The safety of her room rapidly diminished and became frightening with heightened flames, heavy smoke, and falling beams. So hidden was she that the guards would not find her body until it was too late. A small, broken doll with her red hair burned away, and her green dress broken fiber and soot.

The sound of Queen Róisín's screams were so loud, so filled with heartbreak that the palace crystal shattered, looking glasses cracked, and the sound settled into the stones only to release in whispering cries during deep storms. The queen collapsed and young Greer, recently turned ten, stood frozen by her mother's side. Etta wept as she tried to pull Greer away, her mouth an open hole where sobs came out but were drowned by the wails of the queen.

One would assume the queen cried her daughter's name, but such assumptions would be incorrect. Another name spilled out in desperation.

Kayl, Kayl, she screamed repeatedly, calling for her childhood friend who arrived that morning. He only needed to hear the queen's cries to know what she was saying, what she was begging for: *Save her, save her, save my daughter.*

The man rushed into the room where the queen still screamed, and guards laid the small form upon a bed. The queen collapsed at his feet —*Kayl, Kayl*—and he placed a reassuring hand on her shoulder, stopping her screams before he laid his hands upon the girl's bloodied, burned corpse. He worked his magic into her body and mind, seeking the spirit of the young girl in realms beyond the waking world and beckoned it back to her body. He stroked her face and whispered to her soul, *come home, come home, return to us; you have so much more life left in you.*

If you ask any of the palace workers what they witnessed that day, they likely will not speak. The palace workers, haunted by the queen's cries for weeks, months, and years, find their minds immediately go blank and their memories become wisps. The actuality of the events was witnessed by many and yet, the memory is recalled only deep at night when they find themselves tossing and turning in their beds, unable to find sleep.

There is another reason those who witnessed the attack of the white dragon find they cannot speak of that day. Miracles are discussed far and wide, worshiped with hope and desire by those who are most lost. But a miracle twisted into something that binds the receiver to a fate worse than death is not even shared in whispered hushes. It remains within the confines of the mind as a memory only released with sudden realization while the world threatens to fall to pieces once more.

CHAPTER FOUR

AILITH

They traveled in the dark; in Ailith's opinion, there wasn't any other option. Caitriona was shattered, filled with tears and lost in thought. Ailith didn't pepper her with questions after the shades were killed, sensing the princess was trying to process what happened and wouldn't provide many answers. She ushered Caitriona to gather their things while she picked through the brush to retrieve her spent arrows. Amongst the darkened shrubbery, she saw the true damage Caitriona caused: burned shades, mostly husks and some simple piles of ash. The ground covering beneath their feet turned black and ashen from the quick flash of heat and flame—the flames Caitriona somehow created from her hands were forceful enough to scorch and kill everything as quickly as they appeared. Ailith paused at a shade she stabbed. In some ways, Ailith understood why King Cearny and King Donal were so fearful of magic users and creatures that defied what worldly laws humans and animals abided by. It only took a moment of seemingly uncontrolled power to kill them whole while Ailith, with no power to speak of, had barely made a dent in the number of creatures. Ailith felt a quivering certainty she was lucky she hadn't been lost to the flames as well.

While she suspected whatever shades escaped wouldn't attack again, she was nervous and unsettled, and didn't want the princess to discover how many she had killed—four—or how mutilated their bodies were; could you say mutilated if they were reduced to ash?

Ailith made the executive decision to skirt along the woods, a few yards from Gilway Road as they had before, and make their way to the outpost by starlight. Better to move along and get away from the scene than to linger.

Caitriona followed in silence, staying close. Every time Ailith glanced back, the princess kept her eyes downcast. The longer they walked, the longer Caitriona remained quiet, and Ailith found herself growing increasingly concerned. As dawn lit the landscape, casting the world in a slate-gray glow, Ailith reached a tentative hand to Caitriona and gently squeezed her shoulder. Her attempt to reassure was accepted as Caitriona didn't pull away but sidestepped closer before glancing up and offering a thin smile that didn't reach her eyes. Her eyes were no longer glowing and nearly returned to their usual sea of blue, beside a few small, gold flecks that flickered in the low light of dawn. As Caitriona looked at Ailith, her smile turned downward into a frown and she leaned closer, eyes narrowing.

"Wait." She grabbed Ailith's shoulders and scrutinized her face. "Stand still for a moment."

"What's wrong?" Ailith's senses ignited, and awareness sharpened. Caitriona pulled the hood of Ailith's cloak off and turned her toward the light of the coming dawn before gently touching the guard's cheek.

"Oh, Ailith," she gasped, her voice heavy with sorrow. "You're burned! I did this to you! I'm so sorry."

Ailith touched her cheek and felt heat, similar to a bad sunburn. The memory of the white-hot flames passing over her head flared to life, her lungs recalling the ache of the wind being knocked from them. As they walked through the early morning light, she registered her face was slightly sore but hadn't thought much about it.

"It's fine," Ailith batted Caitriona's hand away from her face. The princess looked hurt and frustrated. They had gone long enough without speaking, but this seemed to push them to a precipice and force their attention to what was previously unmentionable. Ailith touched Caitriona's shoulder again, her fingertips gentle, uncertain if she was pushing boundaries. "It's like a sunburn, right? It feels like that at least. I'm fine. It's fine."

Caitriona considered Ailith, her pale face peeking from the shadow of her cloak's hood, and her eyes shimmered with tears. The exhaustion of the last two days and spent adrenaline subdued Ailith's stubbornness, and she couldn't help but want to comfort the princess. The guilt the princess felt was obvious, but Ailith couldn't ignore what occurred anymore, taking the bite out of her tone and leaving her voice softened, she asked the one question that had been bubbling at the surface. "Please, can you tell me what happened back there?"

Caitriona sighed and raised a shaking hand to touch her forehead as she briefly closed her eyes. "I told you; I don't know." She dropped her hand and turned away, walking a few steps forward before spinning on her heel and turning back, her expression pleading. "It was my mistake that we were attacked because you fell asleep, and I was supposed to keep watch, but I fell asleep too. Then you were fighting until you weren't. When you fell and I saw those creatures rushing at you, I just … wanted to help. I wanted to protect you like you protected me. And suddenly it was just … happening."

"The flames," Ailith whispered, and Caitriona nodded. She looked down at her hands then reached into the folds of her skirt, pulling free her traveling gloves.

"I never created flame before." Caitriona pulled the gloves on. "At least … not like that."

"So, this isn't a normal occurrence." Ailith attempted, taking a step forward toward Caitriona. "But one that *has* happened before."

"Greer noticed first. My mother, Greer, and I ate a meal together to celebrate my birthday in the spring. Etta, Callan, and his father even attended. Greer convinced my mother to include them. They were thrilled, and so was I. But I was also angry. My father didn't show … he brushed it off. When I spoke my disappointment to my mother, she brushed it off, too. It was just a meal, she said. But she knows how little interaction I have with him. She knew I hoped he would join us. I grew angry with her and after we finished our meal, I retired to my quarters to pout.

"Normally, Greer's quick to ridicule our father, but she attempted to defend him, and I knew she was doing so to calm me, but it enraged me. I don't remember what I said but the flames in my room grew. The candles, the fire in the hearth, they all lengthened and reached toward the ceiling. The flames caught onto one of the curtains.

"We assumed it was an odd coincidence. Yet days later it happened again. I attempted to speak to my father. My entire life he's kept me at arm's length despite that I'm second in line to the throne. He's always had this sense of shame and distaste toward me. I followed him to his chambers, and everything I felt came barreling out. I wanted to understand why he's ignored me my *entire* life and dislikes me so. He said he had no time for my *emotional outburst*. I stormed from the room as Greer came in and she saw it, the flames in my father's hearth becoming wild and tall then calming after I left. She said my eyes glowed gold." Caitriona stopped and swallowed.

Ailith shifted on her feet, uncertain. Despite traveling together for two days, this was the most Caitriona had spoken at any given time. The princess seemed to be drowning in her emotions, overwhelmed by sharing her experiences, and Ailith stood before her in silence, allowing the woman to share her truth without comment, until she saw a tear slip over Caitriona's cheek.

"That must have been frightening." Ailith forced herself to make eye contact with Caitriona, knowing her words had more emphasis if she did so. "To find out that change about yourself. But also, to have these powers with your father present ..."

"It was awful. We knew whatever was happening with the flames and my eyes was *my* doing, *my* fault." Caitriona pressed her hands to her chest repeatedly with each admission of her apparent wrongdoing. "I tried to hide it away. I intentionally kept my distance from my father since he triggered me before, but it still happened beyond my control multiple times through the summer: my eyes changing color and then glowing, and flames responding to my presence."

Unable to remain quiet any longer, questions persisting in Ailith's brain found strength to gather into words and birth from her mouth. "What brought you two to hire me and look for Kayl?"

Caitriona laughed; a painful sound created from the frustration of the situation. "Because Greer has always been a problem solver.

Considering the laws, neither of us have experience with magic, but she found healers from the city; do you know of them? The old women who make remedies for ailments?"

The women were notorious in her part of the city. Those who lived in Ailith's neighborhood couldn't afford the medical care the royal family had, but Ailith secretly thought their care was better. The old women, often believed to have capabilities they kept hidden since magic was outlawed, were more knowledgeable than simply knowing what herb could cure a person's ailments. An unspoken rule within their neighborhood was to never share the location of the healers, but it was interesting to hear Greer knew to go to them. "What did they say?"

"Greer told them it was one of her guards. Someone whose eyes glowed and they could control elements. They said it was magic awakening and if the person didn't gain control, it could be harmful. They suggested sending the guard to a magic user who could provide a better understanding of what was going on. Greer immediately thought of Kayl."

Ailith considered this turn of events, her interest in Kayl perking up. King Donal found magic unnatural, strange, and banned it from the city years ago; King Cearny took it a step further by threatening magic users with death if caught displaying powers. Neighbors began reporting one another and distrust became constant. The herbal women hadn't dared to pass on their teachings to younger generations, and if they did it was a well-kept secret. "So ... Kayl is a magic user?"

"Yes, he has great powers. He knew my mother before she became queen; they were both orphans and lived together at a home. Greer went to our parents and asked about Kayl, she said she remembered him visiting and wanted to know more about him. Our mother was upset, but our father was enraged."

"He visited Braewick Valley before?"

"He was here when the white dragon attacked. Were you in the valley then? Greer said you began training for the guard when you were sixteen, but I must admit, I don't know much about your life prior to that."

The blood drained from Ailith's face and a chill formed in her stomach as it always did when the dragon attack was mentioned. She and her parents were having a picnic at the Elder Tree that day when the brush—previously filled with the sound of afternoon birdsong— went silent. She hid with them against the tree as a hushing sigh repeated itself from the east and grew louder with each repetition. The still forest—devoid of birds and insects, the ground squirrels gone and hidden away—began to breathe. Air stirred, moving across the ground in waves before seemingly sucking back towards the east, before the roar of the dragon upended all sense of safety Ailith previously had.

Blinking, Ailith swallowed, returning to the present. "We didn't see much ... but we heard it all. My father responded to the king's warning bells but a wall collapsed. He was injured—that's why he can't work anymore."

"Oh," Caitriona said, falling still. "I'm sorry, Ailith."

Ailith waved her hand; she didn't want to talk about her father or that traumatic day.

Caitriona continued. "Kayl just arrived that morning to meet my father. Greer said he wanted to discuss something about the area he and my mother grew up in. Father didn't want to meet with him and only agreed to do so on behalf of mother. Then the dragon attacked and ..." The words left Caitriona's mouth, invisible yet floating away. She fidgeted with her hands; a nervous tick Ailith had come to notice. She chewed at her lip for a moment before bracing herself. "I was killed during the attack. But Kayl ... saved me. He used magic to bring me back to this world and heal me."

Ailith's eyes bulged. The rumors she heard for years flicked through her memory, one after another. Hushed voices whispering that the princess was injured, couldn't be seen in public, or dead. Ailith's father always said rumors were influenced by truth.

"So that's why we're searching for Kayl? Because of your magic and his?" Ailith said with a stab of embarrassment. "This was never to convince the king to stop his conquests, was it?"

Caitriona grew still and pressed her lips into a thin line. Ailith's mouth went dry and her jaw set. Greer lied to her; they all did. Her breath quickened and she pushed her hand over her hair. Her cheeks burned and her eyes shifted from Caitriona, unable to maintain contact.

She berated herself for believing such a falsehood to begin with; she should have known better than to trust Cearny's daughters.

"It took a few months before Greer figured out where Kayl was." Caitriona's words came fast and her tone higher, nervous. Her brows rose with concern as she stepped closer, but Ailith could only stare, agitated. "We couldn't ask our mother, she never speaks of her upbringing and after how badly she reacted to Greer asking about Kayl, Greer felt she wouldn't get anywhere with her. And my father practically frothed at the mouth when Greer mentioned Kayl. I'm not surprised, it's how he's always been when magic is discussed by us. Can you—can you imagine if he saw me move flames? Can you imagine if he saw me push them from my palms?"

The women stared at each other. It was easy to imagine the king's reaction given the dead magical creatures and the regular disappearance of magic makers in the city. Ailith thought of the caroling countess' dead hand outstretched toward her just days prior as if reaching for help that never came, the scent of her blood still easily brought to mind.

Ailith studied Caitriona. She studied the unshed tears in her frightened eyes and pinched brow, the quiver in her voice, and the nervous wringing of her hands. Her hands that were full of heat and flame just hours before could so easily be left cold and still under her father's decree. Ailith swallowed down the sense of betrayal, if only for a moment, if only to listen to the princess.

"Greer found details of the white dragon attack and that Kayl left the castle a day after by carriage to Caermythlin. It seems the town disbanded though; it's near the southern base of the Endless Mountains but Greer couldn't find any additional information on it. She began sending letters requesting memory keepers and librarians to provide any information on his whereabouts. All we got was that Kayl lived near the Endless Mountains, north of the fog-touched valleys within the Mazgate Dominion." Caitriona dropped her hands and stared at Ailith pleadingly.

"So, you feel that what happened back there," Ailith waved toward Braewick, "May happen again and you're hoping Kayl can stop it. But all of that ... you had no control in it?"

Caitriona nodded, then looked at the ground. When she spoke

again, her voice was heavy with tears. "I didn't realize it would kill them. I only wanted them to stop. I wanted to protect you. I'm sorry, I'm so sorry for all this."

The tightness in Ailith's chest eased as she moved forward and slipped an arm around Caitriona's shoulders with the light of morning erupting around them, the chorus of birds heralding in the day.

"Well, look at it this way." She tried to sound reassuring despite her heightened nerves from the shades, the princess's illegal and explosive powers, and her mission becoming quite different—and more dangerous—than she originally perceived. "It was to our benefit. I failed you back there, I should've been able to hold my ground. Had you not done that, I don't know how it would have gone."

Caitriona relaxed under Ailith's arm. "Without you there, I would've been attacked in my sleep and ended up dead. And I didn't even make the flames happen, it wasn't a conscious thing, just an accident."

"Perhaps a blessing in disguise," Ailith replied. The words, at first, felt like a lie fed to someone to simply calm them. But Ailith spoke to herself as much as Caitriona. She considered her next words carefully before continuing. "I suppose it's scary to suddenly do that. I think if it were me, I would've been quivering in my boots. But despite your father's laws, there are still magic users in the world. The fae, the witches, the mages all existed long before your father and grandfather ruled. Although it's outlawed currently, it doesn't mean magic makers are bad. Magic used to be legal; it was accepted for generations, and magic makers were and probably are still good. Surely, they'll see one of their own and be able to help you. *Kayl* will be able to help you. Perhaps you'll be able to control it with time and do good with it."

Caitriona touched the corners of her eyes with her gloved fingers, wiping away tears, as the crease between her brows lessened and the tightness of her shoulders fell away. Ailith gave her shoulder a squeeze then let go.

Caitriona looked shyly at Ailith. "I suppose we're continuing to the outpost?"

If Ailith were to quit and go home, now was the time to do it. And yet, she was never one to ignore someone who needed help. "I suppose we are."

CHAPTER FIVE

AILITH

When the outpost was fully visible, the women made their way onto Gilway Road with cloak hoods pulled up. The road curved toward Avorkaz and the battlefields, but halfway up stood the inn nestled against its side. Its back faced east where Umberfend Marsh lay, its front overlooked the Braewick Valley hills. The post was a frequent stop for travelers between Braewick Valley and the northern lands before King Cearny turned his sights toward taking over Avorkaz. Now business from travelers was replaced by soldiers heading to post in the fields south of the Avorkaz wall while they awaited the king's next order. But the outpost still had a heartbeat: a pasture with horses across the road, and a barn beside. A number of stable hands settled horses that just arrived and prepared ones whose owners were ready to depart. The outpost itself was a two-story structure next to scattered trees, immense and old, that stood taller than the building itself. Beyond were homes for the employees, making a small hamlet of sorts.

When they reached the post, they paused, reading a crooked sign nailed over the doorway that stated The Wandering Nook.

"Stay by my side." Ailith stopped before the door and looked at the yard of The Wandering Nook. Travelers moved about, loading their horses, smoking, or conversing with others. "Don't speak; your royal accent is too telling out here. We'll go in, get ourselves a room, and go straight to it. We can send a letter to Etta or Callan after, and I'll get us food."

Caitriona nodded; her glove-covered hands pulled her cloak hood tightly over her face before they stepped over the threshold. Pausing in the entrance of a large room, they observed the space with a single fireplace at the northern end and a bar circling the base of a staircase in the center. Scattered tables and benches filled the opened area, and a few people ate meals or drank as they conversed. Ailith focused on the bartender. She edged around a bench and made her way to the bar with Caitriona following close behind, head bowed and eyes on the ground.

"Hello, barkeep?" Ailith's unfamiliarity with the situation made her voice crack. She'd never rented a room at an inn before and only visited a few taverns with her fellow guards, but even then, she kept to herself and never spoke to the employees.

Her awkward greeting drew the bartender's attention. He was at least a foot taller than both women, with a thick brow and thinning hair, and ears that ended in the slightest upturned point. Ailith couldn't pull her gaze from the man. The fae, who were often born with magic, were pushed from the land before Ailith was born. She heard from other guards that a few still remained beyond Braewick Valley, those with little magic or none at all, but she never met anyone with any noticeable fae attributes. "Um." Ailith's words felt like molasses on her tongue. She blinked and tried again, "Do you have any rooms available?"

He stepped closer, looking over both women as he dried a stein, and sniffed. "Separate rooms or one together?"

"Together. Two beds or one, it doesn't matter."

"One silver for the night paid upfront." The man's voice was deep and rough. He placed the stein and towel down and leaned his muscular arms on the edge of the bar. "Meals cost extra."

"That's fine." Ailith pulled a silver piece from the coin bag she was given and slipped it over the counter. "Could I get the meals later and bring them up to the room?"

The bartender shrugged, grabbing the coin and shoving it into his pocket before he reached under the bar to withdraw a key. "If that's what you want, it'll cost the same. The afternoon mealtime just started. I think it's a meat stew, so you have time."

He tossed the key and Ailith snatched it out of the air. She clutched the heavy iron key in her hand.

"Go up the stairs, turn left, then go to the room on the right at the end of the hall. Last room there."

Ailith turned and ushered Caitriona to the stairs. The steps creaked as they clambered up and the worn wood of the dark hall emphasized shadows. She tried hard to ignore sounds of coughing, snoring, arguing, or moans from rooms they passed, but the sense they were eavesdropping colored Ailith's cheeks as they reached the door the bartender mentioned. After a shared glance, Ailith pressed the key into the lock and opened it.

The room was small and cramped, but perfect for their needs. A small table with a gas lamp stood between two narrow beds with a small fireplace filled with fresh logs on the opposite wall. Another table sat below the single window with a wash bowl and candle atop, and two chairs tucked beneath. Despite the aged smell and stuffy air, it looked clean. Ailith suspected that by this point she would have been happy even if it was filthy, so long as it was dry and warm.

"Let's get settled and then I'll get stew." Ailith held the door open for Caitriona and locked it after the princess entered.

Caitriona moved across the room and pulled out a chair, dropping her bag upon it before pulling her cloak hood back and reaching to untie it. The morning dew dampened their clothes as they traveled, and the edges of Caitriona's cloak hung heavy as she draped it over the back of her chair.

Ailith mirrored Caitriona's movements, hers weighed down by exhaustion from last night's events. The rest of the walk had done her well, removing her lingering upset from Greer's lie and leaving behind only a glimmer of frustration. If she was going to do this task, she would see it through, and perhaps demand more coin for Greer's lies when she returned home.

Caitriona placed paper, ink, and a quill from her pack on the table between them. Ailith considered her eyes were playing tricks as Caitriona was cast in light from the window.

"I never realized you have a touch of blonde in your hair," Ailith murmured. "I thought it was a deep red, maybe I was wrong." After all, she was wrong more than once in the last few days. The shades approached them with abundant ease, too; perhaps she wasn't as observant as she thought.

"I don't, it's just red," Caitriona replied, as she reached for her long, now-messy braid and pulled it over her shoulder, and looked at the plait which had the undertones of red just before, but now was highlighted in gold. She ran her fingers along it. "At least I didn't used to."

Ailith slipped her cloak from her own shoulders and draped it over the back of her chair. "Maybe the sunlight brightened the color of your hair," Ailith began, seeing the look of concern on Caitriona's face and uncertain how to comfort her. "My father used to have blonde streaks in his hair by the end of summer when I was younger."

"I've worn my cloak hood up and it's only been two days," Caitriona mumbled, pulling the tie from the end of her braid and brushing her fingers through to undo the plait. She crossed the floor and sat at the foot of the closest bed. "Maybe it's the same as when my eyes glowed. Maybe my hair is changing."

Ailith sat beside Caitriona and watched her fingers pick up speed, rushing to undo the braid with nervous energy. She frowned as her fingers tangled in the mix of red and gold.

Ailith reached to touch Caitriona's hands, which stilled. "Maybe it is, but your eyes, they turned back to their blue. Your hair may turn back to its normal colors as well." Ailith smiled at the princess then hopped to her feet. "I'll get a fire going. Settle in; it may be a few days before we're able to sleep with a roof over our heads again."

Ailith visited the bar repeatedly over the course of the afternoon, first to purchase stew and bread, then to retrieve water for the washing bowl and two pitchers of mead, and at last their evening meal. Within the room, they looked over the map and studied their path forward, deciding to leave in the morning and head to Stormhaven. It would be quicker to go straight to the Avorkaz border and travel east on Mazgate Highway to the Endless Mountains, but that wasn't possible with the battlegrounds between them and Avorkaz's gates. They would have to take the long route around, and perhaps they could gain insight into Kayl's location along the way.

"I wish I could've made a map of the Endless Mountains as well." Caitriona's fingertips drifted over the map. "But we haven't any."

"Made?" Ailith repeated.

"I made this map." Caitriona tapped the paper. "I've been transcribing maps in the library. I made this for our trip."

"Oh." Ailith looked back at the map and saw it in a different light. The handwriting indicating towns was Caitriona's, the details of little buildings and trees her artwork. It suddenly took on more meaning knowing she had drawn each little house, each crooked stream, than just a map for travel. "You've been planning this for some time, haven't you?"

"Ever since Greer realized this was a repeated occurrence," Caitriona said, her lips turning down and color flushing her cheeks.

Caitriona spent the remainder of the afternoon fussing over the letter to Etta with multiple false starts. "Do you think this will do?" she asked as the shadows began to grow long and Ailith lit the gas lamp. Ailith reached for the slip of paper, the neat, curling handwriting matching that on the map.

~~We arrived without issue.~~ *We arrived at the outpost. I have seen many birds flying to the southern waters. I wonder if they will still see winter's snow? - C*

Ailith raised an eyebrow and held the paper out. "The southern waters?"

"I figured Etta would understand we're going to Stormhaven. We decided I would be subtle in my messages, leaving clues Etta could figure out or talk to Callan about. We agreed I would write about birds." Caitriona bit her bottom lip as she shyly smiled before Ailith had the time to laugh.

As evening drew to a close and the bar began to fill with tired travelers, Ailith ordered their meals and gave the letter to the barkeep to send with a messenger. Whenever Ailith descended to the bar, she listened to the conversations of those in the tavern. There were murmurs about the ongoing tension between Wimleigh Kingdom and Avorkaz, a drunken argument over the weather and crops, jokes about romances gone sour, but no mention of a missing princess. When Ailith and Caitriona began their evening meal in their room overlooking the marshlands from their window, Ailith finally relaxed.

CHAPTER SIX

GREER

G reer moved with purpose, which was no different than any
other day; she always moved with purpose. She learned at an
early age after much observation that people took her all the
more seriously if she remained carefully guarded of her emotions and
forever gave an air that she had somewhere more important to be. It
made people reconsider if it was worth interrupting or delaying her
from wherever it was she was going. She rarely had the patience for
boring conversation, and she certainly didn't have time for small issues
within the palace; it was better to let her mother deal with those.

But in recent months, Greer took up frequent visits to the royal
library and servant quarters to seek out her former nurse maid turned
Caitriona's handmaid. She read numerous volumes on previous battles
and reigns. She sought all information about magic users but found the
library with little pertaining to the subject. Although no one dared
bother Greer with silly questions, the people of the castle often turned
to each other and whispered their observations. While it wasn't unusual
to see her interact with Etta, what caused this sudden rejuvenation of
their relationship? Could she perhaps be with child? Was she avoiding
royal duties? Was she preparing for her role as queen when the king

departed this earth? Was this study of battles a silent protest to her father's military strategies? Perhaps a stance that she sided with those beyond Braewick Valley and their growing resentment of the king? Despite trying to keep gossip away from the heir to the throne, Greer was well acquainted with all that people questioned about her.

No one dared ask Greer. No one dared consider such things even in her presence. Her brown-eyed gaze felt strong enough to pierce a person's mind and rifle through their thoughts, and so palace workers only exchanged glances and kept their rumors amongst themselves, far from earshot of anyone with ties too close to the royal family. Despite these provisions, the questions flit between ears in the hollow shadows of the castle halls and Greer felt them peppering her skin as she moved through with intentional steps. No matter how hard the servants tried to keep their opinions to themselves, Greer was observant enough to sense a change in the air and notice more studied glances that came her way. It only took one look from her to see the gossiping servants scatter. Still, she ignored it all and continued with her day-to-day tasks with little expression passing over her face. It wasn't the first time her family was subject to rumors and speculations, and she rather they be placed on her than her sister.

Late one evening after Caitriona and Ailith left, she returned from the library with heavy eyes and her bed calling. She nearly made it into her quarters before a guard outside her door cleared his throat. She looked at the man. "That's never good," she said, and the guard at least had the grace to look sheepish.

"I apologize, Your Highness, but you have a visitor," the guard replied, keeping his eyes trained down the hall, his face never turning toward her.

"That's *truly* never good," she said before straightening her back and brushing her hands over her hair to ensure it was tidy. There were only three people who would visit her quarters when she wasn't there. One had left the valley just the morning before, the other retired to bed early like always, but the third—

"Hello, father," Greer said as she stepped into her room and closed the door behind her. "Is there anything you need?"

In his youth, King Cearny was a broad, tall man with the same sandy hair and brown eyes Greer inherited. As he aged, his broad shoulders became more curled, his wide jaw more sunken, and the smirk that often played on his lips when Greer was very young turned into a flat, thin line. He held that expression now as he fidgeted with the fraying edges of a tapestry hanging beside Greer's bed; a poorly done unicorn in the center, surrounded by mayflowers and fairy lights. Greer worked on the tapestry with her mother before she turned ten. It was the last thing she did with her mother. After the dragon attack, the queen's behavior toward her daughters shifted. She kept Greer at arm's length from then on. There were no tapestries made, and she told no bedtime stories; she became a ghost of herself and the mother she once was.

The king tucked his hands into the pockets of his dark pants, his brow furrowed already, and tension radiated from his body. "Where were you?"

"The halls, walking," Greer replied with ease, moving further into her room to pull the dagger free from the holder at her waist and placing it on her dressing table. After years of working beside her father and encountering his frequently poor moods, she became quite skilled at maintaining an air of calm around him. She often compared it to tiptoeing past a sleeping beast you didn't want to provoke. Most times if you were careful, you could avoid detection.

Most times.

"And do you know where your sister is?" He continued, his voice louder than needed and his words sending Greer's stomach down to pool at her feet. Greer swallowed but kept her face blank, her body still turned away. She reached to her hair and began to loosen it from the tight bun she kept it in, pausing to glance at her father's reflection in the looking glass. He began to pace behind her, a sign that his emotions were filling him whole, and he needed to move to let out the energy from it or explode.

"I suppose in her room." Greer maintained the same relaxed tone and pretended not to notice his agitated state as she shook her hair loose and dropped pins and ties to the table. She moved through her evening routine as normal, not turning towards him.

"But she's not," the king hissed. Their eyes met through the reflection of the looking glass. "She hasn't been seen in two days."

Greer shook her head, her blonde hair falling down her back and around her face as she continued feigning confusion. She turned to the king, pitching her eyebrows with pretend concern. "Perhaps she's holed up in the library? You know how interested she is in drawing copies of the fraying maps."

The king paused his pacing and turned his attention fully to her; Greer braced herself. For years he had become more explosive, more aggressive, and while his physical abuse was rarer than when she was a child, she felt she came close to experiencing it as an adult more than once. She suspected what stilled his hand from being raised was the fact that he could not mark his heir who was so constantly in the public eye. There was an image to maintain, after all, and his image was more important than his relationships.

It was in moments like this where his anger was barely restrained that he grew very still and stood very close. While age shrunk him, his rage inflated him, and he towered over Greer, making her feel incredibly small as his body vibrated with emotions.

"Greer." He was practically growling like a beast. "I've had her room searched, I've had the library searched, and I've had *your* room searched as well. She's gone."

Greer sucked in a breath and held it. It was the right response, as her father seemed to deflate slightly. He only saw the shock of an elder sister finding out her younger sister was missing, which was what Greer wanted him to see. Surely it wasn't the response of a sister realizing she hadn't considered the king would discover their secret within two days' time. For a brief moment, she was grateful she hadn't written any plans down, that she hadn't left a paper trail for her father to stumble across.

"What should we do?" Greer whispered, her gaze lowering.

"A search party and a reward for her safe return. Word travels fast when coin is involved, particularly from the crown," he replied. She remained planted where she stood as the king bobbed his head. "I'm gathering my most trusted men to search the city, but I'll also send messengers beyond its walls. If she left the city, perhaps talk of a reward will beat her to her destination."

"You think she left?" Greer asked, honest confusion bleeding into her expression. She assumed, if anything, her father would immediately pin the blame for Caitriona's disappearance on his foes. "What if she was taken? Perhaps by someone tied to the Mazgate Dominion."

The king frowned and turned away. "There's no sign of a struggle, no ransom note. I've asked the servants who clean her clothing and room, and they haven't seen her. They made her bed the morning two days past and never found any indication she returned to the room. They didn't consider raising an alarm, too stupid to think of such a thing, and now they can reflect on their stupidity as they figure out how to feed their families. The idiots. I've fired them all and I may have their heads by the end of this.

"Upon going through her room *myself*, I found a drawer with her writing. She wrote how desperately she wished to leave the castle, how she wanted to see the world beyond Braewick, that she dreamt of going to other *libraries*, of all things. After all these years I would have thought she would be *well behaved*, but perhaps she foolishly felt the need to rebel," he spat. His hand tightened into a fist as he slowly shook his head with disbelief. "I was making progress in finding a suitor for her, someone to bring us more prosperity and a chance to extend our kingdom overseas. Her selfish behavior could ruin it all."

Greer let out a quick breath, annoyance for her father snarling in her chest and setting her blood on fire. It was the first she heard of her father planning to marry Caitriona off, which likely meant her sister had no clue. His concern over a broken business contract for impending rule rather than the safety of his daughter made her all the more enraged. But she couldn't ignore the rush of adrenaline from the surprise that Caitriona left behind writings. Her sister always had her head in the clouds and her eyes on the horizon; she always wanted more than what the palace walls could provide. Marriage to a person she didn't know was not the way to obtain that.

Greer promised herself years before that when she became queen, she would send her sister abroad immediately so she may see the world. She would free Caitriona from such careful observance that was thrust on her since the dragon attack. It made sense that Caitriona would write down her hopes; Caitriona didn't have any friends to share them with, but Greer prayed there were no details of her powers or their actual plans included. Then again, if she wrote of her developing powers, Greer suspected this conversation with her father would be very different, which drew her irritation back to her father for his reaction. Caitriona went missing and he focused on her rebellion and a failing transaction, rather than her safety. This girl who was hidden away and protected at all costs surprised her father when he learned she dreamt of adventure. Then again, how would he know? He had very little to do with Caitriona. In reality, he seemed to genuinely dislike the girl.

Greer blinked with sudden clarity: for all of Caitriona's life it was their mother who fought to keep Caitriona locked away and safe, never their father. It was their mother who stayed with Caitriona continuously after the dragon attack. Her mother would tell Greer that Caitriona was not to join her during guard ceremonies or to sit at court when the citizens of Braewick attended the Day of Royal Greeting. She always had control over Caitriona's life at the castle while the king had his sights on more power.

Their father viewed Greer as a piece of his legacy. If he could live forever, he would, but since that was impossible, he planned to live out his glory through his daughter's footsteps when she was set to reign. But what about Caitriona? Greer heard him comment in the past about her beauty, her desire to please and how perfect of a wife she would be to another royal. A pawn in his game as he bided his time until he could use her to gain more influence on another land. That was Cearny's true upset of Caitriona's disappearance; how demure of a wife would she be if she rebelled?

Whenever Greer was around her father in private, he was quick to show how little he knew of either of his children and how he only viewed them as political tools. Greer's lips turned steadily downward, the disgust she developed for her father coating her tongue and choking her like the most bitter fruit.

Her father sniffed, satisfied by what he said and misreading Greer's expression for one of upset over the news. He was incapable of assuming she would ever be upset with him. He nodded, perhaps content to have caused an emotional tidal wave—he'd use this as a teaching lesson later—then walked past Greer and out the door, leaving her where she stood. She remained silent, unmoving, then realized she held her breath and gasped for air. Compartmentalizing her emotions and focusing on the issue at hand, Greer began to calculate what steps to take next, until the king's thunderous footfall in the hall reduced to nothing.

CHAPTER SEVEN

CAITRIONA

"How many shades did I kill?" Caitriona asked, her meal of steak, potatoes and carrots sitting untouched on the little table. It was heavily seasoned with herbs and the scent lingered lazily in the air. Her stomach growled. Ailith had a fork of food halfway to her mouth when Caitriona spoke; her eyes flicked to meet Caitriona's then to her plate.

"Perhaps only one. The rest ran off."

Caitriona felt the tender rush of nerves along her neck as she saw through Ailith's lie. The guard continued to eat, avoiding eye contact whilst doing so. She wasn't one to meet Caitriona's eye very often, but this seemed intentional.

Caitriona knew the guard was trying to protect her from reality. She saw three shades, at least, rushing to bite at Ailith when she fell, not including the one hunched over her body. The fire came rushing from Caitriona's palm so quickly in response that it startled her. She could still smell their burned meat and rot, and suspected she would always be able to recall the scent. It wasn't something easily forgotten.

"Eat your food, we need strength for tomorrow."

Ailith still kept her eyes down, which allowed Caitriona to view her without hesitancy. Her brown hair was loose and hanging, but still her cheeks, forehead, and the tip of her nose were bright pink from the burns Caitriona caused.

"Can I wash your face?" Caitriona blurted, making Ailith pause her eating for a second time.

The guard lifted her gaze. "Why would you do that?"

"Your skin is burned. I caused that, so I want to help tend your wounds."

"You don't have to do that."

Caitriona was unmoving from her position. She wanted to do this simple thing, if only to make herself feel better. But she suspected, based on what little she knew of Ailith, that she wasn't particularly used to being tended to by others.

The flames in the fireplace crackled, insistent on keeping the silence at bay. Caitriona tensed her jaw, determined not to let this go. It was the least she could do after hurting her guard, and more than she had done for any of the monsters she set on fire back at their camping spot. She hadn't meant to hurt anyone; she didn't honestly know what she was doing when the fire came forward. It hurt to see Ailith's cheeks so red. If she could take this small step towards righting her wrong, perhaps it would also serve as a way to promise that Ailith's choice to stick by her was the right one.

The guard shifted, eliciting a creak from her chair; her discomfort from Caitriona's gaze apparent. "Fine. If it'll make you feel better."

She sat stony faced as Caitriona gathered a cloth and dipped it into the cool water they had set aside for washing their hands after eating. Kneeling beside her, Caitriona raised the cloth to Ailith's reddened face and smiled as the tension in Ailith's shoulders relaxed and her expression softened.

"Is this alright?" Caitriona pulled the cloth back.

Ailith opened her eyes, their gazes locking and she managed not to look away. "It is, thank you."

Caitriona felt both relief and pride warm her skin and relax her muscles. Turning back to their dinner, Caitriona's appetite at last returned.

Ailith hunched her shoulders forward and softly placed her utensil on the table.

"Back at the Elder Tree, when we met, your sister said so many things ... so many *awful* things about your father. I agreed with her. I agreed that I heard talk about his mental state, that I understood his irrational decisions. I agreed to things that could get any commoner sentenced to death if the king knew. But it was a lie, she was only covering up your magic."

"Not entirely," Caitriona quickly replied to comfort her, her food forgotten. She was so consumed with her own fears, she hadn't considered Ailith's feelings, and the weight of that realization was heavy on Caitriona's shoulders and settled into her aching chest. "Everything Greer said about our father is true. All of it. Those fighting Avorkaz *are* exhausted, there's growing resentment from guards *and* citizens, and my father seems all the more unhinged. Greer and I ... we don't agree with our father's way of rule. When Greer is queen, we want it to be different. But we couldn't expose my magic to you right away. We—*I*—was frightened you wouldn't understand."

Ailith's shoulders dropped. "I don't understand your magic, but I can see it isn't all bad, not like your father perceives it to be."

Caitriona leaned back and couldn't help the small smile she gave. Greer was the only one in her corner for so long but perhaps Ailith would join her. The idea felt ... nice.

THE SUN SLIPPED AWAY AND NIGHT CURLED ITSELF AROUND the outpost, pressing against the windows of the rented room to watch the pair ready for bed. Ailith took the bed closest to the door, propping her short sword on one side of the bed, her bow and arrows on the other. Caitriona watched from the bed closest to the window as Ailith secured the door with the lock and a chair braced beneath the latch. She silently slipped the dagger from her thigh holder under her pillow. Caitriona wanted to comment that they had even less protection in the woods but kept that to herself. There wasn't much defense in it; they were, after all, attacked by the shades. At least for this night they could sleep and feel safe and secure.

The hum of people in the pub below gained volume as the evening dragged on, but the warm fire, cozy blankets, and soft beds coaxed both women to retire early. Ailith fell asleep the moment her head hit the pillow, her breathing soft but deep, while Caitriona found herself taking longer to greet sleep.

Sitting up with a sigh, she turned to the window with the rising sliver of the moon in the east. This was the furthest she'd ever traveled, and she couldn't help but wish Greer was with her. After every trip Greer took, she arrived home and crawled into Caitriona's bed to tell her what she saw. Whenever she could, she brought Caitriona a trinket from her trip. When she traveled to Stormhaven, it was the most pristine seashell; other trips she'd return with a flower pressed in her battle plans or a book from a far-off town. Caitriona cherished the gifts, keeping them in an honored place in her room as a reminder that while she was forever at the castle, at least she traveled to other places in her sister's heart.

When Caitriona was younger, she asked her parents to travel outside the city walls and beyond the valley.

"When princes are courting you, then you'll travel," her father grumbled, not even lifting his eyes from whatever map or paper he was looking at. "You'll see the world when you marry and move to their kingdom."

It was the answer he always gave, which sat in a pit of Caitriona's belly, growing with nervous uncertainty. While she knew marriage was expected of her, the idea of leaving her home entirely made her pulse quicken and her heart flutter with apprehension. When Caitriona spoke to her mother, she received an entirely different response.

"Don't bring up such things." The queen flushed, her chest breaking out in a rash as she fanned herself. "It's better to keep you home where you're safe. Don't you understand?"

"I'm sorry, mother. It was a joke. Forgive me."

Caitriona retreated from the topic; there was no sense pushing the subject. Her parents wouldn't budge. Her father would only send her off for marriage and her mother deemed the castle as the only safe location. How safe was she at home anyway? After all, it was where she died.

She imagined her first trip from the valley to be substantially different from this, but Caitriona didn't mind. She loved seeing the forest, the sky, the valley from above and the marshes down below. She even found herself enjoying Ailith's company. The guard was serious and stern when they first met, but now Caitriona dared to think that a friendship was forming, even after Ailith discovered that she and Greer lied about the true reason for this trip. They overcame that. And yet ... the shades took away the immature belief that their travels would be easy. Caitriona had gone from a princess in a castle with her nose in a book, to one capable of harm. She hadn't thought of killing the shades, she only wanted to protect herself and Ailith, and yet they were dead and it was by her hand.

Her eyes began to burn from gathering tears. The feelings battled one another, tormenting her brain. How could she regret killing those beasts with her gifts yet find joy in the release? What did that make her?

Caitriona lay back down and pulled up the rough blankets. Curling on her side, she looked at Ailith. The guard's brown hair spread over the pillow; her cheeks still pink from Caitriona's flames.

The release of tender flame was frighteningly pleasant, something Caitriona enjoyed more than she was willing to admit. It was as if she slowly filled with power, until it consumed her whole, choking her throat and leaking from her skin. When the flames let loose, she felt herself grow light, her whole body feeling instant relief. But also, confirmation of what she and Greer suspected. Magic was coursing through her and finding ways to make itself known.

Greer had suggested being forthright with Ailith but Caitriona wanted to keep her developing powers a secret. She couldn't fathom Ailith handling it well, at least based on her preconceived notion of her. Guards worked for the king and followed his laws. Magic was outlawed and the guards were expected to deal with it accordingly. Why would Ailith be any different?

Caitriona had braced for Ailith's shock and confusion after killing the shades, even her anger, but it seemed to only solidify something in Ailith. In fact, it seemed to soften her to Caitriona, who hadn't realized how badly she needed the guard to warm to her and know her secret. It made her feel less alone; it made her feel safe.

Caitriona fell asleep enveloped in restful peace and savoring in her heart Ailith's quiet acceptance. Enveloped in restful peace. For so long, she feared her father discovering her magic, but now that she had escaped and Ailith knew her secret, she finally felt at ease.

Hours later, thunder rumbling in the distance jostled her awake. Rolling towards the window the familiar flash of lightning lit the room. An early autumn thunderstorm, common as the summer heat fought against the cool breaths of autumn, nothing more. Settling into the blankets, she began drifting to sleep when the room flashed bright from a nearby bolt. The following crack of thunder, right on its heels, was loud enough that Caitriona felt the sound in her chest. But fright from the thunder was twofold when Ailith let out a wailing scream.

Caitriona jumped, turning to Ailith who threw herself upright in bed, hair plastered to her face and eyes wide as she breathed hard.

"Ailith?" Caitriona scrambled from her bed, nearly falling as her foot tangled with a sheet. "Ailith what's wrong?"

Another flash of lightning, too close but not as near as the previous one, followed by another wall-shaking bang of thunder and Ailith cried again, pulling her knees close to her chest and burying her face in her hands.

Caitriona stood still, her hands hovering over Ailith's quivering form for a moment until the guard shook from further rumbles of thunder—further away now. "Ailith? It's alright, it's alright," Caitriona repeated, slowly sitting beside her. "I promise, it's just a storm."

Ailith held still for a moment before letting out a single sob. Caitriona leaned forward and slipped her arms around her. She hushed her, and Ailith grew rigid from the embrace for only a moment before relaxing. Caitriona curled against her, clutching her tight until the thunder lessened as the storm raced on toward the east.

"I'm going to add a log to the fire." Caitriona patted Ailith's shoulder who had ceased crying. She still remained with her face turned down and her arms wrapped about her knees as Caitriona slipped off the bed. Kneeling before the fireplace, she placed a log onto the dying flames before grasping the iron poker and stoking the fire back to life.

"I've woken from storms like that since I was a child," Ailith mumbled miserably. Caitriona turned and found Ailith lying on her belly where she peeked over the edge of the bed, her dark eyes rimmed red and still filled with unshed tears. "Ever since the dragon attack, if a storm passes over at night, I wake screaming. It's like I hear the thunder, but in my sleep, I dream it's the dragon again and it's all vividly real. Half the time I can't even wake myself up; it's as if I'm trapped in the nightmare."

"Terrors." Caitriona got to her feet and returned to the edge of Ailith's bed. Ailith sat up and wiped her eyes, curling her feet under her as she made room for Caitriona to sit. "I've heard of people having those." She didn't mention that her mother was one. Caitriona recalled her doing it her entire life, but Greer said it was only since the dragon attack. Caitriona's room was near Róisín's and often she woke to the sound of her mother's screams and the rustle of palace workers in the hall as they attempted to help.

Ailith frowned and picked at the frayed edge of her blanket. "It's my worst-kept secret. I was the laughingstock of my guard training class. It happened only once, but once is enough. I hate storms. It's better when I'm awake. If I can *see* it's a storm, I *know* it's not the dragon, but when I'm asleep my mind plays tricks on me."

Caitriona reached for Ailith's hand and squeezed it. "Is there anything I can do to help? I imagine we may see another storm or two."

"You spoke to me." Her voice was uncharacteristically small. "Your voice was something I could find in the haze of it all. Talking now, I feel more grounded."

Caitriona nodded and pulled her feet onto the bed, tucking them beneath her as well. "I hadn't thought of how terrifying the attack must have been for you ... for anyone in the city, really. I have such vague memories of the attack; I think it is, unfortunately, one of my first memories. Being afraid, trying to hide, and waking days later. But we never discuss the attack, not really. Growing up, I asked questions and my father ignored me and my mother shushed me. Greer and I spoke about it, but she was also young.

"Even beyond the castle, I feel so much focus is placed on those who died. People forget that there can be peace in death, while those who lived continue suffering with memories of it. It must have been horrifying."

Ailith shrugged. "I didn't see much of the actual attack, but I heard it. It reminded me of thunder then, and I think my subconscious latched onto that. Walking home was scary, to see the bloodied people, the ruined homes, and all the dust and smoke. We didn't know if my father was alright, not for hours. That was the scariest part of it all. But it's nothing compared to what happened to you."

"No." Caitriona lifted a hand to stop Ailith from continuing.

When Caitriona began working in the library, she asked Callan's experience of the attack and he spoke similarly. He dismissed his ordeals due to what happened to her—something she couldn't clearly remember—and it left a sour taste in her mouth.

"We both experienced something terrible. While they are different, they're awful all the same. If you told your story to someone who wasn't in the city at all and never witnessed a dragon attack, they would feel your suffering and understand the horror of it all. Trying to justify your trauma as less than mine only buries yours. You're allowed to feel poorly over a horrible thing; there is no competition over grievances to be had."

The two fell silent for a moment and the laughter of drunks in the pub slipped through the floorboards and filled the room. Ailith's lips curved into a shy smile, and she reached forward, touching the back of Caitriona's hand with her fingertips. "Thank you."

Ailith gathered the energy to move off the bed and slipped her feet into her boots. She tucked her shirt into her pants that she hadn't bothered to remove for sleep as Caitriona looked at her questioningly. "I'm going downstairs to get us a pitcher of water," she explained, flashing a tentative smile to Caitriona. "I just need to move a little bit, shake out the nightmare before I try to go back to sleep. Get your rest; I'll be back in a moment."

Ailith slipped out, taking the key to lock the door as she went. Caitriona was left alone in the room once more and climbed back into bed, curling up with the blankets and closing her eyes. Her body settled into the lumpy mattress and grew heavy when the scratching of a key at the door announced Ailith's return.

"Cait?" Ailith whispered; her tone panicked as she slipped inside and locked the door shut behind her. "Cait, wake up!"

"I'm up. What's going on?"

Ailith rushed to the little table, placing the pitcher of water on it before grabbing Caitriona's bag and tossing it onto her bed. Ailith paused, breathing heavily and raking a hand through her hair. "I went— I went downstairs and there was a—a messenger! From the castle! I don't recognize him and I don't believe he recognized me, but he has the Wimleigh crest." She worked as she spoke, lighting the oil lamp and folding clothing she scattered about the room before stuffing them in her pack. "He was telling the remaining drunks that he was here to spread word that the *princess is missing* and there's a reward for the person who can find her."

Caitriona's chest tightened and all sensation in her face dropped somewhere into the depths of her belly. "Oh no."

"I know." Ailith rewrapped the cloth around the bread that was quickly growing hard and thrust it into her bag. When she looked at Caitriona, her frantic movements went still. "It's okay, Caitriona. We'll just gather our things and slip out."

"How?" Caitriona looked around the room at their belongings and the darkened sky outside. Pressure filled her chest and her hands trembled. "There still are people downstairs and we don't know if they're going to ever go to bed. If there's a reward, I'm certain anyone who sees us down there will question who we are."

Ailith chewed at her shirt sleeve and glanced around the room before answering. "We can climb out the window. The roof of the woodshed is right outside. We can step onto it, then hop down to the ground and head toward Stormhaven. The messenger just arrived tonight, possibly in the storm, so it sounds like perhaps they only *just* realized you're missing. If they're going to continue on from here, they probably won't ride until later tomorrow, and we don't know if they'll go directly to Stormhaven. There are other little hamlets between here and there. Other small towns they'll have to stop at. We can try and get ahead of him."

Caitriona got out of bed and wrung her hands as she tried to gather her wits.

Ailith's hand reached forward and fell upon Caitriona's shoulder, drawing her attention. "It's going to be okay." Ailith's voice was soft and reassuring. Her brown eyes even met Caitriona's. "I don't think it's worth the risk to get horses. I don't want anyone to notice you or become suspicious, so we'll go by foot. Come, I'll help you pack your things."

They worked in silence, the thunderstorm forgotten as they repacked their bags and put on the rest of their travel garments. Their wet shoes and cloaks had dried by the fire, and both made quick work of braiding their hair. Caitriona's hair was so long and bright, and the risks so high, they pinned the braid upon her head as well as secured the hood of her cloak to her hair, hoping to avoid any risk of her red locks being exposed. Even with the few blonde strands that hadn't returned to crimson, she was still noticeably a redhead.

The sounds from below gradually fell silent, the drunks having fallen asleep at tables or in their rooms. Caitriona threw open the windows and the pair leaned out, looking at their escape route. The covered area for firewood didn't stand directly beneath their window, but to the side by a few inches. If they sat on the edge of the window and stretched their legs, they could likely get footing on the roof.

"I'll go first, then you follow. If you fall, I'll catch you." Ailith said this with such sincerity Caitriona nearly believed her. They were both close to the same height, although Ailith was taller and broader, but Caitriona doubted if she fell it would be an effortless catch on her part. Briefly, Caitriona pictured herself being dragged back to the castle with a broken leg sustained from jumping from the window. Unable to flee again, trapped under her father's watchful eye, and the fire magic growing steadily within her, the thought brought a chill up Caitriona's spine.

Sitting on the window's edge, Ailith swung her legs out and held onto the frame as she stretched to the side, getting her footing on the storage roof before carefully adjusting her balance to stand. She inched to the edge before dropping her legs over and finding logs to support her weight. Lifting her gaze, she met Caitriona's, and licked her lips before gripping the roof edge and climbing to the ground.

After a moment, she appeared beneath the window and raised her arms, waiting. Caitriona tossed Ailith's bow and their bags before climbing out as well. Holding tightly to the wooden window frame, she looked into their little room one final time. It was pleasant to spend time there talking with Ailith and getting much needed rest. But now there was a quality of discomfort that lay its heavy hand on Caitriona's shoulders, gripping tight and unwilling to let go. All she could do was move forward.

Her knees quivered as she tried to mirror Ailith's form. She inched her feet to the little roof and discovered it was slick from the rain earlier. Not making a rush of it, Caitriona shifted her weight and found her balance despite her shaking knees as she let go of the sill. Once she was hanging from the awning, her feet dangling briefly, she took a deep breath and let go. It was a short drop, but she breathed a sigh of relief when Ailith's arms caught hold of her, slowing the rush of her body greeting the ground.

Ailith pressed her finger to her mouth, stopping Caitriona from speaking. They paused, listening for any movement from the inn, and looking to see if any of the windows had lit candles or curtains pulled back, but no one stirred. Hoisting their packs in silence, they circled the building and began their way toward Stormhaven.

CHAPTER EIGHT

AILITH

It took two days to get to the coastal city. The marshlands were
warmer than the hills near the valley, but also left a dampness in
the air that clung to their clothing and sunk into their bones. They
avoided the hamlets, wary of being spotted, but stayed on the roadway,
not daring to drift far from it as the murky waters were filled with
drowning dukes. When Ailith was a child, she thought the name
implied dukes were being drowned at a continuous rate, like a strange
sacrifice, but they were nothing of the sort. Drowning dukes were
creatures who appeared like pale, water-logged corpses. Wrinkled and
rotting from the bottoms of the pools during the day, in the evening and
through the night they lifted their heads and appeared more solid and
youthful. Former soldiers for various sovereigns past, when the sun set,
they became handsome men who hunted any who drew too close to
their shores. Young men that sipped blood from the veins of their
victims and tore muscles from bone.

Ailith noticed they watched the women each night as they camped.
Their eyes glowed along the shore, silently taking them in, although
occasionally chattering to one another in glugs and laps of water. Stories
told that the dukes only hunted other men, that women were safe, but
Ailith and Caitriona refused to find out if the stories were false.

While Ailith never saw it take place, there were tales of old or injured guards who were on death's door being offered to the dukes. If the dukes found the offering honorable, they took the guard, performed whatever magic ran through their dead hearts, and transformed the guard into another duke—destined to continue their afterlife within the marshy waters. If the offering wasn't honorable, the dukes fed off the body and gained strength from the offering. The dukes could leave the water and fight in battles for sovereigns they found worthy. While Ailith thought the dukes incredibly interesting, she didn't quite get the appeal of becoming a monster, forced to live for eternity in a bog.

But Ailith did appreciate that their very existence was in defiance of the king's desires. If Cearny attempted to wipe them away, he wouldn't have the support of his own guards. Better to outlaw old practices and ignore their existence until the traditions were forgotten. Ailith never heard of a funeral procession to the dukes in her lifetime. They must have gone decades without broadening their ranks. Would they rise from the water for battle if they hadn't been honored all these years? Ailith doubted it and wondered if it made them all the more ravenous for flesh.

The wet air was a hex leaving the women shivering through most of the first night and Ailith cursed at the perpetually damp logs and reeds she picked up.

"Go kill an idiot man, why don't you!" Ailith yelled at the dukes when they gurgled with seeming laughter after she kicked a log with frustration. Surely there was some semblance of their human minds that understood what she meant.

Ailith made Caitriona move further down the road to a spot where fewer dukes watched them freeze as they awaited dawn. By the second night, Ailith lost her patience and cursed at the sky, the earth, the dukes, and her own tears of frustration. Kicking the logs she carried through the day, with hope they would dry enough by sunlight to catch fire, she stormed off from their site into the reeds of a dried-out pool bed, looking for any branches that could work as kindling. When she returned, a fire was lit and Caitriona's eyes glowed gold. Ailith stopped short.

"I wanted to see if I could control it." Caitriona pulled at the ends of her shirtsleeves sheepishly to cover her hands, but her nails glinted in the firelight, noticeably longer than before. Just as they were when she last used her powers. She gave a small shrug. "It worked."

Ailith studied the princess with her jaw clenched as Caitriona fingered her red hair, inspecting the flush of gold strands threaded through it. But the momentary control of her magic seemed to bring more encouragement to Caitriona than Ailith's words could ever provide. Over the final day on the road, Caitriona made small sparks of fire in her hands, gently cupping the flame before snuffing it out. Each time Caitriona's eyes took longer to lose their golden glow, even longer for them to return to blue. Every use of her power added golden strands to her hair, and they never returned to her natural red. Her nails lengthened, growing talon-like, before shrinking to their shorter length after a few hours passed. Ailith could no longer deny the magic was leaving Caitriona changed. She also couldn't ignore the creeping sense of dread breathing down her neck that she should urge Caitriona not to use her magic, at least not until she learned more about it.

Simultaneous to her concern, seeing Caitriona more confident in her strengths made Ailith ... happy. For a time, Ailith was convinced her positive outlook towards Caitriona's confidence was built on relief; if Caitriona was confident, maybe she would feel better defending them should they be attacked again, but that didn't explain the feeling of pride simmering in Ailith's chest.

At some point between the first appearance of Caitriona's secret powers and Ailith waking from her night terror, she grew to like the princess. She felt an expanding warmth towards her kindness, eagerness, and sweet nature, even if the realization that all Ailith's preconceived notions of the royal were wrong left a burn of embarrassment.

With a night of rest behind them, the pair powered through the last day of walking until they came to the gates of Stormhaven. A sea-port city with white buildings reaching multiple floors and tight wagon pathways twisting throughout, it was old and thick with the scent of salt water. Vines and roses climbed along walls, seagulls and other birds perched on top of the tile roofs and lent their voices to the sky, and trees with autumn fruit gave shade on the cobbled streets.

"The walls of the city reflect the changing colors of the day, appearing pink at dawn, bright white by noon, gray in storms, and red or orange by sundown." Caitriona pointed out as they walked the main roadway into the embrace of the city. "At least, that's what Greer told me."

They found Sunset's Ray Inn, which overlooked the western skies toward Braewick Valley. Braewick Valley's ridge was long lost to sight and the land that Stormhaven rested upon jutted out into the sea, the coast curving inward, so the view was only of the water and sky. Their room's window was large, and Caitriona quickly opened it to the sea air. It was warmer in the city, the ground lower than where Braewick City sat, but the breeze carried a coolness that indicated a pleasant night's rest.

Ailith sat at the table in their room, dragging her finger along the roadways of Caitriona's map. "We can head north, toward the Mazgate Dominion. I suppose we'll skirt around the base of the Endless Mountains and continue up Death's Mist roadway; it goes straight into the northern range of the Endless Mountains where Kayl should be. We can avoid Avorkaz entirely; your father was intending to battle them again soon, no?"

Ailith looked at Caitriona leaning against the foot of one of the two beds. Now in privacy, Caitriona had tossed aside her cloak and the afternoon sunshine coming through the window made her hair a sunburst of fire and molten gold. She pushed to her feet and crossed the floor. Bending over Ailith, she peered at the map. "I don't know how soon. Every time he sends people to the lines, they end up having to retreat. He's taken other cities with greater ease, to my understanding, but Avorkaz has proven strong. It's probably for the best that we avoid it."

Ailith spaced out the distance to the Mazgate Dominion border and groaned, pressing her forehead into the palms of her hands. "We need to get horses, that would help so much."

"I can do that," Caitriona suggested, her tone eager and excited. Ailith dropped her hands and looked up with a look of uncertainty. Caitriona's shoulders sagged, her disappointment that Ailith didn't immediately agree obvious. "Please? I've ridden all my life, even if only within the castle grounds, but I know horses. I just ... haven't much experience with buying them."

"I don't know how smart that is. They're looking for you."

"They're looking for a princess with deep red hair." Caitriona crossed her arms over her chest. She had a point. Her hair was, without a doubt, no longer deep red. She looked vastly different than at the Elder Tree. Her clothing sported stains and grime, her skin pink from their long walks in the sun, her hair the altered color it had become, and even her blue eyes had captured a mixture of green they previously didn't have.

"Fine," Ailith replied, plans already neatly sorting into an orderly list in her mind. "You can purchase the horses and I'll see if I can get any additional information about Kayl or what's going on in Braewick at the market. Better for us to have as much information we can get than none at all."

Caitriona grinned triumphantly and Ailith returned her attention to the map to hide her own sneaking smile.

Pressing her finger onto the map, she retraced their steps back to Braewick Valley and the city. The castle was drawn in finer detail while Braewick City had a mixture of various buildings, none of which particularly stood out. Five days since she last saw her parents, the longest she ever went without them. The thought made her smile fade, her face going blank as a dull ache of homesickness grew.

"Where do you live in the city?" Caitriona squatted beside Ailith, grasping the edge of the table and resting her chin upon her fingers. Caitriona gazed at the edge of the paper where Braewick City was detailed with a sprawl of simple little houses drawn in a cluster. Her shoulder pressed against Ailith's arm and Ailith made no effort to move away. Ailith tapped at the southern edge of the city, on the eastern side.

"Ah," Caitriona responded, reaching for the quill for their letter to Etta. She swept it over the paper to that spot, filling in the outline of a building so it stood out. Beside the little building, she drew a small stick figure. "There." She returned the quill to its holder. "This way we can both find our way home."

CHAPTER NINE

GREER

Greer sat in her mother's quarters, back stiff and hands delicately at her sides, an image of accurate behavior for a royal family member. It was a behavior her mother expected, one Caitriona fell in line with easily; she was the picture-perfect princess, the one learning to paint or draw, embroider and sing. Greer often tossed such behaviors aside, finding it much more enjoyable to ride on a horse with a sword in her hand, mud on her boots, her hair a windswept mess, but she felt it appropriate to put on her princess-airs in certain moments, particularly now.

Greer had clear memories of her mother being more present and active in her life prior to the white dragon's attack. She wasn't necessarily playful, but she expressed love to her children. Kisses, hugs, and stories when they were going to bed were normal. She often sang them to sleep in a language that was faint in Greer's memory now. When she was very little, she tried to sing her mother's songs and when her mother caught her, Greer was quickly scolded.

"*Never* sing these songs," her mother hissed, gripping Greer's arm too tightly, her green eyes wide and fierce. "*Never* repeat the words. They are filled with danger that could get you killed." After that, the queen stopped singing, but hummed to them instead, and the words slipped from Greer's mind.

After the dragon attacked, Greer clung to her mother and sister's side, terrified by the events and worried that if either disappeared from sight they would be gone for good. She slept beside Caitriona, her mother too, and didn't leave her mother's room for days.

Her father hated it and before long dragged Greer away despite her tears and pleading to remain. He forced her to follow him each day and watch as he conducted meetings and made decisions. When she asked to return to her mother and sister, the king marched her to the medical wing to see the injured and dying from the dragon attack. This went on for so long that by the time Greer was able to interact in close proximity with her mother again, she found her mother different. Distant. And over the fifteen years since the attack, the queen only became more reserved, more serious, more stern, more foreign. But Greer knew—and often had to reassure Caitriona who was too young to remember those times before—that her mother loved them both deeply.

The news that Caitriona vanished swept through the castle, swelling until it burst out onto the city streets, coating homes and infiltrating the ears of the citizens. The king was sour, still nursing the damage to his ego that this would sully Caitriona's price as a bride while simultaneously trying to spin that she left against her will. The queen, however, remained straight backed and professional. A true queen, but with obvious fractures to all who beheld her. Her eyes were constantly red-rimmed, tears came frequently, and after a few hours of the city knowing the princess had vanished, the queen retired to her quarters.

Amongst the chaos of rumors, the king put aside his plans for further conquest of Avorkaz. His emotions waved between anger at Caitriona and concern for his portrayal to the world, and all who were in his path took the brunt of his fluctuating emotions. It was safer for Greer to sit in the queen's quarters, better to try and comfort her mother. But having to witness her distress only left Greer feeling incredibly guilty and a little annoyed.

"She'll be alright," Greer attempted after they finished their tea and sat in silence long enough to make Greer uneasy. She reached for her mother's hand and took it in her own. It was delicate and thin, reminding Greer of Caitriona's. Greer had not been blessed with her mother's build, coming out broader and more similar to her father than she ever liked. Her mother's hand lay limply in Greer's grasp. "She's so smart."

"She has no experience with the world." Róisín's green eyes quivered with tears that had not yet fallen.

Greer sighed and withdrew her hand. She heard her mother say this before and it always irritated her. "She would've if she had the choice. But you always kept her so close."

Róisín glared at Greer, a spark of fierceness lighting up her eyes. "I did what I could to keep her safe. She *died*, Greer. Do you not remember? You have to, you were old enough, you were there. I couldn't have her harmed again, not after all of that."

"So, you kept her shuttered up in her own home? How's that living?" A fire burst within Greer, swallowing her reason whole. She hadn't realized there was flame to this argument festering within her for the last fifteen years, but now the situation Greer placed her sister in poured oil on that flame, consuming her. For fifteen years she witnessed her sweet sister trapped in the cage of the castle, growing too big for the space and looking on with desperation for adventure in the great world. She braced herself every time Caitriona built up enough courage to ask for small freedoms, already knowing she would be denied, but ensuring she was always there to wipe away Caitriona's tears. In the last ten years, Greer tried to bring the world to Caitriona, but when Greer had to leave again, the pain in Caitriona's eyes only increased. Her sister wanted to live, just like any person. "She died in the safety of her *home*, mother."

Róisín's eyes flashed, something fierce rose within her and Greer thought she was going to get somewhere, that she'd finally watch her mother snap and give substance to a lifetime of behavior, but it quickly receded.

"You don't understand." Her voice shook and she touched the edges of her eyes. "Things are different with Caitriona."

Greer breathed in. She tasted fire on her tongue. "I suppose I don't. I love Caitriona deeply, she's my only sister, but it was never fair of you to keep her safe while simultaneously waving goodbye as I left to follow father's latest conquests."

"That's unfair of you, Greer." Róisín at least had the grace to look ashamed. Her fingers clenched at the green fabric of her dress and the tip of her nose was pink. She looked away toward the window. "You've always been strong and determined. You already had a taste of the world when the attack happened. Do you think I would've been successful keeping you at home? Do you think your *father* would've allowed it?" Róisín turned back to Greer and held her gaze with a dare in her searing look. "You're the heir to the throne. The moment I bore you I lost you to him. And Caitriona ... she's never *not* been in danger. She survived the dragon attack and has been in danger ever since. I've done what I could to keep her safe. I kept her close to ensure something like this wouldn't happen."

Greer blinked; a question arose that she never had the chance to ask as a knock took away her chance. It quieted the queen as well, her eyes still flashing with assumed pent-up frustration of years of being unable to control most things, particularly when it came against the king's own intentions. She closed her mouth and brushed her skirts, wiped her eyes once more and straightened in her seat. She quickly covered her rage with a curtain of coldness. Her acting was so strong that it left Greer gaping. "You may enter."

A guard stepped in and the slight pink tinge to his cheeks showed that their argument was clearly heard outside the room. Greer sighed, wondering if gossip of what was said would make it back to the king. "Queen Róisín, Princess Greer." The guard bowed deeply. "King Cearny discovered a guard missing from the city ranks. He believes she is involved with the princess's disappearance."

"She?" Greer asked, feeling tightness forming in her gut, already knowing his answer but hoping she was wrong.

The guard nodded. "Yes, ah, her name is Ailith MacCree. A city guard often stationed to the north gate, known to work frequently but took time off the same day Princess Caitriona disappeared. Her superior went to her home to request she take on shifts due to an illness with another guard and she wasn't there. The king questioned her parents directly, they said they haven't seen her. King Cearny has put out a call for her capture."

CHAPTER TEN

AILITH

For the remainder of their first day in Stormhaven, Ailith and Caitriona went to a bath house, paying far too much gold—in Ailith's opinion—for a private room where they could bathe, and handed over even more coin to have their travel clothing cleaned.

"Why is everything perfumed?" Ailith asked, sniffing the bottles and jars of oils and lotions laid out along the edge of the soaking pool.

"Why wouldn't it be?" Caitriona undid her hair and disrobed before slipping into the water. Ailith's cheeks grew hot and she turned away, opting to drop their dirty clothes into a basket for cleaning and finding her movements flustered.

"There's rose water for your skin." Caitriona turned to the edge of the pool, reaching for the bottles. "It smells lovely. And that jar smells like rosemary which makes your hair less brittle."

"Look at you," Ailith teased despite her stomach flipping and her cheeks continuing to burn. Better to joke than to admit the fluttering in her chest. She slipped into the pool as Caitriona's back was turned, crossing her arms over her chest until she sank beneath the water. "If being a princess and making maps doesn't work out, you can always become a conveyer of scented oils."

"Hush yourself." Caitriona laughed, splashing Ailith.

After they bathed, they dressed in their spare clothing; Ailith in pants and a tunic while Caitriona pulled free a simple, sage green dress. "Making maps doesn't require pants." Caitriona pointed out when Ailith gave her a look as she stepped out of the changing room. "I also find a dress more comfortable."

They ate the evening meal in their room, dragging the little table to the window to look over the water while eating fried fish and vegetables. Ailith found they had become companionable, their conversations not always lingering on travel, nor the man they sought, and to her surprise, she liked that.

"I want more freedom," Caitriona confessed, spreading her arms wide as if she would fly out the very window they sat beside. "I want to travel and see the places I've drawn. I like the library well enough, but I hope when Greer is queen I'll do more than transcribe old maps."

Caitriona turned her attention to Ailith, an eyebrow raised as she waited patiently for Ailith to admit her own desires.

"I ..." Ailith bit at the edge of her sleeve as she considered her next words. "I want to move up in the guard. I've never wanted to be in the royal guard because I didn't want to work too closely with the king and I didn't want to go to war, but they do get to travel, and I think if I'm trapped at that gate much longer it will shorten my lifespan due to boredom."

Caitriona laughed, providing the encouragement Ailith needed.

"I want to make enough money that my parents are cared for and we aren't living in a house with holes in the roof. I want us to be able to buy all our winter supplies and groceries in one week without worry of expense."

Caitriona sobered at that, her hand coming to rest on Ailith's shoulder. "I want that for you as well. I'll talk to Greer; I'll see if I can make that possible."

Caitriona wrote to Etta after they decided on their next steps forward:

I've heard the snow geese remain in the Endless Mountains. I understand; why leave a land where they could blend into the white of snow and feel so safe? We are very well. – C

Ailith sent it off, but not before adding her own note to the bottom upon Caitriona's urging, "*Please, share the news with the stone mason.*" Hopefully Etta could figure out who she meant.

They slept the full night. Deep and long, without waking from the fright of a thunderstorm or having to flee. They ate a breakfast of eggs, meat, beans and potatoes, and paid for a second night at the inn after brief discussion. Neither, it seemed, wanted to leave. They weren't certain if it was smart to remain in the city another day, but the morale boost would aid them forward. More so, Ailith knew the royal guards would be meticulous in each location they searched, giving the pair at least a few days' lead before the guards reached Stormhaven. Deciding to depart the following morning, they dressed and headed out the door into the morning light that made the city a butter yellow hue.

"It's so beautiful here," Caitriona marveled. She still wore the light dress but kept her cloak on with its hood pulled up to remain discreet. However, her smile was so broad, it drew attention on its own, drawing Ailith to walk closer to Caitriona and give dirty looks at any whose gaze lasted on Caitriona too long.

"It's nice to be out. It feels ... *normal*?" Ailith hadn't felt this carefree before, and perhaps their gold and platinum-filled purse helped a little. They wandered the marketplace lined with vendors with canopies made from different colored cloths propped upward with thick tree limbs weathered by the ocean or tied to hooks from the corners of buildings. Conversation filled the air and music knit its way amidst the voices. Lazy cats slept on windowsills and dogs begged for scraps of food dropped by vendors.

"I'll grab food for us. Should I purchase horse supplies?" Ailith looked over to a stall with riding apparel.

"Wait on the supplies." Caitriona nodded towards the stables down the street near their inn. "I may be able to get that myself. If not, we can come back before we leave."

Ailith could ride but knew very little of what made a good horse. She was given a horse during training and learned how to care for it. She even enjoyed her time with the horse before passing the course, and never seeing the horse again. There wasn't much use for a horse when your job was to check individuals entering through a gate.

Caitriona was more knowledgeable. "The only regular trips I'm ever granted outside of the castle is to care and walk the garden grounds with my favorite, a mare named Teacup. It'll be nice to have a horse, even if for a little while."

"Aren't the gardens still within the castle walls?" Ailith had never seen them, but her father mentioned the expanse of green and rich scent of flowers when he worked at the castle before his injury.

"Need you remind me? So, I've never left the castle grounds but at least I have my mare."

Ailith took some coin to purchase additional food for the next leg of their journey. She never knew a time when she had more than enough money to buy what she needed. But now she didn't have to concern herself about the costs or figure out what item was worth taking or being left behind. Ailith purchased fresh breads and sweet treats. Nuts, dried meats, and heftier fruits were less likely to be crushed or rot. She spent coin on a bottle of rich cider—a treat for her and Caitriona to celebrate making it as far as they had. It was perhaps premature, but Stormhaven had taken hold of Ailith and Caitriona, breathing life and energy into them. As Ailith circled back to the stables, Caitriona was beaming and waving goodbye to a man at the entrance.

"Two lovely horses," Caitriona announced as she approached Ailith. "They're beautiful and good for long trips. One is a nice tan color, and the other is white with black spots."

Caitriona's cheeks flushed and her lips pressed together as if bursting to share some secret. "What?" Ailith asked, finding herself growing excited as well, as if Caitriona's energy was catching. "What else?"

"The stable doesn't have names for the horses, not anything nice at least. So, I've named the tan one Butterscotch and the other Inkwell. I also purchased tack for them. It's all paid for and we can come for them when we are ready to depart."

"Butterscotch and Inkwell ..." Ailith glanced at the man standing at the entrance of the stables counting coins. "You likely made his week."

"I certainly paid more than I should have, but I felt it necessary."

"We should really monitor how much coin we spend. We don't know how much we'll need later on." Ailith considered with a frown as her hand lowered to her own bag of items.

Caitriona swiftly snatched the bottle from it and raised an eyebrow.

Ailith shifted on her feet and looked away, hiding a smile with her hand. "I said *we*."

Caitriona laughed and replaced the bottle. She looped her arm around Ailith's before dragging her forward a few steps. Ailith stumbled into pace with the princess, allowing her to hold her close and lead her on. "Perhaps we can sit by the water for a little bit."

Ailith's smile grew as if she had already drunk the cider and was pleasantly inebriated by the seaside air, or maybe just the company she kept. "Perhaps we can."

Stormhaven's sea walls were built on the three sides of the isle that jutted into water and stairs often led to the beach filled with white sand, aptly called the White Coast. Leaving their purchases at the inn, the women headed there. Ailith secured her short sword to her waist and draped her cloak over her shoulders, covering the weapon within its folds, and Caitriona adjusted her hood.

While they confessed their hopes and dreams into the open air the night before, hoping they would take flight, they realized a simple dream was achievable together right there in Stormhaven: neither had ever stepped foot on sand or touched the sea.

After following the tight, turning curves of roads and narrow alleys, the cry of seagulls grew and the hush of waves eased through the paths, indicating their proximity to the shore. Stepping around a white building and down a short path, the world opened before the large expanse of water and the sandy shore. "Look at it," Caitriona sighed as if presenting a long-withheld creation of her own making.

Rushing down the steps, past families and fishermen, they couldn't help but laugh at the soft sinking of their feet in the sand. Caitriona balanced on one foot then the other to pull her shoes off and skipped ahead of Ailith into the edge of the lazy waves. Her skirt kissed the glittering liquid and as she spun, the fabric showered the air with sparkling flecks of water that shone like gems in the sunlight.

Ailith stood back and laughed as she watched Caitriona. For a moment, she could almost believe they were simply two women, two *friends*, free and traveling the world without threats growing darker and broader. Her entire life had taught Ailith to proceed with caution.

Never assume things are as perfect as they seem, always prepare for the worst; it hurt more to think things were fine and find out they were the opposite. But in that moment, Ailith risked believing in possibility. Caitriona was so proud to control the flames she produced, perhaps Kayl would teach her how to better use her powers, and they would be free to return home without issue.

Perhaps when they returned home, Caitriona could leave the castle and live life rather than being tucked away like delicate crystal.

Perhaps Ailith could do more than guard the northern gate.

Perhaps she and her parents would never have to worry over the cost to live again.

Perhaps in that, Ailith would feel free.

"Come along, Ailith," Caitriona called as she ran forward. Grabbing hold of Ailith's hands, she pulled her from her thoughts and planted her back on the seaside. Ailith stumbled forward and the princess let go. Caitriona placed her hands on her hips. "How often have you had the opportunity to stand in the sea?"

"I think I'm alright here." Ailith took a step backward but Caitriona's expression turned mischievous as she skipped forward, hands reaching and grabbing the guard's, holding tight to swing her around and send Ailith teetering close to the sea's edge as the waves grappled desperately to soak her boots. Ailith pulled away, laughter filling her whole and making her chest ache. When was the last time she allowed herself to feel this much joy? Pulling her boots off, she tossed them beside Caitriona's, a heap of leather shoes dusted with sand.

Caitriona snatched Ailith's hand again, knitting her fingers between the guard's, and pulled her toward the water. She paused by the lapping waves and turned her blue-green eyes to meet the chocolate-brown gaze of Ailith's. "Ready?"

Ailith's cheeks ached from smiling so much.

"Ready."

Tightening her grip on the princess's hand, they both jumped forward into the cold waves. Feeling the rush of sand over their bare feet and the poke of shells from beneath, as well as seaweed tangling with their toes, made Ailith feel abundantly alive. When she looked at Caitriona, she suspected the princess felt similarly.

They held each other's hands and spun as if discovering in that moment that this was what their existence was meant for: to be together, laughing with their minds focused only on the joy of movement and sunlight, fresh air filling their lungs, sea spray sparkling and the clinging sand. The worries of the valley, power-hungry kings, and secret powers seemed far and away, if only for a moment, while the evening sun sunk down, making the city turn into a blush of warm colors and the sea to honey.

CHAPTER ELEVEN

CAITRIONA

They walked to the inn barefoot, picking along cobblestones with boots in hand, and leaving a trail of footprints in their wake. Caitriona exposed her pale legs whilst her skirts and the edge of her cloak were curled over her arm. Ailith let her wet cloak hang behind her, slapping against her ankles with each step, her pants soaked from the knee down.

Caitriona felt full in a way she hadn't felt in years. Her body sparked with life and her senses heightened from a day spent in such gleeful exuberance rather than the constant hum of escape and search and caution. She couldn't think of a single day in Braewick that compared with the joy she felt in the last number of hours. Still, she remained serious on behalf of Ailith, because that seemed to be what Ailith was most comfortable with. But as Ailith relaxed, so did she. A smile frequented Ailith's face more than not, and Caitriona felt a certain pride that she helped produce that radiance.

Night settled over the city as the women finished a meal purchased from the inn's kitchen and the cider Ailith splurged on. Between the two of them, the bottle provided just enough to leave them giggling as they packed their supplies, readying everything for the following morning. As the light faded from the sky, they sat at the table by their open window. Bare feet propped on the sill, they continued sharing life experiences and observances of the world.

Caitriona listened with rapt attention as Ailith described how her father could look at a rock and know the exact place to crack it with a hammer for a clean break—something he learned from a fae stone mason, and how despite her mother's dwindling sight, she still artfully braided strings and yarns, and even pie crusts for elaborate borders. Something shifted inside Caitriona as Ailith spoke, from the way Ailith's nose wrinkled when she laughed, and how she often tried to keep her face carefully blank of emotion when trying to be serious—yet her emotions were conveyed through her eyes. When Ailith grew shy of something, she brought her wrist to her lips as if to hide her face, but the more they spoke, the less often Ailith did that.

Caitriona's fascination with the guard only grew as they became more comfortable with each other. She noted Ailith's many attributes with warm interest, observing the details of the woman privately and keeping them close to her chest. The ridge of her nose curved, similar to a hawk yet feminine; her skin browned rapidly while in the sun and didn't seem to burn, yet her hair gained streaks of lighter brown amidst the dark tresses; and Ailith's eyes were lined with the darkest, thickest eyelashes that made her appear like she had paint lining them.

They spoke for hours until their commentary tapered to silence. The hum of the city below filled the void of their voices and eventually led them to their separate beds.

Morning dawned early and cool. Both Ailith and Caitriona slept soundly and woke clear headed, despite the cider, as the birds began chirping in earnest. They ate their morning meal in the corner of the hall after leaving their room, before the world they left behind rushed to catch up.

"A guard, yes," a tall man said to another as he opened the door to the hall. "A female guard no less, and there aren't very many of those. But it seems she took off from work all of a sudden, right around the same day the princess disappeared. They questioned her parents and they hadn't seen her—they assumed she picked up shifts which she'd been doing frequently."

"Maybe saving up money to travel?" the shorter man asked with humor in his tone as he followed the man to the bar counter.

The tall one shrugged. "Perhaps."

With the last spoonful of porridge halfway to her mouth, Caitriona went still and looked at Ailith. Already finished with breakfast, Ailith was taking one last look at their map before they set off. Now she sat hunched over it, frozen, with eyes wide and boring holes into the table.

"No horses are missing, so they likely went by foot," the man continued, leaning against the bar as they waited for the owner to step out.

"What does the guard look like?"

Caitriona lowered her spoon, gently placing it in the bowl so the clink wouldn't draw the men's attention.

"Brown hair, muscular, I hear. The king placed a reward for the safe return of the princess and another for finding the guard—alive or dead."

Caitriona slowly moved her hand to rest on Ailith's. They remained motionless, listening as the men were greeted by the barkeep and returned the keys from their rooms. The two didn't move until the men left and the barkeep returned to the kitchen, disappearing from sight.

"We need to go," Ailith murmured, her face pale and brow furrowed as she stood. She helped Caitriona adjust her pack so her cloak's hood didn't accidentally dislodge. Ailith tugged her own hood up with a quick, forceful gesture.

Caitriona gently touched Ailith's chin, turning the guard's face upright as her other hand tucked back stray wisps of the guard's brown hair beneath the sheltering cloth. Ailith studied Caitriona's face and the princess paused. For a breath, they held each other's gaze before Ailith offered a ghost of a smile that didn't reach her eyes and turned from Caitriona's touch to pick up her supplies.

Leaving their inn key behind and a few coins on the table, they went through the early dawn light to the stables. Caitriona asked the owner to ready their horses and slipped him a single platinum coin when she realized he was studying her.

"I trust you won't admit to anyone that you've seen me or my companion." Her heart raced as she placed the coin into his palm. His eyebrows rose and he nodded quickly, pocketing the coin and turning to gather the horses without another word.

The city was to their backs by the time the sun was fully in the sky, the air turning warm as they trotted north on Death's Mist Road. Caitriona shifted on Butterscotch and glanced over her shoulder at Ailith. Ailith was obviously less comfortable with her horse, but Caitriona doubted that her inexperience kept her silent as they moved. Allowing Butterscotch to slow and Ailith to catch up, Caitriona remained by her side in silence until she grew desperate.

"Is it due to the search?" Caitriona thought of the men at the inn, her stomach dropping.

"It's more so due to the fact that your father doesn't care if I'm found alive or dead." Ailith looked up, not meeting Caitriona's glances but staring straight ahead at the road. She blinked, tears in her eyes.

"Oh, Ailith, I won't let anything happen to you," Caitriona reasoned. "I'll put myself in front of you, command them not to touch a hair on your head."

Ailith let out a small, sad laugh. "You make it sound simple." She looked down and sniffed. "I left the valley completely understanding that I may not make it home. But I didn't realize the gravity of what that would mean or how it would feel. How do I know that my parents will be cared for? How do I know they won't be questioned further, that they won't be hurt?"

"I'm sure Greer has a plan for your parents. And if anything happens to you, I promise I'll make sure they're alright." Caitriona kept her voice low, despite that few people were on the road. She didn't want to risk anyone hearing anything. "Not that anything *will* happen."

Ailith looked back at the horizon. "Ensure that Gwen, their caregiver, is paid and she's actually taking care of them. She's a good girl, but she's still young. Maybe she'll get married and want to leave, so if you could just make sure someone can be there to help out. And visit them, please? Or, I don't know, send Etta or Callan to check on them. I suspect your father will keep you in the castle if we're caught."

Caitriona disliked this line of conversation, but even more so, she hated that it wasn't an overreaction. Ailith wasn't wrong, she'd likely be back to the life she led before but more controlled. She had freedom to pass through the castle as she pleased prior to leaving Braewick, but if she was dragged back and her abilities were discovered ... "Whatever the situation, I'll make sure your parents don't have anything to worry about. If you can't return to Braewick, perhaps we can find a way to move them from the city, so that you all may be together."

Ailith squeezed her eyes shut for a moment. "I wouldn't want to upend their lives because of something I did."

Caitriona offered companionable silence. Their future was a series of unknowns with varying degrees of fear and dread. What could Caitriona say that would truly lessen Ailith's concerns?

They continued north, leaving behind the sandy edges of the coast and surpassing the outer region of the Umberfend Marsh. The ground dried, gentle grassy hills appeared, and trees became more frequent in passing. The rubble of former buildings dotted the landscape, broken stone walls, the frame of a house without a roof. Occasionally, they passed settlements. A house, maybe two, with large fertile gardens that were being harvested and animals in pastures. They spoke to no one, keeping stony silence as they progressed by any dwelling or person. By midday, they moved beyond the crossroads that could take them west to Braewick, or east to Sage Hill on the coast. They took the road going northward where the Endless Mountains appeared on the horizon; their white peaks thrusting through the white clouds of the mist.

"How much do you know about the Endless Mountains?" Ailith asked. They were back on their horses after stopping to eat their midday meal. Continuing onward with the sun hidden behind thickening clouds drifting in from the west, the Endless Mountains stood tall and foreboding before them. Caitriona remained close to Ailith whose silence persisted through their meal and the question released tension in Caitriona's shoulders.

Caitriona studied the mountains for a moment, considering all she read about them and what she heard through stories her mother, Greer, and the castle workers shared. "I think as much as there is to know in Braewick. I always thought they were magical."

"The mist that people get lost in, right?" Ailith glanced at Caitriona. She nodded, pressing her horse onward as they began up a steeper incline. "There are so many guesses about why the mist is there and what it could mean. My favorite is that it's a portal to another land."

"I guess that would explain why no one comes back out."

"It always struck me as odd though. If the mist is an entrance to another world, are the white peaks that we see truly part of this one? Or would it be a part of another?"

"Oh." Ailith considered this for a moment. "That's a good point."

They slowly gained ground and the air grew noticeably cooler. As they reached the top of the hill, the crest allowed a view of a valley with a scattering of trees filled with changing leaves and those already appearing to have lost them due to the higher elevation. Standing upon the hillcrest with the gray sky behind them, they were in perfect view of a band of travelers further along the road. Crows cawed overhead, flying above the pair and further down the road toward a cluster of trees near the mountain base before it funneled upward and disappeared into the mist. Caitriona gripped the reins of her horse, continuing at a slow trot, while Ailith adjusted her cloak hood and pulled her bow free to rest loosely on her lap.

A few horses grazed in the field while smoke curled into the sky from a fire where many of the men gathered. A deer hung from a tree, blood pooling on the ground beneath it with flies flitting around. Based on the cache of arrows, Caitriona suspected this was a band of hunters for one of the nearby settlements.

"Should we just continue through?" Caitriona murmured, keeping her attention on the men.

"Yes, follow the road. Hope they let us pass and we don't have to speak to them," Ailith replied with the outtake of her breath, the words slipping forth and barely audible. Ailith's knuckles grew white from her grip of the reins. She looked serious, and her stiffness upon her horse showed further tension.

They continued to approach and more crows took off from the tall grasses beside the road, black dashes against the sky as their deep caws racketed in Caitriona's chest, a rattle against the drumming of her heart. The men, at first, appeared too busy eating and chatting, but when the pair began to ease past them, one of the men stepped out from the bushes and into the roadway before them.

"Where're the two of you heading?" the man asked, his voice loud enough it drew attention from the men near the fire. They lifted their heads and got to their feet, their eyes on the women. Ailith and Caitriona's horses slowed to a stop as the man centered himself in the road before them. "We're a long way from anywhere two women should be traveling."

Caitriona lowered her gaze and remained silent, the predetermined approach to anything like this, while Ailith straightened her posture, her horse stomping its hooves impatiently. "We are heading north towards Avorkaz on business. I'd appreciate if you let us pass."

Some of the men looked the women over as they mounted their own horses and turned the steeds to circle them.

"Of course," the man said. Caitriona glanced up and saw him staring at her, smiling. He was missing a tooth on the top of his mouth. "But we ran into some messengers from Braewick Valley; they asked us to keep an eye out for two female travelers. You see, the princess of the royal family's gone missing, and they suspect she's traveling with a female guard."

The mounted men continued lazy circles around the women, causing their horses to grow skittish. Caitriona glanced at a man passing by within arm's reach before continuing his path around Ailith. Her gaze shifted to Caitriona and she swallowed, her lips pursing as if she were ready to speak but decided it was better to choke on her words. The man tilted his head to the side and lifted a hand to his ear. "Yes? Did you have something to say?"

Ailith took a deep breath before meeting the man's eyes, ignoring the others who continued to circle. "If she's traveling with a guard, it sounds like she's simply traveling, rather than missing."

The man shrugged. "Either way, the king wants his daughter back and the guard found, dead or alive."

One of the men on horseback reached out, snatching at Caitriona's cloak and pulling it backward. She gripped her reins, trying not to lose her seat off her horse. It was a swift moment capable of causing time to slow into dreadful, sluggish seconds as events were suddenly pushed into motion.

First, Caitriona's horse reared, and the movement caused Ailith's horse to do the same. Caitriona clung to her horse, her cloak hood falling back and her gold-lined red hair releasing from its protective cover. The men yelled and seemed to move with separate focus and intention, yet all toward one equal goal. Ailith's inexperience left her unable to remain mounted when her horse reared and she tumbled to the ground, her head bouncing off the hardened earth of the road in a sickening way.

The man who stood before them rushed to grab Caitriona's horse as Ailith's galloped away. The man who grabbed Caitriona's cloak pulled hard, choking her, and reached to yank her off. Caitriona issued a choking scream, her feet kicking as the man pressed her against his chest. Her horse reared again, panicked by her flailing and kicking, causing the man on the ground to let go of its reins. It bolted, leaving Caitriona struggling against the hold of the other man, his own horse growing skittish under Caitriona's struggle.

Ailith lay flat on the ground, her eyes big as she took long blinks. Her hand blindly reached for her sword, her bow dropped a few feet away, but she seemed lost in a haze from the fall.

"Ailith!" Caitriona yelled with what air she could get.

Ailith slowly got to her feet, shaking her head as she tried to find balance with drunken movements. Her sword was in her hand now, her head turning to take in the men who circled them, but she never had the chance to swing.

"*Ailith!*" Caitriona screamed as an arrow flashed through the air and struck Ailith's left shoulder. She wavered on her feet and fell again.

Caitriona's fighting renewed and the man lost his grip. She dropped to the road, falling onto her hands and knees as another arrow went through the air, nearly hitting Caitriona as it sung past toward Ailith, but glanced off Ailith's side. One of the men yelled to hold back as Caitriona got to her feet and rushed forward, collapsing on her knees beside the guard and bending over her body.

Her chest heaved from rage. "Get back," she snarled, spit flying from her mouth as she glared into the face of each man within reach. "Don't come closer. *Leave us alone.*"

"Princess," a new man said, stepping closer with his hands held up and empty of weapons. His voice was kind and perhaps he truly was, but Caitriona's eyes narrowed, seeing him only as a threat. "We won't hurt you, but we need you to come with us."

"I told you to get back." Caitriona's hand flew forward, her palm facing outward. The rush of fear, the turmoil of concern, the rage that any of this was happening and Ailith was hurt because of *her* made her skin tingle and her palms ache.

It wasn't a conscious decision to create flame so much as desire to release herself from the boiling emotions and the need to strike fear in the hearts of these men. It was driven by the necessity for safety and to provide protection to her friend, and the flames responded as great fire often does: a surprise to the men, but an element with chaos running through it, and Caitriona was at the helm.

It roared forward and outward, spreading fast and gaining strength. When fire first spilled forth from her the night the shades attacked, it took no heed to attempts for control. But this fire was different. Caitriona saw its benefit now, she enjoyed the creation of her own making, and the protection it could provide so long as she directed it.

Half of the men fell back, their faces long with shock, but the others hadn't grasped what happened and moved in. Were their movements gallant? Were their thoughts to save the princess from the flames? Or were they selfish, desiring to capture her so they could be paid well with the king's coin? Caitriona refused to consider their intentions before moving her open palm in the direction of the other men moving forward.

Caitriona easily beckoned the flames now. With her lips set in a stern line, she could tell the fire where to go with thought, and watched as they raced forward, flying through the cool air and catching the dry autumn grasses at the feet of the hunters. She requested the fire to create a ring and it rushed to answer her call. Spreading outward from their place in its center, the flames reached high, dimming the sky overhead from their brightness and funneling smoke while men yelled from beyond the flames' deadly reach. Caitriona dropped her hand, satisfied that the flames continued, and turned her attention to Ailith who was slumped on the ground.

The princess lifted Ailith's bow and shoved her short sword into its holder. She paused, staring at her hands as she reached for Ailith's shoulders. They had grown paler, the skin of her fingers displaying a glittering gleam, slick and gold. Her nails were lengthened as they had before, pin-pricking Ailith's shirt sleeve under her touch. Her throat tightened from the sight of the change, leaving her swallowing the knot that formed there.

Monster, she thought, but the voice was her father's.

Pushing the thought away, ignoring her hands and how they both frightened and fascinated her, she attempted to move Ailith. An arrow stuck out from the guard's left arm muscle and her shirt rapidly turned red from the graze on her side.

It was the fall from the horse that worried Caitriona most. Ailith moaned beneath Caitriona's urging to get her to her feet, her head rolled backwards, her brown eyes dark with dilated pupils. "Ailith, I've got you. Just walk when I do. That's right, one foot after another."

As she stumbled forward, pulling Ailith along, Caitriona looked at the ring of fire that guarded them and to the sky where the smoke rose. More crows flashed overhead, flying ever north, and Caitriona turned her sights in that direction, willing the flames with her mind to spread outward and release the earth to create a pathway for them.

As the fire bowed and stepped backward, listening dutifully to its maker, Caitriona shifted Ailith's weight against her and found no inkling of surprise that the flames were so easily persuaded—this magic fire of her own making. She allowed the blaze to follow behind as a heated entourage and moved northward with her guard held tight against her side.

To the men beyond the flames, unable to tame the fire no matter their method, they saw the princess moving forward with the determined step of a queen wearing a crown of smoke.

CHAPTER TWELVE

AILITH

Ailith came to consciousness with a gasp. The pain in her left arm and along her side was suddenly true, then the throb of her entire body followed. Her eyes and head immediately ached from the light surrounding her, and her gasp turned to a moan as she squeezed her eyes closed, lifting her right hand to cover her brow.

A quiet hush, an intake of breath, then the shuffle of footsteps and rustling fabric sounded as someone sat near her.

Open your eyes, open your eyes, a part of Ailith urged herself. *Make sure this person isn't a threat.* But she couldn't for the life of her think why. Her head ached too much to consider it further and she wanted to return to the sweet embrace of sleep.

Fingertips grazed the top of her head and brushed through her hair; the gentlest touch that was comforting. Ailith turned her face toward the figure, squinting as she stifled another sound as the light broadened the pain in her head.

Caitriona knelt beside her, her round face only a few inches from where she rested her chin on her hand. Her elbow relaxed on the edge of the bed Ailith lay on; her other hand lifted to brush at Ailith's hair. Their eyes met and Caitriona smiled.

"Hello." Caitriona pulled her hand back. Her hair, brushed and loose, hung over her shoulders in a mixture of gold and red, so evenly blended it was impossible to call it red any longer. Strawberry blonde was more accurate. The blush on Caitriona's cheeks matched it perfectly.

She offered her hand, the tips of her nails curled, thick and white, and talon-like again. The skin on her hands sported a faint, gold-like glimmer, fading back to Caitriona's tone past her wrist. They had never taken on that color before. Meeting Caitriona's gaze, Ailith realized the blue of her eyes were flushed out by a mixture of green and gold. "Do you want to try and sit up?"

"Oh, Cait." Ailith's voice was a sigh, weakened from pain and weighed down by concern. She took Caitriona's hand, the pads of the princess's fingers cool against hers, the texture of her skin different. Caitriona shifted forward and slipped her other arm behind Ailith's back as she assisted her to sit up, her hand lingering on the small of Ailith's back for a moment before withdrawing. Ailith couldn't pull away from Caitriona though, her eyes locked on the princess's changes. "What happened?"

Caitriona withdrew her hand, avoiding eye contact as she shifted to kneel beside the bed again.

Ailith took in their surroundings. They sat in a large room with a giant hearth in the middle of one wall. Garlic and herbs hung from the ceiling, and root vegetables and grain covered a table against a wall. She rested upon a bed in the opposite corner with a multi-colored quilt. Covering the floor up to the fireplace, blankets and furs were strewn as makeshift rugs. Resting upon a wooden chair beside the fireplace were both of their travel packs.

Caitriona placed her elbow on the edge of the bed, resting her head onto her claw-like hand. "You were shot with an arrow in your shoulder. Another glanced off your side but cut pretty deeply near your ribs. I think it was the tumble off your horse that did the most damage. You don't remember vomiting, do you?"

Ailith shook her head, immediately regretting the movement.

"Well, you did. A lot. You hit your head when you fell off the horse. But we got you here, and Isla was able to call the horses and find our bags."

"Isla?" Ailith asked as the wooden door opened and a huddled mass of dark cloth and gray hair shuffled in.

The woman was old, her face deeply carved with wrinkles and her eyes a light blue that seemed nearly white. She smiled with yellowed teeth and dropped a bundle of wood beside the fireplace.

"I see you've gotten your senses back." The woman's voice was a deep croak. "You've been fading in and out for the last day."

"The vomiting happened primarily overnight," Caitriona added.

Ailith looked between the two and pulled Caitriona toward her. "Cait, what's going on?"

Caitriona turned and entwined her fingers with Ailith's, her face growing more serious. "What's your last *clear* memory?"

Ailith pressed her lips together as she gathered her thoughts. "The men circling us and falling off the horse. It gets foggy after that."

"It happened again, just like with the shades." Caitriona lowered her voice but didn't seem shy by the use of her powers, more so that she was seeking privacy from Isla.

Isla was stuffing logs into the fire and stirring a cauldron that hung above it, ignoring the two as they spoke.

"I created fire, a lot of it, but I controlled it. I moved the men away and got to you. I tried to get us out of the area and keep the fire around us, but the men tried pushing through. Then Isla showed up with her crows. This is her home; near where we saw the grove of trees down the road by the mountains."

"The crows ..." Ailith remembered them flying overhead as they approached the men on the road. In the feverish, gray haze she was in after falling, she thought she heard their caws.

"The crows and Isla work together," Caitriona finished.

"A companionable truce, I would say." Isla stepped back from the fire and brushed her hands off. "I promise to feed them and they promise to be my eyes for the world."

"Isla's watched our progress since the beginning," Caitriona added. "She knows things about our trip that she truly has no reason to."

"I only hope to ensure your safe passage." The woman shuffled to the table on the opposite wall, pulling the towel from a basket and uncovering a still-steaming loaf of bread. She reached a hand toward a shelf, and a jar of honey drifted through the air and placed itself in her waiting palm.

"A magic user."

"A witch," Isla corrected without turning. "Those of us with gifts who are not fae in heritage are witches."

Ailith leaned back further. If they were caught in this household, it was certainly over for her. Not only would she be found to have taken the princess from the city but engaging with a witch was a damnable offense.

"It's alright." Caitriona's expression was sincere, her golden-red brow furrowed and her hand squeezing Ailith's. "We came here yesterday afternoon. She brought on a fog that left the men unable to track us, and she's helped care for you. She willingly told me about our travels and even knows Kayl. She can help us, Ailith, and I trust her. What else could we do? Particularly with you hurt."

Ailith still felt the tingling rush of unease in her shoulders. Her fingers entwined with the clawed hand of the princess kept the feeling there. Ailith lifted Caitriona's hand and gave it a tender shake. "And what of this?"

Caitriona's cheeks colored. "They were worse before, but they're returning to normal. I'd live with it if it meant keeping those men from killing you."

Ailith lied to herself that Caitriona's hand in hers was a comfort after the fright and exhaustion of injury. But the tickle in her belly conveyed the truth of the matter.

Swallowing and shifting in the bed, pain flared and put the quiver of excitement to rest. Ignoring her discomfort, she looked to Isla who spooned broth into bowls, focusing instead on her unease of strangers. "And why have you watched our progress? How did you even know we were taking such a trip?"

"When Princess Greer sent out letters in search of Kayl, there were some murmurs amongst my kind. It piqued my interest." The woman hobbled over to offer them bowls of soup. Caitriona shifted on the floor beside the bed and balanced the bowl in her lap as Ailith held hers, watching the woman steadily. "I sent crows to keep an eye on the both of you, sure that you would make your way toward these mountains and along this road."

"And you know Kayl?" Ailith asked while the woman retrieved the plate of bread covered in honey and butter and placed it on the floor in front of Caitriona before easing down onto one of the many fur skins that lay there. Ailith's frown turned into a grimace as she shifted her feet onto the ground. Despite her sore legs from riding, as well as her injuries, Ailith readied herself to get up and offer the bed back to its owner, but her head spun slightly, and she remained seated.

Caitriona shook her head, urging Ailith to stay still.

The woman settled upon her pile of blankets and stirred her soup. "I knew him years ago when he was a child. I knew your mother, too, princess."

Caitriona grew still. "You never said you knew my mother."

"I wanted to keep that little surprise until your guard woke." Isla leaned back and looked at them pointedly. "I figured you'd handle what I had to say better with her by your side. Now eat."

Ailith shifted the soup with her spoon, not hungry at first, until she lifted a spoonful to her mouth. The warm broth drained into her empty stomach, pooling there as its heat spread slowly into her limbs and softened the cutting pain of her muscles to a dull throb. She held back a content sigh as she spooned more into her mouth, savoring the potatoes, carrots, onions and herbs until Isla's voice drew her attention back to the conversation at hand.

"Your mother grew up in a town that once existed in the foothills of the Endless Mountains. Kayl lived there as well," Isla continued. "I remember your mother for her beautiful red hair and heard that when she was of age, she was whisked away to Braewick Valley and married the then Prince Cearny. It was quite the scandal, considering her station in society."

Caitriona's brows narrowed. She placed her spoon down and sat the bowl on the floor, brushing her hands over her knees. "My mother never speaks of her upbringing. I know she knew Kayl from childhood, but that was the extent of it."

"Your mother grew up in Caermythlin. It was a blended community of humans and fae. Most who lived there had magic abilities. Your mother was orphaned as a child and raised in a group home. To my understanding, when your father passed through on one of his conquests, she caught his eye."

"She lived amongst the fae?"

"Darling," Isla said, reaching forward to squeeze Caitriona's knee. "Your mother *is* fae. Or at least partly."

Even Ailith felt the weight of this reveal, her spoon clinked off the side of her bowl as she put it down. Caitriona sat very still as silence swelled in the room until Caitriona's voice rang clear. "King Cearny has never been very ... welcoming of the fae."

Isla took a deep breath and pulled away from Caitriona, brushing a crumb off her skirts. Her icy gaze held a sudden chill. "Well, yes, he's never been very welcoming of anyone other than magicless humans; even then he only likes other people if they've less power than he. It helped your mother was able to pretend she was fully human."

"Is that why I have ..." Caitriona held up her clawed hand.

"Perhaps, but eat your meal. We need to clean that one's wounds, and then we can have tea and chat more."

With their stomachs filled, Ailith endured the torment of having the bindings of her wound changed and the cut in her side cleaned and wrapped. Caitriona busied herself around Isla, accepting direction with ease and grabbing herbs and cloth while Isla tended to Ailith. She straightened out the blankets and furs on the ground and helped Ailith outdoors to relieve herself before settling her on the bed again. She seemed nearly as relaxed as she was that evening on the beach when it was only her and Ailith. She kept her hair unbraided and loose, allowing it to hang freely down her back like a golden-red cloak, and Ailith wondered if this was how she always was when she wasn't trying to hide herself away. Someone who seemed relaxed and unencumbered with a sense that her very presence was something not to apologize for.

After Ailith was cared for, a teapot was set on the grate above the flames and Caitriona led Ailith back to Isla's bed.

"Isla, you should be sleeping here." Ailith slowly settled onto the bed, feeling every cut and muscle in her body. She wouldn't admit it, but each breath and movement seemed to send shooting pain through her torso, and she couldn't fathom sleeping on the floor, but it still felt wrong to see the older woman settling back in the spot she sat for their evening meal.

"Because I'm old?" The woman turned her gaze upon Ailith and gave a sniff. "You need that bed more than I do for the moment, child. I'll kick you to the floor when I think you're well enough, don't you worry."

"Milk? Sugar?" Caitriona called, busying herself near the shelves filled with food supplies. She pulled the teapot from the fire and left it resting on a platter with three mugs, having made tea with herbs of Isla's choosing.

"The tea is better without either."

"What's exactly in this tea?" Ailith asked, eyeing the teapot.

"I can see why you're the princess's guard. You're terribly distrustful," Isla replied and Ailith felt her cheeks grow hot. "They're herbs that'll calm us, and hopefully provide restful sleep."

Ailith accepted her teacup with a little bit of shame as Caitriona passed one to her. Isla seemed to have that way about her, that special quality only some women held where they put others in their place with a few words. Still, she waited for Isla to drink before she tasted it.

Caitriona settled onto the floor, placing herself before Ailith's feet, and leaned back into Ailith's legs. Ailith grew stiff at the familiarity, uncertain of what to do despite having a deep notion of what she *wanted* to do. A moment passed before Ailith reached forward and brushed her fingers through Caitriona's hair, uncertain if she was pushing boundaries but finding her heart thrilling when Caitriona leaned her head into Ailith's hand. The events the day before shook her and Caitriona's close proximity was grounding, just as she was when Ailith woke from the night terror. That was it, comfort was all, nothing else.

Isla cleared her throat and to Ailith's slight horror found the witch eyeing them both with a knowing look. Thankfully, she seemed only interested in continuing her story.

"When the white dragon attacked Braewick Castle, news spread through Visennore. I saw Kayl just beforehand; he'd taken to traveling on diplomatic trips for his home, including the one he and your mother hailed from. He told me he was going to visit the queen. He wanted to see if he could convince the king to stop the genocide of magic users. He hoped the queen would help."

"I'm sorry," Caitriona interrupted, lifting her head from where Ailith had continued to brush her fingers through her hair. "Genocide? He only ever said magic was banned."

Isla sighed and lowered her teacup. "I suspect there is much about your father's reign that's kept from you. Your grandfather began to ban magic and your father continued that legacy, but he did much more than simply outlaw it. Not immediately within the city, but out here in the rural parts.

"He and your grandfather conquered many of the cities in Visennore. For some villages and towns, it came as a relief. The crown could provide safety and help if they were to face famine, natural disasters, or attacks from other more powerful kingdoms. But for many, the crown's presence was not welcome, particularly to those who have fae ancestry and magic makers. Your father's distrust of our gifts is well known, and he has proven quite the tyrant since becoming king. While he left many alone, to live lives as we see fit so long as no magic appears to be present, he killed far more for simply existing."

"There's laws banning the use of magic within the city walls," Ailith said. "Healers in the city are suspected of being witches but they never perform any real magic. At least not like yours. If they can do that, they keep it hidden."

"Because they know they'd forfeit their homes, if not their lives, if they behaved any other way." Isla frowned, shifting her attention back to Caitriona. "Your father is a man who has built a nation based on his own fears and insecurities. He's afraid of others who aren't like him, anyone not human or those who can wield any magic or gift. It provides them with a strength, something they can use against him. His father shared similar fears, but he wasn't as daring or ruthless as your father is."

Ailith touched Caitriona's shoulder, the princess quivering under her hand. "What do you know? Please, I feel you're dancing around truths."

"Some of this is suspicion, other is fact, but this is what I know," Isla said. "Kayl was in the city to ask your mother for help. Your father was conquering town after town along the foothills of the mountains. Lives were lost and Kayl hoped to change your father's mind if your mother sided with him. Then the white dragon attacked, you were lost, and Kayl lent his gift to bring you back.

"It's a well-kept secret in the greater kingdom, but within our community of magic makers, we knew what Kayl did, even if your father didn't release such information to the masses. It requires a great deal of power to heal someone as well as recall their soul," Isla said, her eyes flitting from one to another. "We could feel the shift of energy that was used to save you. However, while Kayl was gone, his village was attacked by men supporting the king. The village was destroyed. I heard that Kayl moved north of the Endless Mountains, into Beaslig within the Mazgate Dominion after he left Braewick Valley and seemed to fade away. I haven't seen him in fifteen years. But your sister was smart to search out Kayl if you're showing these abilities. I fear what your father will do if he sees what you're capable of."

"If the queen is partly fae," Ailith began, gazing at the top of Caitriona's head as she spoke, "is that information the king knows?"

"If he does, he ignores it because the queen looks human. If he doesn't, well, we can assume it's a tightly kept secret."

"And what of my abilities? Why has my hair changed, and my hands?" Caitriona asked. Her voice was patient, even, but Ailith could feel Caitriona tense. Over the course of the evening, Caitriona's nails shortened, the shimmer of gold on her skin receded, but her hands were still not quite normal, and her hair hadn't returned to the deep red it was a week prior.

"And your eyes," Ailith added, drawing Caitriona to look at her. Ailith frowned, realizing they hadn't been near a looking glass and Caitriona didn't know. "They aren't blue anymore. The golden glow from when you make fire has lingered. The blue looks green, too, and they haven't changed back."

"I suspect *that* is something more ..." Isla's hand rose and turned in the air as if she were beckoning the words to form. She paused and eyed the women before speaking cautiously. "Sometimes, when powerful magic is used, as would have been necessary to bring you back to life, it can leach out hidden gifts, or sink into the bones of the person receiving it. I suspect the magic forever changed you and something, perhaps your age, or an event, caused it to begin coming forth. It may be inherited from your mother, or it may be left over magic from what Kayl did.

"Magic is a fickle thing, it's often uncontrollable until the user learns how to wield it, and even then, it can have unknown effects. Some magic users will experience changes to themselves the more they use their gifts. It isn't unheard of, and entirely possible that's what's occurring with your hair and eyes."

"Can you do anything to ... I don't know, teach me how to control it? Or stop my body from physically changing?" Caitriona held her hands out as if waiting to receive an invisible cure. "I don't mind having magic. I feel as if I've searched for years for the final ingredient to make me feel like my true self and I've found it in this. But you're right ... I don't know how my father would react if he saw me sporting these abilities. Or, I suppose, I fear I *do* know, and that's the trouble."

Isla shook her head. "I'm sorry, dear. Your magic is something different from my own. My magic is old and dry, something I've kept as a constant companion since I was a child. Yours is new. You may grow strong enough to control it; however, it is very unpredictable and uncontrollable for me." She sipped her tea and thought for a moment. "But since Kayl is directly tied to your abilities, at least I believe them to be, and because he's much younger than myself, he should be able to help you. So long as you find him."

CHAPTER THIRTEEN

AILITH

They spent a few days with Isla in her cabin nestled amongst the trees. It was shrouded in secrecy; she kept spells set to keep travelers, and gratefully the men who found Ailith and Caitriona, away. Ailith's wounds began healing without complications and the trauma to her head eased. Dizzy spells plagued her for a day, but Caitriona was close to her side, slipping an arm around her waist, and quick to ensure Ailith had anything she needed.

The princess slept on the floor beside Ailith without complaint, although there was no reason for her to assume Caitriona *would*—she had yet to in spite of everything. Despite that she left her home and slept in the wilderness, often covered in mud and bitten by bugs; despite having powers her father would kill anyone for possessing, and hands that turned to claws and eyes that lost their blue; despite being thrust into this venture with little direction of how to fix what was occurring or where they were headed, while forced to follow and trust Ailith's abilities, she remained the same. She smiled, she laughed, she often turned her jovial mood on Ailith, and she never protested about anything. It left the guard staring in wonder and a touch of something else. A flutter in her belly that grew by the day.

Caitriona chatted with Isla while Ailith was at a loss for words. Most caught between her teeth and her lips promptly sealed as the events on the roadway played out in her mind. Unlike Caitriona, being perpetually optimistic and hopeful was not in her making. She always judged herself too harshly and, after encountering the hunters, her self-ridicule only grew.

The men took her down so easily. She should've been quicker to take arms and defend. But in the moment, she hesitated. She thought she could talk their way through it. That she could avoid pulling her bow out or drawing her sword. What if she couldn't defend Caitriona in the future? What if Caitriona couldn't defend herself?

She found herself more frightened of losing Caitriona than even her own life. It left her on edge and only when Caitriona was near did the tightness in her shoulders release and her jaw unclench.

Caitriona's hands returned to normal, but her eyes and hair seemed permanently altered. The mix of red and gold never lessened, and she continued to wear her hair loose in a fiery waterfall, proving a constant temptation for Ailith to reach and touch whenever Caitriona was close to her. It reminded her of sunsets in late summer and smelled like rosemary.

Over a few days, autumn took over the forest with a sudden change in temperature. Warm weather was replaced by the first frost, but the sun still held heat. As the women walked Isla's property, they noted the fading grass becoming a more distinct yellow and leaves sporting reds and oranges. Late summer flowers grew brittle and brown, shriveling into themselves before dropping to the ground. Birds rushed from tree to tree, gathering what they could to fend off the cold, starving months that would soon arrive, and even ground animals were more active. The chickens Isla kept laid less eggs each day and the goats' winter coats grew. The air held a crispness that coated the tongue and throat, encouraging some primal sense of Ailith's to remain indoors and find warmth from others.

"It'll scar," Isla said the morning prior to their leaving as she rubbed more herbs into the arrow wound in Ailith's arm. "But it was a clean enough wound and the arrow wasn't pushed around. Same with the cut on your side. A scar, but what guard doesn't sport one or two?"

She looked up and studied Ailith's eyes for a moment. Her gaze narrowed and she leaned back to call Caitriona who lingered close by. "Go to the stream and gather a bucket of water so you may both bathe before you leave, won't you, dear?"

Ailith sat still, finding the courage to meet Isla's stare, forcing herself to maintain eye contact despite the growing discomfort it brought. Caitriona grabbed a bucket and went out the door as the woman reached a wrinkled hand to turn Ailith's face back and forth. "Your pupils aren't dilated anymore; have you had any additional dizzy spells? Headaches?"

"I'm feeling much better. No dizzy spells, only a little bit of a headache by the end of the day."

The woman lifted her other hand and framed Ailith's face with soft palms. "You must trust yourself. You're exactly what the princess needs. You'll face incredible things in the near future. Both good and bad. But you must trust in the process. Everything was set into motion years ago and you both must follow it through."

Ailith attempted to pull back, but the old woman was much stronger than she ever conveyed. She slumped, remaining held in place by Isla's hands. Her eyes burned and she wanted to look away. "What do you mean?"

The woman let go and smiled. Caitriona returned and placed the bucket by the fire. Isla moved away as Caitriona came closer. "Is she doing alright?"

"Perfect. I think she's ready to travel again." Isla got to her feet and touched Caitriona's shoulder with the gentleness of a grandmother. "I'll get the water warmed and hang up a cloth."

Caitriona smiled and squeezed Ailith's hand. "Do you think you're ready to head out? We can always stay here another day."

"So long as you're comfortable with leaving, I'm ready to go." Ailith tried to smile as she returned the pressure of Caitriona's hand in hers. Ailith relaxed, allowing the mask to slip from her face and concern color it. Caitriona tilted her head to one side, immediately seeing Ailith's emotions with clarity.

"What's wrong? You seem hesitant."

Isla hung the sheet in the corner of the room, preparing a private bathing space, and ignoring the two.

"To be honest, I'm embarrassed. This is the second time you saved me." Ailith found the sudden shame of it all preventing her from keeping her eyes up. She couldn't stand to see Caitriona's expression as she admitted, "In some ways, I feel you'd be better with literally anyone else."

"Oh, Ailith," Caitriona replied, her free hand lifting Ailith's chin so the guard would discard her shame and see her sincerity. Ailith's stomach twisted and her palms grew warm. Her embarrassment was a rich, hot thing that covered another feeling Ailith was not yet ready to face, but it festered and made her nervous, bringing color to her cheeks. Caitriona's lips parted, her cheeks pink as well. "I would want no one else but you."

The next morning dawned gray and misty. The sun shone like a glowing orb in the white air, pressing in to burn off the fog but making slow progress. Caitriona braided her hair for the first time since they arrived and pulled her cloak hood up. Both women dressed in their travel clothing: pants and shirts, but with the addition of sweaters Isla provided, they found warmth in the rapidly cooling temperatures. Isla also gave provisions and when they took to their horses, they felt better prepared for the journey ahead.

"Steer clear of the mist from the mountains, never step into it. The mist should linger along the eastern side of the roadway. Continue north following Death's Mist Road. The road will split in about two days' time, less with your horses. Take the road to the left, directly to Avorkaz," Isla instructed, looking over Caitriona's map.

"Avorkaz and Wimleigh are in active combat though," Ailith said. "Wouldn't it be better to stay on the road that runs directly north toward the northern mountains? At the very least, it's more direct."

"You'll need to prepare for the cold weather and get more supplies. The sweaters and food won't sustain you in those elements. Autumn may have just begun, but in these higher lands, it passes quickly. We're too close to winter and in the mountains, they see snow much sooner than you're used to in Braewick. So go to Avorkaz. Why would they care that the princess of Wimleigh Kingdom is missing or that a female guard is with her? And the princess's renowned red hair is now changed. I think you'll arrive undetected.

"You both have strong Braewick accents. Use it to your advantage. Say you've left Braewick as you have magic. If that doesn't grant you admittance, mention my name. I pass through the gates to the city in the spring and summer months, so they'll likely know me. Purchase warmer clothes, get potions to aid against the cold, gather food. Ensure you have more than you think you'll need."

Ailith thanked Isla and mounted Inkwell, shifting with slight unease from the dull ache of her healing wounds and still-sore thighs. Caitriona embraced the older woman before climbing upon Butterscotch and began to move toward the exit amongst the trees. Ailith clicked her reins, but her horse stopped short as Isla stepped forward. "Remember, Ailith. *Trust* yourself."

Ailith swallowed before giving a single nod. Isla slapped Inkwell's rear, sending them forward. She waved her arm outward, parting the fog to a clear pathway out of the trees and toward the road, leaving behind the witch with her horde of crows.

There was no evidence of the men from days before. In fact, the woods where Isla lived was further up the road and long past where the scuffle took place. Now they traveled alone and unencumbered amongst the rolling foothills of the Endless Mountains, with the tall cuts of earth jutting upward along the northeast side of their path and trees with colorful leaves sprinkled along the landscape. To the east of Death's Mist Road lay the blue-white mist that perpetually twisted and turned, blotting out all visibility on that side of the road. Corners of it reached out as if to taste the clear air, but never moved past the base of the mountain range that went on for miles until it vanished on the northern horizon.

"How are you feeling?" Caitriona asked after the grove of Isla's forest disappeared.

Ailith shrugged and internally cringed from the discomfort the gesture brought. "Fine enough. Glad my injuries are on my left. I can still wield my short sword without issue ... but it may take a bit before I'm back to normal with my bow. I think by the time we stop for the night my legs will be sorer than anything from riding.

"But I should be asking how you are. Isla gave us more information than we've ever had, and I haven't had the chance to ask how you're doing after … you know."

"Those men?" Caitriona looked away from Ailith, focusing her sight ahead. Holding her head high, the picture of eloquent bravery, she seemed to consider her next words. "My biggest concern is what happened to them. Isla said she didn't alter their memory, she only cast a fog to make them lose their step and get momentarily lost. They're still out there and I feel uneasy."

"Do you suppose they'll go to Braewick and tell the king?" Ailith didn't want to place the thought into the world, but she was unable to hold back. It crossed her mind frequently in the last few days and she wanted to verify if she was overthinking the possibilities or not.

"If we have any luck, they'll go to my sister with the information. And she can figure out what to tell my father. It's interesting though; I wonder if they'll share what I did and yet, I don't care if they do. I know it's foolish, but a part of me wants to dare my father to know what I'm capable of. I was so terrified of the prospect when I was still in Braewick, but I can't deny that creating flame with a simple thought feels remarkable. I don't want to be rid of this ability, so what else am I to do? Hide away this power from my father for the rest of his life?"

Caitriona looked at Ailith and her bottom lip dared to pout. The hesitant yet determined appearance of any young adult taking a step away from the pressure of a parent, ready to declare themselves wholly their own person, no matter what the parent thought. But there was still an element of fright to it, made obvious by the furrow of Caitriona's brow. "I don't want to return to my life before. I don't want to be shuttered away in the castle, never allowed to interact with others. Magic or not, I'm not sure I can go back to that."

Ailith chewed on the inside of her lip as she considered the king's reaction if the men informed him that his missing daughter created flames from air, or better yet, how he'd react if Caitriona refused to comply to his wishes when she returned.

"It would be nice if we could just never go home," Caitriona continued. "If we could have a little cottage in the woods like Isla. We could do as we pleased and never hold ourselves back, never hide ourselves away."

Ailith considered what Greer paid her to do. "Cait, we have plenty to go home to. My parents, your sister. Your father can't continue this behavior where he focuses his vitriol on every creature that is different from him. Perhaps you'll be the person to show him that you're still very much yourself. You're his daughter, even if you can make fire with your mind. It doesn't change your entire making."

"I suppose I'm actually angry. I don't think it would go that way; I don't think he's capable of change. When you consciously choose to hate for so many years, it reaches a point where I fear there's no chance to change back and it won't matter that it's me. He'll only see it as the magic claiming more of what he feels he has a right to."

"I'm sorry, Cait," Ailith said. Caitriona was likely correct. It was fine to hope for the best outcome, but the more she heard of the king as they traveled, the more she realized her life-long distrust was justified. Reaching over, Ailith brushed her fingers down Caitriona's arm. "At the very least, you've changed *my* mind."

Caitriona twisted around; her lips quirked. "Changed your mind? About what?"

Ailith's face warmed. While she grew more comfortable with meeting Caitriona's eye, now she found herself unable to. "I despised the royal family for most of my life. I wanted nothing to do with your lot and I never wanted to work for the royal guard despite how much it pays and all the travel they get to do. Granted, I sometimes fantasized about it, but I wanted nothing to do with *you*. After the white dragon attack, you vanished from the public eye and there were many rumors about you. I saw Greer on occasion, and I didn't like her either. I didn't trust your father and I disliked your mother."

"But why?" Caitriona laughed. "You never met us!"

"I know!" Ailith responded, daring to look at Caitriona and laughing too. "I know, it's stupid. When my father was injured, I was both enraged and frightened. I grew to hate your father; I hated his decisions *and* his wealth. I think when I was a child, my hatred towards him turned into petty jealousy toward you and your sister. You lived in a castle, you had fine clothes and never worried about food or heat. You had an able-bodied father and mother. Everything I struggled to obtain, everything that caused our heartache, you were without, and I was deeply jealous of that. It's easier to distrust something you don't understand, or someone you never met, when you're left to struggle.

"My opinion of your sister began to change when I joined the city guard. I saw she worked hard for her position and that felt honorable. But I never saw you, or your mother or father, so my negative opinion remained secure. I assumed you lived a privileged life and never had to lift a finger or worry about a thing."

"You didn't like me when we met?" Her tone still lilted with humor but after traveling with Caitriona for a fortnight, Ailith spotted the strain in her forced tone and knew Ailith wounded her. The cheerful expression Caitriona often sported was frozen now, a mask of happy humor to maintain the previously silly conversation.

Ailith felt her stomach twist. She shook her head, feeling flushed with shame. "No. You were part of a job. I imagined you'd be more of a hindrance than anything. Someone who complained every step of the way and got us killed. But I was wrong. *So* wrong."

Caitriona smiled but her eyes filled with tears and if Ailith could take back each word she uttered, stuff them into her mouth, and choke on them until she swallowed them whole, she would. Instead, she began to ramble, trying to get out as many words in record time, all her thoughts over the past few days in particular. "You were cheerful and at first, I thought it was a show but then I realized you're genuinely such a happy person who sees light in the darkest days. You've traveled alongside me without complaint and when I've failed, time and time again, you stood up and took charge. You shouldn't have had to do that. I was hired to protect you. But instead, you've comforted me and protected me and ..."

Caitriona was fully crying now, wiping her tears with one gloved hand and gripping the reins of her horse with the other.

Ailith also had tears rolling down her cheeks, her embarrassment mixed with the honesty of the topic making her emotions high. Sniffing and rubbing at her face quickly, a poor attempt to cover her emotion, she urged Inkwell to step closer to Caitriona so she could better reach her hand.

"Please don't cry. I didn't mean to make you cry. I'm sorry."

"Don't be sorry. I appreciate your honesty. You know, you're right, I did have everything handed to me. I've never experienced the strain and struggle you have. But I want you to stop thinking that you've failed me. You haven't. You've shown me kindness and compassion and, despite that we've heard nothing but the dangers of magic, you accepted what I could do and continued on without question. I liked you as soon as I met you, but I'm glad you like me now."

"I do. Probably more than I should say. I wouldn't want you to get too full of yourself, being a princess and all."

With weeping eyes and sidelong glances, their cheeks mirroring a flush brought on by something other than the chilly temperatures, they gripped each other's hands for a moment longer before letting go to continue further up the road with the mist of the Endless Mountains watching their progress, skirting along the roadside, waiting.

CHAPTER FOURTEEN

AILITH

Evening drew close and the sun never found its way through the cloudy skies. A northern wind grew stronger as the pair traveled, blowing into their faces and painting their expressions with frowns. The temperature dropped both from the progression in elevation, the loss of the sun, and the gusting air. They dismounted their horses and searched for an appropriate place to rest for the night where a fire could keep them warm and not immediately blow out from the gathering wind.

The wind-swept women led their horses to a grove of trees with a thicket of holly bushes to help block the wind. The horses startled, blowing air from their noses with distrust and drawing Ailith's attention. The mist of the Endless Mountain gathered its courage to creep over the roadway. It inched forward, not daring to make too much progress.

"I thought the mists didn't cross the road." Ailith brushed her hand over Inkwell's neck and stepped closer to her horse. Caitriona paused from the far side of the road where she was leading Butterscotch toward the thicket of trees.

"That's what Isla said, at least." She squinted at the mist, her lips turning downward.

The mist skirted the horses' hooves and circled around as the women grew nervous, drawing closer together and holding their horses' reins tightly.

"We should move forward and get away from this." Caitriona drew Butterscotch back from the mist that licked at its hooves.

"If you step in the mist you're lost." Ailith wanted to pull her blade or bow, but there was no defending themselves from heavy air. "We can't go through; we have to hope it recedes."

It hesitated for a moment, then tumbled forward to gather itself to become tall, standing above their heads and blanching out sight of the land. It hesitated before leaning down, curling forward to touch their cheeks and kiss them both, forcing them to be lost to the world.

It was gentle, the hush of the mist as it fell upon the travelers. The sound of birds and wind vanished and in its place was quiet stillness beside the nervous whinny of the horses and quick breathing of both women.

"Ailith?" Caitriona reached for her companion's hand as she looked about nervously.

"It's fine," Ailith lied, taking Caitriona's hand in an ironclad grip that conveyed her true feelings. "It'll be fine. We can walk together; keep hold of my hand, so we don't lose each other."

Every childhood story she'd ever heard flit through her mind. Stories of travelers not only vanished forever when entering the mist but lost anyone they traveled with as well. They slipped from each other within a blink of an eye. When Ailith was older, she questioned how anyone would know this since no one had, reportedly, returned from the mist. But as the world grew white, and even the horses faded in color, she didn't want to find out if the stories held any truth.

They gripped one another, exchanging uneasy glances while their free hands pulled at the reins of their horses, leading them forward slowly without any knowledge of which direction they went. Even their footsteps were silent, giving no clue as to where they walked.

They stopped.

"Are you thinking 'what is the point?'" Caitriona murmured.

Ailith nodded. "I haven't the faintest idea where we're going, do you?" Ailith looked at Caitriona who studied the white wall.

"No, I don't," she said softly, blinking and licking her lips. She shook her head, as if trying to rid herself of discomfort. Turning toward Ailith, her now-green eyes watered, and her brow furrowed. "Do you feel a little off?"

"No ..." Ailith studied the princess, feeling a twinge traveling up her spine. Slowly, with each passing second, Caitriona's eyes grew more golden in color. "Cait, I think—"

Caitriona gasped, letting go of Ailith and dropping Butterscotch's reins as she grabbed at her shoulders, trying to reach over them to her back while her legs buckled. She collapsed to her knees on the misty ground, the white air fluffing out around her, before sinking onto her side with panicked sounds. The mist shifted from her movement before settling to cover her like a ghostly blanket.

The horses stepped away, growing nervous and quickly forgotten. Ailith dropped her lead, solely focused on Caitriona who writhed on the ground as a sound grew from her chest and churned into a scream.

"Cait? Cait!" Ailith fell to her knees and alighted her hands over Caitriona as the princess clawed at her cloak. "Cait, what's wrong? What's happening?"

Caitriona cried with anguish and pain, her eyes clamped shut and her teeth clenched. Her hands frantically grabbed at the fabric of her cloak before trying to untie it from her throat. In Ailith's confusion, she reached forward, untying the cloak and pulling it off. Caitriona's nails, now turning sharp, pulled at the cloth of her sweater, her shoulders pointed, angry things. Her teeth bared as she clenched her jaw from the pain that seemed shining and sharp.

Ailith ran her hands over the bulges, her throat tightening as air trapped in her lungs. She stared, her jaw hanging slack. Angry, sharp pressure under Caitriona's sweater met Ailith's touch; something was rising directly from Caitriona's shoulders and demanded release. Ailith pulled her dagger from its holder, hastily cutting through the layers of cloth to expose Caitriona's bare back, now bulging and pointed, bruising and suddenly bleeding as bone pressed through her skin.

The release of the bones brought forth a final scream from Caitriona before she fell silent and still, the jagged bones protruding from her back as if wings were snapped off at the base by invisible hands.

Blood spread from the broken skin, discoloring the white shirt under Caitriona's sweater, and growing heavy as the blood gathered in the knit material. Ailith's hands shook as Caitriona's blood dripped off them to disappear into the mist below.

Her brain attempted to catch up to what happened but was stunted from shock.

Slipping her dagger back into its holder, her hands fumbled and it nearly fell from her grip. It took three tries to get the dagger secure. She ran her hands over her pants to clean them of the blood before wiping her nose. Ailith allowed one sniff to escape as her eyes filled with tears. Caitriona's screams echoed in her head, making her quiver with fear and concern. She never saw so much blood come from a person's body and a flush of spit filled her mouth, her stomach churning as she neared heaving.

Ignoring her own healing injuries and nausea, Ailith got to her feet and slipped her arms under Caitriona's shoulders to pull her dead-weight up. Embracing her chest to chest, she reached for the lead of Caitriona's horse who thankfully hadn't vanished in the mist and pulled it close.

Attempting to shift Caitriona onto Butterscotch proved difficult. Caitriona wouldn't wake, and Ailith tried desperately not to touch the bones protruding from Caitriona's back. With a bit of jostling and cursing from pain and frustration, Ailith finally managed to drape Caitriona across the horse. She squatted to reach for Caitriona's cloak, but found it was lost to the mist.

"Wonderful," Ailith muttered. "At least that's the only thing."

She removed her own cloak and pulled it over Caitriona's slumped body. Moving before the two horses, their leads tight in her grasp, she began walking backwards, watching the way Caitriona's body shifted on Butterscotch, before she paused.

"I don't even know where I should go," she said out loud, looking at the horses for a moment. "I suppose neither of you have a suggestion?"

They observed her; quiet now, their nerves settled, and blinked their large dark eyes.

Ailith turned away, looking at the wall of white. Her eyes welled with tears as the mist stared back. Her heart rate and breathing came fast, and Ailith closed her eyes to the expanse of white as she willed everything to slow down. Perhaps the mist was changing her too, or the mist had some message to share, but it remained empty, silent and cold.

She never felt so lonely.

Uncertainty kept Ailith still. Time seemed odd in the white maze and her thoughts were too loud, becoming a heavy, present companion to her loneliness. What happened to Caitriona was both excruciatingly long and incredibly fast. Perhaps the fear rushing through Ailith twisted time; she felt similarly after her father was crushed by the stones of the castle. When the cart wheeled to their home and Ailith stepped outside to see her father crumpled and broken in the back, his face pale from pain and his eyes closed, time changed. The few steps it took to reach the cart stretched the course of a year, but she knew it was only a few steps, a few seconds.

Perhaps it was only a moment that uncertainty locked Ailith in place, it may have been hours, but even the horses remained still which didn't hurry Ailith forward. She had to help Caitriona, but how could she? She knew how to tend to broken bones, but these were broken bones that did not previously exist. The pain and blood loss swiftly took away Caitriona's consciousness and, while Ailith knew a few tried and true methods to wake someone who fainted, why would she if it was only to endure further pain? If she could find their way out of the mist, she would bring Caitriona to Isla. Surely Isla could help.

Ailith sucked air deep into her lungs as if she was readying herself to plunge underwater. Suspecting that at any moment the mist would press in around her and make her lungs burn, she stepped forward and paused. There was no change in the mist-covered surface she stood upon, yet she couldn't tell if it was grass or stone, only that her pathway forward was clear and level. The horses followed, their hooves making no sound as they stepped. For a few minutes, or perhaps a few miles, maybe a day or only an hour, they moved.

Since entering the mist, her surroundings were void of sound. But a soft, rhythmic step came to Ailith upon the air. She paused, was it only her heart hammering so loud that it echoed against the air to fill the void of this strange place? The footsteps sounded again, progressively louder, closer, and Ailith reached for the hilt of her short sword, pulling it free and holding it aloft.

The mist breathed, expanding outward from Ailith's center point, and releasing her to a worn path along a rocky ledge. A tree was nearby, the visual of it rapidly coming to clarity as the mist drifted backward; its trunk reaching high and its leaves leaned low as if to kiss the ground. The mist continued to move, rushing ahead of Ailith and up the path of a steep incline before curving around the rockface. A lantern post stood out along the pathway and the flame of a torch slowly came into view and glowed gradually.

Behind, a thick veil of mist remained, but it was unmoving, no longer chasing her heels. It seemed what cleared intended to remain that way, churning in spot and not moving closer. Ailith wondered if the mist was no longer interested in consuming them and leaving her lost.

Ailith touched Caitriona's back, ensuring she was still wholly there. The princess breathed, but the bone spurs still protruded from her shoulders. The blood congealed on her back and dripped into her hair.

"I guess we'll move forward," Ailith told Caitriona as if she could hear. She wanted the princess to agree with the decision, to be awake and fine, but her comment remained unanswered.

Looking up the clear pathway, Ailith didn't have any true choice in the matter, and began moving, leading the horses and Caitriona along the curving path toward the misty light.

CHAPTER FIFTEEN

GREER

The echo of Greer's boots ricocheted off the stone walls of the castle, announcing her arrival before she was seen, and providing a signal for those who worked in the castle to quickly move out of her path. It wasn't often Greer rushed through the castle halls—that was her father's way to incite terror amongst the staff —but when it did occur the staff knew something was truly wrong and to steer clear. In recent days, there were considerably more moments that Greer glided through the castle, and she suspected this would continue until her father found Caitriona.

After Ailith was listed as the suspected guard who took Caitriona from Braewick, Greer made the quick decision to move Ailith's parents and caretaker from their home and place them somewhere safe so the king wouldn't question them further, or worse, execute them for simply being related to the guard.

She was so careful to have only a handful of people know what was going on, but the list of people was rapidly growing. First, she had to find a home to send the MacCrees. Returning to the healers whom she asked about magic, she paid for their secrecy and recommendation of safe lodging. They gave directions to a cottage they used during the summer months when gathering healing herbs. It was located in the northern valley and Barden retrieved the MacCrees and Gwen late one night, leading them to the little cottage through the darkness.

That spurred another rush through the castle when Greer was called to meet with her father while he raged over the MacCree family's sudden disappearance. It solidified Ailith as the guilty guard, but even if she had been innocent in the entire matter, Greer knew her father well enough to understand Ailith's life would be endangered for simply being considered as having partook in Caitriona's disappearance. At least this way, her parents might survive, and they could figure something out in the future.

But now a group of men arrived at the castle gates, unknowingly ruining Greer's day and sending her to the halls once more.

"They came early this afternoon," Barden said, rushing to keep up with Greer's fast movement. He stood a foot taller than the princess, but Greer was quicker and nimbler. He struggled to match her pace while explaining the situation. Brushing his wavy, auburn hair that hung to his shoulders back from his face, Barden kept his blue eyes on Greer, not looking where he walked as he continued to explain. "They told the gate guard they saw Princess Caitriona and Ailith and had to meet with the king immediately."

"And the guards, what, took them *right there*?" Greer hissed. She took in the man rushing beside her and her glare nearly caused him to stumble.

Greer expressed to the royal guard that she wanted all information about her sister to go through her first. A concerned sister, wanting to present the information to her own father, that was how she wanted it viewed when in reality, she was trying to avoid a situation like this. She had to stay ahead of it all and question people herself before the king became involved.

They turned a corner, nearly colliding with a woman carrying folded sheets. Barden stumbled back, bowing his head to the woman and pausing to let her pass, but Greer stormed forward. He rushed to catch up to her as she moved toward the doors of the throne room.

"As soon as I heard what happened, I rushed to find you," he swore. Dashing ahead of Greer, he stopped outside of the doors, and looked desperately at the heir to the throne.

Greer faced the doors for a moment, her breath coming fast and her face heated before she turned toward Barden.

Barden, her Barden. Her best guard and her best friend. The only person beside her sister that she trusted entirely with any burden she might carry.

"I know, Barden." Greer squared her shoulders before reaching out to touch his arm. "Thank you, truly, for coming straight to me. I'm just ..."

"I know," Barden said quietly. The two shared a knowing look. He could read her moods better than anyone. He knew what she thought and felt, he always did. That's what came from years of working together. They had trained together since Greer was old enough to join the royal guard and upon her graduation, with Barden a few years her senior, he was quickly chosen to lead Greer's personal guard. After all this time, he seemed capable of knowing her thoughts by energy alone, and that level of understanding never ceased to thrill her.

Greer took a deep breath, gave a final nod, and turned to the doors. Barden stepped forward and grasped the brass handles and pulled them back to allow her entrance.

The throne room was stately, and meant to appear rich and foreboding to any outside guests. The ceiling stood far overhead with windows leaving shafts of light to cascade to the floor. Dark green banners with the silver outline of the Elder Tree—the royal crest—hung from the tall walls and a deep red rug ran down the center of the marble floor.

At the far end sat a pedestal with dark mahogany chairs for each family member—all but Caitriona who never was permitted to attend hall gatherings—behind a gray stone balustrade that separated the royals from the rest of the room. Above the pedestal, hanging close to the ceiling, was the head of the white dragon, the embodiment of the king's squashing of magic and monsters. The beast's head looked down the length of the room, its mouth forever open with its pointed teeth on display as if ready to bite away anyone who drew near. Its horns, creating a crown atop its skull, curved upward to the ceiling. A few finches had snuck into the hall overtime and nested there, leaving the head dotted with feces.

Greer always hated the damn head and hoped that one day, with enough birds roosting on it, the ties keeping it aloft would break and bring the whole thing down. If not, she only had to wait until she became queen. It would be the first thing to change.

The door Greer entered through was closest to the pedestal. Barden followed right on her heels, hand on the hilt of his sword and eyes scanning the room. The king already sat on this throne, a scattering of his personal guards to his back and sides, and more on the main floor where dirty men waited uneasily on the red rug.

Ian, one of his most eager guards, stood a few feet to the side of the king and narrowed his eyes as Greer moved into the room. He would clean the king's boots with his own tongue if Cearny requested it. Irritatingly, he was smart enough to see that Greer was different from her father, that all Cearny worked for would likely be altered when she came to rule. The king, thankfully, would hear no such talk from Ian, and so the guard took to barely withholding dislike whenever Greer was present.

Greer stepped onto the pedestal and slipped into her seat beside the king, ignoring Ian's judgmental glance. Many of King Cearny's men were deeply invested in the political advancements of the dynasty. They served under Cearny since he was young, fully embracing the king's opinions on non-humans and those with magic abilities. While Greer didn't openly reject his decisions, there was the clear undercurrent that Greer and the men who made up her royal guard would bring change to the kingdom, much to Cearny's guards' disgust. Even a few of his own guards stood a little straighter when Greer was present, men that Barden told Greer practiced the old ways in secret, but the list was short.

Other than Barden, those men weren't present today.

King Cearny was hunched in his seat, elbows resting on the edge of the armrests and as he rubbed the scruff of his chin. He lifted his eyes toward Greer as she sat and held up his hand. "Please repeat yourselves for my daughter," he asked, his deep voice filling the room.

The men below were filthy in their hunter's garb. Their hair, greasy and clinging to their brows, and sweaty faces made Greer want to frown, but she kept her face carefully neutral. Barden stood at Greer's side. His face was carefully blank, eyes forward on the men, but a quick glance to meet Greer's gaze was all she needed. He had that way with her. A simple look could convey so much meaning, and she knew what this one said: he was ready to do whatever needed to be done. Greer relaxed into her seat, returning her attention to the men before her.

"We were in the eastern lands, south of the Endless Mountains," the shortest man in the group began. He stepped forward, wringing his hands as he looked toward the pedestal, seemingly unsure who to look at. "Our hunting party was camping for the evening when two riders traveled north on Death's Mist roadway. One fit the description of the guard MacCree. Dark hair, dark eyes. She had a bow and short sword; she seemed to take the lead. The other woman stayed quiet, shy, and didn't speak. One of my men pulled the cloak from that woman ..."

He hesitated, realizing how this sounded. Finding the princess was one thing; forcing her to reveal herself was not something to admit. It disclosed they approached her, touched her, and any form of a "reveal" was inspired by force. Greer clenched her jaw.

"She had reddish hair. We tried to convince them to come with us, but they refused. The guard fought us, and while we wounded her, the princess created fire. She pushed us back with flames."

"Reddish hair? You sound uncertain, sir." Greer jumped at the bait to dismantle any belief they found her sister. "Princess Caitriona has deep red hair and there are plenty of guards with brown. Plus ... fire? Really?"

Greer glanced at her father, shaking her head in disbelief. Her palms grew damp.

Her father, thankfully, laughed. Greer inched her fingers back from the arms of her chair and ran her hands over her pants, all the while training her face to portray careful disbelief.

"No daughter of mine can create fire out of thin air," he grumbled. "She must have had a torch with her." He looked at Greer, laughter still bubbling from his lips, but his eyes were flashing and dangerous.

Greer offered a tight-lipped smile, feigning humor.

The men shook their heads, the shorter one began to speak but was cut off by another from his group. "She made a flame with a turn of her hand and spread it around her like a ring. She was protecting the guard from us." This taller man with graying hair stepped forward, desperation to be understood by the king clear on his face and clearly coloring his thoughts. Why would anyone dare to insist when the king had the look of flame in his eye? Or was Greer just particularly attuned to his emotions? Still, the man continued. "She moved forward and the fire followed her, then a fog fell upon us and the fire died. We were lost for hours until the fog lifted and she and the guard were gone. Even their footprints disappeared. But the scorched earth remains."

The king's laugh died and Greer couldn't help but glance at him with nerves gathering in the pit of her stomach. He sat straight backed, his large hands made into fists and his cheeks flush. The angle of his jawline indicated he clenched his teeth. The men fell silent.

"Magic is *outlawed* in Wimleigh Kingdom. I repeat: *no* daughter of mine can make magic. It must have come from the guard. Perhaps she kidnapped Caitriona to protest the laws of magic." The king looked at Ian who nodded in agreement. Cearny turned back to the men, his hands quivering as he grabbed the armrests of his chair and the men shrunk before them.

"Despicable. Have these men mark on a map their exact location for their claims and send guards to confirm these burn marks. Let it be known whoever can kill the guard MacCree will be rewarded." His tone was surprisingly calm and the hair on the back of Greer's neck rose. Whenever there was an air of simplicity or ease about the king, particularly in dealings with magic, Greer knew he was ready to explode. Like a storm gathering to the west and the earth growing quiet and still before the winds and lightning were unleashed, there was danger ahead.

Three men in the back of the group whispered to each other, arguing and stealing glances at the king. *This won't end well*, Greer thought.

Turning to Barden, Greer tilted her head in the direction of the hunters. He frowned as they gathered their courage to blurt out whatever other damning information they had, but the king was on his feet. The men's voices grew with their courage but Barden was already moving forward.

"Greer, find out where these men live," the king muttered, his back turned to the men, oblivious to their rising murmurs.

Beyond the king, Barden approached the men, his hands up to hush them before they spoke further. King Cearny was red faced, one eye twitching slightly, and Greer knew better than to get in his way.

"Of course," she replied quickly. "I know the protocol."

Cearny didn't meet Greer's gaze but nodded as he moved out with his attendants and guards following at his heels. Greer was left behind with Barden and a few other guards.

"But the king needs to know," a man argued.

"*I* can hear whatever it is you're bursting to tell the king," Greer said loudly, turning to the men after the room's door slammed shut and the king was out of earshot. The men froze and Barden looked on, his face stern.

"Princess Greer."

The shorter man stepped forward, passing Barden who looked down at him and began to follow, keeping his eyes on the man and a hand on the hilt of his dagger. "You need to understand, there was something ... *odd* about the princess. It wasn't only that she created fire with a wave of her hand, she *changed*. Her eyes glowed a heavenly light, her hands turned to claws. It didn't seem ... human."

"Her *form* changed?" Her heart shook as anxiety knitted tender fingers around her throat to choke her.

"It began to. The guard fell from her horse and seemed unconscious, yet the princess lifted her with ease. Her eyes were like white flames and fire upon the ground bowed to her; it was completely at her command. The fire was like walls protecting the guard. She did it all by raising her hand, which looked like a monster's. Her fingers were long and pointed, and the flames moved out of her way. She didn't seem human. There's something wrong—"

"That's enough." Greer's voice was louder than intended. Her words chased after each other as they echoed through the hall. "I urge you to keep these thoughts to yourselves and not share your experiences outside of this room. I doubt this was the princess. As the king said, no daughter of his has magic. We can investigate the situation, but if there's any rumor spread of the princess making magic—*of all things*—know it'll anger the king that you're spreading such conspiracies about a member of his family."

The men fell still and she returned their gaze unblinkingly. "Barden, please gather the information we need from these men and ensure a guard escorts them home."

"What about our reward?"

Greer tilted her head to the side.

"You didn't deliver the princess safely to the castle, correct? We don't know if you did, in fact, see her. There's no reward for you.

"Barden, please take these men now. And gentlemen, remember that if I catch wind of rumors that Princess Caitriona is a monster, that she can make fire or her hands are clawed, I'll know it came directly from you." Greer rose to her feet, pointedly looking at each hunter's face. She committed their profiles to memory as they squirmed under her gaze before turning and leaving through the door she previously entered.

It wasn't until she reached her own quarters that she sunk into a chair and covered her eyes, feeling the burn of tears and a sob gathering in her throat. If she didn't have the threat of her father appearing at her door at any moment, she could allow her tears to freely fall. She attempted to swallow down the pure, burning emotion gathering in her chest and throat, burying it as she buried most things to be dealt with later—although later never seemed to come.

Greer considered her list of 'ifs' and quivered.

If Ailith was injured or dead, what would her sister do?

If her sister was changing physically, was there still time to get help from Kayl? Was there even a possibility she could be saved?

This all was beyond her understanding of magic—what little understanding she had. Cearny and his father not only banned magic use, but allowed no education on the subject, leaving Greer performing a series of guesses and tries.

Was it normal for magic users to change shape?

An hour later, a soft knock at her chamber door roused her from her thoughts. Barden paused at the doorway, their eyes meeting. One look was all it took for Greer to drop her composure. Her feelings choked her as she got to her feet and moved toward him.

"It'll be alright. The men saw her near the Endless Mountains days ago; by now she may have already found Kayl or is all the closer to reaching him." His blue eyes were sincere as they met in the center of Greer's room, standing before one another.

Greer rubbed at her forehead, closing her eyes as she tried to string together words and dig up energy to speak them. Her head ached with stress and worry that was a persistent presence since Caitriona left yet grew considerably worse in the last few hours.

Barden touched her hand. Hers was small in his as he gently guided her hand away from her eyes. His palms were rough with calluses similar to hers, but for a moment, Greer marveled at how gentle his touch was. It was enough of a distraction to snap her out of her emotional drowning.

"I'm finding myself at a loss over what we should do, but I feel we must do *something*. Sitting here in the castle isn't enough anymore, particularly if Ailith's injured."

"Maybe ..." Barden began, trailing off as he considered for a moment. "Maybe we can ride out to the Endless Mountains? Your father said he'd send guards to see the scorch marks. We can find Caitriona ourselves and bring her the rest of the way if that's necessary. We'll convince your father that if Caitriona is alone, she may be scared, and it would benefit her to see you."

Greer dropped Barden's hands. "A friendly face ..."

"He may be completely void of feelings nor understand what love *is*, but he cannot deny that you and your sister share an incredible love for one another," Barden reasoned, drawing a faint smile to Greer's lips. "Who else to go but you?"

"Perfect, yes." Greer's energy returned. She was quickly on the move, a blur as she headed toward her door as the wooden heels of her boots echoed against the stone floor. Barden turned to follow close behind as Greer spoke of her plans that would fall neatly into place, so long as she was in control. "We'll go straight to my father and announce our departure. We'll get to her in a few days' time."

CHAPTER SIXTEEN

CAITRIONA

Caitriona groaned, her head so heavy that at first she couldn't bear to turn it or open her eyes. Her muscles ached like they did after a fierce fever, as if they were spent through the activity of fighting heat, and she was so very tired. For some reason it was a necessity to open her eyes, but she couldn't remember why. It was easier to remain in this pretty twilight and let her heavy body rest.

But a memory pressed upon her mind, something familiar and delicate like the fluttering of butterfly wings cupped in one's palm. Her heart picked up to the whispering of familiarity she could not quite grasp. It took only a moment for her to regain her wits and return to reality.

She had to find Ailith.

After repeated attempts, Caitriona forced her eyes open and found herself in a room with a curving white ceiling, softly glowing from candlelight. The sound of trickling water close-by greeted her but beyond there was only silence.

Caitriona shifted upright, her back protesting. She sat in a comfortable bed with soft blankets covering her, and a light, white night gown on her body. Beside the bed, a wooden table was lined with lit candles, a looking glass, hairbrush, and basket with herbs and strips of fabric. The sound of the waterfall came from a window across the room, its glass panes open wide to a lush forest.

Caitriona compelled herself to slide off the bed. The stone floor was cool as she pressed her bare feet down and tested her strength to stand. Her chest felt tight and inspecting fingers along her torso found wraps beneath her nightgown. Her movements reflected in the looking glass and Caitriona's eyes widened. Leaning forward with a groan of discomfort, she gripped the silver curve of the looking glass and held it aloft, her lips parting in silent shock as she saw her reflection for the first time in weeks.

The red-gold hair she had at Isla's was completely gone and in its place was a mass of shimmering gold. Not blonde like her sister's, which was the color of summer wheat, but warmer and richer. *Gold.* There was no other way to describe it. Light shined off as it glimmered unnaturally. Caitriona's fingers ran over her brows, also lightened to the shimmering color, as were her eyelashes. She paused at the reflection of her eyes; no longer blue or green, but gold as well. Sucking in a shaking breath of air, making her back ache against the wraps, she pressed a hand to her chest. Her heart quivered as she returned the mirror to the table and held out her hands, running her fingers over each other and inspecting her nails and skin. They weren't like the claws they shifted into when she and Ailith were found by the hunters, but something obviously happened to make her eyes and hair change further.

Ailith. Her hands dropped. *Where was Ailith? I have to find Ailith.*

Caitriona's body throbbed with exhaustion, but she slowly made her way to the window where she gripped the sill and looked out, hoping the view would provide some locational clue.

The full moon lit the trees beyond the window, muting their varied colors of autumn. The air held a chill she hadn't felt yet this season and dried leaves stirred on lantern-lit pathways below. Footsteps beyond the room caught her attention, growing louder, closer. Her body was too tired, too sore for her to search the room for a possible weapon. She could only be bothered to turn toward the door as it creaked open, deciding that if a threat entered, she would face it directly.

The door paused halfway before swinging open fully. The quick steps of heel on stone matched Caitriona's rushing heart as Ailith stepped into the room with her mouth open, her brown eyes on the empty bed.

"Ailith?" Caitriona whispered from the window, beyond the bed and Ailith's gaze. The guard startled and snapped her head in Caitriona's direction, her eyes growing wide before she rushed forward.

"Cait, *Cait*." She repeated the princess's name as if convincing herself that was who stood before her. Caitriona moved forward, arms out and heart singing as Ailith closed the distance between them and embraced her lightly, gently, as if Caitriona could break.

Caitriona sighed. Breathing was suddenly easy. She slipped her arms around Ailith, tucking her chin into the space where Ailith's shoulder met her neck and breathed in her scent as she closed her eyes—she could have sworn Ailith's were full of tears. They stood silently for a moment, the only sound their rapid hearts and the trickle of the waterfall beyond the window.

"I'm glad you're awake." Ailith withdrew from Caitriona's embrace, but their hands still trailed over one another's bodies as if mooring themselves. Hands on hips, then shoulders and faces; Caitriona looked at her from an arm's length, convincing herself that Ailith was there.

"I only just woke," Caitriona replied. She had a multitude of questions, and the unease of waking in a foreign room was still a leaden ball in her stomach. It helped that Ailith looked well-rested and cared for. She wore the sweater Isla made and a different pair of pants, unfamiliar to Caitriona. Her hair was clean and in a neat braid down her back; even her eyes seemed clear and it brought a smile to Caitriona's face.

Ailith blushed. "What?"

"I was thinking you look well-rested. How are *your* injuries?"

Ailith laughed and slipped her hand around Caitriona's waist to guide her toward the bed.

"I should be, we've been here for a few days and after the first, I was forced out of your room and made to sleep next door." Ailith held onto Caitriona as she lowered her onto the edge of the bed, then sat beside her. "And I'm nearly completely healed."

"I was asleep that long? What happened?" They hadn't even been on the road for a full day after Ailith's injury when Caitriona's memories went foggy.

"Are we trading moments of missed memories? Do you remember the mist?" Ailith bent to rest her elbows on her knees as she twisted to keep eye contact with Caitriona.

Caitriona blinked and considered for a moment. She remembered the mist beginning to inch over the road toward their feet and then the memories faded. She shook her head.

"The mist triggered something in you," Ailith began, her voice soft as she kept her eyes glued on Caitriona's face. "You were in pain. I didn't know what was wrong, I tried to help but I couldn't understand what was happening. You kept pulling at your cloak and your shirt. You had ..." Ailith paused, cringing at the memory and swallowing. "You had bone growing from your back. You passed out and we were lost in the mist. But suddenly, it lifted and I was on a path. It led me here—we're in Ulla Syrmin. That's what's beyond the mist! A town! It's part of a whole queendom called Invarlwen and the mist protects it!"

"And we're safe here?" Caitriona took in the room with a new understanding. Not just a place to recover but an entire town beyond the mist she always heard stories of.

"Abundantly," Ailith replied. Caitriona never saw Ailith so quick or certain. She was grinning now and took Caitriona's hands in hers, holding them tight. "Cait, the people who live here are *fae*. They may be able to help you."

"Really?" Caitriona lifted her free hand to her chest, touching the wraps beneath her gown before twisting to look over her shoulder. "Where are the ... bones?"

"They disappeared," Ailith replied, letting go of Caitriona's hand and brushing one down Caitriona's back, smoothing the dress and showing no protruding ridges. "Like when your hands change, they slipped away. The fae seemed to hurry it along and they tended the wounds where the bone came out. But, Cait, your hair and your eyes—"

"They're gold," Caitriona reached to her hair, braided down her back, and gathered it over her shoulder so she could inspect the strands. "I know, I saw the looking glass before you came in."

"Your hair grew blonder when you were unconscious, and when we were trying to get you onto the bed to look at your back, your eyes opened briefly and they were gold. The fae said they don't believe they'll turn back considering they seemed to gradually change this whole time."

Of all the things that could change, she felt both an odd thrill and deep concern that her hair and eyes could alter so much. Her red hair was a tie to her mother, who often seemed a little distant and cautious to express love to Caitriona or Greer. When she was young, her mother gathered Caitriona onto her lap to braid her hair, and when she was older, the queen came into Caitriona's quarters to style it. It was their bond, the two red-headed women of Braewick Valley, and it felt odd to have lost it.

Alternatively, as was the consistent feeling through her developing powers, Caitriona harbored a deep sense of fascination and pride. If she lost her powers, at least she had this to show for it. At least she had some proof of what transpired. But something else also felt off ...

"Do they know what's happening to me?" Caitriona dropped her braid.

"I think so. Perhaps we won't even have to find Kayl. Maybe they can help."

Caitriona turned her hand over, stretching her fingers apart so Ailith's could knit into hers.

"That would be too lucky, I suspect," Caitriona said with a wry smile.

A light knock drew their attention toward the door and a woman with pointed ears peeked in. Her gray eyes stood out against her dark-skinned face, and her black hair had strands of silver and gold braided throughout it which caught the candlelight, glittering similarly to Caitriona's.

"May I come in?" The woman's accent was one Caitriona never heard before. Then again, she'd never knowingly met a full-blooded fae either.

"Yes," Caitriona replied as she got to her feet, her back aching as she shifted. Ailith moved her hand under Caitriona's arm as she helped her stand. Caitriona offered a faint smile of gratitude, finding that she didn't want her time with Ailith to be shared. But the fae woman walked on silent feet, unknowing of Caitriona's feelings as she drifted around the foot of the bed to stand before Caitriona and promptly dip into a curtsey. Caitriona's eyes widened and she uttered a single, "Oh!"

"Princess Caitriona," the woman said as she knelt, gaze turned downward. "It's an honor to have you here."

"Please." Caitriona's cheeks flushed as she reached toward the woman but stopped short of touching her. "Please, you don't have to do that. Stand. Tell me your name."

The woman rose, slipping her hands into the folds of her deep blue gown that hung to the floor and clung over the full curves of her body. She kept her eyes lowered.

"My name is Ceenear." Her voice was deep but soft, like a warm bath filled with floral oils. "How are you feeling?"

"I'm feeling quite fine. My back is a little sore and I feel somewhat weak, but nothing a little additional movement couldn't cure, I assume."

"Wonderful. Is there anything I can do for you?"

Caitriona looked at Ailith, hoping the guard would offer some guidance but found Ailith maintaining her peaceful demeanor. "I would change out of this nightgown if I could. Where are our things?"

"Oh," Ailith cut in, "They're in my room. Your bag as well. We didn't want to trip over it if we needed to help you. Our clothes have been getting hemmed and washed too."

"I can get you a gown, or pants and top if you'd prefer."

"A dress would be lovely," Caitriona responded. Ceenear nodded, her footsteps still silent as she closed the door behind her. "She walks so quietly!"

"They all do. This is a whole city of sorts. The buildings are built into the sides of the mountain and some homes are in the trees. There are lantern-lit paths all over, but despite how many fae live here, it always seems quiet somehow. They're soft spoken, like you, and they move silently."

"I hope I can see more of it." Caitriona turned toward the window.

"I'll make that happen before we leave." Ailith brushed a loose strand of hair over her ear. "To my understanding, Invarlwen makes up the Endless Mountains, but it's the fae name for them. Each peak is a different city, and the mountain range as a whole makes the queendom. There's an overlook outside in the hall that shows a good bit of Ulla Syrmin, we can walk over once you're dressed."

Caitriona felt all the more awake the longer she stood, the confusion clearing and her anxiety from waking somewhere strange drifting away. Ailith's general ease was more comforting than any offering of care or dresses from Ceenear. Ailith remained the judge of what was safe, and her excitement left Caitriona smiling. "That would be wonderful."

Ceenear returned with a gray dress that looked like rippling water in moonlight. Another fae with porcelain skin and white-blonde hair paired with deep green eyes that looked dark in the candlelight came with Ceenear. She wore a dress similar in style to Ceenear's, as white as her hair. She introduced herself as Lumia, the healer, and checked under Caitriona's bandages before announcing they could be removed, allowing the princess to take deep breaths for the first time.

"I'm not sure," Lumia trailed her fingers over Caitriona's back, "but there may be scars in the place where the bones pushed out. I'm sorry."

Caitriona thought of her sister and the many scars that littered her skin from the various battles she partook in. Even practicing in the guard yard with her team, Greer sustained blows that left marks. Caitriona never had such opportunities. "It's perfectly fine. Scars provide personality, don't you think?"

"Certainly." Ailith gave a knowing glance as Ceenear came forward with the gray dress. "We'll both come out of this venture with new marks."

The women helped Caitriona put on the dress although Ailith brushed the fae women aside to work on the ties and buttons at Caitriona's back which left her cheeks feeling warm and a smile unable to fade from her face. Caitriona felt a little more like herself in the new clothing and less like she was in recovery.

"Scars are proof of an interesting life." Ceenear stepped back, her hands returning into the folds of her dress. She and Ailith gave each other a knowing look. There was a sense of familiarity between them, that they obviously spent time together while she slept.

A funny twist in her belly tugged at her consciousness. It flushed outward, twisting her heart and coating her tongue with a bitter taste; the pains of jealousy were foreign and new. Looking between the guard and Ceenear, she felt an odd pressure, like a chill of air along her skin. Someone was watching *her*. Lumia's eyes bore holes into Caitriona, her face blank beside one slender eyebrow arching. Caitriona busied herself with studying the embroidery on the cuffs of her sleeves. These were feelings she wasn't quite sure she could admit to herself, let alone a stranger.

"If you're feeling well enough," Ceenear began, "We're hoping you'll join us downstairs for our evening meal. Perhaps a change of scenery will benefit you as much as the meal would?"

Caitriona relaxed. "That would be wonderful."

Ailith remained beside Caitriona as they eased down smooth, white-stone steps. The stairwell curved and the walls had small inlets where candles were placed. Behind the candles, tin reflected the candlelight, providing a soft, calming glow to the steps. Ceenear and Lumia drifted ahead in silence as if gliding, their skirts following them like pools of water.

"The food here is divine," Ailith told Caitriona. "Best I've had the entire trip."

Ailith's relaxed manner did her well; gone was the scowl she always wore, her perpetual frowns disappeared, and in its place were a myriad of facial expressions that were all synonyms of happiness. She lowered her walls and opened up. Perhaps these moments in the Endless Mountains would be ones with a lasting effect on her.

Ailith glanced at Caitriona and tilted her head slightly. "What?"

"You seem happy and I'm glad."

Ailith ducked her head, her nose wrinkled as her cheeks darkened.

They rounded a corner to a large room made from the ever-present white stone and candles casting a glow on all surfaces. Across the room were floor to ceiling windows open to the night air. They overlooked the valleys beyond the Endless Mountains that were aglow from the soft-blue shine of the full moon. A table covered with platters of food sat in the center of the room. Steam rose from the plates and the air was rich with the scent of herbs. Caitriona began salivating. Flourishes of greenery nestled about the platters with candles in the middle, cast soft light and reflected against the silver plates placed before each wooden chair.

"I told you the food is divine," Ailith whispered in Caitriona's ear; goosebumps rose down her neck. Caitriona felt slight pressure on the small of her back and glanced down. Ailith walked closely beside her as she guided her toward her seat. Caitriona looked up and fought off a smile. Alright, perhaps she *was* ready to admit her feelings to herself.

CHAPTER SEVENTEEN

AILITH

A ilith was nearly honest with Caitriona.
"You seem happy," Caitriona had said.
Ailith almost responded, "because I'm with you," but the words stuck in her cheeks, making them as pink as cherry blossoms. The terror she felt when Caitriona fainted as bones burst through her back stuck with her—leaving her heart racing and hands shaking until the fae tucked Caitriona into bed and told Ailith repeatedly that the princess would be alright—and was not something easily forgotten.

When they first arrived, the fae's serums and oils were rubbed on Caitriona's skin after they pulled back the tattered cloth covering her back. When that didn't work, they gathered around her and spoke in a language foreign to Ailith. An ethereal light formed and grew all the brighter until Ailith closed her eyes and turned away. The bones were forced to recede by whatever magic they did, leaving behind open wounds the fae promised would heal quickly.

After the bones were gone, Ailith watched Caitriona. She fell asleep herself, curled at the foot of the princess's bed only to be woken by Ceenear. "You have to get your own rest," the fae woman said softly.

"But I need to make sure Cait's alright," Ailith replied, groggily sitting up on the bed.

"She'll be fine, and all the better if you regain your own strength and have the energy to continue caring for her." Ceenear helped Ailith to her feet and led her to the room across the hall.

"I wish I knew what was wrong with her so I could better protect her." Perhaps something was triggering these explosive changes, something beyond Caitriona using her powers. Perhaps they could avoid it all entirely to save her from this pain.

Ailith was so tired; she couldn't control the tone that conveyed how deep her misery was. Ceenear gently touched Ailith's hand, pulling her attention. The candlelight caught the hue of the fae's eyes which held compassion and pity.

"Ailith, do you not realize your friend is cursed?"

Such a simple sentence carried so much weight and made so much sense. It was as if the sun shone down on a foggy morning and burned the low visibility away to provide a clear path forward. But that path was filled with sharp stones known for cutting at ankles, and branches that reached down from overhead with the intention of clawing at hair. A curse made sense, but what to do about a curse was another path Ailith had yet to wander down.

Caitriona slept for three days and after the first night, Ailith slept in the room across the hall. She kept sneaking to Caitriona's bedside to keep vigil, watching the princess's breathing and fighting the temptation to check Caitriona's back to ensure the bones hadn't reappeared. During daylight hours, the sun shifted across the cuts of the mountainside as Ailith sat beside Caitriona, telling the sleeping princess secrets Ailith realized she barely allowed herself to linger over.

"I've never had many friends. I think I'm incapable of being cared for by anyone but my parents," Ailith began the first day. "I've also discovered that if I act like everyone else, people tend not to notice me as much. When they do, I'd rather sink into the floorboards. It's easier to mirror the behavior of those around me. It's safer."

The second day, Ailith perched herself in the open window of the room while she spoke. "I've cared for my parents for years and I hate to admit that I wish I didn't have to. I feel so guilty about that. I just wish they had the means to care for themselves, but I also can't fathom anyone else doing it."

Before Ailith went to bed, she confessed deeper secrets. "I've only ever had feelings for one other person. She was a city guard like me and it was a quick romance. Romps in the stables during the summer and one night in a room she rented at an inn. But she joined the royal guard, and then died in a skirmish with Avorkaz the following winter. While I wasn't in love with her, I miss her sometimes. She didn't deserve to have her life ended so soon."

Ailith opened up about her most shameful thoughts as well, that she doubted her abilities constantly, and didn't know what she would do if she couldn't return to life as a city guard. She shared she was plagued with a creeping sense of worry and fright over things she couldn't control.

And when she grew tired, she revealed her most recently created secrets. "I'm fascinated by you. Do you know that? You terrify me, the very thought of not completing this mission terrifies me. But I'm also frightened that no matter how this goes, I'll lose you either way."

Ailith left the room to eat meals with Niveem, whose home they were staying in, and a few fae who worked with her—Ceenear, Lumia, and a guard named Raum. She listened as they shared information about the fae, mentally taking note to tell Cait later. While King Cearny certainly persecuted them and took the most egregious measures, the fae of Visennore were threatened for generations.

Long ago, the most powerful fae used their gifts to create the mist, birthing it to the world and letting it free at the base of the Invarlwen Mountains—the true name of the mountains before King Donal tried to wipe the land clean of fae names and replace them with common ones. The mist had a simple mission: those who traveled into it and had ill intent or darkness in their hearts would die. The mist would suffocate them and devour their bodies. Those with good intent survived, and the fae would move the mist aside to welcome them into the cities of Invarlwen. There they would befriend the fae, dine with them as Ailith did, but have their memories altered at the end of their visit, leaving them to forget they ever stepped within the mist, as well as the acquaintances they made. Through this, the fae continued to live in peace while also learning about the outside world beyond the few fae who were permitted to travel to it.

"I understand your need for protection," Ailith admitted over one dinner, unable to withhold her thoughts anymore. "But it saddens me that Caitriona and I won't be able to remember this when we leave."

"Oh, you shall," Niveem replied, drawing the stares of the others and Ailith, too. "I feel it's a necessity for you both to take this knowledge with you. Share it with those you trust. It's been too long that we've remained hidden, and I suspect great change is in all our futures; you never know when it'll be helpful to have friends in other kingdoms."

Ailith asked about Caitriona's abilities, but beyond what Ceenear said, they remained tight lipped, promising to answer what they could once Caitriona woke.

Now sitting opposite Caitriona at the immaculate table lined with roasted pheasant, spiced gourds, and steaming vegetables, Ailith's sense of urgency returned. She couldn't help but want the discussions to begin immediately; she'd waited three days for answers.

Caitriona was still pale and after a few days of not eating, Ailith was willing to spoon feed her if necessary, so long as it allowed Niveem to admit all she was clearly holding back.

Lumia sat beside Caitriona with a friendly smile and Ceenear took a seat next to Ailith. They barely settled when two other fae entered the room. During the first meal together, Ailith scrambled to stand and bow to her hosts, but they quickly admonished her and told her to sit.

"We are all equal parties here," Niveem said as she walked to her seat at the head of the table.

Now Caitriona's hands tightened on the arms of her chair, ready to stand, but with a slow shake of Ailith's head the princess settled.

"Princess Caitriona," Niveem's voice was polished and held depth like the lingering taste of smooth honey. The elder fae was tall with straight dark hair and a sprinkling of gray. Her ears curved up into a point, poking out from her long, loose hair, and her almond-shaped eyes were like a starless night. "I'm glad you've the strength to join us for our evening meal. Welcome to my home. I'm Niveem; you already met Ceenear, one of my diplomats, and Lumia, one of my healers. This is Raum, one of the Invarlwen guards."

Raum tilted his head at Caitriona before slipping into his own seat at the end of the table between Caitriona and Ailith. He was noticeably larger and broader than the rest of the fae in the room, towering over Ailith when he came beside her upon their first meeting.

When Ailith was young, her mother told her the fae she saw as a child were waifish or with soft curves, but Raum was every bit angle and muscle. His physique matched those of many Braewick royal guards. And with olive skin, brown hair and brown eyes, he could have been mistaken for a distant relative of Ailith's, if not for the pointed ears.

"Welcome." Niveem sunk into her seat. "I do hope you're hungry."

"Very." Caitriona's accent was crisp like when Ailith first met her. Nerves, Ailith realized, as something within her went soft as she recalled their first meeting. Caitriona's royal accent became stronger when she was nervous. "Thank you for having Ailith and me. And thank you so much for tending to my wounds."

Niveem waved toward the food and Ceenear lifted the serving platter of roasted pheasants and selected pieces of the moist meat. Niveem observed the progress of the platter making its way around the table before turning her gaze to Caitriona. "We're happy to help you. The mist told us a relation of ours was traveling along the mountains. And I do apologize that the mist caused you harm. It's a protective barrier, meant to keep our home safe. It brings forth the true identity of anyone who passes through. In fact, we often have to ask the mist to part ways so we may retrieve those who are worthy that are lost and wandering. It's meant to part on its own, but often it's too curious for its own good and keeps the travelers hidden. Your guard managed to find her way. I can't recall that happening before. All other travelers remain lost until we find them."

Caitriona studied Niveem for a moment, then blinked to attention as she accepted the platter from Raum, taking a serving before passing it to Lumia. Licking at her lips, Caitriona subtly rolled her shoulders and sat a little straighter as she found the courage to speak. The slight line between her eyebrows was something Ailith noticed when Caitriona was weighed down with concern, making the weight of her question unsurprising: "And what did the mist reveal about me?"

Ailith looked to the head of the table for Niveem's reaction but found Ceenear staring at her. Ailith shook her head; no, she hadn't told

Caitriona what Ceenear admitted to her. Ceenear exchanged a glance with Niveem, conveying the message. Niveem bowed her head for a moment before speaking. "Well, my dear, there isn't an eloquent way to divulge such dark crimes, but it appears you are cursed."

"Excuse me?" Caitriona's shoulders grew rigid, the muscles in her neck tightened, and her nervous movements froze.

"The mist caused the bone to come out of your back," Ailith offered. Caitriona's wide eyes locked on her and her brow wrinkled further. Ailith took in the golden irises, not yet used to the change in color. "The bones have something to do with the curse, so the mist showed that."

"When we tried to force the bones to recede," Ceenear began, "we saw the dark webs of the curse over you. It's a part of you and the bones coming from your body, your hands changing, they're all caused by this curse."

"And my making fire?" Caitriona's gaze turned distant.

"Also a result of the curse, I believe," Niveem said. "Ailith explained that your hair and eyes change every time you create fire. The curse was created by magic, and that magic is bleeding out and changing your form."

"Wouldn't I have known I was cursed though?" Caitriona asked, her voice raising slightly. Her hands, resting upon the arms of the chair, shook. Ailith sat straighter, ready to rise from her seat to go to her. "I've spent my entire life within my home. I've encountered no one that intended ill will towards me, not to my knowledge. My—my social circle is quite … small."

"Curses are not always known." Lumia turned in her seat and took Caitriona's hand. Caitriona went rigid from her touch but slowly began to relax. Ailith watched the exchange between the two with cautious interest. Lumia wasn't simply a healer of ailments. She had a gifted hand, and her touch could create emotions. Ailith was subject to Lumia's touch after she was discovered sitting vigil in Caitriona's room that first night. She calmed Ailith, relaxed her, and took away her anxieties. It was temporary, that was key, but it helped Ailith calm down so she could sleep. Now the white-haired fae worked her magic on Caitriona, calming her building reaction. "While some have a mage say to their face 'you're cursed!' others will have a curse passed down to them unknowingly, generationally, or slipped through while they slept."

As Lumia held Caitriona's hand, Caitriona's breathing calmed, the panic in her eyes receded, and Niveem continued. "Perhaps the curse was placed upon you this year. Ailith informed me your gifts only began to show themselves recently?"

"Yes, earlier this year," Caitriona admitted. "But I've found that I can make fire more at will than before. I can control it. Would it be a curse if it's something I can control?"

Niveem gave a small shrug. "Curses are fickle things. They may appear as an explosion of chaos, or they may come upon a person a little bit at a time—nearly innocent at first, or perhaps only a nuisance. But they're all made the same. They're created out of rage, anger, greed, or the desire for revenge, and they cannot be stopped unless the maker of that curse allows it or the intention of the curse is fulfilled."

"Wait," Ailith broke in, ignoring the platter of roasted gourds Ceenear offered her. "Are you saying that the curse can't be resolved at all?"

"Not by us, unfortunately." Niveem frowned. "We would help if we could, but this curse must play itself out, or you can find the one who placed it on you."

"What about someone who used magic on me, but not to curse?" Caitriona asked, glancing back and forth at those around the table. "When I was young, I was greatly … *injured* when my home was attacked by a dragon. A man named Kayl healed me. To my understanding, it took a great deal of power. Do you feel he could help me?"

The four fae exchanged glances, all eyes settling on Niveem who knit her long fingers together and held the tips of her fingers to her lips. She didn't answer immediately, her gaze downcast and she let out a small hum before lowering her hands. "Perhaps, since he poured his magic into you before, he can help slow the speed of the curse, or maybe read its fibers in your making and see who set the curse upon you in the first place. That information is blocked to us, but he may push through those barricades due to his ties to you."

"Do you know what's happening to Cait?" Ailith asked. "Her

hands, her eyes, the bones in her back. I understand it's a part of the curse but ... why? Why is she changing? Why are some things no longer changing back?"

Niveem shook her head. "I suspect that whatever is upon Caitriona is slowly changing her physically. She's turning into something. What has changed may be permanent or may only be temporary until the curse is fulfilled or discarded."

"And the bones from my back?" Caitriona's voice quivered. Ailith slumped in her chair feeling some of her hope that built over the days she waited for Caitriona to wake weaken. Caitriona's golden eyes glimmered as they grew moist and Lumia's hand came to rest on Caitriona's, her focus intense as she tried to calm the princess's understandable reaction.

"Perhaps wings," Niveem said. "Or, at least, the start of them. We are familiar with wings being torn from the backs of some fae, and the bones are similar."

A question rose to Ailith's lips, ready to spill forward, about who would pull wings from fae, but Ceenear's hand gently touched Ailith's under the table. The fae gave a gentle shake of her head, urging her silence. Caitriona sat still, eyes distant as she looked at her plate of food, and the others at the table seemed to fall into thoughtful silence.

Niveem leaned forward to lift another plate of food. "Let's continue taking our servings and eat before this gets cold. Caitriona, I hope you'll find this food favorable."

"It ... it looks wonderful. Thank you." Blinking, Caitriona's attention returned to the room. She smiled at Niveem, although it wasn't her true smile, then looked at Ailith. The two held each other's gaze for a moment as the clink and chime of cutlery rose around them. Ailith vibrated internally. An insistence filled her to move forward, that they should leave right now and ensure they found Kayl.

She thought of all the monsters she read about, and those she saw from the northern gate, comparing them to Caitriona and internally quivering at the thought of the princess becoming any of them. Nothing she knew matched Caitriona though, nothing beside the dragon. Wings, claws, fire, it all made sense. But never did Caitriona's size change. Perhaps it was just the attributes of a dragon she was cursed with. Who knew? Beside whoever placed a curse on her to begin with.

Ailith offered Caitriona a half smile hoping to convey the words she could not openly say.

It will be alright, she thought. *We'll figure this out. I'll ask more questions later. We'll find Kayl.*

Caitriona returned Ailith's look with a tentative flicker of a clearly forced smile. It was the look in her golden eyes that spoke volumes. Something there and gone again like a flash of lightning in a night sky from a distant storm. She quickly schooled her face to pleasant indifference a moment afterward, but Ailith caught it all the same and understood Caitriona's meaning quite well.

The simple, quivering, silent impression of: *I am afraid.*

CHAPTER EIGHTEEN

AILITH

Dinner was pleasant. The food, outstanding. But the mood was reserved and the conversation prior to the meal created a shadow that crouched on their shoulders and brought about general unease. Caitriona looked the most troubled, which immediately set Ailith on edge, and she found herself breathing a sigh of relief when the meal finished and the table cleared.

Niveem left upon dinner's completion, leaving the other three fae turning their gaze to Caitriona. They were already used to Ailith, but Caitriona was the cursed princess they had tended to, now awake.

"How are you feeling now that you've eaten?" Lumia placed a hand on Caitriona's shoulder.

"A bit tired." Caitriona tensed but once more, under Lumia's touch, she softened. "But good. I didn't realize how hungry I was."

"You're still recovering." Lumia leaned forward in her seat to look at Caitriona more closely. "Having such changes to your body can take a great deal of energy, particularly if you aren't familiar with them."

"Well then I should thank you for what you've done." Caitriona shifted in her seat reaching toward where Lumia's hand rested. She gathered the fae's pale hand into hers and squeezed it. "I remember, vaguely, how much it hurt to have that happen and now it feels as if nothing happened at all."

"It'll get better. Any fae who shapeshifts finds it painful at first, but that lessens. Think of it as growing pains."

"I suppose ..." Caitriona frowned, and Lumia mirrored her expression. "I wish I understood what I was becoming."

"There's no sense in worrying over it now. Perhaps the curse is that you're to grow wings like one of the fae, and if so, there's no use worrying over that change. It's wasted time that could be used in other ways." Lumia got to her feet, brushing at the skirts of her white dress. "You still have to find that magic maker, no? And you have many more days of travel ahead of you. We'll ensure you both are well prepared before you go, but first, we should show you our home beyond these walls."

"Ailith, you haven't left yet?" Raum asked as he too got to his feet. He was the one to come across Ailith as she wandered the paths of the mountains with Caitriona draped over her horse. He admitted to Ailith that he spotted her from his post where he watched the passersby on the roadway and sought out anyone who stumbled into the mist. He climbed down to greet her and offer aid, and over the last few days they became acquaintances, sharing meals together as well as stories of their jobs. Ailith went so far as to think she could develop a friendship with him.

"You know I haven't," Ailith replied, glaring as he stood a foot taller than she. He laughed and pushed his chair in. He knew Ailith barely left Caitriona's side.

"Well, Lumia's right, you both should come out for a stroll." He waved them toward the doorway, pausing for Lumia to drift to his side and slip her hand around his arm.

Caitriona stood by her chair, watching Ailith as if waiting for instruction. "I trust them," Ailith whispered. "If you're feeling well enough, we can take a brief walk."

"A walk would be nice."

Ceenear stood beside Ailith, quiet and unmoving. "I'll see you both when you return. I'll bring some tea for a restful night's sleep."

"You're sure?" Caitriona asked, her tone already warming up and her shoulders relaxing.

"Yes. Enjoy your walk. I'll see you soon."

"Come along then," Raum said, turning toward the door with Lumia still on his arm.

Raum led the small party down curving steps to double doors that opened onto a stone pathway. They were on the edge of a steep hillside with stones jutting from the side of the landscape. Switchback pathways curled down and thick ferns grew along the border until it ran to the edge of a gorge. Within the gorge was a deep, blue stream where various waterfalls cascaded down the hillside to end their travel into swirling pools and bubbling baths. In the pools, copper leaves floated in lazy circles before moving along the streambed to lower destinations.

"So, this is what lies beyond the mist of the Endless Mountains." Caitriona looked at the twinkling structures on the mountainside. She was still on edge with panic in her eyes, but her upbringing forced her to pretend to be calm. Lumia's frequent touches to sooth Caitriona helped. Still, Ailith remained close to the princess, offering her reassuring looks whenever the opportunity arose while wishing she could do more.

"All along the mountains, in different clusters, we have towns. A queendom that we surround by mist, hidden to those beyond it." Raum swept a hand toward the flattened lands. "We're located at the edge of the range, closest to Mirkbrynk Road—I believe your people call it Death's Mist roadway? Nonetheless we often have travelers lost on our paths."

"Well, your home is beautiful. I'm grateful you came to our aid." Caitriona paused at the base of a tree which held a white, marble statue of a woman with her hands clasped and her face turned towards the stars. A constant hush of water trickling and the soft songs of nighttime insects was music in the air. The sound of fae life drifted by on the breeze: occasional laughter, music or song, and the low murmur of conversation. The air smelt of herbs and flowers, rather than the stench of city streets Ailith was used to.

"Niveem was right, no one's found their way through the mist before Ailith. Her heart's of good intention." Raum gave a nod to Ailith and she replied with an eye roll and a smile. "The mist exposed the evil of a curse, but you're pure of heart as well, glowing golden like your hair, so the mist didn't kill you."

"Glowing golden ..." Caitriona repeated.

"That's Raum's gift," Lumia chimed in. "It's partly why he's a guard. For those who wander through the mist, he can see their souls, and if a person is hiding something, or they have an ailment, magic or otherwise. He can determine if a person is safe to be welcomed into the city or not, and he can work with the mist and get it to move."

"It's not entirely as easy as Lumia makes it sound," Raum added. "I need distance from a person to see souls. Standing here with both of you, what your souls possess is hidden to me, but from my guard tower it's abundantly clear. The mist does most of the work for me though, we're coworkers."

"What about Ceenear?" Caitriona asked.

"She works for Niveem," Raum replied. "She's somewhat a guard too, but of a different sort."

"She's capable of changing her form," Lumia continued, whispering conspiratorially. "Not into animals or anything such as that; she changes into other humanoid people. Anything that falls under fae or human person. She can change the tone of her voice, how tall or short she is, and have curved ears or wings that work. Any gender. She often travels outside of the mountains if there's a need because she can appear human like you. You'd be wise to talk with her about the wings, she may have some guidance."

"I will, thank you. And what about Niveem? Is she the leader of your home?" Caitriona continued as they turned toward stone steps that led to an outcrop overlooking the stream at the base of the gorge.

"The one and only," Raum said. He turned toward the three women and leaned against the railing. "You've been staying in her guest rooms these last few days."

Caitriona's eyes widened and Ailith smirked. Caitriona's upbringing likely sparked nerves, and Ailith could only fathom the thoughts flitting through the princess's mind.

"But not queen of the fae or anything like that," Lumia added and Caitriona visually deflated.

"Consider her a lady of our portion of the mountains," Raum continued. "Each mountain peak holds a village of fae with a lord or lady to oversee it."

"Are there no kings or queens?" Ailith asked, picking a loose pebble from the ground and tossing it into the stream below. She gripped the railing and leaned forward to peer down and see how long it took for the pebble to hit the water. "Someone that oversees it all?"

"There's Queen Onora." Lumia leaned over the railings and looked to the water, her white-blonde hair cascading down and appearing almost blue in the moonlight. "She lives on the tallest mountain in Invarlwen, understandably, and keeps to herself. I've never seen her, but I've heard whispers of her and her powers."

"Powers?" Caitriona stepped beside Ailith and looked at the water as well.

"Fae have what we call little magics, which we're born with. We can do small tricks; creating light, making it dark, moving objects, making sounds. It's rare for a fae to not have magic, but it happens occasionally. Some fae, about half of us, have specific gifts; we call those simple magics. That's what Ceenear, Raum, and I have. Shapeshifting, healing. Some will only have one of these gifts, a few have a couple. And then *some* fae have huge abilities, we call those grand magics, but that's rare. Raising the dead or manipulating time. Giving a person magic or changing people into new things. Most fae who have grand magic only have one of those gifts and end up in positions like Niveem. But then there's people like Queen Onora, who has multiple gifts of grand magic," Lumia said with a lift in her tone. The fae woman gestured up the river pathway to a tall mountain far away with hillsides and lower mountains rambling up to its feet.

Raum smiled. "She's a great ruler and she sounds wonderful."

"Raum, we shouldn't give them incorrect information," Lumia nudged Raum's shoulder. Her smile immediately dimmed and it seemed her entire presence fell into shadow, like the sun suddenly hidden behind clouds.

"But the *truth* is still *incorrect*," Raum pointed out. Ailith glanced at Caitriona who leaned back from the railing to look at the pair fully.

"What truth?"

Raum shifted his jaw and glanced at Lumia who crossed her arms before rolling her eyes. "Go on, tell the story, I know you love the tale."

Raum turned on his heel and stepped forward, leaning in as he began to whisper. "The queen is married to *Malcolm Fadnach*. He has all the dislike of humans that—well—King Cearny is known for, but in reverse. He goes by king, but it isn't an earned title. He enjoys the thrills of being royalty but does very little else. It's technically the queen's throne by blood. Her father was king, and she had an older brother who became king after their father's death. She was married to that dullard as a truce with fae from Agatiroth, a realm across the sea. He's the idiot younger child of the Agatiroth royal family who was never meant to have true power. But Queen Onora's brother died suddenly, and so she and her husband stepped forward to rule.

"They have one son together, Shad. Malcolm's thrilled his son will one day reign, but *he shouldn't*. The queen has a child she birthed before she ever married Malcolm: Lachlan. His father was human, and the queen was madly in love with him. But her brother insisted on a fae courtship."

"Ah, we know how that goes," Caitriona murmured glumly. Raum nodded.

"The rightful heir to the throne, Prince Lachlan, is rumored to have as much magical power as the queen, if not more. Simultaneously there are rumors he has no gifts at all, but I like to believe he takes after his mother. When the queen was forced to marry Malcolm, Lachlan was rushed off, hidden somewhere when he was an infant, and no one knows his location. He's never been seen. Many feel Lachlan should take the throne when Queen Onora passes. After all, he's the eldest and first born, and better fit for the role if he has all this magic he's rumored to possess."

"What about Shad?" Ailith asked.

"He takes after his father," Raum replied. "Generally magicless. Which isn't necessarily a bad thing, but as someone ruling over fae who primarily *have* magic, it's best to have gifts."

"Ah, the chaos of royal life," Ailith blurted, catching a smirk on Raum's face as he lifted his hand to run his fingers along his jaw and released his laugh into his palm. Lumia blinked and looked at Ailith with a little frown. Ailith raised her hands innocently, smiling as she shook her head. "No, believe me, it's *very* interesting. But it always seems to be the case with royal families. There's stories about love affairs and hidden children, or some dark secret kept buried deep that spills outward."

"Isn't that what brought you two onto Mirkbrynk road?" Lumia asked, turning her gaze on Caitriona. "A hidden daughter and a secret buried deep?"

Caitriona frowned before speaking up. "You aren't wrong. I certainly was hidden away and I created fire uncontrollably before we left. I suppose *that* is a deep secret."

"So, the king let his daughter leave the kingdom with only one guard?" Lumia knit her hands behind her back and tilted her head to the side.

Raum cleared his throat and shifted on his feet, looking uncomfortable. Lumia's questions were too pointed, edging into a territory that made Ailith protective. She felt the need to be vague despite so much already shared. She kept her eyes trained on the white-haired fae, a frown tugging at her lips.

"No, that's another secret," Caitriona admitted, raising her chin as if greeting the challenge. Would she be honest or lie to the fae? Caitriona apparently dared for honesty. "We left together without his knowledge. In fact, that's something that's pestered my mind. I know the fae haven't much relation with my father. But all the same, we're trying to find Kayl —as we discussed during dinner—but we have to do so without my father knowing."

"Well, I think that opportunity is long gone, unfortunately." Raum stepped closer, running his hand over the back of his neck. "We've heard your disappearance is known across Wimleigh Kingdom. A description of both of you was released as well. Weren't you just stopped by a group of hunters?"

"How do you even know that?" Ailith asked, sounding more offended than she intended and she immediately stepped back, a little guilty.

Raum didn't seem hurt by Ailith's tone. A smile spread across his face—one filled with delicious secrets to be savored. Secrets he could dangle in front of their hungry mouths—but in the few days Ailith interacted with Raum, he never seemed to hold out long.

"Easy. The crows told us." Raum turned away, beckoning them to continue on their walk through the winding pathways while Ailith and Caitriona looked at one another with their jaws hanging in surprise.

CHAPTER NINETEEN

AILITH

When the pair returned to Niveem's home, the elder fae was nowhere to be seen and Ceenear was absent from the halls. Caitriona drifted after Ailith as she went to her room, which was much more chaotic and lived in than the princess's. Both of their travel bags were tossed into a corner and used mugs lined the table beside the bed. Ailith's traveling clothes sat folded on the surface, and beside the pile lay the sweater Isla gave Caitriona, tattered from the bones that burst from her back.

Ailith paused midway into the room as Caitriona beelined toward the table, her hands reaching for her broken sweater. But it wasn't the sweater she focused on, it was the ball of yarn and the bone needles Ailith left sitting beside it.

"Have you been trying to mend this?" Caitriona lifted her sweater and studied it. "You *are* mending this."

Ailith's feet grew heavy and froze in place on the floor. She lifted her wrist to her mouth and bit at the cuff of her sleeve, a nervous movement that easily conveyed the answer and yet was beyond Ailith's own perception. While she could often read the moods of others, how she displayed herself was, at times, foreign to her. "Oh, yes, I—I just figured

... you seemed to really like the sweater she made you and the weather's only growing colder, and we'll be traveling further north ..."

"I thought Ceenear took everything to be cleaned and mended." Caitriona rubbed her thumb over the neat stitches fixing the holes.

Ailith's reply caught amongst the fluttering in her chest and came out stunted. "Well ... I mean, she *did* have them cleaned. I just, you know, offered to mend your sweater myself. I ..."

She let out a short breath and rolled her eyes. Dropping her hands to her side, she ran her tongue over her lips and steadied herself before attempting to continue. "My mother taught me how to knit and sew. I can even embroider a little. I couldn't sleep while you were unconscious. I was worried. So, since I was unable to sleep, I figured it was a helpful way to pass the time. The downside is Ceenear couldn't find yarn the same color as what Isla used, so it'll be a bit noticeable."

Caitriona remained still for a moment, long enough that Ailith's discomfort grew. The princess gave a small sniff and gently placed the sweater back onto the table. "Thank you." Her fingers trailed over the stitches, slightly quivering before the strength seemed to deflate from her. Her shoulders slumped and her head hung down. "I'm sorry that happened. I'm sorry I fainted and left you to figure out what to do."

"Oh, Cait, don't be sorry," Ailith replied whilst trying to hide her relief. Discussing her feelings, the reasons behind her feeble attempts to fix Caitriona's sweater, would leave her too exposed, which was never a position Ailith enjoyed being in. But discussing what happened amongst the mist? That was easier. "You had no control in it. Anyway, how were we to know you were cursed?"

"I wish I knew how, or why." Caitriona gazed ahead, her sight looking beyond the room. She bit her lip. "We've been traveling for weeks, and I feel more confused than ever. I was just growing comfortable with the powers; I just moved past the instant shame I felt over them. But now my body is physically changing and ... I'm frightened, Ailith. I'm scared."

Tears filled her gold eyes, making them glitter like riches. What magic Lumia used on Caitriona to keep her calm during their evening was gone. Caitriona's emotions were now pure, honest, and undiluted.

Her voice shook as she asked the question Ailith suspected sat on her tongue since they were at the evening meal. "What am I turning into?"

Ailith stepped forward, her hands out. She wanted to fill them by gathering Caitriona to her and holding her close, by comforting and protecting her, but found she wasn't certain if that was allowed. Gone were the early moments of their travels when Ailith was irritated by the princess's presence. In its place was something more: a heavy heartbeat thrumming wild when she was near, hungry hands that craved the feel of her hair, and lonely lips that yearned for warmth. She wanted to share the secret nature of her feelings but held back. Cearny would hate what was going on with Caitriona, she was frightened by what was happening to herself, and Ailith didn't want to add to that. Despite it all, she wished she could convey to Caitriona that she was incredibly brave and strong. Instead, she stood a few feet away with arms held out, sympathetic.

"I don't know what you're turning into," she admitted, the truth of the statement making Ailith want to cry as well. "But whatever it is, you have me by your side. I don't care if you turn into something tomorrow, I'll simply take you with me and I'll find Kayl myself."

"I know," Caitriona said with a sad laugh. "Greer always knows what she's doing and she was right to ask you to go with me. I know you'll do whatever it takes and that's a comfort, but I'm still scared. What if I turn into something and I can't come back? What if I don't know who I am anymore? What if after all of this, the curse's sole purpose is only to kill me?"

"Cait." Ailith stepped closer as Caitriona devolved into tears. She put her hands over her face as she wept, and Ailith slipped her arms around Caitriona without hesitation. She guided the princess to her bed, sitting down beside her as Caitriona continued to cry. Moving her palm in small circles on Caitriona's back, she remained silent, not attempting to talk away Caitriona's tears but giving her the right to let them fall. Ailith's job didn't allow for many displays of emotion, and she trained herself to keep them locked away, but she knew the relief that sometimes followed after emptying your thoughts through clenched eyes and bleeding heart.

"I don't want to lose myself," Caitriona whispered. She hunched forward, her elbows resting on her legs, her face in her open palms. "I'm so frightened. I would take death as *myself* over *losing* myself entirely."

Ailith leaned forward and reached for Caitriona's face. She guided the princess's chin to turn towards her. When she spoke, her voice was heavy with passion. "If you're lost, I'll find you and *bring you back to yourself.*"

"I know you'd try to, *I know*, but there's no guarantee you'll be able to do anything. No amount of hope, no good will, no valiant guard to stand by my side will matter. And, honestly, I'd find it more comforting to know that if something very bad were to happen, you'd protect yourself first and foremost." Caitriona wiped her eyes and sat upright. She turned to Ailith and her gold eyes still sparkled from her tears.

Holding Caitriona's gaze for a few passing seconds was all Ailith could bear. She hated to consider abandoning Caitriona, but nodded with agreement to the princess's wish. Her fingers found the edge of her shirt and picked at the sewing. They both held the silence between them, liquid and cold; it seeped through their fingers, growing into worry that spread across the floor, and soaked into their souls.

"I'm sorry," Ailith said after a long moment. "All of this isn't fair. I wish ..." She thought of the Elder Tree back home with the colorful strips of cloth and ribbon cascading from its branches filled with wishes and dreams.

"Alas," Caitriona said. "Sympathy and fairness are not in the nature of curses."

CHAPTER TWENTY

AILITH

They remained in Ulla Syrmin for two more days. Time took on a restful quality similar to molasses, spreading slowly, yet thick with lazy activity. Caitriona and Ailith attended meals with Niveem, Raum, Lumia, and Ceenear as before. Each dinner allowed them to grow more familiar with the fae and Ailith was embarrassed to think she ever assumed they were any different from herself. Niveem was married, although her wife was visiting the mountain peak she grew up in, missing them entirely; Raum and Lumia argued like any couple; and Ceenear was a world traveler with stories from all over Visennore and beyond where she took ships to distant lands to visit cities and countries. In the evenings, they rested on a patio higher in Niveem's home that overlooked the curling river gorge below. A few other fae passed through on business with Niveem, their interested eyes glancing at the pair but there was little interaction, and they retained their privacy. At night, when Ailith couldn't sleep, she worked on Caitriona's sweater with one hole closing, followed by the second, and still drifted towards Caitriona's room to ensure the princess was resting and safe.

Caitriona spent her afternoons with Niveem in relative silence. The leader of Ulla Syrmin welcomed the princess to her library, a sprawling, circular room with windows bordered by books. It was there Niveem showed Caitriona detailed maps of the Endless Mountains and the Mazgate Dominion. Caitriona was given ink, quill, and large sheets of paper to copy maps for her own. She was also taken to the flat roof of the home where together, fae and princess, they made fire in the air and controlled the flames to make them twist and rise and fall. Ailith could see the red and orange glow reflecting on the pathways below as she sat on her windowsill in the evening, looking out at the expansive view and savoring the moment. At long last, she achieved her childhood dream of seeing the mist and wandering far beyond it. It seemed right that it was nothing the tales said, with so much more to it than guesses and stories spoken over fires.

In the afternoon, Ailith visited Raum on Niveem's roof. Determined not to repeat what happened with the hunters, she was eager to spar and Raum was happy to help.

"You already know most of this," Raum pointed out, beads of sweat shone on his forehead after they sparred for an hour in the late afternoon sun. It was the final day Ailith and Caitriona were in the mountains. While the air held a crispness and the wind often blew cold, the sun still held heat. "You've been trained, you know how to use weapons. What's holding you back?"

"Nothing." Ailith got to her feet. He'd, yet again, knocked her off balance and stopped with a blade pressed to her chest. While Ailith never was the top of her class when it came to weapons training, she was never this bad. "Are you sure fae can't move faster than humans?"

Raum flashed a smile as he pushed his dagger back into its holder on his hip. "Some can; it's little magic, but generally speaking, no. I think in this case, it's less your ability and more your mind."

Ailith let out a breath and dropped her shoulders, looking at the fae beside her with a tired expression. "I don't know what I'm doing."

"You're training with me," Raum replied with a crooked smile, earning him a punch to his arm.

"I mean ... I don't know what I'm doing with Caitriona. I'm on the edge of failure with her. She's cursed. She's turning into some creature. I couldn't even remain seated on my horse when the hunters found us. *She* saved us."

"Mistakes happen, sometimes multiple mistakes in a disastrous row.

There's no use lingering over them, it'll only get in your head and make you mess up again. What's necessary is taking your blunder and learning from it. Prepare as if you'll face your fault again and have a chance to correct it. And *please*, stop pitying yourself over it." A dark eyebrow rose as he silently dared her to disagree.

"If someone approaches us and attempts to get Caitriona again," Ailith began, turning on her heel and drifting in a slow circle around the roof as she considered her options, "I won't play with caution. I'll act aggressively. If anyone dares to question us, they're a threat."

"Perhaps so. And if they approach you with hostility?"

Ailith stopped and turned to Raum. She hated the truth of her next words. "I'll kill them."

"And that bothers you."

Not a question, but Ailith nodded before blinking rapidly and looking away. "I've never killed someone. I mean, I was trained to. That was part of our training for the guard, how to kill someone. But the city guard, overall, isn't expected to take lives. We're a protective layer for the city. They helped when the white dragon attacked, but the expectation is for the royal guard to do all warfare. I haven't even drawn my sword while on duty; there's never been a need. But out here, traveling with Caitriona, that's the expectation—that's why I was hired, to protect her. I'm afraid I'll fail Cait, and I'm afraid I'll have to kill someone."

"I think you'll have to conquer both of your fears in order to be the best at your job." Despite his taller, broader appearance that gave him a sense of hardened warrior, his gaze softened with sympathy. Not for the first time, Ailith wished she could work with him at the city gate. She suspected she'd find a true friend in him and learn a great deal.

Raum straightened his back and crossed his arms over his chest. "What strikes fear in your heart about killing someone?"

Ailith blinked, surprised by the question and its obvious answer. "That I would have to *kill* someone. That their life would be snuffed out, that I murdered them."

"*That's* where you're getting lost in your thoughts," Raum said. "There's a difference between killing and murdering. Murdering sparks some sense of joy, of satisfaction. It's a predetermined death that gives the murderer an edge, an upper hand. Killing ... that's a death taken without joy. It's a death created by a need to protect, to save; that's the difference, that's what saves you. You wouldn't kill a man at random, but you may if you're looking to protect yourself and Caitriona. It's hard, of course. Taking a life is not something easily done ... unless you're the type to find pride in that type of thing ... which would make you a murderer, which—" he stepped forward and flicked her nose, "—you're not. Do you see? You need to understand that to grapple with killing someone, otherwise you'll be buried under the weight of it all."

Ailith let out a burst of air, a half laugh. "For a guard, you have a firm understanding of what goes on in the minds of others. Is that part of your magic?"

"For a guard, you don't." Raum spread his hands wide. "I'm certain seeing the glow of a person's spirit helps me, but this is all basic lessons fae are taught when they take up weapons and vow to fight for our land. Does Braewick City not speak of the burdens of the mind that war and death bring? Are you not trained to handle these mental loads?"

Ailith shook her head. "Not particularly. We're told we're doing it for the crown, for the good of the city. Perhaps those who continue through the ranks of the city guard and into the royal guard have different training, I wouldn't know, but we never spent long on matters of the heart and mind."

Raum made a face of disgust. "King Cearny must have a multitude of broken-minded guards in his possession. I can guarantee more guards under his rule are fighting internal darkness more frequently than the individuals they're ordered to kill."

Ailith pressed her lips together. He was likely right. King Cearny—and from what Ailith heard, his father as well—was never particularly concerned with how his guards got by, so long as they did their job. Failure to do so meant a swift removal from their position and if how the king treated her father after his injury was any indication, Ailith suspected the guards were left with little aid or options as well.

Raum patted Ailith on her shoulder. "You're worried you'll have to kill someone, but you know you'll do it, because you don't want to fail Cait."

Ailith shook her head. "I *don't* want to fail her. I can't. I'm afraid of that, possibly equally, if not more."

"Well then, I think you know what you'll have to do. Remember, correct the previous mistakes, don't let them create more. Kill to protect if it's necessary. Death created by the need to protect, to save; that's the difference, that's what saves you. Now," Raum spread his legs and held out his hands.,"why don't you try again."

Ailith was finally able to disarm Raum by the last bit of afternoon light. Clasping Raum's knife in her hand, she beamed over his body after kicking his legs out from underneath him. He returned her expression tenfold. "I knew you were just in your head," Raum said before accepting Ailith's hand to stand up.

That evening, Ailith and Ceenear followed Caitriona to the library where two sprawling papers with drying ink lay out.

"So, this is the rest of the road to Avorkaz. We'll travel there and gather supplies before we take the Nordstrak Road to the northern mountains," Caitriona explained, pointing out their pathway forward on the map. While the map Caitriona made in Braewick helped them thus far, Braewick didn't have many accurate or recent maps of the Mazgate Dominion or the mountains due to lack of access. "This should take us to Beaslig. That's where Isla thought he'd be."

"Kayl?" Ceenear asked, looking over the maps with her hands tucked behind her back.

"Yes," Ailith replied. "Isla, the crow woman, she heard he lives there."

"I've passed through Beaslig, to the pass for Norkasser. I haven't met Kayl, or at least I haven't met anyone by that name, but there *was* talk of a magic maker who lived in the town further up the mountain on the edge of the village."

"When we get to Beaslig, we can ask if anyone knows where he lives, and if not, we can look around the edge of the village ourselves," Ailith suggested.

"They're northern folk, happy for those who pass by because it brings business, particularly this late in the year," Ceenear added. "For that region, it's the depths of autumn now and the weather is growing colder by the day. Ensure you buy heavy clothing in Avorkaz and trade your horses for a northern breed that's familiar with the cold. Get plenty of food too, also wood for fires."

"I suddenly feel nervous," Caitriona admitted, a flicker of a smile appearing on her face. "Like, after all of this, we may almost be done."

"It'll still be a few days of travel," Ceenear clarified.

"We understand." Ailith looked up from the maps. "It's a few days but it feels new. We've never experienced the north."

"We also never experienced the marshlands or the seaside," Caitriona countered.

"But they were still familiar in some way," Ailith continued. "They reminded me of home. The temperatures were relatively alike, the trees, the upcoming autumn. We have our snowfalls in Braewick, but it's only for a few months. Here we'll be going to a land that only experiences a few months where there *isn't* snow. And now this completely new place is within arm's reach. Soon all our worries could be cared for."

"Or ..." Caitriona's voice downturned and already Ailith knew her eagerness for the next few days would be quickly squashed. "Kayl won't be able to help at all."

"*Or ...*" Ailith tapped the map, her nail rapping over the little town they would soon see. "If he can't help, he may point us to whoever placed this curse on you. He knows your mother, he knows *you* to an extent, and he's this great magic maker, right? So, he surely has powers to help us, whether it's to stop the curse, or slow it down and figure out what we do next."

"I don't know if magic quite works like that."

Ailith's shoulders dropped, her attempt falling flat.

"Magic tends to follow its own rules," Ceenear offered. "It's very easy to look ahead and see only the possibility of failure. The idea of what may go wrong can come easily. But when magic is involved, you truly cannot assume it will go one way or another, so I'd choose to wish for the best." Her eyes met Ailith's, softening the nervous twist that formed in Ailith's spine. In its place, something else pushed its way in, small but fierce and growing: hope.

Ceenear helped the women pack their belongings and gather supplies for the two days of travel to Avorkaz. Their horses were well cared for, rested and fed, and ready to get on with their travels, and Ailith found she was itching to move on as well. Dinner was more jovial and talkative, and when their regular dinner party dispersed, Ailith's chest felt tight with the bittersweet pain of saying goodbye.

"Perhaps one day I'll leave the mountains and travel with Ceenear," Raum said as he bid Ailith goodbye. "I'll make sure we come and find you at your gate."

"I think it would be better if I came to you." Over the few days they spent in Ulla Syrmin, Raum rose to Ailith's dry sense of humor and jokes, creating a friendship she never experienced with her fellow guards in Braewick. Despite their teasing, Ailith knew she would miss him. "Can you imagine how King Cearny would act if two pointed-eared elves arrived at the city?"

"Well, only one," Raum raised an eyebrow at Ceenear who gave a shake of her head, causing her pointed ears to vanish and then reappear. "I'm sure the blokes you work with wouldn't know what hit them if I arrived. Travel safely; I'm certain we'll cross paths again. Remember our sparring." Raum sobered slightly to reach his strong arms around Ailith, giving her a tight embrace that threatened to break her ribs.

With emotions welling within, Ailith chose silence. There was no way to know what her future held, and she already missed them from the uncertainty of seeing them in the future.

Ceenear followed the pair down the mountain's pathways toward the mist's edge. The mist, for all the defense it provided, didn't necessarily move aside for the fae, beyond those deemed worthy enough to control it. Raum had that power though and climbed to his outpost to push the curtain aside. They paused before the wall of white air that curled forward and gently touched their faces before it stepped aside, offering an exit for the women and revealing the roadway they were on days prior.

"I should forewarn you both before you leave," Ceenear said as Ailith and Caitriona led their horses to the road edge. "The birds have spoken on the wind of movement. People are looking for you."

"Well, I could have told you that," Ailith said with a smirk. Ceenear's serious expression softened with a shadow of a sad smile.

"This is different; a new group, one moving from Braewick City. Be careful while you travel. Camp far from the road and in cover if you can find any. The closer to Avorkaz's wall you get, the more wooded it will be, but it's open fields before that." Ceenear stepped forward and embraced Caitriona. She stepped back, eyeing her for a moment before continuing. "Remember, if there are more changes that come upon you, don't fight it. If this curse is turning you into something, it will be painful the first time, but the less you fight the aches of change the more you can keep your wits about it."

Caitriona mounted Butterscotch. Ceenear placed her hand on Ailith's arm. "Travel well, Ailith."

"Thank you." Ailith grasped Ceenear's arm and gave it a gentle squeeze. Ailith mounted Inkwell and both women pressed forward, stepping onto the roadway and beginning to move further north. The peaceful lands of the fae were to their backs and Ceenear remained at the break in the mist, watching as they moved further away.

Caitriona glanced over her shoulder and raised a hand, drawing Ailith's attention. Ceenear waved, a distant speck framed by the white mist, and Ailith returned the gesture.

"You know ..." Caitriona turned back to the road and picked up speed. "I think she liked you."

"I like her too," Ailith encouraged Inkwell to keep up with Butterscotch. "She's quite nice."

"No, I mean more than that," Caitriona teased. "She *liked* you."

Ailith felt her cheeks grow hot. She rode forward at a faster clip, leaving Caitriona's laughter behind. Any feelings Ceenear felt toward Ailith were completely missed by her, her focus too heavily on the princess who rode beside her. Even that realization left Ailith repeating to herself that Caitriona was only teasing, but the heat of embarrassment was present all the same. Perhaps admitting her feelings to Caitriona wasn't wise. The thought left an ache in her chest that she was happy to ignore as she focused on the ride ahead.

They were in the thick of autumn in this higher elevation. The time of year when leaves gathered their best display of color seemingly overnight and it only took a rainstorm, or a heavy frost, to set them to the wind. The air was crisp and the wind carried a slight bite that urged the women to ride at a brisk pace, no dawdling, with hope to get to Avorkaz's gate soon. Silence was a more preferable companion, something they were able to achieve with greater ease and comfort than in the earlier days of their travels. They learned enough of each other's emotions and understood them fairly well that after their time spent in the Endless Mountains, reflection seemed necessary.

When the sun grew close to setting, they turned their horses off road toward a cluster of trees. As Ceenear said, trees were appearing more frequently along the roadway, as well as circles of pines. This particular spot seemed prime for rest, with broad evergreens blocking some of the breeze. It would serve well to prevent their firelight from being seen on the road whilst affording them privacy. The earth had grown rocky and Ailith made quick work making a fire pit with loose stones along the outer ridge of the circle to block further light from escaping.

"Nothing more we can do, really." Ailith sat, rubbing her thighs that ached from riding. "Other than sleep without a fire at all, which may be wise to do through part of the night, but I'm not sure that's smart with the air as cold as it is."

"Let's do it for part of the night." Caitriona laid out their blankets side by side. Slipping her travel gloves on, she hugged herself and rubbed her arms. "We'll just stick close to one another for body heat when it's out."

Ailith's cheeks heated again, happy to turn her attention toward the grouse she shot on the road yet groaning with each leg movement as she shifted to get it on a spit and over the fire. Caitriona remained quiet, not once gagging over the tufts of feathers Ailith pulled from the dead bird, but her eyes still sparkled with held back humor as Ailith grumbled her complaints of her sore legs from riding.

They were well fed in the mountains, and this meal made them desire to return to Niveem's home. Years of not being able to afford many ingredients taught Ailith to cook with very little, but she wished for the herbs and spices of Ulla Syrmin. Before long, they settled in, buried under their cloaks and blankets as they shared bird breast and legs, and roasted potatoes Ceenear provided.

"When we reach Avorkaz, we'll sell our horses and buy one with the money, and hopefully have enough for new clothing that'll be better in the snow." Ailith poured the coins from her bag, counting what remained.

"I still have plenty of gold as well," Caitriona freed her hand from her cloak and reached into her bag. She tossed a coin purse to Ailith who tipped its contents into her hands and raised her eyebrows.

"Platinum?" Ailith quickly counted the gold and platinum coins. There was more than enough for what they needed. They could afford room and board both in Avorkaz and Beaslig, plus respectable places to rest on the return trip to Braewick. "And you had me counting coins with concern."

Caitriona's cheeks colored. "I never had to buy much before this trip, so I admit I'm unfamiliar with costs. To be fair, Greer prepared everything I took with me, including my coin."

"Well, we're set then." Ailith returned the coins to the purse and tossed it back to Caitriona. She lifted her waterskin and held it high. "Now we only need to make it through tonight and we should be at the city gates by tomorrow evening."

"One step closer," Caitriona replied, lifting her own waterskin. They tapped the two together before focusing on their meals.

CHAPTER TWENTY-ONE

GREER

T hey were ready to return to Braewick Valley, and Greer wasn't sure how she felt about that. One part of her wanted to find her sister, to see her with her own eyes and verify Caitriona was fine; another part of her was terrified that her sister was becoming a monster; and a final part felt that not finding Caitriona indicated she was still safely traveling forward or perhaps had already found Kayl.

It was easy to find the scorch marks the hunters described. Greer was shocked by the vast area it covered. The grass was gone, the earth black and making a near perfect circle except for a centerpiece that remained untouched. They retraced Caitriona and Ailith's steps from the burn marks until they vanished, the trail gone, as if they never existed. Now, unable to find her sister, heaviness settled in her stomach, making her uneasy. They would camp for the night and go back to Braewick City, until an unexpected change of plans arrived.

Coincidence is too simple a word to describe what prevented them from returning home. After a week of travel, they were too close to the borders of Avorkaz for Greer's comfort. They didn't need Avorkaz scouts spotting them and assuming they were on behalf of King Cearny and leading an attack on the city. With darkness falling, they searched for a place to camp, their movement slowing as they scanned the brush beside the road, when luck took their side.

The sky was slate gray. The shadows had already taken the clarity of the land and caused trees to turn into dark outlines. Had it been a few minutes later, had the sun set further or the clouds grown thicker, or the party paused earlier in their journey, they would have missed the slight smudge of black smoke rising into the sky from a group of pine far off the road.

Travelers camping for the night.

"Let's approach quietly," Greer commanded her small band of men. "We don't want to startle any innocent travelers with fully armed soldiers. Only a few of us will go."

They tied their horses to roadside trees, and some men offered to stay behind. Much to Greer's disappointment, Ian—King Cearny's guard who the king forced upon the party that was otherwise of Greer's making—decided to join her. The short man with a thin face and hungry eyes was first to dismount his horse and set off toward the trees. Greer glanced at Barden who rode beside her, and he was an immediate blur of movement. Jumping from his saddle, Barden hurried after Ian while Greer handed her reins to another soldier as she hopped off her own.

"The bastard never listens." Greer moved over the tall grasses that were spent from summer days, the blades turned to yellows and browns, brittle and snapping under her footfall. Crows cawed in the distance; the persistent sound having followed them through most of their journey as all the other birds migrated to warmer climates. Greer narrowed her eyes as Ian all but pranced to the trees. As Barden began running after him, stopping short to move quietly along the tree line, Greer cursed under her breath.

A shout rose from the grove as Barden reached the outcrop, a feminine sound that made Greer's heart lodge in her throat. Barden darted into the shadows and Greer began running, pulling her cloak free from her throat as it caught on twigs and bushes. Letting it go, she reached to her waist and unsheathed her sword before she dove into the brush and stumbled into the circle of pine to find the scene she dreaded.

Ailith was on her knees, back arched and shoulders pinned firmly against Ian's stomach as his knife pressed against her throat. Her hands clung to his arm, her short sword tossed to the ground, bloody, which seemed to pair with a gushing wound coming from Ian's side. Ailith managed a good strike on the man before he bested her. Barden stood a few feet from the pair with a hand held up and eyes locked with Ian.

Feet away stood a cloaked figure, a woman with a short sword held out at the ready. Her form was pathetic, the way she gripped the handle displayed her inexperience, but Greer focused on the gloves the figure wore. Gray traveling gloves she picked out for her sister herself.

"Ian, stand down," Barden commanded as he stepped closer. Ian's eyes flitted to Greer, his face pale and clammy.

"I have the guard." He applied pressure to the knife, making it go deeper in the skin of Ailith's throat. She clenched her jaw, closing her eyes as a red line formed from the blade.

"Ian, what are you doing?" Greer hissed. "*Stand down*."

"The king said to kill the guard when we found her." Ian glanced between Greer and Barden. "Kill her on sight if she was with the princess."

"But I'm not the princess," the figure with the sword said, her voice quivering as it barely escaped through a flood of tears. Ian narrowed his eyes, cocking his head in the direction of the princess, obviously disbelieving her. She reached to the hood of her cloak and pulled it back, allowing gold hair to tumble out and gleam in the firelight. "The princess has red hair, does she not?"

Ian studied the girl, hesitating for a moment. His grip loosened just enough for Ailith to slip down and out of his hold. She moved fast, her hand reaching a knife strapped to her thigh that she quickly held up as she twisted, using her full weight to throw herself forward and push the knife into Ian's chest.

He took a step back, his hand swinging to stab at Ailith but only cutting into her cheek as blood poured down his front. Ailith hissed, but was on her feet, pushing the knife deeper as she yelled, a strangled cry filled with fear and tears. Barden came behind Ian, capturing his stumbling body into his grasp and pulling him back. His knife made swift work that left Ian slumped in his arms as his neck drained what blood wasn't already gushing from his chest and side.

Ailith fell to her knees and made a small, gasping sound. Caitriona wept, but remained where she stood as the scuffle ended. Barden turned with Ian's body in his arms and dropped him into the bushes unceremoniously before returning his attention to the women.

The party was motionless, Ailith bled from her cheek and neck as she knelt on the ground, and Barden was coated in Ian's blood. The guards studied one another before turning to the Braewick princesses, drawing the sisters to look at one another for the first time in weeks.

"Cait?" Greer asked the woman across the clearing. With the fire between them, she was fully lit and glimmering with golden hair and eyes. She had the same face, the same lips, the same shape of eyes. She had the same voice and clothes. But she looked like a golden goddess, standing straight-backed and serious. Someone filled with magic and permanently changed, someone that Greer suddenly wasn't sure she knew.

"Ree." Speaking Greer's nickname, Caitriona's voice didn't convey excitement or fear, but exhaustion. A moment passed before Caitriona looked down at her hair, her hands touching the locks. "I suppose I have a great deal of explaining to do."

"I think we need to figure out what *we* are doing first and foremost," Barden announced, stepping closer to Ailith to offer a cloth for the guard to press against her face. "Ailith's going to need stitches in her cheek, one of your father's guards is dead in the bushes, and we have a troop outside this grove of trees."

"They can know." Greer looked at Barden. She gave a defeated shrug. What else could she do? The number of people knowing Caitriona's secret continued to grow. "Ian was the odd man out. The rest are *our* men, although we do need to figure out what to do about his death."

"Who was he?" Caitriona asked, but her attention was on Ailith who sat silent on the ground. Barden knelt beside the guard and looked at the wound, moving the cloth away from her cheek slowly and frowning. Caitriona shifted as if fighting an urge to join them.

Greer sheathed her sword and rubbed her temples. This was rapidly getting out of control and turning into quite the mess.

"A guard of father's that he requested join us," Greer growled.

Caitriona was never admitted to war discussions or meetings where the king had his favorite guards with him, so she wouldn't have recognized Ian. "The hunters you encountered came to Braewick. Barden and I decided to take a group we could trust to search for you, but father demanded Ian go with us. He is—*was*—a bootlicker. Always quick to side with father and do anything he bid. It makes sense that father would select him to tag along, particularly if he's beginning to distrust my own authority."

"So, everyone else …?"

"They're loyal to me."

Greer looked at Caitriona and internally flinched. It hurt that her sister could go through so much change without her, that she could become this person who she did not visually recognize in so short a time. What were these powers doing to her? Greer took a slow breath to calm her emotions before continuing. "I trust them. We need to dispose of Ian's body somewhere and we can figure out a lie to tell father."

"I'll get the healer's kit." Barden gripped Ailith's shoulder before rising and turning to Greer. "And I'll tell the men to settle down by the road for the night and bring a few to get Ian."

"We should pack to go," Ailith pressed the cloth to her cheek and tried to stand. Her body immediately wavered and she sat on the ground. Her gaze was far away and her skin pale and moist. "This obviously isn't as safe a location as we thought."

"No, it's the perfect location." Greer looked over her shoulder where her men waited beyond the trees. The horses' faint noises were the only sounds. Greer turned back. "My group won't breathe a word about what they see or what we've done. While Barden knew about this situation beforehand, the rest of my men will have to embrace the secret as well, but I trust them. Otherwise, I wouldn't have brought them with me—I knew there was a risk our secret would be exposed.

"You both should continue to rest here tonight. We'll be by the road and see if anyone else comes this way. You'll be safer near us."

"We were so close to the damn city." Ailith groaned as she lay back on the ground, seeming to shake Caitriona from whatever was holding her still. She slipped her short sword into her belt and moved to Ailith's side, sinking to the ground and pulling at Ailith so the guard's head rested on her lap. Caitriona took the cloth from Ailith's hand and pressed it to her cheek, allowing the guard's hands to drop. Her free hand brushed Ailith's uninjured cheek, a gentle and brief movement that seemed to comfort Ailith.

"Perhaps it'll be a blessing for an easy passage into the city," Caitriona replied in a tone that seemed distant, her attention clearly not entirely on the conversation.

Greer stared at the two women as she chewed the inside of her cheek. The logical part of her was glad to see the bond the women created. Caitriona had been tucked away for most of her life and from what Greer gathered, Ailith kept few close acquaintances. She was happy they seemed at ease and were traveling well together. However, it was also completely undeniable that the two meant something more to one another than just acquaintances.

While she was more logical than her father, she also was quick to speak when emotions drowned her, bringing her to spit out, "What the hell is going on here?"

Ailith and Caitriona looked at Greer. She threw her hands up, frustrated as she circled the fire to where the women had obviously bedded down for the night right beside one another, and came to a stop a few feet away from the couple. She wanted to question them about their relationship, to tell Caitriona of their father's plan to marry her off, but every time she looked at her sister, she felt her gut crumble at how different she looked.

"Cait, what … *what happened*?" Greer waved her hands toward her sister's hair. "Your hair, your eyes; what's going on?"

Ailith rolled her eyes up to Caitriona who frowned. Ailith gripped Caitriona's arm in a way to seemingly encourage her. It was an intimate movement that nearly brought a blush to Greer's cheeks if not for her sister looking at her and speaking. "I can still make fire, I can control it in a way, but each time I use the power something happens. I've experienced physical changes that all disappeared, returning me to normal, but my hair and my eyes seem … I don't know, permanent."

"So, the powers did this to you?" Greer's knees bent and suddenly she was sinking to the ground beside them.

"We assume so. It certainly seems tied."

"And the physical changes? What are those?"

"My nails become claw-like. I've had bones break from my back, shooting out like broken wings."

"*Cait.*" Greer couldn't fathom that happening, let alone to her quiet, docile sister who seemed completely undeserving of such trauma. "You haven't found Kayl yet?"

"That's where we're going. We've had some ... hold ups," Cait replied, looking at Ailith. "We just got back on the road. We're heading to Avorkaz to get supplies and then traveling into the northern range of the Endless Mountains. Kayl is likely located in Beaslig."

"Thank goodness," Greer sighed. "Perhaps he'll figure out how to get your eyes to turn back. Your hair ... I'm sure we could find a dye that can bring it back to red."

"I ..." Caitriona began as she reached for her hair and brushed her fingers over it. "I don't know if it'll change back. Even with Kayl's help. And I don't *hate* the color."

"It's lovely." Greer laughed, a bitter sound, her frustration with the situation leaking out. "I mean, you look more like my sibling now that our hair's similar in color, no? But we can't have you return home with golden eyes. Father would immediately see what magic has done to you."

"You're not understanding." Caitriona hands dropped to Ailith's shoulder. "None of this may change back. It may not be possible. I don't know if I'll be able to stop what's going on, I don't know if Kayl will be able to help."

"He brought you back to life and healed your entire body," Greer countered.

The very mention of that day was enough to make Greer pause. She was just a child, but she still could recall the scent of Caitriona's burnt body, could still remember the appearance of her dead, charred form. Her mother screamed so loudly that it hurt Greer's ears and Etta had tried to pull Greer from the room. But she fought her, pulling away from her arms to run to her mother, the one safe spot Greer could reach. When Kayl rushed into the room, robes floating behind as he moved, and his voice clear as he took charge and told the guards to back away from Caitriona, Greer looked to her mother whose cries had cut off. She pleaded and begged with her hands outstretched for Kayl to help Caitriona. His hands ran over Caitriona's body, seemingly wiping the ashes and burns away with the great magic he possessed. It was a miracle, it was magic, and the image never faded from Greer's memory.

Returning to the chilly woods with Caitriona and Ailith before her, Greer shook the memory off her shoulders. "He's an *incredibly* powerful mage."

"She's *cursed*," Ailith groaned, her brows furrowed with pain. "All that's going on is the result of a curse. She's turning into something."

Greer furrowed her brow. "Who would've cursed you?"

"I don't think you need to have any personal relationship with someone to get cursed. So, who knows? It could be someone who hates father for all we know. But we've met with fae who could see a curse in me; it's the reason for the powers and the changes."

"Do you think Kayl can stop the curse?"

"That's what we hope to find out," Ailith replied, sitting up as Barden stepped into the clearing with a bag.

Caitriona got to her feet, making room for Barden who kneeled beside Ailith and turned her cheek away to look at the cut. It was still badly bleeding, deep and rough enough that Barden's nose wrinkled before pulling free a waterskin filled with wine.

"Drink this," he said, shoving it into Ailith's hands who lifted it to her lips, flinching as she chugged the red wine.

Barden leaned back on his heels, taking in the sight of Caitriona, his face expressionless as he studied her. The younger princess was oblivious and only had eyes for Ailith. Barden raised an eyebrow and looked at Greer, who couldn't return his unspoken question. She was far from all right but had to stay strong for her sister's sake.

"Is anything happening in Braewick?" Caitriona asked, looking between them. "Tell me about home."

"Father is ..." Greer bit her lip. "He wants you home. He's *determined* to get you home. He's ... upset. The hunters who saw you came straight away to the castle and reported what they witnessed."

Caitriona's hands slipped around her waist as she embraced herself. "Everything?"

Greer's frustration rose like a tide; she had so much power as the heir and yet so little. She wished more than anything she could order her men to travel forward with her sister and finish this mission themselves. She wished she had the power to set things right. But the power was still in her father's hands and his reactions ruled everything.

"*Everything*, and luckily, he didn't believe them ... at least not entirely. He's in one of his moods. All rage and secrets behind his eyes; you know it's not smart to ask him what he's feeling. He declared Ailith the one with powers, even though the men insisted it was you. Ailith, dear, you certainly have a price on your head now."

"Yeah, I gathered that," Ailith groaned. She repositioned herself against a nearby stump of a fallen tree as Barden pulled out a needle and thread. Ailith's eyes went wide before she clenched them shut, a small whimper escaping her lips. "What about my parents? Are they alright?"

"I relocated them, the girl that cares for them, too. They're safe and away from my father. I doubted he would trust my opinion to leave them alone if he turned his sights on them. It seems he's losing trust in me overall."

Caitriona moved closer to Ailith and squatted down opposite Barden to take her hand. "Do you think so?"

"I don't know why else he'd send Ian along with us. He's never had much issue when I've made my own selections for travel before, and I doubt he'll be pleased to find out Ian's dead."

Footsteps drew closer to the circle. Two of Greer's men stepped into the clearing, pretending to focus on finding Ian's body, but their continuous glances at Caitriona reminded Greer she needed to have a long sit down with her men.

"We can figure it out though," Greer continued, turning back to Caitriona. Her eyes were cast down, a frown plain on her face as Ailith gripped her hand hard. Barden was making quick work at sewing a few stitches into Ailith's cheek. The blood from the puncture of the needle made her face look all the more gruesome.

"This is going to give you a hell of a scar," Barden wiped Ailith's cheek with the bloodstained cloth. Greer pitied the guard. Getting field dressings, particularly stitches, was always a dirty, daring affair that could lead to scars or worse, infection. Every one she ever received was by an actual medic and thankfully not on her face.

"And I didn't even kill him." Ailith moaned as Barden pulled away, a few stitches standing out against her cheek.

"Oh, you did," Barden replied as he cleaned the needle and put his supplies into the bag. "He would've died from the side wound alone, but that stab to the chest nearly finished the job. I only helped speed up the process."

Ailith slumped against her pack and Caitriona was over her in a heartbeat, hands gently touching her chin as she looked over Barden's work. She pulled a clean cloth from her pocket and wet it with water from her waterskin before wiping away more blood. Caitriona and Ailith moved as if pulled together, entwined without touching, and a devotion Greer never saw Caitriona possess for anyone beyond herself and perhaps her adoration for the library.

"Barden, can you return to the group and begin debriefing them on all that's transpired?" Greer asked, her eyes on the women. Barden got to his feet and gathered his things. "Tell them everything. They need to know what they're dealing with and that none of this is to go back to my father. Tell them that I need their silence on this matter, it's dearly important to me."

"Of course. Should we expect you back shortly?" Barden placed his hand on the hilt of his sword, his medic pack hanging from his shoulder.

"I'll be staying with you lot tonight, don't worry." Greer pulled her gaze up to meet Barden's, her expression sobered. "But I wanted to spend some time with these two first, thank you."

CHAPTER TWENTY-TWO

CAITRIONA

C aitriona helped Ailith settle amongst their blankets as the effects from the wine made her drowsy. Her face swelled from the cut of the knife, angry and red, and Greer fished out a pain-killing powder that Ailith mixed with her water. Caitriona stoked the fire as Greer cleaned Ailith's blade and gathered spent arrows Ailith used when Ian first burst through the tree line. A few crickets began to tentatively sing, but most night insects had fallen silent in the chilly air. The heat from the fire drew them close, encouraging the sisters to finish their clean up so they could settle down and warm themselves. It was only then that Caitriona was able to sort out how their evening had gone so wrong.

Unlike with the shades, Ian hadn't captured the women by surprise. Caitriona hadn't even heard Ian's footsteps when Ailith reached for her bow and let arrows fly into the trees in rapid succession. Ian came forward without pause, running across the clearing with his sword out. He moved with aggression and drew blood from Ailith's neck, just shy of his goal to kill her.

Ailith pushed Caitriona to the side where she fell, hitting the ground hard and sending a shock through her tail bone. She clenched her eyes shut as pain shot up her spine and upon opening them Ian's sword was end over end into the brush and Ailith made a slashing effort against his waist. The scramble turned in Ian's favor. He grabbed Ailith by the throat, leaving Caitriona shaking and scrambling to her feet to pull her own short sword free.

In that moment, she hated her father with every ounce of her body. He kept her locked within the castle, refusing her requests to learn swordsmanship like her sister. She had no faith in her abilities to do anything without hurting Ailith in return. She was as powerful as a child with a stick as she stood there, helpless.

Yet Ailith's hesitancy when the hunters approached weeks before was gone. Something pushed the guard, even though torment flashed in Ailith's eyes when she sunk her blade into Ian's chest.

Greer's arrival was, by far, the last thing Caitriona expected. She assumed her father found them when Ian stumbled into the camp with the Braewick crest on his chest. Her hope rapidly deteriorated, but Greer's arrival was a blessing.

Now her sister deposited the lost arrows and pulled Ian's sword from the grass, holding it up to the light of the fire as she turned the blade.

"If the fool only waited," Greer murmured before sitting the blade against a tree trunk, "perhaps he would've been saved."

"You think you could've talked him out of telling father about us?" Caitriona knelt beside the fire and placed more branches onto its flames.

"Oh, certainly not," Greer replied, moving next to Caitriona where she unbuckled her belt and pulled off her sword before settling on the ground. Slight circles colored the skin under her eyes, dirt was smudged on her skin and caked under her nails. She smelt of horse and body odor. With her hair not well-kept and her clothes sporting stains, it was clear Greer hadn't seen a bed or comfort in days. "Maybe we could've found a way. Maybe Kayl could've offered a serum to make Ian forget. I don't know, in the end that's neither here nor there."

Caitriona rubbed her hands over her arms, the presence of where Ian's body had laid pressing in on her across the opening. A red stain could be seen by the firelight—or perhaps it was only shadow—but Caitriona suspected it would live in her memory as blood lost with a man's life. Her stomach turned into a pit. She never witnessed someone die before.

Greer's eyes settled on her and Caitriona pulled her own gaze away from the reddened shadows to look at her sister.

Her sister.

Greer was the one true constant in her life, the person Caitriona could always confide in. She never quite felt that way with her mother, certainly never with her father, but Greer was always there. She was fiercely protective and deeply loving, and Caitriona would be lost without her.

Before Caitriona's powers appeared, when Greer traveled for weeks at a time, they rejoined when Greer returned home and were glued to each other's sides. But this separation seemed to create a distance between them that Caitriona never experienced before, and it left her tingling with unease.

"Hi," Caitriona mustered to say. Simple. Pathetic, perhaps. But Greer visibly softened.

"Hi, Cait." Greer allowed herself to smile.

Ailith reminded Caitriona of her sister in that way, neither smiled very often except when truly happy and at ease. But this expression was different; a relief to have her near, but it didn't reach Greer's tired eyes. Was she the cause of that? Caitriona's heart felt heavy with certainty that she was.

Greer turned and took in Ailith's sleeping form beside Caitriona. Ailith took time to fall asleep but the wine and pain killer helped her relax and drift off. She lay with her wounded cheek exposed to the air, puffy and angry from the stitches Barden gave. Caitriona reached forward and pulled the blanket further up on Ailith, tucking it under her chin.

"You care for her," Greer observed.

Caitriona shrugged. "Well, yes, we've been together for these past few weeks. We've grown fond of one another."

"No, that's not what I mean," Greer replied. She nodded toward Ailith. "I see the way you look at her. I see how she looks at *you*. You know that even at the end of all of this, if all goes according to plan, you'll never be able to be near Ailith again, don't you? After all of this, father wants to marry you off and will have her head. We'll have to ensure she can live peacefully far from Braewick. She'll be gone from our lives."

"Does the sun love the moon?" Caitriona interrupted. She looked at Ailith's sleeping form and everything within her yearned to reach forward and touch her. She was like a moth to a flame, pulled so immediately the sensation was bewildering. "Even though they're often apart, they still manage to share the sky every once in a while."

"I just don't want you to be hurt."

She didn't respond, she couldn't. It was too embarrassing. For all that she and Greer shared, gossip of crushes was never a topic. They were left to figure out love and lust on their own, their own parents being only an example of what they didn't want in their futures. The idea of her father forcing her into a marriage of his choosing made Caitriona cringe. What type of man would her father pick? Someone like him? Someone harsh and mean? She didn't even want to consider what awful future lay ahead of her when she had Ailith now.

"She won't hurt me. It's all just ... new. The feelings, this experience." Caitriona looked to the ground, blushing. Years prior, she kissed Callan in the shadows of the library. The dwindling light made her fumble, her nerves made her nearly miss his lips, but her heart rushed with quickened beats and her head spun with delight. Would she feel the same if she kissed Ailith?

She always found herself dutifully attracted to men. The number of men she came in contact with were few, but she crushed on many all the same. Guards in training mainly who she watched from an upstairs window. Their forms and voices, and all the parts that were so different from her own, were dreamt of at night. But she also found herself drawn to the softness of women and how they were so beautifully varied. Strong, muscular, thin, curved, she appreciated the striking range as an artist would, someone who takes note of the design and memorizes it with hope to replicate its beauty. That's all it was, that's all it ever was, because she was a princess and there were unspoken expectations of her.

Ailith allowed her to forget her expectations as the second daughter of the king. Ailith allowed her to daydream, and often those daydreams included Ailith by her side, her rough hands holding Caitriona's;

Ailith's brown eyes only seeing her's. Because over the last few weeks, that was exactly what they shared. They fully shared in the newness of all the lands they never saw before and the quiet moments when their eyes met.

Caitriona's feelings shifted in Stormhaven, but when the hunters circled them and she saw Ailith fall, her heart lurched into her throat. She would do anything for her. She hardly allowed herself to admit these thoughts. The first issue was finding Kayl, the second that she was turning into *something*, and third that perhaps Ailith didn't feel the same as Caitriona did—so why risk messing up the friendship they shared for one kiss? But to have Greer so easily pull the truth from Caitriona by simple observance left Caitriona embarrassed and shy.

"Cait," Greer sighed before offering a smile. "I don't care if you like her. I just ... I truly don't want you hurt is all. Not with the way father is."

"I know," Caitriona managed. The fire crackled and spit continuing the conversation while they fell into silence. Greer reached for a thick stick and put it over the flame, using another to push embers around. "Do you think he'll ever welcome me just like this? As someone with magic?"

Greer's eyes flashed, her face stern, and her sister's expression confirmed Caitriona's suspicions. Since leaving the castle, she hadn't just become something her father wouldn't accept, but already *was* something he didn't accept. The curse always existed in her, and somehow, her father sensed that.

Caitriona sighed. "Never mind. I already know."

"Tell me more about how you learned of your curse," Greer prodded, changing the subject like turning a page and Caitriona allowed herself to relax into the safer topic.

"We ended up in the Endless Mountains, beyond the mist." Caitriona smiled as her sister predictably looked up with immediate attention. She thought of Niveem for a moment, and the elder fae's permission to share the tales of the mist. If she could trust anyone, it was her sister. "It was by accident on our part; intentional by the mist. It came across the road and took us. Ailith found her way through it—a first, apparently. Beyond the mist is an entire queendom of fae and the mist is a defense mechanism."

"Amazing." Greer's brown eyes grew wider. "So, they're using magic?"

"They all have gifts. The mist shows the truth of those who enter. It showed I have this curse but that I, personally, meant no harm. It kills those with ill intent."

"And were they able to explain the curse at all?" Greer leaned forward.

"They concluded all that's happened is tied to the curse. We assume, like Ailith said, I'm changing into something. But that's all. They helped us draw maps to Beaslig, which is where Kayl is rumored to live."

"Are you heading there directly?"

"No, to Avorkaz first."

Greer moved her tongue behind her lips, considering for a moment, before shaking her head. "I was going to say it wouldn't be safe, but that's likely the safest city you and Ailith can be in. Perhaps they'd know you if you still had your red hair, but now ..." Greer laughed.

Caitriona smiled, warm from the sound of her sister's laughter, like walking into a firelit room after being out in the cold. Greer's laughter faded but her smile remained. "I should get back to the camp. We'll be by the road tonight. Build up your fire to stay warm. You and Ailith both need your rest, so I'll place men on the perimeter to keep watch. Pass through before you leave in the morning so I can see you off."

Greer climbed to her feet and Caitriona scrambled to hers, the two moving forward to one another, mirroring movements and embracing tightly. "It is so good to see you, Greer," Caitriona whispered, finding she didn't want to let go, not yet. She missed the safety her presence always gave her. "I've missed you so much. I wish you could travel the rest of the way with us."

Greer ran her hand over Caitriona's hair before moving her grip to Caitriona's shoulders and holding her at arm's length.

"I've missed you too and I can't wait for you to be home. But you've already made it so far and I know you're in good hands." Greer looked at Ailith and gave a nod. "Enjoy yourself a little, too. I'm almost certain the feelings are mutual."

Caitriona's cheeks grew hot and she hid her smile behind her hand, nodding as she did. Greer reached for Caitriona's chin, pushing it upward and bringing her gaze forward. She almost looked sad. There was knowledge behind her eyes that Caitriona couldn't place. Something that Greer wasn't ready to reveal.

"I'm serious. With all the calculated moves father does, we don't know how fleeting our chances to be happy may be."

CHAPTER TWENTY-THREE

AILITH

Ailith jolted to the waking world as the wine she guzzled wore off and the reality of what she had done set in. The realization spread through her, taking the discomfort from the cut in her face with it and spreading it through her limbs.

Death created by the need to protect, to save; that's the difference, that's what saves you, Ailith repeated to herself over and over as she lay on the ground, feeling the effects of the pain killing powder wear off and the throb in her cheek grow.

She couldn't pause to consider whether or not Ian would've harmed them; it was obvious when he came rushing through the trees with a sword drawn. She had to act, she had to protect, she had to save herself and Caitriona. She found no joy in taking his life, that was the difference, but she hoped Raum was right. She hoped that would save her. Caitriona listened with quiet sincerity as Ailith admitted Ian was the first person she killed.

"He seemed more of a problem for Greer than not. He would've killed you and he would've dragged me back to my father." Caitriona brushed Ailith's hair back from her face. "You saved me."

Ailith held that comment close to her breast, keeping it alive and bright to chase off the creeping darkness of doubt.

She slept in fitful bursts after that, reassured by Caitriona that her sister's men were nearby and there was no need for them to keep watch. They were granted privacy, but the group was close enough for protection and Ailith was grateful. She found she wasn't ready to share her time with the men she often saw in passing, even a few she worked with. But morning dawned and, as they packed to go, Caitriona urged Ailith to join Greer at the camp before they continued on.

"That's awful looking," Barden called from where he knelt beside the fire when Caitriona and Ailith led their horses to the ring of Greer's men.

"No thanks to you," Ailith retorted, her cheek swollen enough that her eyesight was obscured on her left side and the constant throb in her face made her head feel like it was ready to fall off. Plenty of water when she woke helped her head ache a little less, but then she attempted to eat breakfast and the motion of chewing made her face explode in pain. She stopped bleeding and it already looked as if the outer edges of the cut were starting to heal, that was good at least. The blood congealed elsewhere, gathering around the hasty stitch marks, but she still looked a sight.

Barden shrugged. "You look better than Ian at least."

Another guard grunted with suppressed laughter and began choking on his morning tea. Ailith raised a brow, immediately regretting the movement as her pain flared.

"If I may," said a younger man, with short brown hair and tan skin. His face lingered on the edge of Ailith's memory. It took a moment for her to recall he was in training with her years before but moved on to become a royal guard. He sat in the huddle of men separate from Barden, all working on their morning meal. His expression was one of friendly interest. "I'd suggest you visit a proper healer when you get to the next city, they'll likely pull those stitches out."

"Hopefully I won't die from infection before then," Ailith replied dryly.

Greer prepared her own horse for departure a short distance away, her appearance more orderly than the night before. She looked up from her bag and finished tying its straps to her horse. "So, you're off then?"

"Ready to go." Caitriona stepped forward and threw one arm around her sister, hugging her as tightly as she could.

"I believe you'll be there by evening, sooner if you both go at a quick clip." Greer offered after returning Caitriona's embrace. She turned to Ailith and looked her over once. The queenly pose she maintained at the Elder Tree when Ailith was given this task melted away. She softened around the edges and her jaw no longer clenched. In its place was a woman with plenty of knowledge that was road weary and concerned. "You *should* find a healer once you reach the city. Avorkaz accepts magic; perhaps you can find a magic salve that'll help it heal fast."

"I will, thank you." Unlike with the other guards, and despite that Greer seemed more relaxed, Ailith couldn't throw jokes at her; she viewed her with more cautious respect. "I do have a question though. Once we find Kayl, whether he can help us or not, what should we do afterward? There are people on the roads looking for us; how should we proceed?"

Greer rolled her head, cracking her neck as she looked to the trees with thought. "Take Caitriona to the closest hamlet or town outside the Mazgate Dominion and send a letter with her location. Get an inn for her to stay in so we can retrieve her."

"And what of me?" Ailith's stomach already began to drop.

Greer frowned, only furthering Ailith's discomfort. "If things go well, I'll supply you with gold for your aid, but I fear you'll have to find a new home. There's no possibility you can return to Braewick safely, not while my father lives. But I promise you, I'll ensure your parents are fine."

"We'll relocate your parents to wherever you settle," Caitriona broke in, her voice lilting like a songbird, but her smile didn't reach her eyes. She took Ailith's hand and gave it a squeeze. "And I'll visit. I'll demand to be able to travel."

Greer gave Caitriona a knowing look, who blushed under its weight.

Ailith noted the interaction with a spark of passing interest, but she was too distracted by what Greer admitted. When she set out on this venture, she knew there was a chance it wouldn't go well and she would lose everything, but now facing the possibility of never being able to return home, she wanted to fight off that outcome. No matter how it ended, good or bad, she wouldn't be able to go home, which was harder to bear than she thought.

The Elder Tree didn't grant her wish. It took her scrap of cloth into its heavy boughs and never promised anything, yet Ailith still foolishly assumed her desires would be met. She wished she could see the tree once more, if only to ask why it refused to grant her wish.

With a small sniff that conveyed more emotion than Ailith cared for, she pulled her hand from Caitriona's grip and rubbed her palms on her thighs. "Well, we should get going."

Caitriona hugged her sister once more. "I love you. I'll see you soon, I hope."

"Very soon." Greer's hands brushed over Caitriona's golden hair and cupped her sister's cheek in her hand. "Go on, get on your horse."

Caitriona led her mare away and Ailith stepped forward to do the same before Greer clapped her strong grip on Ailith's shoulder. Ailith grew still, tensing before turning, her face aching from the movement and swelling which made her already serious expression more like a glare. This was the second time an elder with power stopped her before they set off, the second time someone had something important to convey, but Greer scared Ailith more than Isla did.

"Try to save her," Greer whispered, her voice giving way to a slight quiver.

Ailith looked toward Caitriona who was on Butterscotch a few feet away, speaking to Barden who smiled up at her with familiarity displaying the years the guard knew the royal family. They laughed, oblivious to the two or the heartbreak in the elder Gablaigh daughter's voice. "I will," Ailith reassured Greer. "I'll save her, I promise. I have to."

Greer let Ailith go. "Travel safe, Ailith MacCree."

Ailith studied Greer for a moment. She could never fathom being born into the position of heir to the throne. Before all of this, it was due to the sheer amount of wealth and comfort the royal family had. It was nothing Ailith could understand. But now there was something like sympathy for the woman. Greer's entire life was decided for her before she was born, and Ailith couldn't comprehend the pressure she faced beside her growing worry for her sister. For the first time, Ailith offered Greer a genuine smile. "Goodbye, Your Highness."

Ailith walked her horse to the road before mounting it. Caitriona ended her conversation with Barden and led Butterscotch closer to Ailith's side. They waved goodbye and began their northern ride to Avorkaz, picking up pace once Greer and her guards were out of sight.

Travel was swift until noon when the gray skies finally opened and began dumping cold rain. It sank through the layers of their clothing and chilled their bones; even Ailith quivered under the hood of her cloak and knew without looking that Caitriona was likely frozen solid. The horses kicked up mud, coating their legs and bellies as the women pushed them forward at a quicker pace. The land became less desolate; farms and stone buildings peppered the landscape, clustering together then breaking apart with fields between. Fields were dug up, the summer crops long since harvested, and the trees dropped their leaves under the weight of the cold precipitation. The day progressed to something that chased farmers indoors and Ailith envisioned how lovely a warm drink beside a large fire would be.

The closer to Avorkaz they came, the busier the roads, the muddier the horses, and the more miserable the women became. When the massive stone walls for Avorkaz appeared and the road narrowed and grew busy with people waiting to enter the city through the main gate, the rain threatened to freeze anyone it touched with its cold embrace. The pair shivered, raising their faces to the guards who checked on the mud and rain splattered people passing through. Ailith pitied the guards for a moment as a gate guard herself, until one spoke.

"What's your business?" He was middle-aged, standing with his back against the open gate and his hood pulled up. Rain gathered on his hood and dripped off, hitting the tip of his nose on the way down. He took in Caitriona's gold eyes longer than Ailith was comfortable with and only sniffed at Ailith's presence.

"We're seeking safety," Ailith stated, drawing the man's attention back to her. "My friend here, she's begun to develop magic and we know she isn't safe within King Cearny's land."

The man scrutinized them both for a moment before turning his head and spitting into the muddy grass. "What's your magic?"

Caitriona's eyes went wide and Butterscotch took a step back, sensing her unease. "Uh ... flame. I can make flames."

The man narrowed his eyes and studied her, leaving Ailith itching to reach for the handle of her short sword. After a momentary pause the man stepped aside with a sniff. He wiped the edge of his nose with the back of his hand before pointing at a waterlogged pile of wood where a fire should have been. "If you can make a flame, why don't you start our fire?"

"Is this really necessary?" Ailith asked as Caitriona's face visibly paled. "Do you ask anyone who seeks safety such requests?"

"If she can make a flame, it shouldn't be an issue, should it?" the man growled. He rolled his eyes up to glare at Ailith. He took a step back and crossed his arms in waiting. Ailith's lips pressed together; his intention to refuse entrance until something happened was clear.

"It's ... it's fine." Caitriona dismounted her horse and handed the reins to Ailith. "I'll only be a moment and then we can be on our way."

"Cait ..." Ailith hissed under her breath and Caitriona gave her a look that left Ailith empty of words. She was going to make fire, even if it meant burning the gate down. Ailith urged her horse a step back, leading to a chorus of complaints rising in unison from the people waiting behind.

Caitriona faced the wet logs for a moment before pushing the hood of her cloak down and pulling off her travel gloves. Slipping them into the pockets of her pants, she rubbed her pale hands together before raising them before her. Closing her eyes, she took in a slow, even breath.

Nothing happened.

At least from the perspective of someone unfamiliar with Caitriona's abilities. The guard seemed unimpressed, but Ailith held her breath as Caitriona's nails grew thick and white, extending past her fingers and lengthening to points; scales broke out over the skin of her fingers with a white-gold shine, spreading up the back of her hands towards her wrists. Air shimmered before her hands, like heat rising off stone on a hot summer day and quivered down to the wet logs. At first, a sputter, a sizzle of cold rain bouncing off a hot surface. But gradually the sound grew and a curl of smoke inched its way through the driving rain. The air grew thick with the scent of rain hitting hot rocks, reminding Ailith of warmer days, but mixed with something fouler. Sulfur.

A moment later, flame sputtered to life. The once wet logs dried and where a fire hadn't existed before, it now grew into a hearty blaze that radiated warmth. The guard took a step back, a scowl on his face, and shrugged. "I've seen better." He stepped aside and held his arm aloft so they could pass.

Caitriona blinked with surprise, her eyes glowing and her clawed hands lowering. Ailith couldn't contain the laughter that rippled up her throat and rushed from her mouth, her face throbbing with pain from the smile that attempted to spread on her face.

"*Seen better?*" Caitriona hissed to herself as she mounted Butterscotch and took her reins.

"Maybe you should practice your technique," Ailith teased.

Caitriona shifted on her horse, pulling the edges of her cloak over her clawed hands with a pout to her lips.

Beyond the city gates, Avorkaz was a tight pathway between gray stone buildings that stood two to three stories tall, sometimes more. Vendors lined the paths and a hum of people moving about and attending to their own needs bounced off the walls with a splash of uniqueness Ailith never saw in Wimleigh. Where the city seemed gray, the people brought brightness to the scenery.

"You don't have to hide your hands, Cait," Ailith said as they were propelled forward by the crowd and less by their own direction. "Look around you."

Those who wandered the street, whether by foot, horseback, or cart, were a blend of beings Ailith only ever heard of. Fae of different forms appeared; some with pointed ears and others smaller with neat wings draped from their shoulders like a cloak. Dwarves with bushy beards, stout and strong, made their way through the crowd carrying hearty axes and swords. No one seemed to notice Caitriona, or if they did, they didn't care.

The lower building levels were businesses while the top floors held living quarters. Some windows stood open to people leaning out to talk to others on the street. Others pulled laundry in from lines that crossed over the street, the fabrics dripping wet from the rain and their chance to dry in the air gone. The scents of various foods filled the air and Ailith licked her lips with hunger. The further into the city they went, the more hustling people pressed in on all sides. Ailith spotted a stall with a sign for renting, selling, and boarding horses, and she urged them toward it.

"I'm somewhat sad to get rid of our horses," Caitriona said as she dismounted and pulled her bag from Butterscotch.

"I never owned a horse before." Ailith tugged her pack off Inkwell and shrugged it onto her back. "But I hope Inkwell lives a happy life as a city horse. He'll enjoy this much more than the cold mountains."

"Perhaps they'll be here when we return and we can trade our mountain horse for them." Caitriona pet Butterscotch's nose as one of the stall hands approached. Ailith reviewed the collection of horses and picked the largest beast they found, a black draft horse with a glossy mane whose back towered over the women and was broad enough to fit them both as well as their supplies. Caitriona gladly graced the mount with the name Onyx and bid adieu to their trusted horses who were accepted as a trade. After a payment of gold to keep Onyx in the stall until they were ready to leave, they departed for the nearest inn.

The inn wasn't particularly interesting, a gray building like the rest with a narrow staircase winding up to small landings leading to rooms on each level. Dropping off their bags and weapons in the cold room with two beds, similar to their previous ones, they lit a fire, washed the majority of the muck and grime from their faces and hands, and changed into less rain-soaked clothing before returning to the streets.

"We need to get you to a healer." Caitriona stopped Ailith at the bottom of the inn's dimly lit stone steps, her fingers hovering over Ailith's cheek. "Your face looks awful."

"We'll keep an eye out while we look for clothing. Don't worry," Ailith replied, cautiously touching her cheek and grimacing. Caitriona frowned and Ailith couldn't help but take her hand, still slick with scales and the pressure of pointed nails.

She was half tempted to lift Caitriona's hand to her lips, but fought off the urge, instead blushing and sporting a lopsided grin whilst reveling in the feel of their hands entwined. Her smile grew as Caitriona gripped Ailith's hand in return before pulling her onto the busy street.

Somehow, she could ignore the pain in her cheek as her joy was too great.

The rain stopped while they were indoors and they followed a cobblestone boulevard with dancer's steps as they avoided runoff and puddles. They strolled to a square that was bordered by an impressive stone structure with stained glass arched windows depicting flowers and sunbursts. Booths lined the square on all sides; a marketplace, filled with hearty gourds and root vegetables for sale, as well as buckets of ground grain tucked beneath large sweeping tents. Even small pop-up eateries were established on the still-wet streets, and they ate their fill, too hungry from skipping their afternoon meal to ignore the tantalizing scents coming from the fires set in low curves of stone built for such things. They took seats at the scattering of stools and tables and watched the mixture of humans and fae move through the square. It reminded Ailith of Stormhaven. A moist, cold, gray version of the town, but they didn't have to hide and it made Ailith slightly drunk with ease.

After eating, they found a tent filled with heavy, fur-lined trousers and tops, as well as thicker cloaks and sleeping pads. The scent of animal hides hung on the moist air as they inspected the selection. The fur lining was a flourish of colors, grays and whites, blacks and reddish browns.

"Coins from Braewick," the female dwarf shopkeeper said as Caitriona paid for the pile of clothing. She held the coin up, scrutinizing the Elder Tree's symbol with her dark eyes.

"We abandoned our homes there," Ailith offered and the woman glanced from the coin to Ailith, and then to Caitriona's still changed hands.

She patted Caitriona's hand. "You'll find many people here who did the same. Don't worry, this city welcomes all. Well, besides King Cearny and his lot."

Caitriona smiled, tight-lipped, before gathering the armful of clothing from the shop. With the rain ending, the streets continued to fill. People hurried home before the last of the day's light drifted from the sky; others selected food from the market; some found people they knew and chatted. Nearby, the cautious starting notes from two street performers with hair like Lumia's played with a fiddle and pipe. Life was abundantly normal for those around them, while Ailith felt exhausted from the weight of their conquest and all they endured thus far. They sat on the edge of the environment, quiet observers, and no one knew their predicament.

"It's magic," Caitriona said, eyes wide. She nodded towards the musicians. "They're covering their wings, do you see? It's a glamor."

Ailith did not see. She felt the surge of energy around them, a tingling in the air like static that made the hairs on her arms rise, but no wings or any indication of such. "Their backs look normal to me."

Caitriona pushed Ailith along until they stood behind the performers. "You can see the wings pressing into their clothing from this side, see?" But she still couldn't, although she didn't tell Caitriona such. She gave a nod and a smile as they continued, but Ailith's attention remained on the scene. Was this a further step into the curse? This sudden ability to see things that Ailith couldn't? Perhaps doing party tricks for bitter guards wasn't so wise and the small use of her magic pushed her further along the road of the curse.

Ailith coddled this worry as they circled the square until they stood before a large tent pressed against half the length of the building. Jars and bottles lined wooden shelves, herbs hung from beams across the tent roof, and an old man and woman worked beneath. "That looks like a healer," Ailith observed, but Caitriona wasn't paying attention at all. Her face was upturned, eyes locked on the building. "What's wrong?"

"It's a library," Caitriona said. Ailith softened and held out a hand.

"Go to the library and sniff some books."

Caitriona pulled her gaze back to street level. "We have to get your cheek looked at."

"I'm fully capable of doing that by myself. Plus, it's right beside the library entrance. I'll come up when I'm done. Just don't get lost within the shelves."

Caitriona considered Ailith's offer long enough for a smile to flash across her face before beelining for the steps and toward the doors. Libraries were safe havens, that's what Ailith's father always said. They were built to withstand a lot because neither wind nor rain nor humidity nor chill were allowed inside. He always told Ailith that if ever she needed to seek shelter, the library was where she should go.

Hopefully that line of thought worked for the safety of runaway princesses as well.

Ailith shuffled toward the medicine tent, pausing at the entrance to look over the low-lit area and catching the eye of the woman. She was shorter than Ailith, hunched and with deep creases in her face. She reminded Ailith immediately of Isla, which was a surprising comfort. She didn't realize how much she had grown to like the old witch until spotting this woman. The very reminder of Isla made Ailith inclined to remain.

"I suspect you need your cheek looked at?" the woman asked, her voice like gravel.

"That's correct," Ailith replied as the woman waved a hand toward an open table and Ailith settled her new clothing upon it.

"Whoever stitched your cheek did an awful job." The woman waddled toward the back of the tent and pointed at a deep chair. "But I suppose it worked in a pinch."

"I suppose so. I hope you have some herbs or a serum that can help with healing, or anything to better clean out the wound."

"We have it all, dear." The woman smiled, some teeth missing. Tan skin, dark eyes and hair, and ears that ended in a point, but not quite as sharp as the fae from the Endless Mountains, the woman brushed her hair from her face and waved over the man in the tent. He was taller than the woman, likely taller than Ailith as well if his shoulders weren't so hunched nor his back curved, but just as old. He came closer and seemed mostly human, at least from what Ailith could tell. Ailith sat, the old wood creaking underneath her weight and wobbling slightly with uneven legs.

"Ah, so I see you've been stitched up." He pulled out a stool and sat beside her. His accent was immediately familiar, like home, like Braewick Valley. "I'm Declan, and I've worked in medicine for years. My wife is May and she deals in healing magic."

"That sounds like a competitive marriage," Ailith joked, bringing a smile to Declan's face.

"We certainly were competitors when we met but ended up working as a happy partnership on many fronts. Now tilt your head back so I can look." Declan pulled out thin scissors and moved a lantern closer. "Your accent reminds me of a place I once lived."

"I was thinking the same about you." Ailith tried to keep her head still as he poked her cheek.

"What brings you to Avorkaz, then?"

"We left Braewick, my friend and I." Sticking to a truth with little detail was better than lying.

"Ah, as have many before you. I left with May when magic was banned." Declan lifted a paste-like substance and slathered it onto her cheek. Immediately, the pain disappeared and her cheek went numb.

"And has Avorkaz been good to you?" Ailith tried to keep her voice steady as Declan lifted scissors and her body went stiff with nerves.

"I've enjoyed our time here. May misses her home though."

"Don't confuse the girl," May grumbled as she came over with a collection of bottles in her arms, laying them out on the table beside Declan. "Braewick was never my home. I missed home long before we came to Avorkaz. Here, at least, my kind and my abilities are accepted."

"Where was home?" Ailith trailed off, losing her bravery the moment the scissors opened and neared her face. She clamped her eyes shut and gripped the arms of the chair, holding very, very still. Hearing the metal shift of the scissors so close to her face and the tug of the stitches pulled from her cheek made her insides twist. She was glad she hadn't had an evening meal yet, because she was certain she would've lost it to the cobblestones.

"Caermythlin."

"Oh, my friend's mother is from Caermythlin," Ailith mumbled out the corner of her mouth furthest from the scissors.

"Then I'm sorry."

"How come?" Ailith opened her eyes as the pressure receded. Declan moved quickly, gathering a clean cloth and pressing it to her face with one hand as he reached for a different salve with the other.

May narrowed her eyes and tilted her head. "The town was ruined some years ago, all of its people gone, either killed or fled."

"Oh." When Isla said the town was disbanded, Ailith suspected there was more to the story. Much more. She looked away, opting to study the collection of items Declan laid out. "I didn't know that. I thought it dispersed. I'm sorry."

Declan wiped Ailith's cheek clean before rubbing the new salve over the open wound and patting herbs on top. "This should stop the bleeding and prevent infection." He looked at May. "Do you have the broadroot leaves?"

She passed over chopped green leaves in a clay bowl. He scooped them up and pressed them against Ailith's cheek. "You're going to look quite the sight for a bit. Let me wrap your head to keep your cheek secure and the herbs and salves from rubbing off. Wear it for a night and take it off in the morning. Then you can wash your face and you should be fine."

"Thank you." Ailith sat up, remaining still as Declan wrapped white linen under her chin and up the sides of her head, tying the fabric into a knot at the top. "Do you have any items for sale? My friend and I are looking for a family friend. Someone who once knew her mother. Our search is taking us into the mountains by the pass."

"What do you need?" May asked as Declan cleaned his supplies.

Ailith glanced at the gory remains of the thread Barden used to stitch Ailith's cheek closed and hesitated. The woman raised her chin knowingly and turned on her heel, moving back to the herb covered side and pulling items from her shelf. She waved Ailith over.

"This is a tonic that'll chase away any sign of incoming illness and the beginning of fevers." Pulling a brown glass with a red wax seal from the shelf, she handed it to Ailith. She reached for other glasses with different colored seals. "This will help to keep the chill of the cold at bay; if you're riding there from Avorkaz, you'll likely have to spend a night on the road and this will help you survive it. I don't know why they haven't opened an inn at the midway point yet. Anyway, this black-capped one can help ease the pain of any injuries you may sustain."

Ailith held the three glass bottles in her hand, looking at the liquids sloshing about within. "Do you have anything to hold them?"

The old woman reached under the shelf, pulling out a belt with leather pouches sewn on the side, and a small canister about the size of Ailith's palm. "Wear this across your chest, the bottles will be close to your heart and easy to grab. Also, don't forget this salve, it'll help your cheek to continue to heal."

Ailith looked over the supplies and back at May, the old woman smirked with amusement, knowing full well she would get every piece of coin she requested.

A moment later, Ailith sprinted up the stairs of the library, nearly tripping and dropping the winter clothing along the way. With her face free from pain, a spring returned to her step. She was excited to show Cait the supplies she purchased. The closer they were to Kayl, the more she wanted to hope. If *she* couldn't return to her home, at least Caitriona could return to *hers* and continue life as normal. They could move Ailith's parents somewhere—maybe to Stormhaven or even Avorkaz. Caitriona would be able to visit. Things would be alright. But first, they had to reach the northern pass and find the mage. It was coming together, it had to.

"Cait?" Ailith called as she entered the library. The wooden shelves had more books than Ailith ever saw and based on the spines, they were in more languages than she knew existed. Long tables nestled in the pathways between shelves and far overhead lanterns were blazed with flickering flame, casting the room in a soft golden light that reminded Ailith of Caitriona's changed eyes.

Caitriona was, however, nowhere to be seen and after passing the fifth row and not finding her, Ailith's jovial mood lessened and a tightness gripped her shoulders.

"Cait?" She earned a glare from a man with a long beard and small glasses. Ailith cringed. "Sorry."

She reached the tenth row when she saw long golden hair falling down the back of a woman. She sat before one of the stained-glass windows at a wooden table at the end of the row, back bent and head down.

"Cait," Ailith sighed as she turned down the row. Her boots clomped against the hard floor, making far more noise and leaving a trail of muddy prints behind her on the once white, clean marble. "You frightened me; I couldn't find you. Look at this ridiculous wrap I was given for my cheek, isn't it—"

Caitriona turned to Ailith. Her face was wet from tears. A large book sat open before her, a sketch of Stormhaven on one page and small printed words on the other.

"May we go back to the inn?"

Ailith stared at her with surprise, the wrap around her head forgotten as her lips parted with concern.

"Yes, of course." Ailith checked Caitriona over for any signs of physical pain, but it appeared to be only emotional. Caitriona was already rising on her feet and abandoning the book. "Let's go back now."

Caitriona began walking down the aisle, oblivious to the full arms of what Ailith carried. Ailith glanced at the book, her eyes only catching a word or two before she turned to leave. All she was able to obtain from the quick glance of the weathered book's pages repeated in her mind like thunder echoing off the valley hills: *The Conquest of Gil'dathon and Killing of Fae.*

CHAPTER TWENTY-FOUR

C aitriona sat on the floor of their rented room weeping with her knees pulled to her chest as her hands covered her face. They returned to their room swiftly, dropping supplies on the closest bed before sitting on the floor beside the fire, warming themselves as Caitriona poured out all she dared to learn in the short span of time they were separated.

"The Avorkaz Library is a stunning place with far more tomes than I've ever seen," Caitriona had begun. "Even with access to my father's personal archives, they can't be compared. I was completely overwhelmed with choice, but I picked a book about the history of Wimleigh Kingdom. I thought it'd be interesting to read the perspective of our kingdom from an outsider."

Ailith eased to the floor, her attention locked on Caitriona. Through all they experienced, she never saw her this upset or shaken. She fought the urge to touch Caitriona while she stared at the flames, wringing her hands together until she had to wipe her eyes.

"I began at the back of the book. I figured I'd see information on my family there. Right away, there was detail about the dragon attack and even mention of my disappearing from the public eye. Of course, the truth of what happened wasn't revealed. They did include a list of reasons I may have disappeared though, all the ones you've told me. But it was everything in the book *before* the attack that's so upsetting."

Feeling the need to keep her hands busy, Ailith sipped water from a mug, the cool liquid pooling into her stomach. She fed off Caitriona's energy and discomfort spread into her limbs, making her restless. "What did it say?"

"There was a list of every city my father and grandfather claimed, as well as another with the names of cities in their original languages. I read further and the book said these names were bequeathed hundreds of years before by the inhabitants of the towns and cities unassociated to Wimleigh Kingdom. But my father and every tutor I've ever had has always told me the names were changed due to a mutual decision when my family came to control those lands. I was told all conquests were, in the end, a *mutual* decision. That the ownership was handed to my father because those who lived there saw the obvious benefits to joining the empire."

"All except the Mazgate Dominion," Ailith commented as she stretched her legs before her. "They dared to push back."

"Exactly. And what's worse, it seems that every city, every town, wasn't some simple decision. They were taken by force. The original names were removed, their languages squashed and the common tongue enforced. Those with magic weren't simply asked to leave. They didn't choose to travel on roads to new lands. They were slaughtered."

Ailith remained silent, a sick feeling sweeping over.

"I read about the conquest of Stormhaven, or Gil'dathon as it was originally called. This advance happened shortly before I was born, while Greer was still very young. Entire lives were ruined, entire histories," Caitriona wept. "The book details that while my grandfather began these conquests, it was my father who got his stride by destroying entire towns. He led the destruction at Stormhaven's city center. My father's men burned libraries under his direction, they tried all they could to wipe the land clean of their previous history, of their previous rulers. He wanted to present it as this perfect city that was perfectly ruled. The teachers at Braewick taught me it practically fell into his hands, that they were desperate for his help. They only educated us with what my father deemed appropriate. He had final say of everything

Greer and I learned, he decided what the guards were taught, and it's all lies. It's a history of his own making rather than fact. The book says Stormhaven was a bustling seaport that had even more prosperity than it currently does. It had a mixture of people. Humans and fae alike but also creatures that belong to the sea.

"The book described what he instructed his men to do, what he found to be adequate behavior," Caitriona continued. Her skin paled as she shook her head with disgust. "Remember when the fae said the bones from my back looked like something they saw before? *Wings,* fairy wings, snapped from the backs of fae. *My father did that.* He mutilated and murdered people because of how they were born. Because they have gifts they never asked for, but gifts all the same that gave them an advantage over him.

"He lied. He lied to everyone." Caitriona's brows furrowed as her sadness turned to rage. "He's made Wimleigh Kingdom believe this story that we're their *saviors.* These valiant people who came to help a humble yet struggling city, who raised it into gleaming success, and it's all a *lie.*

"What did my mother think of all this? No wonder they seem so different, so incompatible. If he can do this to all these people, I don't think he would let her live if he knew she was fae."

The flood of words ran out and Caitriona fell silent, her palms up as her hands fell to rest upon her lap, as if begging the universe to place facts into her palm and make sense of it all. Ailith stared at the fire, turning her mug in her hands as she considered her next words.

"I was taught much of the same," Ailith admitted, drawing Caitriona's attention. Ailith's shoulders dropped, the weight of the information heavy. "We don't have great schools in our part of the city, but children learn all the same. We were always told that what our kingdom did was a good thing."

She was fooled as much as Caitriona. The difference being that Caitriona was lied to by her father and mother. They had the correct knowledge but chose to block her from accessing it. For Ailith, she had the lack of opportunity. Who were they, the lower class of Wimleigh Kingdom, to know the truth of matters? They didn't have the option, there was no extra coin to travel to seaside cities and visit other lands.

They remained where they were born and were lucky if they rose up to a new home with more space and have a well-paying job before they died. For those who arrived from outside Braewick Valley, like Ailith's mother, questions of how their towns crumbled or why they moved were often met with side glances and silence. Had Ailith's mother partaken in this genocide? Had her mother turned the other cheek to neighbors with magic as they were killed?

To Ailith, it seemed very easy for Cearny to create an elaborate lie for his citizens to believe because how would they ever know any better? She considered May and Declan in the square, and the many others who easily accepted that she and Caitriona arrived from Braewick and Caitriona had powers. Avorkaz was its own city, but it took in many people who abandoned Wimleigh Kingdom for a chance to freely be themselves. She thought of the old women in the dredges of Braewick City, the healers who cured colds and tried to mend broken bones. There was always whispered rumor that once, long before, they were magic users, witches, or mages forced to bury their past. Perhaps it was less rumor but the truth of history trying to resurface like a buried artifact rising from the rock bed.

"I feel utterly selfish," Caitriona blurted, breaking the silence between them. She hastily wiped her face before staring at the fire that reflected in the shimmering tears of her gold eyes. "Because I'm angry. I'm so upset for all those people. I feel guilty, like I had a hand in it. All of this was done by *my* father. Yet my first thought, the one that keeps churning over and over again in my mind is the thought that 'I wish I didn't know.'

"I wish I didn't know and I could just go home, but home in the sense of a place I feel safe, a place I feel loved. I don't know if that's Braewick anymore. I wish I could just be done with all of *this*." She held up her hands, the last glimmering scales that formed that afternoon lingering on her fingertips, her nails still thick, still pointed, but marginally less than before. "But I don't know *how* I can go back. Even if we get rid of this curse, even if my hair turns red again and my eyes blue, I don't know how I can go back. I don't know how I can face my father again after what I've read, because I know without a doubt, that if he sees me like this, if he knows what I am capable of, he'll kill me."

"But a curse was placed on you," Ailith attempted, trying to find some way to comfort her. "You didn't ask for this."

"The fae didn't ask for it either," Caitriona pointed out. "If my father can so readily kill those who look different, and those who have magic gifts, he won't stop simply because I've been cursed. I wish I never knew about all these horrors; I wish I never wanted to travel; I wish I never wished for more. I wish none of this happened, none of it."

Ailith leaned back slightly, the blow of Caitriona's words striking her like a slap. Caitriona, oblivious to the effect of her words, tilted her head back, and slumped against the footboard of the bed, the fight leaving her. A tear fell from her eye and left a wet path down the curve of her cheek. Ailith reached forward and caught it with her finger, wiping it away. She paused before pushing the pad of her thumb over Caitriona's cheek as she continued to wipe away the wetness there, carefully keeping her face blank, and hiding her hurt.

"Perhaps we call it an early night," Ailith said. "This has all been ... a lot. And it's fine to take a minute to recover. I'll get things ready for tomorrow, but you can rest for a little while. We can get a late dinner."

Spent from her tears and consumed by thoughts, Caitriona accepted Ailith's help to stand and crawl into the free bed. She curled on her side, quiet, with her back to the room. Ailith waited until she suspected Caitriona fell asleep before working on their bags. She laid out their warmer clothes for the rest of their travels and organized for this final leg while her mind wandered. Guilt itched at her cheeks and tugged her lips into a frown. Although she hadn't done any of the atrocities the king had, she still had a hand in it because she accepted what histories were offered to her and never questioned it—at least not enough to seek out truth. The entire kingdom was guilty.

Settling on the edge of the bed amongst their supplies, she sighed. Maybe not returning to Wimleigh Kingdom was the right decision. Maybe she could get her parents to leave. The idea of staying there under Cearny's rule knowing what she knew now felt wrong—she had no political power; how could she fight his decisions?

Ailith began replacing her loose bowstring as night settled on Avorkaz, her mind emptying from the upset as she focused on the task at hand. She hadn't done much when Caitriona whispered, "Ailith?"

Her tone demanded attention and secrecy, one best suited between intakes of breath and sheets. Caitriona sat up in bed, her hair like a waterfall around her shoulders, her face pale and her lips flush. "Would you mind laying with me for a bit?"

Ailith blinked and nervously bit her lips, nodding slowly as she got to her feet. She abandoned her work on top of the empty bed and kicked off her shoes.

Caitriona shifted to make room, her eyelids lowered and her cheeks flushed. Ailith thought, briefly, of the night the thunderstorm shook her from her sleep and how Caitriona comforted her. She had never truly consoled someone. Not her parents, and she hadn't many friends. Even in her short relationship years before it was primarily made up of mouths to flesh and quick romps in shadowed places between training. As with everything else, however, it was different with Caitriona. They constantly mirrored one another's needs.

They curled into each other, face to face as they lay on their sides. Ailith lay straight, one arm curled under her head and the other to her side, wanting to reach for Catriona but simultaneously afraid to overstep. But she needn't worry as Caitriona moved first, reaching forward and gently running her still-clawed nails along the wrap that curled around Ailith's head.

"I'm sorry, Ailith."

"For what?"

"Wishing this never happened." Her hand lifted and her fingertips brushed through Ailith's loose hair. "Despite all that I said ... you're the one thing I don't regret. You're the one thing I want to take with me."

Caitriona's honesty hit Ailith squarely in her heart. The weight of it all squeezed Ailith tight. The concern of failing her mission and Caitriona, the worry for whatever was before them, the fear of never being able to see her parents again, the heaviness of having killed Ian only the night before, and the knowledge she would do it again if given the opportunity was all too much. Caitriona's words were enough to undo the strength of her carefully constructed will. It filled her until she burst. The mask that kept her emotions tidy and concealed slipped.

Ailith's eyes burned as tears began to spill, she sniffed and groaned, embarrassment washing over her. "I hate crying." She wiped at her tears and rolled onto her back. Keeping her eyes to the ceiling, Ailith avoided eye contact with Caitriona until soft hands and the gentle press of elongated nails touched Ailith's uncovered cheek, urging her to turn and look again.

Caitriona shifted on the bed, moving closer. They were only a breath apart now, and Caitriona's voice a whisper. "Ailith MacCree, I swear to you, you've been the one constant source of safety and the one constant thought on my mind, during this entire time. Everything feels like it's crumbling and I don't know if I'm going to survive this, but I'm glad that if it all ends in the mountains, if I'm doomed and I never go home, then at least I get to have you by my side."

Their breaths were in sync, air meeting and mingling between them like a pulsing light ready to expand over shadowed places and bring warmth to areas touched by cold.

"I wish ..." Ailith whispered as Caitriona's thumb made lazy circles on her uninjured cheek, her nail scratching lightly along Ailith's skin. The sensation sent a shiver down Ailith's spine and her breath caught in her throat.

"Hmm?" Caitriona urged, her gaze steadily meeting Ailith's.

"I wish I didn't have this stupid wrap around my head."

Caitriona blinked and laughed, her hand pulling away as color formed on her cheeks like the bloom of a rose. She rolled onto her own back as she smiled.

"Wait, no. Don't move away."

Ailith reached for her shoulder, urging her to roll back into her waiting arms. Ailith studied Caitriona's eyes—like the richest of spring sunrises and the gleam of jewelry. Most of Ailith's life, she had wishes and desires left unspoken because she learned long before, that to speak them out loud only gave them power to make her hurt when she never obtained what she wanted. But with Caitriona lying beside her, looking as she did, Ailith for once allowed her heart to speak its desires. "Don't leave me."

Caitriona's smile was soft and sincere as she reached to Ailith's face, framing it with both her hands. "I won't."

Ailith wondered frequently over the last number of days how Caitriona's lips would taste. She wondered how they would feel when they were swollen from kissing and how lovely it would be to slip her fingers through the long, wild, golden locks that spilled from Caitriona's head. She wondered about the softness of Caitriona's belly, the curve of her thighs, and if she would ever be able to run her hands down the princess's body and bow between her legs.

As the autumn rains ceased and early snowfall began to softly fall, burying Avorkaz in muffled stillness, Ailith explored something new she hadn't dared to completely imagine because it only raised her hopes. She learned important things as the snow blanketed the gray city. That Caitriona's lips tasted of strawberries and were soft like rose buds, her hair was smooth as silk and glimmered while in her hand, she was ticklish in the curve of her neck, and when Ailith bowed to the princess for the first time, her moans ravished Ailith with glee. Ailith also learned that she could cry from simple joy and the relief of having found her heart's hunger fulfilled and satisfied at last.

CHAPTER TWENTY-FIVE

AILITH

Ailith woke before the sun. She was tangled with Caitriona, the wrap around her head having barely made it through the night, while their clothing was left scattered on the floor. They hadn't gotten much sleep, perhaps a few hours as they focused on each other. Yet Ailith never felt so rested.

She slipped from bed, careful not to wake Caitriona, and tiptoed over the remnants of the dinner they shared, naked beside blankets they wrapped around their forms as they sat before the fire late that night. They were drunk on love and mead, and fully ignoring what lay ahead of them. It was possibly the best night of Ailith's life. They'd enjoyed themselves—truly enjoyed themselves—until they were too exhausted to stay awake any longer.

Ailith tiptoed to a speckled mirror hanging above a wash bowl, a small smile played on her lips as she thought of Caitriona gently running her fingers over the healing scars of Ailith's shoulder and ribs hours before.

Forcing herself away from her thoughts, Ailith lit a candle, then turned to the wrap around her head, untying it and peeling the fabric away from her cheek. The cut was ugly, but less so than with the haphazard stitching Barden had done. With a cool cloth, Ailith carefully wiped away the herbs and salves Declan and May applied to her wound, revealing skin and what looked like the beginnings of a scab. It would certainly scar, but if that meant another kissable place for Caitriona, Ailith didn't mind.

"Magic," Ailith whispered, patting her cheek dry; the swelling already lessened, and the area around the cut was only slightly raised. The smile she couldn't seem to remove from her face didn't even hurt. She fished out a comb from her bag and brushed her hair quickly before slipping back under the covers.

Curling her body against the princess, she pulled the blankets over her shoulders, and Caitriona sighed. Ailith wanted to go back to sleep herself, to dream happy hopes and fantasies of what could be, but she lay awake and considered their path forward. It would take a day and a half to reach Beaslig, and then they had to find Kayl. With any luck, Kayl could remove the curse.

Try to save her, Greer said, and the worry she wouldn't sat like a ball of lead in her gut.

Slipping her arm around Caitriona's waist and pulling her flush against her body, her chest to Caitriona's back, Ailith breathed in her scent and memorized the way the hairs on the back of her neck stood when Ailith's breath hit Caitriona's skin. Caitriona stirred. She rolled toward Ailith, a murmur of a word in her sigh that Ailith caught with her lips, which turned to a hum of pleasure before Caitriona hid her smile in the curve of Ailith's neck. They remained this way, taking note of each other's bodies and memorizing the sight of one another's smiles until the city outside their window grew blue with dawn's light on a recently snowed upon world.

Neither wanted to get out of bed and begin the next leg of their journey. Despite going forward together, their time at the inn would be the last opportunity they had completely to themselves and neither wanted it to end. But as the light went from blue to white, and the sounds of the city increased, they dressed in their layers and left the warmth of their little room behind.

"This is the earliest I've ever seen snow," Caitriona said as they mounted Onyx at the stables. Ailith climbed up before Caitriona and the princess slipped her arms around her waist, giving her a gentle hug before taking the reins and leading them out. Between the two, Caitriona was the most skilled with horses, and Ailith would sit in front with the ability to use her bow if necessary.

They left Avorkaz's gates and turned eastward toward the mountains that appeared like faded ghosts against the snowy land. A powder of white stuck to the long pieces of grass but melted into the muddy ground on the roadway—saturated as it was from the heavy rains the day before, and trails of footprints that already came and went. But the white skies produced a never-ending light snow that caught on Onyx's coat and the fur of their cloaks. The air was dry and crisp, and their breaths curled from their mouths, all the better reason to hold each other close as their horse moved along the rocky incline toward the mountain pass.

With the snow-filled clouds, night came on quickly and they dug through a thin layer of snow against a boulder to find shelter from the wind. They huddled close together, not bothering to pull their hands free from their gloves or remove the hood of their cloaks. Onyx stood nearby, content in the cold with his thick coat and bag of food. Despite that Caitriona brought fire to a pile of sticks, they both suspected it was likely to be a long night.

"The woman I purchased the salves from gave me this to keep warm," Ailith offered, pulling the blue wax bottle from the belt. She worked off the waxy top and pulled the cork free, releasing the scent of heated herbs and spices from the liquid within. Pulling the piece of paper with instructions, Ailith twisted to read them by firelight. "She wrote we should take a spoonful in the evening to warm us through the night."

"And you trust the woman?" Caitriona asked, reaching for the bottle and scrutinizing its contents.

"What's the worst that could happen?" Ailith replied dryly. "You're cursed and I'll likely never be welcomed back in Braewick Valley. At least we won't freeze to death ... probably."

Caitriona sighed and offered the bottle back to Ailith. "You can go first. I'm already cursed, maybe we both can be."

"It would have helped if we had a spoon." Ailith laughed as she eyed the bottle. Shrugging, she tilted it back, pouring a small amount into her mouth and squeezing her eyes shut as she swallowed. The liquid burned as it rushed down her throat and poured into her stomach, bringing out a hearty cough that shook Ailith's ribs. She held the bottle out to Caitriona. "Better or worse, it certainly sets fire to your insides."

Caitriona took the bottle and a quick sip before coughing into her hand. "This is awful!"

But as May said it would, it warmed them. The liquid held a spiciness foreign to most meals in Braewick that warmed them from the inside out. Before the cold pressed in on their heavy wardrobe, they were as comfortable as the night before whilst nude before a fireplace.

"I'd rather we were back at the inn," Caitriona said with a lazy smile as she curled against her.

"You've read my mind." Ailith kissed the top of Caitriona's forehead before wrapping an arm around her, the other hand gripped the hilt of her short sword just in case. "Perhaps after the curse's removed and we head toward home, we can go back to Stormhaven, to that first little inn with the view of the sea and wait for Greer there."

"We'll get one bed this time," Caitriona murmured as sleep laid its heavy hand on her.

Before long, they fell into a dreamless sleep with Onyx standing near, clutching each other as Ailith softened from the feel of Caitriona's body against hers.

They woke in the early hours just before dawn. A thin layer of snow took hold of their clothing and the fire diminished, but the warmth from the potion kept them free from frostbite and chill. After eating, Ailith climbed upon a large stone to mount Onyx. She held her hand down for Caitriona but she hesitated, her eyes looking down the road to the steep incline into the mountains.

"So, this is it."

"You say that as if you're facing a death sentence," Ailith replied, forcing her tone to be lightly teasing but finding her throat tighten as if her heart was reaching up to force the words out. She wanted to believe but found herself doubting.

"Maybe it is." Caitriona continued to stare at the horizon.

"This may be the end of the curse, keep that in mind." Ailith leaned forward, squeezing her shoulder. "And I'm sure Kayl will be happy to see you. You're the little girl he saved, after all."

Caitriona took in a slow, long breath, then let it out bit by bit. She took Ailith's hand. "Just don't leave me during all of this, alright?" Caitriona whispered into Ailith's ear after mounting Onyx. She leaned forward, resting her chin on Ailith's shoulder. "Whatever happens. If Kayl can do anything to help. Please, please don't leave me."

"I think you'll find it quite hard to get rid of me." Ailith twisted her torso and met Caitriona's eyes. "I won't be going anywhere."

They moved at a crawl. The uphill climb was a gradual process that felt all the longer as the skies remained white and snow continued drifting down. They passed only a few travelers along the route, people with carts or multiple horses, and another hunting party, all who left them alone. Every traveler was too focused on getting to their next destination and away from the cold.

The further they progressed, the higher they were, with the lower lands and the city of Avorkaz now a distant, faded outline on the horizon. By late afternoon, the snow lessened to the occasional flake, but the sun still didn't show. On the breeze was the scent of woodsmoke and meats, announcing their close proximity to Beaslig.

It was a small, mountainous town with a single inn offering ten rooms. A pub sat across the broad roadway and a jumble of voices poured from the door with each person coming in and out. A scatter of shops lined the road, but barely enough to adequately call the structures a town; more so a settlement to gather resources before heading for the pass.

"Here we are," Ailith declared as they paused in the clearing between the short line of buildings. The roadway was covered in packed snow, footsteps, hoof prints, and wagon wheels cut in with bits of gravel poking through. This high into the mountains, this far north, the area was under steady snowfall for some time already, and pathways were dug from the entrances of the dwellings.

"I suppose we stable Onyx and rent a room?" Ailith asked as Caitriona hopped off the horse and Ailith slid off after her. "We can get a meal at the inn and ask around for Kayl; perhaps someone can point us in the right direction."

"Alright." Caitriona looked around and adjusted her gloves. "I'm a bit nervous, Ailith."

"I know." Ailith took Caitriona's hand as they led Onyx toward the inn's barn. After settling him into a stall they attempted to get a room, and nearly failed. Despite traveling conditions through the pass growing steadily more dangerous, the inn was nearly full. All that was available was a single room, cramped and set partly under the stairs that led to the owner's quarters on the third floor. The small bed was barely big enough for one person with a tiny wood stove in the corner whose chimney led straight out the wall. They had no available floor space beside where they stood between the door and the bed, so they left their belongings on top of the mattress, along with Ailith's bow and arrows. The short sword and the knife on her thigh she was unwilling to go without.

Still sporting their winter gear and plenty of coins in their pockets, they left the inn to plunge into the dark, snowy world and approach the pub hand-in-hand. Opening the door released bright light and the instant chatter of drunken revelry. People scattered from table to table, all as unique as they were in Avorkaz. A group of dwarven men took a table against the wall, their beer steins sloshing, drinks held aloft and fists pounding on the table as they spoke loudly. Other clusters of people were quieter, travelers with similar winter gear to what Caitriona and Ailith wore; and then those who were obviously locals in less heavy materials, sat and chatted with one another over meals.

Ailith looked around the room, hoping to spot Kayl although she had no idea what he looked like. She only assumed someone so powerful would look regal, but no one met that assumption.

They found open seats at a table off to the side where they ordered whatever the chef made—there was no other choice—and mead. Caitriona pulled off her cloak, her gold hair catching the light of the room and shining bright. She wore it loose again, no longer bothering to have it tied and tucked away in the Mazgate Dominion, and Ailith's eyes were instantly on her tresses, as were others in the pub. Ailith frowned at the onlookers. "Your beauty is drawing too much attention."

"It's so warm in here, I can't keep my cloak on any longer." Caitriona settled back and offered kind smiles to those looking. Half immediately looked away, the others seemed to puff out their chests and contemplate their next move. "Plus, I don't have to worry about anyone noticing my red hair. You should take off your cloak."

Ailith pulled her cloak hood down but didn't bother removing it. While other guests seemed content to disarm, rid their cloaks, and relax, Ailith felt on edge. She was excited by the possibility that everything could be finished, but a gnawing weight on the back of her spine bit down and pushed pulses of concern.

She thought of the moments after the white dragon attacked, when all was silent at the Elder Tree and her mother decided to return home. She remembered the unease of going back through the city streets; knowing it was necessary but frightened to find what was and wasn't there. Buildings she passed by her whole life were dusty rubble. People she knew were injured, covered in dirt and bleeding. As she had traveled toward home with her father missing, her dread increased. What would be waiting for them there?

It was all the same now. She knew they had to find Kayl, but she worried what would be revealed.

A smaller woman with pointed ears placed sloshing bowls of stew and bread before the pair; a meat stew with rice, a colorful selection of carrots, sweet and white potatoes, plus a handful of herb leaves mingling within the broth. They bowed their heads over the steaming bowls and coated their lips with crumbs from still warm bread. The stew replaced the lingering effects of the warming potion and the mead gave the room a softened look. As they ate, the remaining seats in the hall filled with additional guests and the volume increased. With empty bowls, Ailith leaned back in her seat and watched the various groups, hearing conversations discussing the incoming winter, a rockslide by the pass, and wolves in the mountains that already circled ever closer.

Ailith was particularly invested in the gossip shared from a tiny fae man and a human couple about a man they knew caught with a farmhand by his wife, when Caitriona reached across the table and grasped Ailith's hand. Gripping it tight and digging her nails into her skin, Caitriona snapped Ailith's attention back to the room at large. Her peripheral vision took in their surroundings for a threat, but Caitriona was looking straight ahead, behind Ailith.

"That man," she whispered. "He's ... glimmering."

Ailith twisted in her seat and only saw the sea of people filling seats; no one in particular looked unique amongst them beyond their visual differences. Pointed ears, tall or short, but not a glimmer to the air.

"Cait," Ailith turned back. "I don't know what you're seeing. Even the music players in Avorkaz, I didn't see a glimmer like you mentioned and I don't see it now. How long have you been seeing this?"

Caitriona pulled her gaze from the person, her face momentarily skewed in confusion before she licked her lips and narrowed her brow. "When we were in Avorkaz, I could see it with the musicians. I could see it coming from the healer's tent too—from the woman that helped you. And I see it on that man with his back to us. He has dark hair that's receding, he's hunched over the table. There's a shimmer to the air around him."

"Do you think this is something new? Something from the curse? You made flames before we went into Avorkaz. Maybe that pushed the curse along."

Caitriona's cheeks paled slightly as she sucked in a small breath of air. "That sounds plausible ..."

"But it's to our benefit right now." Ailith reached forward and held Caitriona's hand between both of hers. "May can do magic. The musicians in Avorkaz, you thought there were wings on their backs that I couldn't see—it must have been magic covering them. That man over there ... maybe he's—"

"Kayl." They stared at one another for a moment unmoving beyond Caitriona's hand quivering in Ailith's grasp.

"Are you ready? We don't have to do this now if you aren't. I'll follow your lead."

Caitriona's breathing increased and she gave a small nod before gripping Ailith's hand again. "I think I'm ready."

"You're sure?"

Caitriona remained unmoving for a moment, her hand clasping Ailith's hard before she gave a firmer nod and got to her feet. Pulling free from Ailith, she beelined directly toward the man. Ailith scrambled, reaching for Caitriona's cloak that was left behind, and hurried after the princess, whose hair caught the attention of those she passed as it glinted in the candlelight.

The man's long, graying hair was tied away from his face, the top of his head bald as if his hair was sliding off the back. He was pale and silent, not lifting his gaze to anyone around him or noticing Caitriona as she stood next to him for a few moments.

Ailith stopped a few feet behind Caitriona. After all this time, she hadn't quite envisioned what they would do when they met Kayl. She hadn't considered what to say. She realized there was nothing for her to do. Ailith had done her job, she had led Caitriona to Kayl, and now everything going forward was in Caitriona's hands.

Caitriona cleared her throat and asked in her ever-soft voice, "Excuse me? Are you Kayl?"

He paused, his spoon of stew halfway to his mouth; after a second, he lowered it before looking up. The moment his dark eyes met Caitriona's, they widened then grew confused. He blinked.

"And you are?" He wiped his mouth with a cloth, face blank with confusion.

Caitriona sank to the floor, squatting beside him as she held onto the edge of the table. Ailith glanced around, the passing interest in Caitriona from the other diners was over but she still felt on edge.

Caitriona's hushed voice, barely above a whisper, drew Ailith's attention back to the pair. "I'm Caitriona Gablaigh, the youngest daughter of Queen Róisín."

The man leaned away and took Caitriona in. He shook his head and seemed to reconsider, looking at Caitriona again with a suspicious eye. "The princess has red hair like her mother and blue eyes."

"That's in part why we came all this way to find you," Caitriona continued, nodding toward Ailith and drawing the man's attention to the guard. Ailith stood a little taller, her hand itching to touch the hilt of her sword. Caitriona reached forward, her fingertips gently touching the man's arm and drawing his gaze back to her. "You see, it seems I've been cursed and we were hoping you may help us."

CHAPTER TWENTY-SIX

CAITRIONA

K ayl placed a hand upon Caitriona's head, the pressure light and gentle. Ailith immediately stepped forward, her dagger drawn and Caitriona reached to still her movement as the warm presence of magic pressed into her skull.

"It's okay," she said, glancing at Ailith. "I'm safe."

A glimmer wafted through the air as it stretched from Kayl and covered her like a blanket.

"Your sister Greer sent you to find me," he murmured, reading her memories with ease before leaning back and taking Caitriona in as if for the first time. "I brought you back to life after the attack of the white dragon and helped you heal."

"And hopefully you can help me again," Caitriona said with a smile.

His eyes shimmered as he cupped Caitriona's cheek. "Let's leave the tavern and go to my home, shall we? I have all my supplies there that can lend us aid for this situation."

He stood and pulled his cloak over his shoulders. Turning toward the door, he left without a backwards glance. Caitriona looked at Ailith who returned her dagger to its holder.

"I guess we're following him," she said. Caitriona took her cloak from Ailith and headed for the door.

She moved quickly through the snow, her footsteps creating a guttural crunch with each impact. Ailith followed close behind and Caitriona could feel her tension rising. She was on edge ever since Kayl read Caitriona's memories. Caitriona wished she could turn to Ailith, kiss her hard and fast, and whisper *it'll be fine*. Despite her fears in previous days, she was finally hopeful. If Ailith knew that, maybe she could relax. However, that wasn't possible with Kayl rushing ahead along a narrow path up a steep embankment. The path wound around boulders and thin pines covered in snow to a small dwelling built into the side of the mountain. His home, just where Ceenear said.

"I haven't spoken to your mother in years," Kayl said from ahead of them, his breath showing against the cold air. "I've often wondered how you were faring. At long last, my questions seem to be answered."

They reached the end of the pathway that overlooked the twinkling lights of the town. Kayl paused at his door. "Welcome to my home, daughter of the king," he announced before ushering them inside.

Ailith followed Caitriona, remaining close by, silent and observant; her overall mood darker than when they were eating their meal. While Kayl's back turned from them, Caitriona slipped her hand into Ailith's and gave it a squeeze. Quickly leaning forward, she pecked Ailith's wounded cheek with a kiss. To her relief, Ailith softened slightly, her shoulders relaxed and a brief smile brought light to her face.

"*This is a good thing*," Caitriona whispered and Ailith gave a small nod, their hands dropping as Kayl turned back to them with the door closed.

"It's very cold here," he murmured, waving at the heavy wooden door. "Everything's built a little more thickly; the walls, the doors, it helps keep out the cold in the winter."

He shuffled past them to a large hearth and stoked the embers within before adding logs and urging the flames to grow. "Take off your cloaks, make yourselves comfortable." He turned to them briefly as he pulled his own off.

He was surprisingly thin. Caitriona remembered him being much broader, taller; then again, she was only a toddler when he saved her, an age where her memories were flashes of imagery. But now he seemed small, underfed, a person fading away. Caitriona frowned as she placed her cloak on a hook beside Ailith's. Perhaps he wasn't as strong as she and Greer remembered.

Ailith stood awkwardly to the side, but always within arm's reach of Caitriona, and kept a steady eye on Kayl. The fire grew in height, pushing out heat that filled the single room with a bed in the far corner and a table, as well as a narrow staircase up to a loft above. Kayl turned to the pair and looked Ailith over.

"You can remove your sword," he offered, his voice light.

"I'd rather not." Her voice was emotionless. Kayl frowned.

"She's my guard. And a wonderful one."

"Ah, guards," Kayl replied with a thin smile. "Yes, Cearny always had well-trained guards in Braewick. Well, so be it, wear your sword if it makes you comfortable."

"Can you help Caitriona?" Ailith blurted, stopping the words from Kayl's mouth. Caitriona grew still, watching the pair. She forgot, despite all their time on the road, how straight forward and serious Ailith was when they first began their journey. She loosened up over time, but underneath that, she was still very much the guard her sister hired.

Kayl rubbed his hands together and tentatively smiled. "I believe I can. Come, let's hurry and fix all of this. I do most of my work in the loft, follow me."

He set forward, passing the pair and going up the steps quickly, spryer than his thin and older form conveyed. After exchanging a look, Ailith stepped forward, forcing Caitriona to follow her up the stairs. Caitriona advanced more slowly, noticing Ailith's hand resting on the handle of her short sword.

The loft had a large table covered in maps, bottles, bowls filled with herbs, and open books. The far wall built against the mountainside was lined with shelves holding similar items. Kayl moved to the table and reached for a match. Striking it hard he lit an oil lamp and turned the knob to make the flame grow brighter, filling the room with light.

"I knew your mother when we were young." Kayl went to his bookshelf and pulled out a rolled sheet of paper, moving quickly as he darted from place to place, getting what he deemed necessary. "Róisín and I grew up together. We were the closest of friends."

He ushered the women closer as he unrolled the paper and pinned its corners down with an empty bottle, a candle, and a book. The sheet was a map of the Endless Mountains, the similar mist lingering at the base of the mountains but most focus on the land to the southeast of the southern tip of the mountains. A town, with multiple little homes drawn carefully and a roadway that passed through its center to the eastern edge of Visennore. A town Caitriona never drew on her own maps because it simply did not exist. She leaned in closer, Ailith by her side doing the same.

"What is this place?" Ailith murmured, her fingertip brushing over the paper as she traced the outline of a building.

"Caermythlin, a town much like this with a mixture of people. Dwarves, fae, humans. A tight-knit community, one built on magic. King Donal began to force magic users from Braewick and many came to Caermythlin to coexist without persecution."

Kayl ran his fingers over the map, sadness conquering his features as he continued, "Róisín's father passed through a town south of there—he was a soldier for Wimleigh Kingdom—and left behind your grandmother with child. She died when Róisín was small, which was quite the shock as your grandmother was so young. Some say she died of a broken heart. Nonetheless, your mother came to live at an orphanage, the same one I grew up in."

"We met with fae," Caitriona whispered. Such tales about her mother were best spoken in a whisper. Overall, her mother's childhood was an unmentionable mystery. Questioning her mother's past was only met with a cold stare and anger; it was best to leave such things alone but Caitriona couldn't help but find it all the more interesting. It wasn't just her mother's history, but hers as well. She felt her heart ache from the idea her mother was alone without any parents at a young age, and suddenly Róisín's lack of maternal behavior made more sense. "They shared that my mother has fae ancestry."

"Plenty of it. Her mother was fully fae," Kayl replied. "It was quite the surprise when I visited Braewick to see her with curved ears. She glamoured the points away, but I suppose it makes sense considering your father's stance with anyone who isn't human."

Caitriona looked at Kayl, surprised by this admission. Her mother's ears were always human-like. To think she was at least partly fae and married to the king while actively practicing magic, even if small, felt like the biggest lie she ever told. Caitriona looked at Kayl's ears, scarred at the tops and oddly formed, and tried to cover her surprise. He raised a hand, running it over the edge of his ears.

"The points of my ears were cut," he said quietly. "But more of that later ... You see, your mother and I were the best of friends growing up, but she always wanted something more. The little town we lived in wasn't large enough for her, she wanted to see the world."

"I suppose I get that from her," Caitriona admitted with a little smile. Ailith leaned back from the table, keeping a serious eye on Kayl as she crossed her arms over her chest. Caitriona shifted on her feet, her hand lifting to tuck hair behind her ear. "But I don't understand ... if she's half fae, why would she marry my father? He's always been so ... *awful* to anyone not human."

"She once told me she wanted to see if she could change him," Kayl replied, moving around the table and picking up various jars and bottles. He held them aloft and peered at their contents before returning them to the shelves. "Your father was young, still a prince when he came through Caermythlin with other soldiers to establish a trading route on the eastern shores. She caught his eye immediately. This beautiful woman with the most vibrant red hair. She stood out like a flame."

"And she hid her ears away?" Caitriona asked, still trying to alter the view of her mother in her mind's eye.

"Immediately. He was already displaying his hatred towards anyone not human. He made it clear he wanted to free your mother from living with such *filth*."

Ailith cleared her throat, her eyes narrowed.

"I'm shocked you wanted anything to do with the queen after that," Ailith began. "She turned her back on your people."

"She hid her true self as she attempted to obtain her goals. She wanted to see the world. She didn't want to continue living in a home with other orphans. She thought with her wit and her looks, she'd make more progress from within the castle. She thought she'd convince him to stop his actions and allow magic folk to live freely. She promised me before the now-king took her away to marry, that she'd try and right the wrongs Cearny and his father were already doing." Kayl met Ailith's gaze, unbothered by the dark look of the guard's eye. "King Donal died shortly after their wedding. I've always wondered if she was behind his sudden death. But with Cearny in power, things only grew worse, and she vanished within the castle."

"And after all that time, what brought you to Braewick Valley?" Caitriona asked, trying to urge the conversation along.

"King Cearny was pushing to free the countryside of people who were not human. I remained in Caermythlin and took a role leading my neighbors. Many were moving on, abandoning their homes for Avorkaz, and the fae went to Invarlwen. Some took ships to other lands. But those of us who remained, we didn't want to give up our land, or our magic. We wanted to fight to keep it. Seeing I was close to Róisín when we were young, I offered to meet with the king and queen to ask for reconsideration of the laws banning us from magical use and practices, and forcing those who weren't fully human to leave the land behind. And so, I traveled to Braewick Valley and arrived the morning that the white dragon attacked."

A silence fell and the flame in the lantern seemed to be the only thing willing to move. All stared for a moment as they remembered a past they would rather forget; the white dragon haunted memories and plagued dreams for many.

"And you saved me," Caitriona whispered. Kayl blinked and smiled softly. He rubbed his hands together and spread them out. The air around them shimmered and other candles lining the bookshelves flickered alive with new flames. He moved around the table and gently took Caitriona's hand, turning the princess to look at him.

"Your mother's men found me after the attack. Your mother was beyond control of her emotions. You were lost to all of us. But yes, I used what powers I had to tether your soul to this world for a little longer before you drifted too far from our realm. I brought you back to yourself. I healed your body so no mark of the attack remained."

Caitriona blinked, her eyes filling with tears. Her entire life she knew she owed her existence to Kayl. She wondered what she would do if given the opportunity to meet him, to thank him, and now presented with that opportunity she was left overwhelmed. She sniffed and smiled, embarrassed by her emotions, and wiped her eyes, shuffling her feet as she gathered her thoughts.

"I can't express enough how grateful I am. I've always thought of all I would say to you and I find myself incapable of articulating adequately how thankful I am to still be here."

Kayl smiled, lifting Caitriona's hand in his and squeezing it tightly as he leaned closer. "Oh, princess," he said softly, his smile turning knife sharp. "The world is full of monsters and misdeeds. Evil men who only search for greed and women willing to go blind for comfort. You shouldn't thank me yet. You haven't come to fully understand what this curse is that was placed upon you."

Caitriona raised an eyebrow, a nervous laugh bubbling out of her throat. She took a small step back, but Kayl still held her hand tightly and Caitriona felt the hairs on the back of her neck rise as goosebumps spread over her skin. This wasn't right. She reached behind with her free hand, searching for Ailith's grasp.

"Caitriona," Kayl began. "You've spent enough time in that castle library. I can see it in your mind. Does your guard know what happens when fae allow their hearts to grow cold and revenge to become their priority?"

Caitriona glanced at Ailith who stood close behind her, arms crossed over her chest and jaw clenched, her eyes flitting from Caitriona to Kayl as she remained still.

"The fae become the unbound. They become gruesome creatures ..." She looked at Kayl and half expected him to turn into a monster. But there wasn't a glamor over him, making the air ripple; he wasn't hiding anything. He smiled and gave her hand a pat before letting it go. Caitriona stepped backward beside Ailith, her sleeve brushing into the guard who stood resolutely beside her.

"What your history books fail to convey is that this can happen to anyone, no matter what they are. Fae, dwarf, human. The fae are always the focus because their change is so obvious. They slowly lose themselves, their bodies relinquishing to the air as they become shadow and dust. They survive on borrowed power until they lose their minds, or humanity, or their lives, whichever comes first. Until then, they crave the magic of others. They yearn for it and they can take it, supping upon magic makers who draw too close or willingly give themselves to the unbound. It becomes their sustenance.

"I *did* bring you back to life, this is true. But, my dear child, I don't *care* that I saved you once. Understand, your father made me a promise while I was at Braewick. He *swore* to leave creatures of magic alone, he *swore* to allow Caermythlin to continue their peaceful existence. I left Braewick the day after the attack, taken home in a carriage by the king's command. When I arrived to Caermythlin, I was thrust out, kicked to the ground, and lifted my head to discover the charred remains of my home and the death of my neighbors. Families, *children*, all gone. Fae had their wings *torn* from their backs before their throats were *slit*, others were burned, some hung from trees. The guards cut the points of my ears off and rode away, leaving me to breathe in the stench of burning and death. To put out the flames and bury the corpses of my loved ones. All under your father's orders.

"As I sat amongst the rubble of my home with my ears bleeding, I gave my heart to seek justice for those lost. Bless my human ancestry, it slowed my physical changes. Yet I still feel myself drifting, falling apart year by year, becoming lighter and less detached to this earth. But that's beside the point. Caitriona, daughter of King Cearny, I had a splendid idea when I sat there in the remains of my home with the death of my loved ones spread around me."

"Kayl ..." Caitriona whispered, taking a further step back and feeling Ailith resist Caitriona's movement. She turned to Ailith. She still stood with her arms crossed, jaw clenched, and her eyes alarmed. They blinked rapidly as her breath came fast. Caitriona touched her, then tried to pull Ailith's arms free, but found her stiff like a living statue. "Ailith?

"What have you done to her?" Caitriona asked, panicked. She spun on her heel and looked at Kayl, her eyes unknowingly glowing with golden light. "What have you done?"

Kayl's smile curled upon his thin, pale face; his dry lips cracking and bleeding. "When I saw what your father did, I lost my humanity. What better way to find revenge than by allowing you to lose yours?"

"What do you mean?" Her heart beat fast and her skin grew hot with rage. The air was shimmering from tears in her eyes and the rising power of flame gathering within her.

"Darling, *I* unleashed the curse. My magic is so entwined with your very heartbeat, your breath, your soul, it was *easy* to rope myself to your being and place a curse upon you. I saved a child, but never promised to save an adult, and so the curse was laid upon you as your mother cared for you in the castle. A swift promise that when you became an adult, the curse would unleash. You would discover magic for which your father would hate and shun you. Your mother would lose you all over again. If your father didn't kill you for it, the powers would slowly grow, and you'd gradually change. Your father and mother would be forced to face their actions directly. I've heard he's quite proud of that dragon head he has on display. Funny, it's a coincidence that it watched over his rule while hinting to his future end. A dragon in his home. A dragon as his daughter. And his daughter as his killer."

"I'm not—" Caitriona snapped but stopped short. She and Ailith considered what she was turning into and they wondered if a dragon was possible. But they never witnessed someone turn into something and she hadn't changed size, hadn't grown large, so was that even possible? But it made sense now, her clawed nails, the scales that spread from her fingertips and aligned her wrists, and all of this having begun after her eighteenth birthday.

"Oh," Kayl replied. His grin was malicious, hungry in a way that Caitriona had never seen a man possess. "I see you understand."

He turned and went to his shelves, selecting a collection of bottles and placing them into a bag that hung on a peg. "You know, I did forewarn your family. I sent a final letter to your mother and told her she and her husband allowed their destiny to be determined by my hand. I told her that her daughter would destroy the comforts she lied to obtain, and her husband killed to enjoy. I simply left out *how*."

CHAPTER TWENTY-SEVEN

Aɪʟɪᴛʜ

Kayl turned one final time, the smile on his face unnatural and cruel. "Send my regards to your father."

He turned to the stairs and Caitriona stepped forward, an anguished scream spilling forth from her lips as fire appeared in the palm of her hand. It spread quickly through the air and simply ... snuffed out. Kayl glanced over his shoulder at Caitriona as she stood motionless, the scream gone from her mouth and replaced with a quivering gasp. He hesitated, his smile fading slightly, but Ailith never knew why. He said nothing as he looked her over with a quick glance before descending the stairs, slamming shut the door to his home as he left. The loud sound released Ailith from the prison she was thrust into. She dropped to the floor as her muscles loosened and her joints unlocked all at once.

When he used his gifts to light the candles in the room, Ailith simultaneously froze. She could breathe, she could look, but her muscles were locked in place. She tried relentlessly to reach for her sword, to thrust it into the bony chest of the mage before them. She attempted to warn Caitriona, but her jaw and tongue were stuck. Caitriona was too far lost, too entranced by his awful story, to see the signs that something was off. All Ailith could do was stand by and watch with horror.

Free now, Ailith attempted to move to Caitriona who was slowly folding into herself. An awful, choking sound spilled forth from her. Ailith's muscles and joints were sore and stiff, her movements clumsy and slow as she remained on the ground.

"Cait? Cait?" Ailith crawled forward until enough strength returned to her legs to allow her to stand. Caitriona was bent over and grasping onto the table. Her eyes glowed from a light within, her brow glistened from sweat, and her lips parted to form a perfect circle as she groaned.

A crack of the wood rose over Caitriona's sounds of pain. Her fingers tightened on the table's edge as her nails thickened and lengthened, curling into the wood and indenting it with ease. Ailith grasped Caitriona's shoulders, turning her into Ailith's chest as she held her tightly. "Cait, what can I do?"

Caitriona slowly lifted her head. Her eyes were panic-filled. Pulling her hands free from the table, her nails sticking briefly into the grains of wood, she clutched Ailith's heavy, outer shirt, and ripped the thick skins and fur with ease. Ailith's panic was a wild thing, filling her whole and vibrating in her chest as Caitriona worked her jaw, attempting to speak, but only groaned. Arching her neck, she bared teeth that were growing long and strong, and forming fangs along the mouth that Ailith greedily kissed only two nights prior. Her fanged teeth crowded her small mouth, causing her jawbone to crack and the skin to bulge along her face. Ailith fought against her instinct to run as she watched with horror as Caitriona's jaw continued to change and slowly stretch forward. All strength left Caitriona's body and together, the pair sank to the floor as Caitriona writhed in Ailith's arms, whimpers reaching higher volumes until they became screams.

Ailith tried to comfort her, but how do you comfort a person you love when their very body betrays them? How do you bring ease as their body twists and changes against their will? Caitriona's muscles and bones grew at an incredible speed. More bones developed rapidly as the curse ran rampant. Her skin pulsed, the press of new cartilage rose against Ailith's hand as she held Caitriona. It rushed through Caitriona's form, forcing her back to spasm and a long scream issued from her mouth, ringing through Ailith's ears and securing its place in Ailith's mind.

Caitriona's pale face was coated with blood as four horns pushed out the skin on the top of her head, curling upward and turning into thick, heavy bone. Wisps of her long, blonde hair fell freely from her head, drifting to the floor to be forgotten. Her body was breaking and morphing before Ailith's very eyes and she was helpless.

How can you stop a curse from being fulfilled when you willingly walk into the lair of the man who created it? How do you stop a curse at all?

You can't.

Caitriona fell from Ailith with another scream. Her back arched as she choked on words that seemed unable to break past her pain. Smoke rose from her lips, her breath scalding hot. She tried to pull at the fur coat, her hands larger than they were meant to be and her nails full claws now. Her palms had thickened, rough and padded; her fingers were fattened and shorter; and her wrists grew thick as the bones seemed to expand.

Ailith scrambled to pull Caitriona's coat off, then tugged at the clothing beneath that strained as Caitriona's body bulged, and bones pushed through her shoulders once more and coated her back with blood. There was a sheen of gold, the soft plumpness of human skin growing harder and slick as scales pushed forth. Her arm swung wide, pushing Ailith away as she grunted, an animal sound that Ailith's instincts immediately flared from. *Wrong, wrong, this is wrong.*

Turning her head toward Ailith with tears streaming from her eyes, pops sounded from her neck as it rippled forward and grew in length. Caitriona spoke around her fanged teeth, changing jaw, and lips that had grown hard and rippled with scales. A simple, growling direction: "*Run.*"

The curse was unleashed and spreading fast. Caitriona belonged to it. It filled her whole as it reconstructed her, turning into something horrid as the woman Ailith knew was pushed aside. She didn't want to go, but it was the promise she made. Even though in doing so Caitriona was breaking hers.

Don't leave me.

I won't.

Ailith ran down the stairs and grabbed her cloak before reaching for the door. She tried to pull the heavy thing open, but a rumbling wave of sound followed her and left her covering her ears as the dragon found its voice in an expansive roar.

Ailith could only perceive the bright flash of light and the sweeping heat as the dragon set fire to the building and pushed out of the roof and walls. The structure exploded outward to rain books and maps, bottles and potions, rooftop and plaster down upon Beaslig. And Ailith was lost to it all, her world going dark and everything silent.

She was left in the embrace of empty blackness, surely a cousin to the fae's white mist. In the darkness she only felt pressure of what would be bodily pain later on, and a dull ache in her chest where her broken heart was kept. Time was a concept she could not grasp. She was listless, lost, knowing there was something she was doing, that she was someone with a purpose, but unable to reach and grasp the memory. It was fluid, easing between her fingers, and hard to make sense of until voices punctured the darkness and drew Ailith back to night. Fishing her roughly from the murky black until she sputtered awake.

She woke to people speaking in different tongues. Hands grasped her body, lifting it, all before she opened her eyes. As they placed her on the blanket, they told her the explosion shook the very foundation of the buildings they were in, and when they came out they saw the mage's house bursting with fire and light. They explained that a large, golden dragon spread its wings and took to the air from its remnants. It breathed fire on the hillside, thankfully not touching any of the Beaslig homes before gliding into the night and traveling south, from what they could tell. They bent over Ailith's body, inspecting her wounds as they continued to explain that they came to the mage's house hoping to find him, but instead found Ailith in the rubble. The wound on her cheek reopened and she sported burns along her right side that wept with blood and swelled red.

"I need—" Ailith groaned, sitting up on the bedding of cloaks people lay her on. "I need to go …"

The world spun and the shock of what happened made her nauseated, but she knew she had to get to Greer quickly. A dragon was heading for Braewick Valley and likely would destroy the castle, if not the city. With the defenses at the ready for another dragon attack, Ailith shook with fear that Caitriona would be killed in the process.

"You need aid, you're wounded," said a man with dark skin and gray hair as Ailith tried to get to her feet.

"No, I need to go." Ailith looked around and found her short sword taken nearby. She paused and looked at the man, his expression both irritated and concerned. "Where's the mage? What happened to him?"

"They're still searching the rubble," he replied, nodding toward what remained of Kayl's house. "We haven't found him."

"And you won't." Ailith buckled the holder for her sword to her waist and ground her teeth from the pain in her arm and hand. "He left; he fled the house before all of that happened. He's somewhere in town. *He* did this. He's the one that made the dragon."

The man looked doubtful and Ailith rolled her eyes before grasping a cloak and trying to clasp it around her neck. Her right fingers couldn't move properly, the skin already red, wrinkling and weeping blood. She reached to her chest and found the packets of spell jars still there, pulling free the one to help with injury and ripping the wax seal off with her teeth, she guzzled it. It tasted like ice water, a shock to the system that numbed Ailith immediately, and she took off down the corkscrew pathways from the mage's house, towards the inn.

In their room, Ailith wept as she reached for Caitriona's bag. Her tears stung the open cut in her cheek and she miserably wiped them away with her left hand. She found a hole in her chest that was previously filled by Caitriona's presence, and the loss of her made Ailith feel she would drown in her own sorrow. Struggling, her strength weakened from the magic Kayl placed on her as well as her injuries, Ailith made her way down the stairs with both bags and her bow, turning to the barn and finding Onyx within.

"Please, Elder Tree," she whispered as she prepared to ride, hoping the massive tree would hear her plea. "Please keep her safe. Please don't let her die."

As she rode from the town into the dark night gratefully lit by the light of the waning moon, she passed a stream of people. They came from the tavern and their homes, their faces turned toward the hillside, their eyes reflecting the flames of what remained of Kayl's home.

"A dragon!" someone said, "It would've been beautiful if not so terrifying."

"Do you think the mage is dead? We're lucky other buildings weren't set ablaze."

"I pray for whomever is in the dragon's path. I saw the hunger for death in its eyes."

CHAPTER TWENTY-EIGHT

GREER

They lingered in the fields where Caitriona and Ailith left them, taking their time to dig a deep grave for Ian's body and give him over to the earth. But once that was done, they had no reason to continue their search. They found the princess and knew she was fine, but now what to do? Greer and Barden led a meeting with the rest of her troop to explain the truth of the matter and asked if they agree to keep Caitriona's secret amongst themselves. It was a reflection of Greer's leadership that everyone agreed with relative ease. Cearny's continued drive for possession of land was fraying the inner workings of the royal house. The men weren't fools. Cearny's time was fading and Greer was the next person to take the throne; best to side with her early and allow her to remember who stood by her side.

They spent another night in the fields, this time moving back to camp amongst the trees the girls camped in prior. While the men settled, Greer remained by the fire late into the night staring at the flames.

"You look like you're trying to make the fire move," Barden teased as he settled beside Greer. Beyond the two of them, one guard stood on the fringe of the forest keeping an eye on the road. The rest slept, and Barden kept his voice low and private.

"If only I could." Greer rubbed her eyes that burned from the smoke, or something else. "I'd set fire to the damn castle and be done with it all."

"Come now, the castle never did anything wrong."

Greer looked at Barden, narrowing her eyes with mock anger and he smiled, his blue eyes glowing in the low light. Greer turned back to the flames and rubbed her temples. "I've never felt so useless."

"You're doing as much as you can; anything more would threaten your position with your father. At least you can still stand between him and Caitriona if necessary."

"I suspect I'll have to."

They fell quiet. What words could be said? They both witnessed her father's rage and had been on the receiving end of it many times before. The man was driven by negative emotion and never happy unless he had something dead at his feet. He tried his best to color Greer's world view and make her hate just as he hated, but her bond with Caitriona had been too much. Her innocence and sweet nature calmed what flames Cearny tried to build within Greer's mind. Once she traveled beyond the city, all of Cearny's hope to have his heir as awful as he was squashed. Greer thrived on the magic of the world and finally had the distance from her father to truly see him for the broken man he was.

On the second morning they couldn't linger any longer; the close proximity to Avorkaz made them all uneasy, and with lead in her stomach Greer called for them to move out. They would travel at a slow pace and head south toward home. What they would do or say when they returned was an unanswered question that clutched at Greer's shoulders and constricted her throat.

Overall, she dreaded returning to Cearny with empty hands and his favored soldier dead, and so the pace remained slow until the third morning when dawn brought a moving shadow that darkened the rising sun and turned all their attention to the horizon.

"Is that ...?" Barden lifted a hand to shade his eyes from the sunlight.

Greer's stomach dropped as the dragon flew overhead, disappearing rapidly from sight as it glided south, seemingly following the road. Barden dropped his hand and looked at Greer. Everyone was silent and even the horses seemed to know it was best to grow still. Dragons were once plentiful in Visennore, but the last one seen had its head currently hanging in King Cearny's hall.

"We have to get back to Braewick," Greer murmured before kicking her horse into a gallop.

They traveled as quickly as their horses allowed but slowed to a walk by midday while they heaved from the effort. The skies grew dark and gray with incoming rain that began pouring as quickly as the clouds arrived. Before long, the horses slipped through mud that crested over their hooves and barely made any progress at all.

"We should get off the road," Barden yelled over the driving rain. "Get over to those trees. Perhaps the earth isn't as water-logged there."

The ground was strewn with rock and pine needles, but considerably less muddy. The horses were happy to eat the brush and rest after being pushed during the course of the morning. But their human counterparts were miserable.

Greer huddled under her riding cloak beneath a large pine. A number of the guard were scattered beneath the trees as they attempted to find comfort without fire. It was miserable and Greer grunted with frustration as she tightened her cloak around her cold body.

Barden crossed the center of the grove and sat beside Greer.

"You've been tense since we saw the dragon."

"Wouldn't you be?" Greer snapped, immediately a little guilty as Barden leaned away from her tone, his brows raised. "I'm sorry."

"It's fine," Barden replied, straightening in his seat beneath the pine. His auburn hair hung in his face, curling from the moisture and dripping with rainwater. He hadn't bothered pulling his hood up. "You're concerned the dragon's heading for Braewick?"

Greer nodded as she shifted and watched water rush off the edge of her cloak to puddle around her feet. "I don't know why, but it makes me feel like Ailith and Caitriona weren't successful. They didn't find Kayl, the curse took hold, something like that."

"Dragons certainly aren't a good omen, I'm with you on that."

The rain continued, turning the road into a streambed thick with mud. While Greer and her men often camped under the stars, the continuous rain forced them to pitch their tents to find some escape from it. They remained by the trees for two nights, soggy and miserable from the constant downpour as the roadway became a shallow river, and Greer's anxiety intensified. On the third day, morning dawned with lighter skies and hope of the weather clearing.

"Oy!" A guard shouted from the outer edge of the woods. He looked over his shoulder to Barden and Greer. "There's someone traveling on the road; they look hurt."

With her monocular, Greer saw a black draft horse foaming from the mouth and coated in mud, then focused on its rider. She gasped. "Barden, it's Ailith!"

Barden got to his feet, looking toward the road. "There's only one rider."

"Caitriona isn't with her."

Greer and Barden took flight, running over the muddied fields, their feet sinking and boots nearly lost, to reach Ailith as her horse slowed to a stop. She nearly slid from its back, her face pale and her clothes covered with blood.

She held on until they reached her, then fell completely off the horse. Barden darted forward, catching Ailith in his arms. He looked at Greer with raised brows.

"Oh, Ailith," Greer whispered. Barden lifted her with ease and gently held her against his chest. She was soaked but her skin was angry and raw, the rain having washed away blood.

Greer grabbed hold of the reins of the new horse and led it toward the trees with Barden carrying Ailith.

"At least the rain's stopped." Barden adjusted Ailith in his arms, who remained silent, her eyes closed as she was lost to the world.

The other guards came forward, making a loose circle as they stared at the injured guard. Everything was wet, but no rain fell. Greer glanced to the sky; already peeks of blue appeared.

"Well, I had to do something to slow you all down," a gravelly voice said from the shadows of the pines. A gray-haired woman stepped from the trees and smiled. "Hello, Greer Gablaigh. I'm Isla, a friend of your sister's. I've been waiting for you all to pass my way and for Ailith to catch up. Now, how can I help you?"

CHAPTER TWENTY-NINE

 AILITH

Ailith pushed Onyx to the breaking point after leaving Beaslig. He galloped through most of the night until he outright refused to continue. After a fitful rest, he trotted the rest of the distance while Ailith's body began to revolt against her.

As they went, Ailith kept her eyes to the sky and for every crow she saw, she called to them, telling the crows messages for Isla. Perhaps all the crows could speak to her, and perhaps caw that Caitriona was changed and Ailith needed help. Ailith continued south, her exhaustion heightening and the pain returning, until she saw Greer and Barden rushing towards her. That was when everything went dark.

Ailith woke to find herself on the very bed she rested on two weeks prior. In the course of a fortnight, she had more wounds to her body than she ever obtained in her entire life. Besides her previous injuries, her right arm, as well as the side of her neck and face, were now burned.

Isla kicked the men out of her home so she and Greer could strip off Ailith's sweater and tunic to better clean the burns. The fabric stuck to the wounds on her arm, bits of fiber were caught within the ooze and blood, and Ailith felt tears fast and hot running down her cheeks when Isla began treating the injured areas. The pain was a pulse, the world went white and sound vanished. Ailith nearly slipped back into the black void she kept finding herself in until Isla poured a numbing tonic to the mix that finally kept her tethered to the room.

While Ailith had downed May's potions to prevent infection of her wounds, her injuries still left her weak and exhausted. Greer washed her skin, gentle as her sister at the outpost when Caitriona's surprise flames irritated Ailith's cheeks, and Isla covered the burns in salves and wraps. Ailith, all the while, sat in silence with eyes glazed.

"The brunt of your burns are on your right arm," Isla observed, "I think your face is saved. Beside the scar on your cheek, the burns should heal there. I suspect you'll have some scarring on your arm and neck though."

Ailith continued her silence while Isla helped her into a chemise, which fit wide and short on Ailith, but didn't press against her wounds. Greer repeatedly looked at Ailith, pacing and biting at the skin along one of her nails as Ailith dressed.

"I couldn't save her." Ailith lifted her gaze to meet Greer's as tears began leaking down her face. Greer's movements stilled as Ailith continued, her voice horse and small. "The curse took her. I couldn't save her."

Isla paused her wrapping. Greer looked to the ground, suddenly unable to meet Ailith's gaze. "Is she dead?"

Ailith let out a sad, short laugh. She was lost in a sea of dulled emotions that festered in odd ways. Greer's question wasn't funny, nor was the reality of it, but the words bounced inside Ailith's torso and pushed free her exhausted laughter all the same. "I suppose it depends on your definition and how you feel about monstrous creatures. Also, how good the castle's enforcements are and if the cannons are ready."

Greer lifted her gaze, her brown eyes widening. "The dragon."

"The *gold* dragon," Isla corrected. She gathered the unused wraps. "There are many dragons in the world, although they're rare here. It's better to clarify your sister is the gold dragon you saw in the skies. I have the gift of sight. I knew Caitriona was cursed; I could see the dragon was nestled in the depths of her soul."

"You knew she was turning into one?" Ailith leaned away from the woman. Lazily angry, her energy so little she couldn't do more to portray her annoyance than by this small movement. Isla pressed her lips together and met Ailith's gaze without flinching, which only upset Ailith more. "Why didn't you *do* something?"

"The trickery of curses is that no matter what one can see, there is no help to be given. This curse had already begun, and it needed to finish. There was no way to help, at least nothing I could do. Going to Kayl was your best option because it's true, until a curse is fulfilled the only one to stop it is the one who placed it. But I suppose Kayl is too far gone to reason with."

"What do you mean Kayl placed the curse?" Greer turned to both of them.

Ailith held Greer's gaze for a moment until the heir glanced away, as if Ailith's vacant expression pained her. It was clear to Ailith how much Greer loved her sister from the moment the guard saw the two together. She knew that the truth would be a stab to Greer's heart but had to be out with it.

"Kayl admitted to placing the curse on Caitriona. He did it as a way to get revenge on your parents. Your mother is part fae, did you know that? Cait didn't," Ailith started, her voice bitter from the unfairness of it all. "Your mother came from Caermythlin, same as Kayl. She said she was going to change your father's mind and ensure he accepted beings with magic. Either she gave up or your father didn't care, or maybe she never tried. Worse, your father destroyed Caermythlin and killed everyone there. Kayl found out after he saved Caitriona. That's when he placed the curse on her. He was just ... *gleeful* that it was all working out according to plan."

Greer's brow furrowed as she stared at the floorboards.

"It was awful," Ailith croaked before she began to cry again. "I couldn't stop Caitriona from changing. I tried, but I couldn't stop it. Her body—it looked so painful. I don't know how she survived."

"Oh, child." Isla wiped Ailith's tears, her fingers rough and her wrinkled mouth a perfect frown. "There's so much to curses you don't understand. Please, don't fret. There are no rules to what can be done *after* a curse is fulfilled; she's changed, and now stepping forward we can figure out how to change her back."

"Does she even know who she is?" Greer asked. "Is it Caitriona who's flying through the skies right now? Or is she lost and just … a dragon?"

"I think if Kayl had a choice in his curse, he would have decided no," Ailith replied, looking at Greer. "He wants your father destroyed by his own daughter. So, I suspect Caitriona isn't really controlling the dragon. Or perhaps she is, but she isn't the Caitriona we know."

Greer crossed an arm across her torso, grasping hold of her other arm as she looked at the dried herbs hanging from the ceiling. "How do we bring her back then?"

"I don't mean to show off," Isla said with a smile. "But Kayl had to learn how to control his magic from *someone*."

"Isla, you need to stop surprising me." Ailith looked at the short woman sitting beside her.

"I left Caermythlin a few months prior to Kayl visiting Braewick, but I helped raise him and taught him nearly everything I know," Isla explained. "If we can reach Caitriona, I can attempt to call her home to her human body. I cannot promise it'll be lasting or she'll return to her full self—there may be lingering effects of the curse—but I can promise to try."

"That sounds good enough to me," Greer replied, now filled with energy. She began pacing again. "You can ride with Ailith. If we push the horses, we can get back to Braewick in a few days."

Isla held up a hand to silence Greer. "I know you want to rush to your sister's aid, but Ailith needs to rest and I need to gather my supplies. Caitriona's only recently turned. It's a great transition to go from the small size of a human to that of a dragon for the first time. If she's to attack the valley, it won't be for a few days. Dragons, despite their size and capability of destruction, need to rest their bodies, and that's *without* having just become one. We'll leave tomorrow."

"How do you know?" Greer asked, her eyes dark and daring. "Perhaps she flew to the castle first before running out of energy—we don't know for sure."

"The crows." Isla raised her hand to cup her ear.

"The crows?"

"Isla can talk to them and they to her," Ailith said.

"They told me when Ailith was on her way and I've asked them to keep an eye on Caitriona. Your sister is resting in a valley within the Endless Mountains. The fae won't harm her, she's safe, but her energy is spent. We have time."

Greer took a long breath. She held Isla's gaze for a moment before nodding. "Alright, that's fair. We don't need to rush into this blind. Hopefully you're right and Caitriona doesn't make her way to Braewick beforehand."

"I *am* right. Now go inform your men."

Greer spent most of the afternoon outside, coming in occasionally with Barden to help Isla prepare enough food to feed all that camped in her yard. The ground was dry there and the air, while crisp, wasn't freezing.

"I made it rain," Isla whispered as Ailith stood at the window, looking at the guards preparing their sleeping pads and blankets for the night. "Anything to slow them down so you could catch up."

Ailith looked at Isla, her eyes heavy with exhaustion, but she managed a small smile. "You're an interesting woman with a lot of secrets."

"Plenty."

Isla placed a hand on Ailith's shoulder and guided her away from the window to the little bed. It would be another night that Ailith took the bed from the old woman—again at Isla's insistence—and Isla slept on the floor in a makeshift bed of blankets and furs. But despite a large evening meal, Ailith didn't find sleep when she laid down. Isla applied enough salve to chase away pain from her burns and already her magic ingredients worked wonders on the reopened cut on her cheek, but the repeated images of Caitriona convulsing on the ground as her skin shivered with sweat and scales haunted Ailith. When she opened her eyes, Caitriona's absence felt heavier.

"Child, drink this," Isla said, startling Ailith after she laid on the bed with her face to the wall and her eyes clenched shut for several minutes. "It'll give you restful sleep, which you need."

Ailith accepted the mug and drank without comment. In moments, sleep took Ailith in its arms, cradling her into a dreamless rest before she could offer the empty cup back to the waiting witch.

They left early the following morning, a quiet progression with crows alighting to the heavens as they left the pine forest behind.

"They'll fly ahead," Isla said, looking up to the black shapes spreading over the open sky. "And they'll let me know of Caitriona's progress toward Braewick."

It seemed a painfully slow journey, although significantly faster than Caitriona and Ailith's prior travels. Where the girls were slow due to walking by foot or stopping in Stormhaven, Greer commanded her men into an orderly procession that pushed them forward. For each hour that passed, both Ailith and Greer looked to the skies and frowned as they futilely sought out the shape of the dragon.

At night, Ailith was greedy for rest as her body tried to recover from its injuries. She was desperate for her mind to take a break from the repeated thoughts of what happened to Caitriona, her absence, and the constant worry over where she was. They bedded down in the marsh, making a hasty camp far from the edge of the murky waters. Even the fire in the marsh reminded Ailith of Caitriona.

"I wish they wouldn't watch us," a guard murmured from the middle of the clustered group. Ailith raised her head, watching quietly from where she lay on the ground with her pack as a pillow. The guard looked over the water where the glowing eyes of the drowning dukes watched silently. The dukes were significantly more interested in the party now compared to when it was only her and Caitriona.

"They're only living their lives; let them be." Barden smiled as he crossed the clearing and clapped the guard's shoulder.

"I wouldn't necessarily say they're living," the man continued with a frown, his gaze still locked on the glowing eyes.

"I would." Barden stepped closer to the water, but not close enough for any waiting duke to reach for his legs. "Imagine all they've witnessed from the water. Imagine all they've learned. We don't understand it, but it's life for them all the same."

Barden flashed a smile then walked toward Ailith. She closed her eyes as he passed to go to Greer. The heir was hunched over her pack nearby. She struggled to sleep as well, and her mood was generally dark. She'd been relatively quiet as evening drew near, conveying her requests to Barden who would dispatch orders, but still maintained control over the entire progression.

"I know you're worried about her." Barden sat beside Greer, close enough to Ailith that there was no hiding the conversation.

In the marshes with the damp air seeping into their clothes and bones, autumn had progressed enough that what little warmth Ailith previously experienced in the marsh was gone. Everyone sat close together, taking in each other's body heat and the warmth from the little fire. Only Isla seemed unbothered as she took on the role of mother hen and served tea to the group.

Barden's shoulder pressed against Greer's, companionably close. He looked down at her, his deep voice low and weighted with concern. "But you need to rest, there's no reason for you to keep watch. Let go of some of your responsibilities, that's why you have all of us as your chosen guard."

"I've tried to rest," Greer sounded miserable. A misery Ailith felt to her core. "Every time I close my eyes, my thoughts grow too loud."

Ailith got to her feet and shuffled to Greer, holding out the mug of tea Isla just made for her. "Drink this, it'll help you sleep."

Greer looked at her for a moment, shadows deepening under her eyes, then accepted the mug.

"Thank you," she said softly and Ailith shrugged. When she returned to her pack and blanket, a new, steaming mug was already waiting for her.

The next day they followed the roadway along the coast to the central entry of the valley, and Ailith took in autumn's advancement. When they left, the season had just arrived and was now nearly gone. It was always a quick season, but she felt the particular loss of this one. An entire season lost to roadways and shared moments, and her partner now off to the skies. Trees changed color rapidly and if the weather was cool or storms moved through, the leaves dropped quickly. All signs pointed to an early and brutal winter by the flash of autumn's length, and with the graying skies and the sun lower on the horizon, it seemed fitting that she traveled with dread nestled in her ribcage, chilled and quivering as it seeped into her body.

Braewick Valley's ridge came into view, bringing a surge of energy the group desperately needed. They picked up their speed, climbing the hillsides with Greer and Barden leading the line, and Ailith and Isla behind them.

"How do we broach this to your father?" Barden asked, voicing the question all seemed to have.

"We don't," Greer replied. "I fear how he'll respond if we arrive and tell him that Cait is a dragon."

"His own daughter ..." Ailith said, the words slipping from her mouth before she had a chance to think them through. Barden and Greer looked at her and she felt her cheeks warm. Her life was on the line already, her time in Braewick Valley done, so what did it matter? She decided to be honest. "I've always found the king awful. His rage and selfishness are well known, but the fact that you and Caitriona both seem to agree that he'll kill his own child because of something done to her speaks volumes."

Greer swallowed and turned her attention back to the road. "The carefully constructed image that he's tried to maintain for his citizens doesn't seem to work anymore and I must admit, I'm glad of it."

The four pieced together what to do upon arriving at Braewick City. The plan was flimsy and likely to fail, but attempting to make some plan comforted Ailith, and she suspected it comforted the heir and her right-hand man as well. Greer and Barden would go to the king and distract him; the rest of the guards would disperse and take positions at the air cannons; while Ailith and Isla would go to the top point of the castle: a small balcony where Braewick Valley was viewable from all sides. From there, they hoped to capture Caitriona's attention when she came to the valley. From there, they hoped they could save her.

But as things are with magic and curses, they prove to never work in the time hoped for by mortal men. With the crest of the valley hillside close, there came a sound that all who traveled could recall with ease. A hum that repeated once, then twice, and the air took on an ocean-like quality, pulling back then blowing forward. Ailith's throat constricted, the sensory recollection of years before rolling over her as all feeling in her body flushed down and out of her legs. All turned to the sky and Ailith's heart seized as the massive figure of a gold dragon flew towards them with specks of wildly flapping crows trying to beat its speed.

"Get to the castle," Greer called out. "Go quickly, get to your positions!"

The horses galloped, kicking up dust and dead leaves in their wake as they tried to beat the speed of the dragon flying directly for the castle walls. Greer screamed at the gate guards and they rushed to pull back the gates while the fleet of horses pushed through. The guards who caught sight of Ailith cried her name, but she pushed Onyx on with Isla clinging to her torso.

The dragon circled the city, letting loose a roar that shook the buildings. Some city folk stepped from their homes, eyes to the sky with confusion, but most recognized the sound and rushed to gather children and bring them indoors for what protection their flimsy buildings could provide. The castle loomed before them in its white-stoned glory as Ailith followed Greer and Barden, her horse keeping close to theirs as they made their way beyond the ramparts and to the castle entrance. She only visited within the ramparts a few times in her career, and the layout was unfamiliar and threatening with so many of King Cearny's guards eyeing her with their swords at the ready. Ailith threw herself off Onyx, daring any of them to advance as she twisted around to help Isla who was so short—and the horse so tall—to drop into Ailith's arms.

"This way, this way," Greer ushered them forward into the castle where people rushed to placements and heeded orders. The dragon was spotted and the guards were called to arm, the warning bell rang loudly for all to hear. They didn't have much time.

Amongst the fray, standing still and looming threateningly, stood King Cearny. His blond hair was wild and his dark eyes flicked from person to person as he shouted orders. Ailith would have choked on the self-important air he gave off if she wasn't so focused on saving Caitriona.

Greer stopped short and Ailith ran into her back. The blonde spun on her heel and grasped Ailith's shoulders, her eyes serious as she quickly instructed, "Go down that hall, take a left and you'll enter the library. Call out for Callan, he'll lead you to the tower." Greer pushed Ailith and Isla forward just as the king turned, his eyes narrowing on Ailith.

Ailith grabbed Isla's hand and began to run, moving as quickly as the old woman's feet allowed.

"Callan!" she screamed as she burst through the doors of the library. In the hall, far back, she could hear the king yelling and swore she caught the sound of her name being hurled at her as she pulled the library door closed. Ailith spun on her heel looking for the closest furniture at hand —a table—that she pushed against the door to block it from opening. All the while she screamed, "Callan, we need to get to the tower!"

CHAPTER THIRTY

AILITH

Ailith and Callan took two steps at a time, rushing up the curving stairwell past servants who ran the other way. When Ailith entered the library, she explained rapidly that they needed to reach the top of the tower. While mouse-like when they first met, Callan's strength was clearly in his bravery as he led Ailith and Isla behind metal gates into the library's archival section without hesitation. It was scant of books but had a table covered in maps. Toward the back, he pushed a bookshelf aside and exposed an entryway to a stairwell.

"This goes straight to the top of the tower." He reached for a candle. "It's the quickest and safest way, so long as the king doesn't go through his quarters."

Ailith didn't have time to consider that possibility and had to hope the king remained in the entryway of the castle with Greer. She followed him, coughing at the dust in the air that coated their lungs. They continued to push all the same. A distant roar followed by the shaking of the castle walls emphasized they were working with borrowed time before the stairwell would collapse.

"Why aren't there any good windows in this?" Ailith coughed. They passed by another narrow slit in the stonework that provided dim light but little else as they climbed. "We haven't a clue what's happening."

"If you go to the left, there should be a door," Callan said as they came to the landing. "It'll take us into the hall of the upper floors, there are windows there. We can look out before we continue."

Ailith pushed past Callan, leaving Isla behind who made her way forward slowly. Ailith took the corner and opened the door. Stumbling into the hall, her feet skidded on the dust and crumbled stone covering the marble floors. Her arms shot out and she grabbed the doorframe, catching herself before Callan ran into her back with a grunt. They kept their footing, holding onto one another, and froze in place.

The ceiling was gone from an explosion that revealed the sky above. Walls had crumbled, separating rooms with nothing but debris. Across the expanse of floor were divots, as it collapsed in spots.

Ailith stood open mouthed at the sight of the full dragon sitting in the midst of the destruction. On top of its head were four curved, pointed horns above the temple—two to each side. The scales almost looked white in shadow, but where light touched its flesh, gold sparkled. Its hind legs were as wide as a tree trunk and horn-like bones in similar shape to those on its head ran down its spine before tapering off at the tail, which was as long as its body.

Its long neck curled and its head turned down. The golden eyes matched what Caitriona's eyes had become, but seemed foreign, distant, and unrecognizing of its surroundings. It snuffed from its long nose, with puffs of smoke escaping its nostrils, unaware of the humans at its feet.

"Does she know us?" Callan whispered.

Ailith looked at Callan, uncertain, then back to the dragon. Every memory of the trauma she experienced as a child led her body to freeze and lock in place. Her hands shook and her legs grew weak. She felt like she was five again and wanted to hide. She tried to flush out her rising fears and focus on her memories of Caitriona. The way freckles covered her nose in a splatter like stars, that her cheeks tinged rose red when she blushed, and the feel of her small hand in Ailith's. Somewhere beyond the giant creature, somewhere within, was the girl Ailith had fallen for. She could do this, she had to, because Caitriona didn't deserve any of this.

Stepping forward, eyes turned upward to meet the gold dragon's gaze, Ailith inched forward, ensuring she kept an eye on any movements that seemed to hint at aggression.

"Caitriona," Ailith called, her voice shook as she held her hands to the side, "Cait, it's us. You know us."

"We won't leave you." Callan's voice was uncertain. He glanced at Ailith and gave a small shrug before looking at the dragon again. "We're here."

The dragon stared down unblinking.

"What do we do now?" Callan asked softly as they paused a few feet away, his hands held up similarly to Ailith's.

Ailith hadn't the faintest idea. She had two experiences with dragons: her childhood recollection of the white dragon and this very moment. Neither experience told her if Caitriona was there or how to move forward; it was all a guessing game. Caitriona always remembered herself when she used magic, but she was human then. This beast behaved as one, not as a dragon with a human mind. Perhaps she was there, deep inside, and she would recognize Ailith if only she found a way to coax Caitriona's memories forward.

Ailith stepped forward and paused, watching the dragon's reaction before taking another. A shiver ran along the dragon's skin, a shudder of the large scales of its body. Ailith paced closer, fighting against her inherent desire to run the other way. Her breathing was tight, her heart racing, and tears burned her eyes. Every ounce of her being told her to get away, everything but her heart which encouraged her forward to reach for what was once Caitriona's arm. A single claw was the length of Ailith's foot; the dragon's paw could crush her with applied pressure. Ailith didn't know what else she could do; her ideas had run out and all that was left was to try to save her friend, someone she loved.

If Caitriona still existed in the depths of the dragon, somewhere deep and nestled in the back of its mind, Ailith hoped she would hear her. "Cait, I know you're still you, I know you're still in there. This may be your curse, this may be a part of you now, but perhaps it's not *all* you are. You're still Cait, *my* Cait, and we can bring you back to yourself. Come back to us, please, come back."

She reached forward, not daring to turn her eyes away from the dragon's and touched the dragon's front leg. Another step forward, a pause, and she embraced it as best she could with her chest pressed whole against the cool scales of the dragon and her wounded cheek against its breast. Ailith closed her eyes, her heart racing. "Come back to me, please come back to me."

All was still beside the dragon breathing against her. She could hear its heart beat under the scales, rhythmic and consistent. She remained motionless, her arms tight in the only embrace she could manage and waited for something to happen. Above, a snuff of breath came from the nostrils of the dragon and a wave of warmth washed over Ailith's body before it shifted. Ailith's eyes opened, and her nerves made the hair on her neck rise. The dragon stared at her for a moment before closing its eyes and breathing out a puff of hot air again.

Ailith couldn't withhold the laugh of relief, it burst from her mouth, and she began to cry freely, her tears hot against her cheeks. The dragon opened its eyes and gazed at her with some interest and perhaps, the faintest recollection. For a moment, she felt hopeful—it would be fixed, and Caitriona saved—until a flash came overhead and a thick bolt pierced into the shoulder of the dragon.

Immediately it reared and Ailith fell backward onto the marble floor. The dragon roared, its breath hot, and its forepaw reached to pull at the crossbow bolt that stuck from its shoulder. A flash, and another hit its forearm, eliciting a growling roar.

Ailith rolled onto her hands and knees, looking towards the doorway she'd entered through. Callan's face was pale with shock. Behind him, Isla and Greer stood with another woman. Red hair, green eyes: Queen Róisín. Greer stared, her mouth parted briefly before she screamed, something Ailith didn't hear over the roar of the dragon. Another bolt stood out, far too close to where Ailith imagined the heart to be.

"No," Ailith exclaimed, climbing to her feet. The dragon was pumping its wings and making dust and rubble whip through the air.

Greer yelled as she pushed through the doorway, her hand going to the sword at her side.

Ailith spun on her heel, the broken shards of the roof making her footing uncertain, and looked for the source of the crossbow bolts. King

Cearny stood beyond the crushed floor, lifting the crossbow and sighting his mark as he prepared to shoot again. "No!"

Ailith ran forward, determined to plunge the sword into the king's chest if it was the final thing she did, but a hand grabbed her shoulder, pulling her around and pushing her toward the doorway. Greer was panting, her hair covered in a film of dust, but her eyes were flashing with rage. "I'll talk to him. Go with Isla and my mother to the tower. *Go.*"

Ailith looked between the king and Greer. She wanted to kill the king. For all he did, for all he would do.

"Get moving, MacCree," Greer hissed, her sword out. "You're still under my order. I command you go and save her. Hurry!"

Ailith nodded and turned on her heel. The dragon's mighty wings lifted into the air and its tail hit the roof, bringing more wood and rock down. The last crossbow bolt went flying and Róisín rushed forward, pushing past Ailith with her hand raised to the sky. A wind, cold, sudden and stronger than that created by the dragon's wings, swept past them to knock the bolt off its path, causing it to end its journey in a wooden beam.

Ailith and Róisín looked at one another. Magic, the queen had magic. Callan cursed from the doorway, drawing their attention. "We have to go! Come on!"

They scrambled up the stairs, continuing their climb to the top of the tower and Ailith couldn't bite back her rage anymore. "Why are *you* here?" she snapped at Róisín who'd picked up her skirts and moved with them. Ailith knew what she saw the queen do, but she couldn't reason with it after hearing the queen sat by silently for years. "Why did you decide to help now? After all these years and your hidden powers, you choose now to do something?"

The queen nearly tripped and Ailith was flooded by a rush of satisfaction, hot and wild in her veins.

"Greer said you'd have my head." The queen held her skirts high so she wouldn't trip again. "She explained what happened and, in the end, the only thing I ever wanted was for my daughter to be safe. I tried to help, but my magic is weak from lack of use."

"You still pushed that last bolt away," Isla huffed from behind.

Ailith clenched her jaw, not willing to let her anger go. "You could've helped before all of this! Kayl said he told you of the curse. *You knew*! You *knew* there was a curse. You turned your back on your people *and* your daughters."

"Yes, I knew there was a curse, but the king was ready to be rid of Caitriona the moment she came back to life. He knew I hated him and threatened to kill Caitriona if I stepped out of line. What could I have done that would help her and not place the king's rage on her? I'm a foolish woman. I never said I was not. But I'm learning and I'll right my wrongs."

"You couldn't have thought of—"

"Must we do this *right now*?" Callan cut in, supporting Isla as they continued their ascent, silencing the pair as they circled and came closer to the top. Natural daylight began to make the stairwell glow with a soft white light from an exit ahead.

Ailith pushed forward and came upon a door. Throwing her body against it, it opened to a narrow deck that circled the top of the stairwell. She turned and reached for Isla, helping her onto the landing as she took in the damage to the castle. Primarily, the eastern side was ruined. Walls were crumbling and the roof was on fire. The city itself appeared undamaged and still stood in hazy silence—all the residents seemed to have found places to hide. And above, the golden dragon circled, its eyes searching the ground below. Letting out a stream of flame, more of the roof caught fire.

"Hold onto me, dear," Isla asked, taking hold of Ailith's burned hand. Ailith had taken all the potions she had to help keep away infection and pain, and they were starting to fade. She clenched her teeth but followed Isla's lead as she guided her to the north-facing portion of the deck. Beyond the castle stood the red leaves of the Elder Tree, the only tree to still have all its leaves in the valley and beyond. Isla looked at Ailith. "Call to her."

"Caitriona!" Ailith immediately screamed, turning to the sky. In the distance, black spots filled the air and grew closer—Isla's crows. "Cait! Please!"

The dragon turned its head and straightened its wings as it began to glide, making a large arch through the air as it turned toward the tower.

The pain in her hand grew worse as Isla gripped harder. It spread up her arm, through her shoulder, and into her chest, nearly taking her breath away. "Caitriona," Ailith gasped, her head spinning from pain. "We're going to help you!"

The dragon flew closer then seemed to pause, its wings curling around the air and flapping to hover over the Elder Tree. It was listening. Somewhere beneath the surface Caitriona was fighting for control from the urges of the dragon.

"It's all you, my girl," Isla said as she waved her arm toward the dragon. "You have to speak reason to Caitriona."

Ailith looked down at Isla, her jaw dropping. "I thought you could do magic, I thought you could help?"

Isla glanced at Ailith and frowned. "It's never been about what magic I can or can't do. A series of events were set into motion, and you made yourself the key to saving her. If anyone can speak to her through the glare of what happened, if anyone can reach into the haze of this curse, it's you, Ailith MacCree. You were destined to go on this journey, you were destined to help the princess find her humanity. Now as I said, *call to her!*"

Ailith looked at the dragon, stationary before them with its large wings flapping to stay aloft and its eyes glinted as it looked upon the tower with interest, a growl rumbling deep in its chest that reminded Ailith of thunder. The air from the dragon's wings blew Ailith's hair into her face, stirred her clothing and pushed at her body.

A memory sharpened in a flash. It was Caitriona who called Ailith out of her night terror, and it was Ailith who Caitriona focused on when she produced the fire to protect them from the shades and the hunters.

"Cait," Ailith said, her voice quiet now, yet she knew it didn't matter. What she had to say wasn't for the dragon to hear, but for Caitriona. "Remember when I taught you how to build a fire? Remember dancing in the sea in Stormhaven and watching the sunset in Ulla Syrmin? Remember the first snowy night in Avorkaz? I want more moments like that. I want you to see more of the world with me. Don't leave me, Cait. You promised me that. Come back. *Come back to me.*"

Ailith remained motionless. The sound of crows cawing

overwhelmed the warning bells. The birds grew ever closer until they filled the sky. They circled the tower as they flew in a whirlwind of black but Ailith remained unmoving, unblinking, as she stared at the gold dragon. The crows flew toward the dragon like smoke, blurring it from Ailith's sight. All she could hear was a singular cry from the beast as a bright light broke through and scattered the black crows. They flew back, exposing the dragon once more as its head tilted upward and wings arched out. Then it began to fall. Down, down, down toward the Elder Tree. The crows flew after it and Ailith's view blocked by the ever-moving darkness of the hundreds, if not thousands of crows. Golden scales, golden wings, a golden tail all obscured by feathered darkness until there was a loud breaking of wood and the shattering of limb. The Elder Tree collapsed beneath the weight of the gold dragon and everything grew still.

CHAPTER THIRTY-ONE

AILITH

She left everyone in the tower. The queen wept while Callan tended to her, and Isla had sunk to the floor of the outlook with a smile on her face, her energy spent. So Ailith abandoned the lot of them to scramble down the staircase and into the library. She pulled the table away from the door and ran into the main hall.

The hall was chaos; people coughed from smoke and dust. Guards let Ailith pass without comment as royal employees rushed about, called by the warning bell as her father had been years before, taking directions from guards who shouted orders. Ailith stumbled into one guard who looked her over then stepped aside to let her pass. Apparently, word spread that Ailith was not the convict the king thought she was.

The king was nowhere to be seen, nor was his crossbow. Ailith was disappointed; she still wanted to press her blade into his chest. Her rage was so great that she wanted him to choke on his blood and watch life fade from his eyes. She thought of Raum's lesson and shame tingled along her jawline. She wasn't a murderer; she wouldn't kill him so long as Caitriona was still alive.

Barden barked orders at the far end of the hall, past the entrance they came through earlier. She waved to him, shouting his name as she ran to his side.

"What's the quickest way to the Elder Tree?"

"Why do you need to get there?" Barden held up a hand, pushing off a guard who ran to him for direction.

"Caitriona. She fell there. I don't think she's a dragon anymore, I need to get to her."

Barden looked over his shoulder and pointed. "Go through that door into the gardens. Straight back to the wall covered in rose bushes. You have to push behind them, against the wall. There's a door there that will bring you out to the woods where the Elder Tree is."

Ailith was already moving past Barden when he grasped her shoulder. "You need a key to get through."

He reached beneath his shirt and pulled free a leather cord with a key hanging from it. "Don't lose it or Greer will have both our heads."

Ailith smiled at the key as she backed toward the doors. "Thank you!"

She prayed to the Elder Tree the bolts that hit Caitriona hadn't done permanent damage and the prayer repeated with each step toward the garden.

It was rich with the scent of late blooming roses and dust from the castle. The bushes were full, the leaves still green, but red petals had begun to fall and scattered across the ground like drops of blood. Ailith skidded to a stop at the end of the first row of plants, looking at the tall wall making up the edge of the large garden with the hidden door.

A voice called her name, one Ailith recognized. She turned on her heel to find Greer rushing from a castle door. The tidy braids and pinned blonde hair Greer always wore was now a mess. Locks as long as Caitriona's flowed behind her as she rushed forward. She had blood beneath her nose, which was already swelling, and deep red was splattered across her face and chest. Dust covered most of her clothing as she sprinted to Ailith's side. "Where is she? Where did she fall?"

Ailith pulled forth Greer's key and held it out. "The Elder Tree. She collapsed in the sky; she fell there. Barden gave me a key to a door."

"Follow me!" Taking the key from Ailith's hand and thrusting the leather cord over her neck, Greer ran toward the roses covering the far wall, just as Barden instructed. Greer pulled her sword free and hacked at the plants, not wasting any time. They forced their way through to a thick wooden door with steel covering the surface. Greer quickly worked the key in the lock to free them from the garden. Together they stepped beyond the castle grounds and into the low-lying bushes that surrounded the base of the Elder Tree.

"The boulder blocks the entrance and there's more bushes, but we aren't far," Greer explained as Ailith followed close to her heels.

The ground was covered in branches and fallen leaves. The rainbow of ribbons and glittering coins were scattered on the earth. So many wishes that wouldn't be granted and Ailith thought her own might be amongst the wreckage.

The Elder Tree, while it still stood, had suffered a great deal of damage. It splintered down the middle and half of the tree was lost to the earth. Sap already gathered from the break, dark and thick as it dripped down the sides of what remained. Greer and Ailith scrambled over the partial trunk and limbs while calling for Caitriona. They separated, searching the tangle of tree bits and discarded dreams. There was no body of a golden dragon, that much was obvious, but the body of a young woman was harder to find. Brushing past ribbons and leaves, Ailith peeked beside curled roots and jagged tree limbs. The bells from the castle grew silent and the forest was quiet beside the pounding of her heart.

"I found her!" Greer cried a few yards away.

Ailith rushed forward, tripping over fallen branches. Greer was bent over, pulling limbs away from a little mound of leaves. A hand, a human hand with no sign of scales or claws, lay visible from the pile but it was unmoving. Ailith grabbed another branch, tossing it over her shoulder and ignored the pain in her arm. She dug at the leaves until she found Caitriona's body beneath. Laying amongst the leaf litter, her hair still gold, her body bare and covered in scratches, and bleeding from where she was struck by the crossbow bolts, she was motionless. There were changes, alterations from the girl Ailith knew, but all she could focus on was the rise and fall of the princess's chest as she breathed.

"And so, the curse is *truly* fulfilled."

Greer and Ailith looked at one another then turned toward the sound of the voice. Isla stood on the outer edge of the damage. "A dragon to destroy the king's house and death by his daughter's hand."

Ailith's brow furrowed and she looked down at Caitriona then back to Isla and Greer. "No, I saw the king, she didn't kill him. She began flying away after he struck her. Even if she did, she wouldn't be able to live with herself if she—"

Greer mouth flattened in a line, jaw tight and her breathing fast. While her nose bled freely, having been hit by something, the rest of the blood splattered on her chest and face was dry and not her own. Ailith blinked, the understanding coming suddenly.

"*Death by his daughter*—he has *two* daughters." Ailith sighed as Greer's shoulders sank and she looked at the ground.

"Even after I told him what happened, he didn't care. He knew it was Caitriona and he was going to kill her all the same," Greer whispered, her gaze moving to take in her sister's form. "And I couldn't allow that to happen. I couldn't allow all of this to continue, all of the hatred and vile behavior. I should've stopped him before this, but I couldn't let him kill her."

Caitriona moaned, drawing both of their attention.

"Best to get her inside before anyone sees her," Isla called, circling the outer ring of the clearing. "I'm sorry I couldn't help or reveal more. But this was meant to happen and to meddle would have brought dire consequences to the kingdom. Know that I did all I could."

Ailith looked at the old woman who offered a toothy smile before her form fell apart, turning into hundreds of crows that took to the sky and cried to the heavens the story of one princess who turned into the dragon and another princess who took the life of a king.

EPILOGUE

Aɪʟɪᴛʜ

The Following Year

When Caitriona was first found, she was in a feverish sleep for days, waking briefly only to sip water. Nothing could stir her from that place of rest and all hoped she only needed time.

The elder MacCrees and Gwen left the little cottage toward the north behind and returned to their home in the city. A few days after their return, Ailith was released from Braewick's royal healers. With the help of May's potions, Ailith avoided greater injury to her weeping burns, but they still needed attention and she needed rest. Free from work by Greer's demand to recover her strength and heal from her wounds, Ailith returned home to her family.

"Did you see the sea? Did you travel the mountains?" her parents asked, trying to pull Ailith from the silence she sunk into. She wanted to tell them what she saw and experienced, but she found her energy spent, her words dried up, and conversation something she was incapable of.

Ailith went to her room and slept for a day. Even when she woke, she couldn't speak. It was too much; it was all too much.

"Sweet girl, you must tell us what's wrong so we may help you," her mother said, having climbed the stairs to Ailith's room while her father waited at the bottom, his brow furrowed deeply with worry. That was when Ailith began to cry.

The fear of never returning home, the fright and horror of watching Caitriona forced into a being against her will, and how close she came to losing it all—her home, her parents, Caitriona, and her physical abilities as her arm wept with blisters from the burns—broke Ailith. In silence, her parents comforted her. They weren't unfamiliar with times that the world became too much and Ailith found herself unable to speak. They understood. Just as it would take time for Caitriona to wake from her sleep, so it did for Ailith to recover enough to find her words again.

It took a few days of rest and tears before Ailith felt the blockade disperse and her energy return. She found her words, telling her parents what occurred before being welcomed back within the castle to take her position at Caitriona's bedside. She helped where she could, but otherwise spent the passing hours beside the sleeping princess whispering to her as she had in Ulla Syrmin, but this time it was nonsensical because Caitriona kept sleeping. Nothing Ailith said did anything to wake her.

A week after returning to Braewick, Ailith arrived at the castle in the chilly morning. A crow called from overhead. A black shape glided past and something fell. Ailith stepped back and watched the object flutter to the ground. A small scroll of paper, tightly wound and tied with yarn that matched the sweaters Isla knit.

His name is Crowley, the letter stated in scrawling black ink. *A teasing name—one of my favorites, but he's always at odds with me and prone to wandering west. I felt he'd be happiest in Braewick. He's quite good at letter delivery, should you ever find the need to write to those of us who remain near or within the mist. He enjoys nuts as a reward. Should you fail to serve such a recompense, he'll likely defecate on you when you least expect it. –Isla*

Ailith couldn't help but laugh. She flipped the paper over and found small writing on the back: *Mugwort may help.*

Mugwort, brewed into a tea that Caitriona sipped while half asleep did help and Ailith celebrated by feeding Crowley his weight in nuts, which easily convinced the corvid that Ailith was worth sticking by.

A day after Caitriona woke, Etta waited on Ailith's doorstep as she came home from the market with another bag of nuts under her arm.

"I'm sorry, dear." The woman clutched a letter in her wrinkled hands, her eyes lowered and her voice heavy with sorrow. "But the princess ... she doesn't want to see you right now. She explains it all here."

In her curled handwriting, Caitriona expressed her shame and sorrow, and admitted her reluctance to face anyone, including Ailith, and only wished to heal. Rather than wallowing, Ailith wrote a letter to Ceenear with a simple request, sending Crowley to the winds as the first snowflakes of winter began to fall, and received the response she expected.

Still barred from seeing the princess, Ailith passed the news to Etta with another letter. "Give this to Caitriona or Greer. It's an invitation for Cait to continue her recovery with the friends we made beyond the mist."

Within a week Caitriona was gone, taking a carriage to Isla's and traveling from there to Ulla Syrmin. Ailith didn't even have the opportunity to say goodbye, she was only left with a letter from Caitriona requesting she write.

A month after, Gwen burst into their bedroom with her face red and her chest heaving from running up the flight of stairs. "Ailith, you need to come downstairs now!"

In their doorway stood Greer with Barden behind her. Wrapped in a fur-lined cloak, her hair in a tight bun, the new ruler of Wimleigh Kingdom glanced at the worst attributes of Ailith's house. A new roof had been built just as a cold snap with early snow arrived. The living space and side of the house were still littered with sawdust and wood scraps, but the interior was rich with the scent of fresh wood.

"Ailith, I'm glad to see you." Greer's informal tone was a surprise to Ailith's household, but it softened Ailith.

Ailith hugged herself, feeling underdressed with Greer in her fine clothes and Barden standing behind with the crest of the crown stamped on the chest of his own heavy coat. He winked at her before schooling his face to remain serious. It only made Ailith more confused.

"I'm happy to see you too. The both of you. Is everything alright? Is there something wrong with Cait?"

Greer smiled at this and Ailith realized the queen was quite pretty, her face changing entirely when she was happy. It wasn't something she saw before all this. "She's fine, don't worry. I came to see you. You see, you've proven yourself in more ways than most royal guards have, and I wanted to make an offer. Join me. Become a royal guard. I won't destine you to battles if that isn't what you want. But I want you by my side. I think your upbringing, your experiences, your *voice* is needed."

Years before, Ailith would have immediately refused. But that was before Ailith learned there were often multiple sides to situations, and it was best for her to remain open minded to possibility.

For nearly a year, Ailith wrote to Caitriona. As her burns healed and she strengthened the damaged muscles and skin of her hand, the letters grew longer. She wrote of her day-to-day experiences and news of her parents—and Gwen—moving into the homes set aside for royal guards. She knit on her days off, her stitches awkward and messy from lack of practice and her right hand stiff. But she sent a scarf, and eventually mittens, to the Endless Mountains. Caitriona sent pressed winter flowers from Ulla Syrmin and poems. She transcribed fae stories she learned and drew pictures of the places she wanted to take Ailith someday. Each letter had pieces of themselves, their memories and secrets scratched into the paper with quill pens. It was through these correspondences they grew closer and yet there was never an answer to the final line of every letter Ailith sent: *when will I see you again*?

As autumn put on its best display after a long, warm summer, Caitriona penned a simple message to Ailith, the one she'd waited for: *I hope you will agree to see me the morning of Greer's coronation. If so, please come to my quarters just before the midday bells. I've missed you.*

The city dutifully mourned the unexpected death of the king for three whole seasons as was the standard practice, but now that the mourning period ended, the jovial crowning could commence. The trees were torches of orange and gold, while what remained of the Elder Tree blazed with fire in the deep reds it was known for as it persisted despite its injury. The season lingered in brightly colored celebration, as if to say, change would continue for better or for worse.

The sunshine was warm, but in the shadows of buildings was the chill of oncoming winter and the whispers of frost. It left the people of Braewick City uncertain of what to wear for the long-anticipated crowning of the new queen, and so they came in summer shirts and dresses with shawls and coats to cover chilled shoulders.

Braewick Castle was a work in progress for the second time in less than two decades. Half the roof of the living quarters was destroyed, and much of the top floor ruined. It was decreed by the new queen that the royal family would leave Braewick Castle behind, turning what remained into a university and expanding the library once a new castle was built on the western edge of the city, high enough into the hills that the ocean would be viewed from its windows on the west, and the valley to the east. Until then, what remained of the royal family lived within and very little was seen of them in the year following the attack.

Ailith walked quickly down the hall of the castle, pulling at the sleeves of her white shirt and fidgeting at the brooch on her throat. Her hair had grown longer in the last year; she wore it half braided, half loose which obscured part of the scar on her left cheek. Her right hand itched and she pulled at the sleeve of her shirt again, attempting to adjust the fabric over the ripple of scars on her arm and hand from the dragon's breath. It took her half a year to retrain how to shoot her bow with her non-dominant hand. The skin on her right proved too tight, the muscles weakened, but she was improving with guidance from Barden and his father, as well as a steady supply of creams ordered from Declan and May and sent all the way from Avorkaz.

She reached the room at the end of the hall and came face to face with Barden who stood outside in a vest similar to Ailith's, the same quality of deep blue fabric and the embroidery of the Elder Tree stitched into the breast. His shoulders relaxed when he saw Ailith, an encouraging smile alighting his lips. He and Ailith had grown close over the past year as they worked and trained together.

"Is she in there?" Ailith asked and Barden nodded.

"Just remember to breathe," he offered, a hand reaching to grip Ailith's left arm—her good arm—reassuringly. "You look like you're ready to pass out."

"Well ..." Ailith began and lost the words. She shrugged.

"I know. It'll be fine though, it's just your nerves getting the best of you," Barden replied before unlatching the door and pushing it open for Ailith's entrance. Ailith brushed at her pants and pushed her hair over her shoulders, before taking a breath and stepping into the room.

Queen Róisín, soon to be the queen mother, looked at Ailith and rose to her feet. She wore a gray-blue dress, and her vibrant red hair was braided in a way to pull it back from her face, placing her pointed ears on display. After the death of the king, she removed the glamor and Caitriona wrote to Ailith that her mother began sharing memories of her time in Caermythlin when they exchanged correspondence. She also gathered funds to send to those who left Caermythlin before it was destroyed, and worked diligently with Ailith's father to design an orphanage that would be built in Braewick Valley. It wasn't enough to make up for her deceit, but it was a start.

Ailith let her dislike of the woman diminish to a murmuring irritation. Through working with Greer, Ailith began to understand the queen mother a little more. They both were wounded creatures from their experiences in life, unwilling to trust strangers and preferring to keep their distance. They both had the same drive, too: to keep their loved ones safe and protected, even if the queen's way of showing that was a bit odd. All the distance the queen maintained with her daughters was due to the king. The moment magic was used to bring Caitriona back to life, Cearny viewed Caitriona as tarnished goods, touched by magic and nearly as awful as any human who wielded such gifts. He was suspicious of the queen, assuming correctly she had magic at her disposal. The queen's desire to protect Caitriona made all the more sense. In that, Róisín and Ailith bonded over their love for Caitriona and desire to keep her safe.

She nodded to Ailith before brushing past her and out the door, slipping away quietly with whisper-soft footsteps that reminded Ailith of her time in the Endless Mountains. Greer met her searching eyes next and offered a half smile. In the past year, Greer came into her own. She stood tall and, while constantly serious as she always was, she shared more smiles with those around her than her father ever had. Already the people of Braewick had high expectations of Greer and it seemed she'd satisfy the desires of the townspeople. People were eager to see how Greer would perform as a queen, and many hoped to convince her to follow their own political interests. Ailith suspected emotions would boil over in the future, but for now, the citizens were content to sit back and see what her moves would be.

Now, the morning of the coronation, Greer shifted around the tall chair that faced the curved windows of the room, stiff in her movements. She was forced into a gown for the coronation that she repeatedly complained about, but looked beautiful in. It was a deep blue with maroon attributes and pearls stitched across the bodice to create a crisscross design. Her sheer, bell-shaped sleeves shimmered in the light, the tips brushing the floor. Her hair was loose and fell in waves to the small of her back, her head unadorned until shortly after noon when she would receive the royal crown. She patted Ailith on her left shoulder, similarly as Barden had done, before moving from the room, and leaving her alone with Caitriona.

Ailith froze in the middle of the bedroom of her former traveling companion. How Caitriona looked was no secret to her. Word was gently released to the public that the princess had survived a curse, that she was the golden dragon, and she was changed. The fact that the dragon only had sights for the castle softened the news to many, but the coronation was the first time many would see the princess and nerves were high.

Ailith opened her mouth then closed it. Her hands tingled and she felt lightheaded with nerves. When alone, she often ran dialogue in her mind of conversations she'd have with Caitriona, but now she was tongue tied, and shifting from foot to foot in the center of Caitriona's spacious room.

"Hello, Ailith," Caitriona spoke from the other side of the tall-backed chair, her voice immediately making Ailith's heart beat faster.

Ailith was released from her temporary hesitancy and moved forward, circling to the front of the tall-backed chair to face Caitriona. She grinned.

"Hello, Cait." Ailith knelt into a deep bow.

"Oh heavens, please don't do that." Caitriona's voice hedged toward a laugh. She leaned forward and took Ailith's hands into her own, urging the guard to stand upright but pausing as her thumb passed over the scarred tissue of Ailith's right hand, her brief smile stilling on her lips, then fading. "Oh."

Ailith attempted to pull her hand away, but Caitriona held on tightly. She slipped her hand along Ailith's and pushed her sleeve up to examine the ripples of skin. Ailith carefully wrote that she suffered some burn damage, but this was the first Caitriona saw it. "I did this, didn't I?"

"It's nothing," Ailith said, but frowned when Caitriona's golden eyes narrowed. "Okay, well, it covers most of my arm, but it's healing. It'll just take time. I have wonderful salves from May. It's okay."

"I really am a monster." Caitriona let go of Ailith's hand.

"Oh, come now," Ailith replied, turning to grab hold of a fancy little stool that sat nearby. She dragged it closer and sat, leaning forward and resting her elbows on her knees. "I don't see a monster."

"Really, Ailith?" Caitriona asked, raising her hand to touch her temple. Much like the dragon, on each side of Caitriona's head were two sets of horns pushing up and out, curving slightly toward the sky. When the light hit them, they gleamed white with a slight golden shine; the first horns closest to Caitriona's temple were only an inch long, but the horns behind were double the length. Ailith thought they were beautiful, like a crown. Caitriona did not agree.

Greer mentioned that Caitriona was mortified when she realized none of the Gablaigh crowns fit over her horns, and they worked with a jeweler to create a new crown that now lay on a pillow close by, waiting to be worn.

But the horns weren't the only permanent changes: a sheen of golden scales covered Caitriona's shoulders and peeked from the neckline of her dress like glittering light on her skin. Beyond the horns and scales, Caitriona's hair and eyes remained golden, and scars from the crossbow bolts her father shot peeked from the edging of her maroon gown. She was, otherwise, herself again, at least physically. Caitriona wrote to Ailith, explaining a little with each letter, that mentally she was burdened by the experience and trauma done to her body. She could recall changing into the dragon and how it felt; after a period of time, she recalled *being* the dragon.

"Cait, the curse was embedded in you for most of your life. That wasn't your choice. Being a monster, I feel, is entirely based on choice. You choose to do evil things; you choose to hurt others—*that's* being a monster. *You* didn't choose to do anything. You were forced into it."

Caitriona frowned but didn't argue, which Ailith considered a success. What went unspoken was the choices Kayl made. He was never seen after Caitriona became the dragon. There were rumors that some who knew him caught sight of him on occasion, a wisp of the man he once was, more shadow than substance and falling apart closer to nothing than existing. His decision to curse Caitriona was a choice spurred by King Cearny's actions. Of all the monsters, it seemed the king was the worst of all.

"Do you remember when I said I wished none of it happened and I was home?" Caitriona asked, tilting her head back, the horns caught the light of the sunny day. "I take it all back. What I really wish is that we were back in Avorkaz, in the little room at the inn."

Ailith grinned and reached for Caitriona's hand, leaning forward with a hungry look. "You know we could always do that again."

"I regret to inform you I can no longer slip in unnoticed," Caitriona said with a sigh, but a smile appeared like a glimpse of sun during a cold, cloudy day. "I'm pretty sure the world knows Wimleigh Kingdom's princess is part dragon now."

"Ah, damn." Ailith snapped her fingers. "We'll just have to find somewhere to go within the valley. Perhaps that cottage your sister put my parents in? I'm sure your sister would let us slip away for a few days."

Caitriona made a small laugh. Ailith mentally captured the sound and placed it in her heart. She looked at the oddly shaped crown and back at Caitriona, raising her eyebrows. "How about we put that on you. It won't be as much fun as we had in Avorkaz but ..."

Caitriona frowned as if it offended her. "I suppose I better just get it over with."

Ailith hopped to her feet and lifted the delicate crown. It was made to rest upon the top of Caitriona's head with sparkling opals at the center of her forehead before the metal work curved around the base of each horn with additional jewels dripping down between them, leaving them to glimmer against Caitriona's hair. It curved back around the rest of Caitriona's head with delicate metal work of curled smoke and rounded suns spotted with diamonds. Caitriona got to her feet and stood before Ailith for a moment, gathering the hem of the long maroon skirts of her dress. Ailith smiled.

"You're taller than me now with those," she pointed out, her eyes on Caitriona's horns. Caitriona glanced up, cracking a small smile.

"I suppose you're right."

Caitriona settled onto Ailith's little stool as Ailith circled behind her, gently placing the crown onto her head. She leaned around to see if the front was centered and found Caitriona reaching for her cheek, fingers gently brushing over the scar, her touch igniting Ailith's heart to divine humming. She sucked in her breath and met Caitriona's eyes. They froze in place for a moment, the pair falling into the pool of each other's gaze before Ailith blinked and pulled back, circling Caitriona fully to kneel down on the floor before the princess.

"Cait. I promised Greer something before we went to Avorkaz, and I fear I failed her and you."

Caitriona's brow wrinkled. "What do you mean?"

"I promised to save you. That's what she asked of me, and I failed you both."

Caitriona shook her head and lifted Ailith's hands to her lips, kissing them and pressing the back of Ailith's scarred hand against her cheek. "Oh, Ailith, you have it all wrong. When I was in that other form, you were the shimmering spot in all the haze. You were the thing tethering me to the world. You did what you promised."

The midday bells began to chime beyond the room. Caitriona sat up a little straighter and looked at the window. "I suppose it's time."

"It'll be fine." Ailith got to her feet. "I'll be there with you."

Caitriona smiled but didn't reply, her gaze lost in the view out her window for a moment before turning to the guard. "Ailith? You mentioned at one point you left a wish at the Elder Tree. Did it ever come true?"

Ailith led them toward the door, holding Caitriona's hand in her own. She thought of the moments in the early dawn light at the Elder Tree and the scrap of cloth she tied to a branch before Caitriona's arrival. Ailith traveled to the tree shortly after returning home and pushed her way around palace workers gathering sap, fallen limbs, and branches. It took ages, but she finally located her cloth and pulled it free from the tree, not wanting the tree to take her granted wish back. She had all she wished for: to be home and happy.

"It did," Ailith grinned. "Did you leave a wish? Did it come true?"

"Before I left for Ulla Syrmin." Caitriona's eyes sparkled as brightly as the jewels of her crown. She pressed her shoulder against Ailith's and stepped closer to the guard. Brushing her lips against Ailith's cheek and holding Ailith's hand tightly in her own, Caitriona sighed. "And I think it's coming true."

BONUS CONTENT
THE CASCADING SKY

THE CASCADING SKY

AILITH

Fifteen Years Ago

The first day of autumn held the honey-sweet taste of possibility. Sunshine turned gold and dripped betwixt the Elder Tree's tear-drop leaves that once shone bright green. Now they displayed veins of butter yellow preluding the deep reds that would follow in a few weeks. The day dawned with persistent exquisiteness as the sun approached its peak in the sky. Children slept through the night, bread dough rose then baked to perfection, chickens laid impeccable eggs, and the citizens of Braewick Valley were abundantly cheerful for no particular reason. The early harvests were plentiful, the city richly scented with smoked meats, and preparation of fruits and vegetables for winter happened without the annoyance of bugs. The arrival of autumn cast magic on the land, and even the fearsome royal guardsmen were caught exchanging pleasantries with peasants.

To fathom the future in the glory of a new season was impossible. Reflection of the flawless morning would occur for years to come whilst citizens stood before broken stone and weed-covered memorials. With hushed tones, they would note how the morning hours slipped to peaceful early afternoon as they searched memories for cracks, shimmering weaknesses they missed, anything to indicate the shattering of their safety. A reminder that perfection is fragile and never long lasting, while destruction may appear as rapidly as the breeze can change.

At least, the memory of the day would appear that way for most. For those too young, the memory would present itself in dreams, nightmares, and the near constant unease found when safety is never truly known.

Midday bells tolled and dappled sunshine shone off five-year-old Ailith MacCree's summer-browned skin from where she rested beneath the heavy boughs of the Elder Tree. She sighed and turned her face toward the sunlight; a smile played over her berry juice-stained lips. Through her closed eyelids, the sunlight was red and yellow, creating a pattern of swirls and pulsing design that only she could witness. The breeze brushed her cheek, tickling her neck with wafts of her brown hair.

A few feet away, her parents laid out a blanket beneath the Elder Tree's stretching canopy as they shared stories from their workday. Ailith felt a nap close at hand from the gentle murmur of her parents' voices and the sweet berries stolen from the satchel digesting in her belly. Cari's work as a seamstress continued going well, but Taren finally received an offer a week prior as a top stonemason for the royal family and they at last could celebrate. It was a rarity Ailith's parents spent a day together—too often one would be working—but their schedules aligned. Another gift of autumn.

After a week of work, Taren brought home a larger pouch of coin than he often made in a month. Together the family of three splurged on late summer fruit, fresh bread, smoked meat, and rich cheeses at the street markets before following the city roads along the castle to paths to the Elder Tree.

There weren't many trees in the lower ward. One flowering tree struggled outside the MacCree house, and Ailith found it charming, but it couldn't compare to the majesty of the Elder Tree. She adored the massive roots and deep curves of the bark. She loved the soft leaves and shades of color they wore through the year. With her eyes closed, feet pressed against the trunk, and the sun smiling down, Ailith could happily remain there all her days.

Ailith pressed her palms against the earth. Her fingertips traced the curves of bark-covered roots to where they plunged into dirt. There were stories that the tree gave life; root hairs spread and birthed the ground-clinging drowning dukes, marrow maidens, and fool makers. Taproots swelled and sky-bound dragons, wyverns, and cockatrices burst from them and crawled outward. But as the tree grew, limbs spreading and leaves unfurling, men, fae, phoenixes, and dryads were found nestled in the blades with the tissue curled around their bodies.

Could she sense future creatures lurking beneath the soil in the roots? Or perhaps a fallen leaf would birth a fae child right before her; someone who would be her playmate. Her imagination of what powers the Elder Tree held took flight since she learned the history of her kingdom in the single-room classroom she attended once a week. The tree was powerful; anything that could create life was. But there was more to it than that, a greater power that particularly drove Ailith's fascination.

Wishes. The tree heard wishes and made them *come true.*

Ailith's teachers explained the founder of the kingdom, Baldwin Gablaigh, discovered the Elder Tree towering over the forest. He walked across the land that later became Vissenore searching for a place to establish his home. He was starving, weary, and cold. Wrapping himself tightly amongst the scraps of his torn and weathered cloak, he settled beneath the tree and spoke to it like a friend.

"Please," he begged its branches. "I want a full belly and a soft bed. My feet are swollen and my body weak. I want to find a home."

He did not expect the tree to answer and so he wasn't surprised when the tree remained silent, yet he was compassionate to this mighty hardwood that lived through many years. A broken branch hung above him, likely an injury from the freezing wind and rain that passed through just days prior. The jagged edge looked sharp and dangerous compared to the majesty of the rest of the tree, and it dripped a dark sap steadily to the ground like blood from a wound. Taking pity, Baldwin climbed to his weary feet and tore his tattered cloak from his shoulders. He wrapped the broken branch with its cloth, as if attempting to heal a fracture, then settled against its roots to fall asleep. When he woke, he was inside a stone building, in a soft bed with a fire roaring, and food prepared and waiting. From the window, the Elder Tree stood. The cloak fell from the broken branch to show it healed and the sap no longer flowed.

Braewick Castle now sat on the spot that the Elder Tree placed the little stone building, and the people of Wimleigh Kingdom honored the Elder Tree and all its magic. The royal family—the Gablaighs—placed the Elder Tree on their family crest. It was designed in its glory with silver against a green background on their shields and hung from banners. Citizens of Wimleigh Kingdom traveled to the tree and spoke softly of their dreams. All honored it and the gift it provided: that it granted wishes, so long as you left an offering and took the offering from the tree's branches once your wish was granted.

If Ailith could leave a wish, it would be to befriend the Gablaigh princesses. She saw them the summer prior at the king's birthday celebration. King Cearny seemed stern and frightening, but he was of little interest to Ailith. She only had eyes for his daughters, the princesses. Stoic Greer, five-years' Ailith's elder, and little Caitriona who was a smiling toddler spinning circles around the queen. Ailith's loneliness as an only child gave her endless opportunities to play pretend and a specific hunger for their friendship.

"May I leave a wish?" Ailith opened her dark eyes as her fingertips pressed into the soil and her feet remained sturdy against the trunk. Sunlight made the coins sparkle and wink, and colorful threads and cloths of offerings waved in the breeze.

Soft footfall approached over the grassy and rooted ground. Cari stepped closer to Ailith and looked down, smiling with wrinkles already standing out at the corners of her eyes. Gray streaked her long, braided, black hair that swung over her shoulder as she bent down. Cari ran her fingertips along the curve of Ailith's cheek and the tip of her braid tickled her nose.

"I'm sorry, dove." Her voice was clear, soft and reassuring. "We have all we hope for and we mustn't be greedy. Let the tree grant wishes for those who truly need them."

Ailith blinked, feeling a chill prickle at her neck. Her mother's words rang out, solitary, too loud in the brush previously filled with afternoon birdsong which was now silent. Cari's smile froze and began to fade as Ailith's spine curled with discomfort. Ailith sat up fast, pulling her feet off the tree trunk and twisting to look at her father across the undergrowth.

He crouched with eyes turned upward and lips parted while his chest rose and fell. His breaths came fast. "It's time we return home."

Ailith scrambled to her feet. She'd only heard this tone from her father once before when he woke her one night a few months prior. "*It's time we go for a quick walk*," he had whispered, stirring Ailith from her sleep and picking her up. It wasn't until they hurried down the narrow road Ailith saw the glow of flames in the night as fire from a burning home in their neighborhood spread.

Presently, her father shook his head and raised his hand toward them. "Ailith, stay by the tree."

She slunk backward like a cornered cat, uncertain why he changed his directions yet feeling this was necessary. She pressed against the Elder Tree's trunk, while her mother returned to the picnic area. They gathered their items, remaining silent while haphazardly placing each piece of their rich meal back into the satchel. Ailith helped fill it an hour prior, gently placing the items inside the basket with care, but now that care was gone. Her mother balled the blanket they ate upon. The unwrapped cheese was tossed within the confines of the satchel and the paper it came in forgotten. The berry stems were scattered to the earth, and the silence of the woodland pressed forward.

A pregnant pause grew to suppress ear drums until it was so thick it transcended to humming vibration along skin that raised hairs. It was then their movements were triumphed by another noise, rising from the distance with repetition, a hushed sigh from the east growing louder like the earth had a heart beating all along. Ailith's parents arched their necks and looked to the skies. Abandoning the picnic supplies in unison, they rushed toward Ailith.

The air lifted from the ground. Strands of Ailith's hair drifted upward toward the tree limbs as the bottom of the leaves flipped over and exposed their soft undersides. Her parents leaned in, wrapping their arms around her and the tree. They pressed into her like a barricade from an invisible force. They didn't speak and all the same Ailith knew to remain silent, still, and watchful.

Then the forest quaked.

Swaying back and forth, air rushed forward into Ailith's face before retreating just as quickly as it arrived. A sharp crack broke the air and a treetop fell yards away, a heavy sound that shook the ground and mingled with the rush of falling leaves. The Elder Tree's branches swayed, following the breathing of the forest back and forth, back and forth, as unfulfilled wishes and dreams shook loose in a downpour of coins and shower of ribbons.

While the air shifted, another sound grew. Filled with a rage Ailith had not experienced in her short life, yet knew instinctively, it descended upon them like thunder. Ailith clutched her parents, her fingers knitting into the thin cloth of their shirts as she shrunk further against the tree. Beyond the canopy, the face of a fanged, white dragon appeared. Its eyes shone like silver, its horns spread like the antlers of a deer, and the expanse of its wings were broader than could be seen through the breaks of foliage.

Its white body slipped over the sky, flying effortlessly while the wind its wings created made the forest bow to its power. The cries from its throat made leaves fall and as it disappeared from sight, Ailith realized her body was quivering with fright.

Perhaps it was gone, a nightmare passing, but her parents clung to her and did not move. Through their stillness, the lesson was passed to Ailith. Remain still, listen, wait. They were small creatures, insignificant, and fragile in the sights of the dragon, like rabbits in a burrow with an owl passing overhead.

It flew over the Elder Tree again and released a final cry before the world brightened in a flash and heat ran its burning fingers along the landscape.

The sound of massive, sudden flame was something Ailith would stumble over to describe in future years. It was an experience one only felt and words could not contain. The force of rage built within the creature and balled into a single breath. It pushed outward into something heated with molten anger, hunger, and lust. It wanted, it sought, and it claimed. The heat of the flame hit its targets and luckily it was not the Elder Tree, but somewhere else. Still, the world smoked, the air grew heavy with soot, and the sky became a dangerous form of red. Bells rang, somewhere in the distance like peals of panic, and Ailith's father shifted against the tree.

"I have to go." He lifted his face toward the flakes of burning ember drifting down like forbidden snow. Ailith and her mother looked at him with confusion and he gave a weak rise of his shoulder. "The bells; we're to report to the castle if the warning bells sound."

"There's a *dragon*, Taren," Cari hissed, her arms shifting to pull Ailith closer as if to overcome the void of where Taren's arms once were. "You aren't a royal guard, you're a stone mason!"

"King's orders." Taren voice was small and filled with the precursor of regret. "The bells toll, and all able-bodied men are to report to the castle, even us lowly masons."

He got to his feet as if they were made with led. Cari snatched forward to grip him and keep him in place. He paused, his gaze falling on Cari's, and Ailith looked between them with fear and confusion that made her heart tremble. They both had tears in their eyes. Both of her parents—her parents who rarely shed tears. This wasn't good, this wasn't right.

"Stay here until you don't hear the dragon anymore, then go home. I'll find you there." He stepped backward and Cari's hand loosened.

King's orders. There was no fighting against what the king wanted, even Ailith knew that. As he vanished into the thickening smoke, Cari ran her hand over Ailith's hair and pressed her against her chest. Ailith curled into the embrace, burying her face as tears flooded her eyes. She wept as her mother's tears dripped onto her hair while the dragon roared, and the world grew redder and the air smelt wrong. She wept until the roar of the dragon stopped and all that remained were the tolling bells.

Ailith remained with her mother, crouched beside the Elder Tree, but after a time, they rose together. Holding onto one another, they inched away from the tree and its fallen wishes, and picked their way over broken limbs and brambles to retrieve their satchel. They found the path they took earlier, now rough with leaves and shattered stone that made its way so far from the castle walls. The air pressed into them, red with the heat of fire and ash. Ailith wiped flakes from her eyes and clutched her mother's hand. She fought the urge to glance at the sky and search the smoke-laden air for threats. A habit she would keep for the rest of her life, birthed from the attack.

The moment of terror was brief in time yet grew powerful by expanding each passing moment. It became long-lasting in the minds of witnesses. People meandered lost and confused, covered in dust and sticky with blood beside the clear tracks down their cheeks from tears shed. Royal guards ran past, sightless to people stumbling from shattered homes as shouts rose from the castle walls. The destruction was scattered, the castle and buildings closest to it hit the hardest. Words made their way through the haze, bouncing off crumbled stone and floating on ash, loud and shrill and settling into Ailith's veins—*the fields, the fields northward, the dragon in the fields, dead, the dragon is dead*—and Ailith realized what was missing. Beyond her sense of safety, beyond her father's absence; the warning bells were missing from the air. They were, at last, silenced.

ACKNOWLEDGMENTS

Often there is an impression that writing is a solitary activity and for many years, I thought this was true. But writing *Tarnished* taught me it isn't solitary at all, but something best done with a solid support group who surround you with encouragement in the best of ways. This group helped me so much that I do not know where I would be if I did not have them.

First, I want to thank the creative team that helped make this book shine. Jean and Staci from Creative James Media, thank you for championing my novel which subsequently became a trilogy. You both truly helped guide my dreams to life and I appreciate your encouragement, knowledge, and support. Luxury Banshee, you've depicted all of my girls with such eloquent art and I am grateful that we have such an amazing artistic relationship. To the wonderful artists that have given visual uniqueness to my story, thank you, in particular Michelle Connor for my chapter headings, Triumph Covers for my cover and Dewi Hargraves for my map.

Second, I am forever grateful that I've been taught by such an incredible group of English teachers and professors throughout my life. Most of my favorite education stories are tied to these teachers who taught me to love reading and writing. They encouraged me to create stories and saw the best in me when I didn't see it in myself. Thank you all.

Thank you to my beta readers and friends who have seen *Tarnished* at its worst and encouraged me to get to its best: Meredith, Christine, Lucie, Andrew, Eliana, Hannah, Amy, Jennifer, Anshul, and Josie.

To writer friends who supported me every step of the way by accepting random questions no matter the hour, helping put out fires I self-created in my mind, who cheered for me and comforted me, and were all-around people I've come to deeply love: thank you. Particularly Corinne, Taylor, Diane and Teagan. To my friends— Mere, Leo, Lyss, and Wren—who are the best cheer squad, I'm thankful to know you and have you in my court. Ali, one of the first people who encouraged me to go full throttle with this idea, thank you. Melissa, who's been my biggest source of encouragement and has read every single version of this story without growing tired of it, I am abundantly grateful for you and our friendship. My Finger Lakes Scribblers, I love our write-ins and chats, and I'm grateful we're part of the same community. My elemental authority—Courtney, Kassidy, and Christine—you've brought me an abundance of joy, laughter, and pride over the last year, and I'm so happy to be on this publishing journey with you.

You all are amazing people who've made this entire experience all the better. What would I do without you? I never want to know.

Thank you to my family who endured the flurry of intense focus over weeks (months ... years) while writing and editing this book, as well as enduring rants, raves, and tears of sorrow and joy. Particularly my mom and dad who were my earliest fans.

Most of all, thank you to Bruce who is such a cheerleader despite not at all being a reader. Thank you for being a team player, giving me time and grace while I worked, and delivering meals and drinks to my desk. Your encouragement helped get this story done.

At last, but certainly not least, to my son who gave me the greatest hugs and yelled "yay!" the loudest for every step along the way, you will never understand how deeply I appreciate your abundantly bright presence. Hearing you say "congratulations, Momma" is the sweetest thing. I hope you retain the splendor of the world and carry the magic of dragons and deep forests with you always.

ABOUT THE AUTHOR

Erica Rose Eberhart grew up in the Catskills and spent many formative years in both Eastern Pennsylvania and Northern Virginia. She now resides with her family and cat in the Finger Lakes region of New York. A technical editor by trade, she has a master's degree in English and Creative Writing. Erica has written stories since she was able to write sentences and has found comfort in fantasy her entire life, whether by consuming fantastical stories or creating her own. Beside the comfort of books, Erica adores nature walks, crocheting, embroidery, cats, baking and autumn. This is her first published novel.